# He's Gone

# He's Gone

**Alex Clare**

First published 2016
by Impress Books Ltd
Innovation Centre, Rennes Drive, University of Exeter Campus,
Exeter EX4 4RN

This is a work of fiction. Names, characters, businesses, places,
events and incidents are either products of the author's imagination
or used in a fictitious manner. Any resemblances to actual persons,
living or dead, or actual events is purely coincidental.

*British Library Cataloguing in Publication Data*

*A catalogue record for this book is available from the British Library*

ISBN 13: 978–1–907605–94–9 (pbk)
ISBN 13: 978–1–907605–95–6 (ebk)

Typeset in Garamond MT
by Swales and Willis Ltd, Exeter, Devon

Printed and bound in England
by Short Run Press Ltd, Exeter, UK

To A.

# MONDAY 18 JULY

# 1

Gillian folded the receipt once, twice and tucked it with the others. She called over her shoulder, 'Benjamin, we're going now.' Shoving the purse back into her sagging handbag, she allowed herself a moment of satisfaction for having finished the chores when it was still only eight-thirty. She needed a second to unhook the purse, which had snagged on the bag's lining. 'Here, please.' The shopping centre was tacky but the shops opened early and managing someone else's toddler inside was easier than on Meresbourne's congested High Street. She took another second to balance the bags, then turned. 'If you're hiding …' The boy could be very irritating. The pharmacy was empty.

The pharmacist gave a futile scan around the tiny shop and shrugged. He'd had his head down, answering her prepared sheet of questions about the ingredients for head lice treatments. Gillian stepped into the aisle; there was no need to run or draw attention to herself. Opposite the pharmacy were the doors to the car park but Benjamin could never have opened them on his own. She looked left, looked right, at knee-level; the height of a boy who's almost two, tuning her eyes to spot any flash of red that might be his sweat-shirt, then shut them, overwhelmed. Red was everywhere: sale signs, fast-food litter, artificial flowers. She pressed her fingers to her fore-head and went back into the shop. 'He's gone …'

* * *

This was supposed to be the 'first day of the rest of his life' as maga-zines put it but there was no euphoria, more a queasy feeling, like ver-tigo. Although the worn steps to the staff entrance of Meresbourne police headquarters were only fifty yards away, the walk seemed an impossible distance. Detective Inspector Roger Bailley wondered whether any of the people walking past to start their normal Monday mornings had spotted him: he'd been skulking in his car since quarter past eight. He realised he was gripping the steering wheel, his painted fingernails glaring against the black leather.

He studied his reflection in the rear-view mirror. He'd have to resist touching anything; getting his face and hair as he wanted them had taken ages this morning. The last two weeks at home had been a succession of steady steps to shed his maleness, experimenting with make-up, watching his reddened lips say 'I'm Robyn now.' After a week, he'd ditched the unforgiving crimson for a warm peach shade which went better with his newly-dyed hair and the words came more easily. Though only an inch longer than before, no one could miss the change of colour and style. There had been no other option: the wigs he'd tried had been hot and uncomfortable, with the added worry of it flying off when chasing a suspect.

Missing two haircuts, the most he could manage without comment, had been part of the months of planning before she could start the 'real-life experience'. His doctor had refused to consider prescrib-ing hormones or surgery before he'd demonstrated he could live as a woman, adding that this period helped to weed out those who were 'just confused'. Before writing out the specialist referral, there had been an awkward session where he'd suggested Roger took up a

4

hobby less solitary than photography and hinted it was time to start dating 'real' women.

In his own mind, he was so certain. He repeated, this time out loud: 'I'm not Roger any more – I'm Robyn.' He'd meant to tell the team, or at least Janice, before he started his leave. Then the superintendent suggested that a memo go out while he was away and it meant one less thing to worry about. The problem was that Superintendent Fell's notes always avoided awkward subjects so Roger's new appearance might still shock everyone. The only person that really mattered was Becky but he'd chickened out of telling her and sent a letter instead, hoping it would explain why her father felt the need to do something so shocking. She hadn't responded yet, which didn't feel like a good sign. Men: always rubbish communicators.

It would be good for everything to be out in the open. For the last few months he'd felt sneaky, dodging questions about his holiday, shopping for new clothes over the internet and leaving six large bags containing all his male things outside a charity shop in the middle of the night.

The car radio babbled. *Quarter to nine on North Kent FM: hope your Monday's started well because it's going to be another hot one. After the news, we have an exclusive interview with Meresbourne Town's new manager and we'll ask him his plans for the Dockers …*

Now, when Roger got out, he'd be Robyn and he wouldn't have to hide anymore. He turned off the radio, made a final check of his make-up and got out of the car, nerves under temporary control. As he twisted, the waistband of the trousers pinched, while spare material bagged at the hips. At the top of the steps, he reached for his security pass. It had been the first thing he'd packed into the new handbag, which meant it was now right at the bottom.

He cradled the handbag, conscious for the first time of a CCTV camera staring at him from above the door, prompting an urge to escape. He could still turn back, say everything had been a misunderstanding, get in his car, drive away. The door clicked open, pushed from the inside. Now or never.

# 2

Robyn scurried through the door into the dim lobby of the police station. The desk sergeant was playing with his mobile, top two shirt buttons undone, no tie. Robyn opened her mouth then decided she couldn't face a confrontation over the dress-code at this precise moment.

'Good morning.' The voice was too squeaky because she hadn't practised enough. Talking to herself at home had made her feel crazy.

'Morning, sir.'

The usual response. Robyn kept moving. She was determined not to stop, not to let others' reactions bother her. She knew he didn't mean anything bad, reasoning that if it had taken her over forty years to have the confidence to declare herself a woman, she had to allow everyone else time. She concentrated on walking because the tape between her legs was pushing them apart making her feel like a gunslinger entering a saloon. The new shoes, bought over the internet in a size nine-and-a-half, claimed to be for women but didn't look much different to her old ones. She was grateful she hadn't risked heels.

Along the corridor, the notices on the staff board had new ones pinned over them. The same bulb was out near the lift where a knot of people waited, a woman in a black suit standing apart, tapping into a BlackBerry. Chatter about a local girl's chances on *Superstar Seeker* stopped, leaving a sudden absence of conversation. The thought of standing and waiting in silence wasn't appealing so she kept on moving towards the stairs. Robyn was past the group when she heard the HR Business Partner.

'Ah, DI Bailley, welcome back. Good break?'

Robyn opened her mouth but the woman hadn't finished. 'Relaxing, I hope? We're all glad to have you back.' One civilian worker was gazing at Robyn and another, with equal intensity, at the floor. Robyn stopped, wondering what to do with her hands as the speech went on. 'It's always good to take holiday early in the summer I think, don't you?' The woman flicked her highlighted hair behind one ear. 'You get a good break and things aren't so crowded. I'm going away soon myself ...'

The lift arrived and people shuffled forward. The tall woman answered an unspoken question by holding the doors open with her briefcase.

'Well, good to catch up, DI Bailley. If you need anything, do let me know.'

The doors closed. There had been lots of meetings with HR in the last few months and presumably there would have to be more. Robyn made a note to keep arranging them for late in the day when she could have a stiff drink afterwards.

As she trudged up the stairs to the second floor, Robyn wondered what conversations were now taking place. The tape around her groin rubbed every time she raised her foot but being back in the bland, familiar building was soothing. She took a deep breath on the last landing, clinging to the belief that everything would be fine. The team's morale was strong, she'd spent two years building it up, which was why she hadn't taken up the superintendent's offer of a transfer to a new station. But it didn't say much for her opinion of them, when she hadn't even told them what she was going to do face-to-face. Now it was actually happening, there seemed to be lots of things she could have handled better. Robyn stood outside the CID office, gripping the handle, still hesitating. She'd come this far …

In the office, Detective Constable Ravi Sharma was sorting through piles of statements. Talking to his back seemed cowardly so Robyn dropped her handbag onto a desk with a thump. Ravi spun round, eyes widening with shock, narrowing with scrutiny, before finally crinkling with welcome.

'You made me jump. Ma'am. Good break?'

Robyn paused before replying. Ravi was blinking a lot.

'Yes thanks, Ravi. Good to be back. How are you?'

'Fine. Thanks. Ma'am.'

Robyn sat down, wondering which short person had been sitting in her chair and reached under the seat to adjust it. 'Now which of these does the height – ah.' When she sat back, Ravi was still standing, wearing the same fixed smile, making her wonder when he'd last taken a breath. 'Janice has been keeping me up to date with texts. She said everything had been quiet, apart from the new burglary.'

'Yes, ma'am, same as the last five, another pensioner but there's a witness this time, a neighbour who was able to give a description. Lorraine's following it up.' Ravi's chest swelled as he gulped air.

In the pause, a buzz of conversation in the corridor rose then fell.

'And you got the result in the hit and run – good work.'

'Thank you. Ma'am. The bloke pleading guilty meant they didn't need what I'd put together but at least he went down.' Ravi's rigid grin had returned.

Robyn smiled back, willing him to relax. 'Your work meant he'd no choice but to change his plea. Avoiding a trial is good news.' Ravi's hands unclenched. 'A confession is best because getting someone to make a clean breast …'

Ravi twitched, sending half the statements sliding to the floor. As he scrambled to retrieve them, Robyn switched on her computer, reflecting if this was the reaction from Ravi, aged twenty-seven with a sociology degree, things were going to be at the lower end of her expectations.

There was a shriek of laughter as Detective Constable Lorraine Mount barged in, holding the door for Detective Sergeant Graham Catt, both laden with bags from the canteen. After the laugh died, no one said anything for a moment.

'Right, let's get started on these while they're hot. Here you go, Raver.' Graham handed Ravi a fried-egg sandwich, the yolk already seeping through the napkin. 'And there's your hot chocolate – careful you don't fall asleep.' There was a pantomime between him and Lorraine as they worked out which of the bacon rolls had brown sauce. 'There's yours, Guv.' He reached into another bag. 'And tea as well. One sugar, not much milk.'

Robyn reached for the cup, conscious of the tension in her shoulders. As her number two, of all the team, she'd worried most about how Graham would react and now he'd offered a neat way out of one problem. She'd always hated 'Guv' because it was how the previous DI had been addressed but anything was better than 'ma'am'. 'Thanks, Graham. Morning, Lorraine. It's good to be back.' And for the first time she believed it might be. The voice was OK – not too deep or high. 'Anyone seen Janice this morning?'

'Holiday today, Guv – her birthday.' Ravi spoke through a mouthful of sandwich.

She'd forgotten. Unlike Janice, who always remembered everyone else's special occasions. 'Oh yes. Have we got her a card?' Three blank faces. 'OK, Ravi, pop out and get one today and we can all sign it. And some chocolates or something too.'

The team settled around Robyn's desk as, for once, it was free of clutter. 'Right, let's get started. Lorraine, where are we with the burglaries?'

Lorraine stopped in mid-chew, nose powdered in flour, white against her dark skin. Normality was restored, until Robyn noticed Ravi staring at the lipstick mark on her cup.

The door opened. As it swung closed, the reek of Superintendent Fell's sweat moved with the air. His presence in the incident room was unusual and there was an immediate hush, apart from furtive flicks as napkins removed grease.

'Welcome back, Bailley.' Fell's gaze was fixed somewhere above Robyn's face. 'We have a missing child at Whitecourt Shopping Centre. Uniform are there but the local news has already picked up the story so I need a senior officer to take charge.' He glanced down at a heavy watch. 'Give updates to Tracey as I have meetings all morning.'

The door closed, leaving the room with a penetrating reminder of Fell's presence. It focused the mind. Robyn's worries over what she was wearing seemed less important now she was needed.

'Right.' Robyn stood up. 'Graham and I will take this. Ravi, get the kid's name and run background checks with Social Services. Let's hope this is a false alarm but it never hurts to be prepared, especially if the press are already on it. Lorraine, keep working on the burglary.'

If there were stares in the corridors on the way out, she didn't notice them. Her mind was checking off things to be done. As they walked outside, Graham tutted and pointed to where DC Janice Warrener was bending to lock a small van.

Janice met them at the bottom of the steps, her blouse buttoned into the wrong holes. 'Morning, Robyn. When I heard the news on the radio about the missing boy I thought I'd better come in. Then my car wouldn't start and I had to take Martin's …'

Even though she appeared flustered, Robyn could feel a gentle gaze taking in details of her new appearance. She touched her own buttons. Janice looked puzzled before she glanced down and blushed.

Hoping she hadn't upset her, Robyn smiled. 'Thanks for thinking of us, Janice, and thanks for the updates while I was away. And Happy Birthday. Let's hope the lad isn't far away and you can be home before long. I've set Ravi getting background: can you let him know where everything is?'

Walking between cars, Robyn had a moment of panic when she touched her thigh: her car key was not in the pocket. Then the realisation. Nothing was in the trouser pocket because the woman's suit she was wearing didn't have any pockets. Everything she needed, keys, wallet, phone, was all in the black handbag swinging from her shoulder. Graham pulled out his own keys.

'I'm driving, mind. Bloody women drivers.'

# 3

Robyn fidgeted in the car, aggravated by the peculiar pressures of her bra, which dug in just where the seatbelt crossed. She told herself again there was no way the breast prostheses could fall out, however fast Graham took corners. When he slowed to fight his way across lanes to the shopping centre's slip road, Robyn acknowledged her uneasy feeling was caused by more than Graham's driving. She couldn't have picked a worse case to deal with on her first day ... Anything involving young children disturbed everyone, but Roger Bailley had had the sort of quiet authority needed to deal with distressing subjects. Except he'd gone, replaced by a tallish attempt at a woman in a size sixteen blouse.

'Guess who I met last week when you were on holiday?' Graham paused.

Her irritation that he actually wanted her to guess was tempered with relief that any conversation was flowing at all. 'I don't know. Tell me.'

'Kenny Prentiss. I ran into him in Willingdon nature reserve walking his new dog, a lovely little Norfolk terrier puppy. He asked how the team was getting on and the super's memo had come out by then. He wished you luck with your, ah, new life.'

So Prentiss knew. It was the sort of personal detail Meresbourne's ex DI had loved to play with. Still, as everyone at the station knew, once they'd told their friends and family their DI was changing sex, everyone in Meresbourne would soon know too.

Robyn tried to sound casual. 'What's Prentiss doing now?'

'Enjoying retirement. Three more years and I'll join him. Kenny's got it sussed – he's a member of lots of societies, keeps busy. He said we should all meet up for a drink, the old team.'

'No.' It was sharper than she'd meant.

Graham's eyes were on her so Robyn kept her face forward until he turned back to the road. 'Why not, Guv? We never go out for drinks any more …'

'Not everyone appreciates a culture where you have to drink to be accepted. When I joined CID, I wanted to be a detective, not an alcoholic. The main reason I left Meresbourne and transferred to Bristol for fifteen years was to get away from working for Prentiss.'

Silence, one, two, three, then Graham swore at a scooter, keeping up a string of abuse until he'd got across all three lanes and swerved the car under an archway. 'Easier to park here, don't want to get stuck in the multi-storey.'

Robyn thought the abuse was really for her. She'd never criticised Prentiss before, hiding her frustration at the cliques and sloppiness she'd inherited. Her flash of regret at the outburst started receding.

They got out of the car in the loading area. Robyn's scan took in the bays, racks and pallets; so many places you could hide a child.

'We can take the access passage right to the middle.' Graham pointed to a scuffed set of doors. 'That's where Uniform are supposed to bring shoplifters out so they don't scare punters.'

Robyn stretched her arms; the jacket's tight shoulders stopped the movement. 'No, let's go in the proper way.'

The quarter-chime on St Leonard's church could just be heard outside the centre's Northbank entrance. All doors except one pair were shut, two women complaining as they left.

'Ten minutes I had to wait and it's stifling.'

'Well, if a little lad's missing, something's got to be done. We don't want another case like the kid on the railway line.'

Graham approached a uniformed sergeant who broke away from his conversation with a woman jammed into a mobility scooter. People in the queue fretted and stamped – somewhere a child was screaming. The officer didn't do a good job of hiding his double-take or sharp breath when he saw them: his Adam's apple jerked and was still.

'Morning, ah, ma'am, Graham.'

Graham gestured at the queue. 'Blimey, Phil, it must be serious if you've been dragged in from Gaddesford. How'd the cricket go over the weekend? Have you got anything?'

They were giving the crowd something to look at. Robyn heard muttered conversations and sensed an undercurrent of hostility. Biting her tongue, she told herself it was frustration at waiting – she was just part of the delay. She fixed her gaze on Phil, who rubbed the back of his neck.

'A draw. Nothing so far, Graham. We've got teams on all exits but if someone took him, they'd be long gone because we weren't called in until twenty minutes after the boy went missing. And they're having trouble getting the CCTV. Right bunch of showers, the security team here.'

Robyn tried to shut out the pop music. 'What have we got from …?'

'How much longer are we going to be kept waiting? I've got a meeting.' A man strode forward from the queue, shiny patches on his suit jacket.

Robyn waited for quiet. '… from the mother?'

Phil made a placatory gesture in the direction of the crowd. 'Not his mother, it's a nanny.' He swallowed. 'Ma'am. She's in the administra-

14

tion office.' He handed over a picture of a boy with pale brown skin and solemn, dark eyes. His red sweatshirt had an ostentatious blue crest. 'Ben Chivers, the missing boy. He'll be two in September.'

'A face made for television,' Graham held the photo at arm's length. 'Can we keep this?'

*Now it's holiday time, everything you need is here at Whitecourt Shopping Centre. Make the most of our free parking and family-friendly space ...*

The tannoy cut across the rising noise from the crowd. Phil nodded. 'We've got copies. Lucky the nanny had some pictures on her phone. It's been circulated to all the usual places. Should warn you, ma'am, we've already had someone from the *Gazette* here. Taking pictures.' Phil's glance to Robyn lasted too long.

There was a second's pause. Graham shrugged. 'Not surprising. This would be a big story for them.'

The man in the suit barged forward, tie undone. 'I asked how much longer?'

Graham clapped Phil on the shoulder. 'You'd better get back to it. Has the mother been contacted?'

Phil nodded. 'Yeah. She works locally so has gone home, somewhere in Upper Town, in case he turns up there. Family Liaison is sending someone.' He turned back to the queue and dismissed the woman in the mobility scooter, who reversed, wheels crunching over the man in the suit's briefcase.

They walked down the slope to a door marked *Staff Only* between a Pound Shop and an empty unit: there was still a faint echo of raised voices. They went up a dim staircase, notice-boards on both sides, to the first floor where there were just two doors, marked with a stickman and a stick-woman with drawn-on tits. Continuing up, a dark trail on the lino ran into a room resembling a bedsit with a corner counter crammed with dirty crockery. At the end of the corridor, they walked into an office where grimy windows gave a view over the shop floor. A woman in a tight suit leant over a paper-strewn desk, plastic bands for various causes slithering around her wrists. Discarded on top of

15

the muddle were papers with bright red headers denoting B23-08 Customer Sickness and B23-04 Acts of Vandalism.

On a chair in front of the desk, someone sat swaddled in an olive cardigan, grey wisps of hair visible above the shawl collar. By the window, a young woman with spiky, cropped hair saw Graham and looked relieved. She was familiar – a constable from the station, in civvies. Robyn nodded to her as she searched her memory for a name: Claire? Kate? Graham muttered something to her as he got out his notebook.

A sniff came from inside the cardigan. Robyn pulled her mind back. 'Madam? I'm DI Bailley and this is Sergeant Catt. Please can you tell us what happened?'

The woman raised her face towards the voice, hearing but not seeing. Sixty, Robyn concluded, seeing the powder in the lines of the face and a slight tic fluttering in the left eye.

The young woman took a half step forward. 'Perhaps I can help, DI Bailley, Graham? Constable Chloe Talbot.'

The broad Yorkshire accent sounded too big for her small frame. Robyn nodded for her to continue.

Chloe tucked her hands behind her. 'I was doing some shopping.' Her eyes widened. 'Only because I've got the week off, you see. Well, at quarter to nine, I saw this lady getting agitated with a security guard. They hadn't even started first response though the lad had been gone since half past. I called it in then got some staff and public organised into a search but there was no sign of him.'

'Thank you, PC Talbot. I appreciate this is very difficult for you, Mrs …'

'Green, ma'am,' supplied Chloe. 'Gillian Green.'

'Thank you. Mrs Green, we need you to tell us what happened in your own words. Can we get you anything – a glass of water?' There was a small nod.

Robyn appealed to the skinny woman, now pulling more files from the shelves. 'Could you get Mrs Green a glass of water?' The woman didn't even look round. Robyn rapped on the desk. 'A glass of water, please.'

'I have to find our missing child policy.' The woman dumped more files on the crowded desk. 'The index says it's B23-10.'

Graham stepped into her eyeline. 'I think it's a bit late, don't you?'

'I'm the manager of this centre, I have to follow the policy.'

'Good for you, it's your centre.' Graham held a file shut as the manager tried to open it. 'Least you can do is get this poor shopper some water.' She glared at him and swept out.

Gillian kept her cardigan tight around her, despite the heat.

Robyn felt a creeping sensation on her skin as each second passed. 'Tell me what happened this morning.'

There was no answer or acknowledgement. One of Gillian's hair pins fell to the lino.

'Mrs Green, what time did you get here?' Robyn raised her voice.

The manager returned and spent huffy seconds finding a mat for the plastic glass with a scratched Minnie Mouse picture.

Robyn jerked her head at Graham, who took the hint. He blocked the manager's route back behind her desk. 'Why don't we go and make sure the CCTV footage is ready?' He steered her to the door and out.

Chloe stepped forward, squatting directly in Gillian's eyeline, taking a liver-spotted hand. 'Hey, it was an accident. Just an accident. You mustn't blame yourself.' Her voice was friendly, soft and at last there was an answering nod.

Chloe pressed on. 'Now, when did you get here? I bet you were like me, here early to beat the crowds, yes?'

'I listened to the end of the news on the radio then started the chores.' The husky voice filtered through the collar of the cardigan.

'So about five past eight.' Chloe smiled in encouragement. 'And what did you do downstairs?' Robyn moved behind Chloe, perching on a corner of the desk.

'Uh, the health-food shop, got shoes from the menders and picked up dry-cleaning. The pharmacy was the last stop.'

'Did you notice anything peculiar?' Chloe looked up to Robyn, who nodded she should keep going.

'No. Everything was the same.' Gillian's voice wavered. Chloe passed a tissue from a quilted box on the desk and Gillian blew her nose before composing herself. 'I always do the chores on a Monday morning as it's quietest and Benjamin doesn't have school.' Her shoulders shook and tears seemed imminent.

Chloe cocked her head on one side. 'Ben goes to school? You mean nursery?'

'No, Benjamin attends a special school for gifted children on Tuesdays and Wednesdays and I teach him at home the rest of the week.' Gillian dabbed around her face with the tissue.

'How long have you cared for him?' Robyn leaned forward.

'A year and a half.'

'And what else can you tell us about him?'

Gillian drooped leaving Robyn wondering why she wasn't making a connection. A nervous voice in her mind whispered that no one would want to talk to her because she must seem odd, maybe frightening. A more practical voice said her appearance couldn't be important as Gillian wasn't focusing on anything.

Robyn leaned forward. 'Mrs Green, Gillian? We need to get this information ...'

Gillian lurched to her feet, knocking Chloe backwards and began to pace – step, step, turn.

'What can I tell you about Benjamin? Everything, because I'm with him all the time except when he's with a tutor or in school.' Step, step, turn. 'His mother works so hard and I've lost him.' Step, step, turn. 'He's such a gifted child, he wouldn't go anywhere on his own, someone's taken him, someone's ...'

Step, step, crumble. Gillian collapsed back onto the seat, tears beginning to fall. Chloe passed another tissue, making soothing noises. Graham and Phil appeared in the doorway and behind them, the manager could be heard demanding her office back.

18

'And where's Ben's father?' Robyn had to speak louder than she wanted: it sounded like an accusation.

Gillian's swollen eyes peered into Robyn's. Uncomprehending, she turned back to Chloe.

'Gillian? How can we get in touch with Ben's father?'

The answer was so muffled, Robyn couldn't catch anything but Chloe reacted, leaning forward. 'You must know something, Gillian. Does he live a long way away?'

'I became Benjamin's nanny when he was six months old. His father has never been mentioned.'

Most single mothers lived in the Docks or New Town estates, not Upper Town so Robyn filed the father's whereabouts as a question for when they spoke to Ben's mother. She straightened. 'Thank you. I assure you we will do everything we can to find Ben. Phil, can you radio for someone to take Mrs Green home?'

Gillian left, arms wrapped around herself, forgetting the shopping bags piled by her feet until Chloe called after her.

# 4

Robyn sat with Phil and Chloe in a corner of the shopping centre's staff room.

'A right shambles, ah, ma'am.' Phil flicked back pages in his notebook. 'There are supposed to be three security staff on duty at any one time. Gillian was in the chemist's when the lad went missing. She had a look up and down but the boy had gone. The pharmacist pushed his emergency button at eight thirty-eight. The only guard actually working was removing a rough sleeper and didn't get there for another ten minutes.'

'That's when I heard Gillian yelling and assumed she was a shoplifter.' Chloe had her feet up on the chair, arms wrapped around her knees. 'I went over to see if I could help the security guy.'

Graham slipped in, holding a disc and settled on the sofa next to Robyn.

'We got a couple of cars here before nine.' Phil pointed to his notes. 'Chloe had got both sets of doors shut but it was too late. Nothing was going out on the tannoy because the guy on the ground was Polish and the one in the office was Greek.' He paused, as if expecting a reaction. 'Barely speak English between them—'

Chloe cut across him. 'And all this time, Gillian was just left outside the chemist's. She didn't want to leave in case Ben came back.'

Phil's eyes narrowed. 'As I was saying, the office didn't help and no one wanted to disturb the manager because she was on the phone to a potential tenant.'

A locker was banged shut: Robyn shifted on the hard sofa. 'Thanks, Phil. Got the CCTV, Graham?'

Graham scowled. 'Yeah. Don't get your hopes up though. Nothing but blue sky from the cameras at the Riverside end because they were out of position but …' He held up a disk. 'We've picked up Gillian and Ben at the Northbank entrance.'

A constable hurried in. 'Sir, we've got something from the shop-to-shop.' Robyn gritted her teeth, until she realised the woman was addressing Phil.

The officer handed Phil a camera. 'The photography shop said someone was taking pictures with this in the aisle about the time the boy went missing.'

Phil's big fingers jabbed at buttons as he squinted down at the small screen. 'There's nothing here.' He held out the camera to Robyn. 'Just blurs.'

Robyn scrolled through the six images: the text of a fast-food sign, litter amongst the plastic flowers, a couple holding hands. 'He's testing the camera's features.' She scrolled through them again: a girl sucking on a straw; the support struts of the roof; a mannequin in a first-floor window, fuzzy figures below. Zooming in, one of the blurs resolved itself into two distinct shapes. 'Here! Look at this.' Robyn held the screen so that everyone could see. 'Can we blow this one up?'

'If you think it'll help, ma'am.' Phil hauled himself to his feet.

Robyn made a larger-than-needed gesture to check her watch, impatience growing at the lack of urgency. 'It's five to ten. The child's been missing an hour and a half. We'll need an all-ports alert and extend the searches into town.' She bit her lip, tasting lipstick. 'Phil, can you get on with that? I need to arrange a press briefing.' She stood up. 'Anything else? Oh, has the loading bay been searched?'

'Of course it has. Ma'am. We've searched the whole place. Teams are in the High Street and Victoria Park now. More units are on their way to cover the rest of town.'

Dealing with Phil had always been hard work. 'Thanks, Phil.' Robyn turned to Chloe. 'Good work today. Lucky you were there.'

Chloe lifted her elbow from the table, then screwed up her face and began scrubbing something sticky off her skin. 'Not lucky enough, though. Guess I should go back to the station – they might need me for searches.' She stood up.

As she towered over Chloe, Robyn was struck by how ridiculous she must appear in comparison. Chloe hesitated a moment then turned to go, grabbing her bag from the sofa.

Robyn suddenly realised she didn't know where her own handbag was. Her phone was in it and she needed to call Fell. There were a few panicky seconds before she worked out she hadn't picked it up from the car.

'Graham, can I borrow your phone?' She found her hands were flapping and went to put them in her pockets, before giving up and clasping them behind her. 'I left my handbag in the car.'

Graham pressed his lips together but held out his phone. Robyn turned away to make the call, nearly bumping into a plump woman in a yellow uniform who gave her a look of curiosity and suspicion.

'Superintendent Fell's office.'

'Hello, Tracey. It's Robyn.'

'Robyn.' Tracey seemed to roll the name around her mouth, as if tasting it. 'Welcome back.'

'Thanks.' There was a constant crackly hum. 'Can you hear me?'

'Just about – it's an awful line.'

'I wanted to update Fell on the missing boy as it looks like an abduction. We'll need to get an appeal out as soon as possible. Could you organise one here at the shopping centre as soon as possible?'

'Let's see. Ten o'clock now – I'll arrange the session for eleven to give enough notice for a reasonable show.'

'Thanks. We'll have finished interviewing here by then.'

'Anything else you need?'

'We'll need some bodies to answer phones.'

'I'll get a team together. Oh and the superintendent would like to see you sometime this afternoon.'

Robyn shut her eyes for a second. Of course he would. Just a routine, she would have to get used to now that DCI Golding had been signed off sick again. Fell needed an update, nothing to worry about. 'OK, Tracey. Thanks.' As she finished the call, the phone rang. 'Hi, Ravi.'

'Oh? Hello, Guv. I tried to calling you and just got voicemail. I've got the info you wanted on Ben.'

'Go ahead.'

'Well, he's not known to Social Services. There's no father listed on his birth certificate, just his mother. Her name's Melissa Chivers, no record, one speeding fine – I've sent a text with her address. She also made a complaint about someone threatening her, three months ago: Janice investigated.'

'Interesting. Anything else?' The woman in the yellow uniform said something into her own phone and shrieked with laughter. Robyn changed the phone to her other ear.

'Yeah, one other thing, Guv: there's a lot online about this case.'

'What's being said?'

'CCTV from Whitecourt has been posted to YouTube. It seems to be Ben just before he goes missing and it's got thousands of hits already.'

'What?' Someone had seen Ben disappear and done nothing. Her angry gesture got Graham's attention. 'Hang on, Ravi …' 'Graham, someone's put a CCTV clip from here on the internet – can you find out

23

what the hell they saw and why they didn't tell us first time?' Graham scowled, nodded and left. '... sorry, Ravi. Can you keep a watch for anything else online? Tracey's rounding up a squad to answer phones so can you and Janice get the office organised? OK, thanks. Bye.'

Five minutes before the briefing was due to start, Robyn returned to the office suite and stood on the first floor landing, desperate for the loo. There were voices coming from the women's changing room. She hesitated, then ducked into the men's toilet, grateful to find the cubicle free, before fleeing upstairs, face burning because she couldn't face the possible confrontation.

The press were already crowded into the staff room with no sign of Graham. Robyn scanned the faces as people settled themselves on the mismatched chairs. There were representatives from the local weekly paper, the regional daily and a couple Robyn didn't recognise, who had the polished look of TV people, confirmed when they set up a small camera. Everyone seemed to be taking pictures of her. She hoped they were just checking light levels.

Graham slid in, holding another disc. 'I've got the extra CCTV footage, Guv. The little twerp in security admitted he was having a fag when Ben went missing. When someone told him what'd happened, he checked the footage, then posted the clip "so people would spread the word". Thought he was being a bloody hero.' He pulled a face.

Robyn shook her head then scanned the room again. They couldn't wait any longer, even though she'd been expecting to see Ady Clarke, from the *Meresbourne Gazette*. Everyone was taking a good look at her and who knew what they were thinking.

'Ladies and gentlemen, thank you for coming. I'm DI Robyn Bailley.' The sudden flurry of scribbling didn't help her composure. 'This briefing is to ask for your help in finding Ben Chivers who went missing from this shopping centre two and a half hours ago.' Robyn held up the photo of Ben in his school sweatshirt and tried not to blink in the flashes. 'Ben is nearly two years old, of mixed race. We'll show you evidence that this was a deliberate snatch so we need everyone in Meresbourne and the villages to be vigilant and report anything suspicious.'

Ady had appeared and was now watching with the rest. Robyn wondered whether he could imagine them now going for the pint they'd talked about a few times. Another person who should have been told beforehand. It was a relief when she was able to stop talking and show the CCTV. From high up in the pharmacy, they watched Gillian and Ben walk in: the door was propped open. All that could be seen of the pharmacist was the dome of his bald head as he faced Gillian. Ben approached her once, the angle making him disappear behind the counter. Gillian looked down, her stiff gesture making the lost words unnecessary. Ben wandered back into view, moving to the doorway, looking out, his backpack a lighter square on his dark sweatshirt. He turned back for a few seconds but Gillian was still talking. There was a collective sigh from the watchers as the boy toddled out of the top of the screen.

Graham loaded the centre's CCTV, just five frames. The grainy blob that was Ben stood alone in a patch of empty floor. Next shot, four lads, all caps and loud logos, were occupying half the frame, one pushing another, Ben just visible behind them. Then the screen was full, a crowd of teenagers, girls and boys, mouths open, laughing or jeering. In the fourth shot, the first of the group were already out of the top corner, half a screen of empty floor behind them. Finally, only two remained, almost out of shot, empty space where Ben had been. Robyn finished with the blurred image from the camera shop, blown up as large as they could make it. The digital display showed eight thirty-four. Two shapes, joined in the middle, walked away from the camera, a small one in red and a larger, yellow one. Ben was being led away by a figure in a long, patterned frock.

# 5

There weren't a lot of questions at the end of the briefing and, to her relief, the most personal was how to spell 'Robyn'. Ady had left straight away, without saying goodbye, which she hoped was simply because of the deadline for the local evening paper. She and Graham walked back up to Northbank, past the pharmacist, who was gesticulating for reporters. Graham pushed at the door to the car park with one finger, then one hand but the heavy door barely shifted. 'These would be hard to open if you had an unwilling toddler. Someone might remember.'

Robyn peered into the corridor. 'If so, Phil's team should find them. Right, time to talk to Ben's mother.'

They got back into the car, Graham taking advantage of the lighter traffic to go faster. Robyn was grateful when they turned off the ring road onto Albert Avenue and started the climb towards Upper Town.

'I think I've only been to Upper Town once since I came back to Meresbourne, when that accountant embezzled from the mayor's charity fund.' Even under the shade of the plane trees, it was hot and Robyn leant towards the window to catch any hint of breeze.

Graham waited for two women with enormous buggies to cross the road. 'Of course, the estate agents don't tell you how often little Timmy and Jocasta raid mummy and daddy's drinks cabinet and start trashing cars.'

Robyn laughed then checked herself. They were about to meet a mother who'd lost her child. She needed to bring her comfort and reassurance.

'Oh, by the way, did you hear about Gold-Top? Signed off with stress, this time.' Graham snorted. 'The only thing he's got to be stressed about is his golf score.'

Robyn always wondered where Graham got his information from and how he got confidential HR information on DCI Golding. In the short term, it was bad news, meaning she would have to spend more time in meetings.

The road was rising steadily, parallel turnings on either side filled with neat rows of Victorian red-brick terraces behind pocket-hand-kerchief front gardens. After three junctions, the slope slackened, the side roads now broader, lined with pale brick town houses. Just before the crest of the hill, they turned off the avenue and began the hunt for a parking space in the grid of streets.

A lot of people seemed to be walking around so progress was slow. Robyn wondered whether she was being paranoid or whether the hard looks people gave the car were aimed at her. Graham swore as the first parking space he'd seen in five minutes turned out to hold a stone trough filled with flowers. They continued up into the two rows of detached villas crowning Upper Town.

'So she hasn't quite made it ...' Graham craned his neck in the hope of a space. '... still not got a place at the top of the hill.' Leaving the car hanging over a junction, they walked back to the last row of town houses.

A tall officer in uniform stood at a crossroads. In response to Graham's wave, he ran over with a smooth, easy motion, clipboard gripped like a relay baton.

'Morning, Clyde. Found anything?'

'Morning, Graham, sir.' Clyde turned to Robyn and almost bowed. 'Good morning, DI Bailley.' He turned back to Graham, shoulders relaxing. 'Nothing so far but everyone's asking how they can help. We're getting volunteers to check sheds and report anything suspicious. Teams are doing house-to-house.'

That explained the scrutiny of the car as they drove in. Graham nodded. 'Keep going. We're seeing the mother now. Good luck.'

They walked on through a contemporary conformity of façades with two-step front gardens and blinds at the sash windows. The only thing distinguishing number twelve was a 'To Let' board nailed to the fence. The family liaison officer answered the door, multiple bracelets jangling together. From the way she scrutinised them, you wouldn't believe she was in the doorway of someone else's home.

Robyn coughed. 'Can we come in, Susan?'

In a swirl of printed skirt, Susan stepped past them, to scan up and down the street. 'We haven't had any reporters yet ...' She stopped, focusing on Robyn before checking the street again. 'But I'm expecting them soon.' Graham sniffed.

As Robyn stepped onto the quarry-tiled floor, cold rose through the thin soles of her new shoes. The air was thick with scent; there were two plug-in air-fresheners but none of the usual hallway litter, just a series of close-up photographs of lilies on the walls. High contrast, soft focus, just the sort of bland shot a couple of bores at her camera club specialised in.

Graham had already scanned around the front room. 'Well? Is there anything we should know?'

Before Susan could answer, a woman appeared at the end of the passage, stopping under one of the ceiling spots, the white light glowing on her black hair. Her suit was the colour women's catalogues described as taupe but Robyn considered beige. In the deep shadow under her chin, a heavy gold cross glowed against her brown skin. She scrutinised them both without blinking before turning back into the kitchen. Robyn thought she'd caught a downturn in the outlined lips but it could have been a shadow.

Susan folded her arms. 'Melissa Chivers, Ben's mother.' Graham kept his eyes on the end of the corridor before turning to scowl at Susan.

After the dim hallway, the kitchen was dazzling with ceiling spotlights and the noon sun. Melissa stood poised, a spread of shiny tools on the worktop, a flat-pack shoe-rack half way to completion. Susan hovered in the doorway: Robyn had never seen her so subdued. Despite the brightness, the room was stuffy with the same persistent scent as the hall. There was no invitation to sit on the white bar stools. Robyn cleared her throat of the cloying smell of pine. 'Ms Chivers, I'm DI Robyn Bailley. I know this is a traumatic time for you so first, I want to reassure you we're doing everything we can to find Ben. Susan will be keeping you up to date with our progress and will screen approaches from the media. Are you feeling up to a few questions?'

'My son has been gone for nearly four hours. *Four hours.*' Melissa put down the screwdriver and gripped a hammer. She turned to face Robyn, pale patches showing on her knuckles. 'How can you stand there and say you are doing everything to find him? And his name is Benjamin.' The voice was low, each syllable distinct and the words hung in the air until Melissa rapped the metal frame twice with the hammer, the sharp sounds cutting the silence.

Robyn cleared her throat. Melissa snapped her head around to glare at her then slotted the hammer back into a tool roll and tucked herself onto a bar stool, sitting with her back rigid, one pink nail tapping the counter top.

'I'm sorry, Ms Chivers. We'll try and make this as quick as possible.' Robyn ticked herself off for misjudging her approach. Roger had never had that problem. 'Now, can you please tell me about Benjamin? Is he an adventurous boy?'

'No.' She made an angry gesture to the paved yard. 'He doesn't like to go outside. Benjamin is a studious, obedient child.'

Graham's eyebrows rose as he started taking notes. Fortunately, he was out of Ms Chivers' eyeline.

'So could Ben, Benjamin, have seen someone he knew?'

'He does not associate with the sort of people who use that place.'

'How can you be so certain? We understand Benjamin goes to school – could he have seen another pupil or a teacher?'

Melissa tutted. 'No one from the school would have taken Ben. Why aren't you questioning his nanny?'

'We've spoken to Gillian Green. Can you tell us how long she's worked for you?'

'Have you not already asked her?'

'We have asked her, ma'am, but we need to cross-check every fact.'

'Sixteen months. She came from a top agency and had references, even though she lives in the Docks.' Melissa pursed her lips.

'Thank you. And before?' Again, she was couldn't establish any rapport with a witness. Robyn wondered what else she could do.

'I had a specialist nursery nurse from the same agency.' Melissa was aligning the next shelf within the shoe rack.

'So apart from Gillian, who else does Benjamin have regular contact with?'

'He sees the teachers at his school and two music tutors, for piano and violin.'

'Could you give us their details please?'

Melissa spoke over her shoulder to Susan who was still loitering in the doorway. 'In the office, at the left-hand end of the shelf above the desk is an address book.'

The bangles on Susan's wrist rattled as she folded her arms. She looked back at Melissa and opened her mouth as if to say something.

Robyn caught her eye. 'Susan, please – we need those details.' Susan shut her mouth, blinked and disappeared into the hall. Melissa made an impatient noise in the back of her throat.

Another shelf was secured. Graham was shifting from foot to foot, a soft shuffling against the tiles. Susan reappeared, placing an A4 book on the counter and retreating to the doorway.

Melissa inserted a manicured nail into a tab.

'I'm glad you do things the old-fashioned way.' Graham turned to a fresh page of his notebook.

Melissa stared at Graham for a second, his bald head glowing under the spotlights, then she smiled. To Robyn, it all seemed rather predatory but Graham swallowed, his pencil poised. Melissa read out the details, pausing at the end of each line until Graham confirmed. To Robyn, watching, the process seemed to take longer than it needed to as Melissa's voice had slowed to a drawl.

Closing the book, she turned to Robyn. 'I saw you at the press conference. Why did you do that without my permission?'

Robyn swallowed. 'Ms Chivers, when a child goes missing and we suspect foul play, time is of the essence. We try to get as much early coverage for the case as possible so the public are on the alert and ready to report anything suspicious.'

Melissa held the book across her chest. 'Let me be clear. I meant, why were *you* speaking at the press conference? Now, rather than thinking about Benjamin, everyone will be focusing on you and your deviance.'

# 6

Robyn stood in the hallway of Melissa's house, fumbling with the front door catch. She had concluded it was better for her to go and leave the interview to Graham.

Susan had followed her. 'Typical, bloody Graham.' She reached past Robyn to click back a lock. 'Of course she's happy now. She's got everything under control.'

Having Susan glowering next to her reduced Robyn's temptation to slam the door and it was reassuring that it wasn't just her who found Ms Chivers hard to get on with. From what she had seen, Susan, with her offerings of chamomile tea, hadn't built up a rapport either.

'You'd better find her boy quickly. She's so tightly wound, I think she'll snap.' Susan began twisting a strand of hair between her fingers. 'And you need to have a word about Graham. He shouldn't be allowed anywhere near women in case he starts dribbling.'

That was a conversation Robyn didn't want to start. 'Keep me posted, Susan.' She realised she'd been holding her breath. Two steps to the gate and she was on the pavement under the shade of a plane tree. To the right, Clyde stood with a group of people. Susan was watching from the doorway so Robyn turned the other way, towards the main road, then left, up the hill. She let her mind go into neutral. Melissa Chivers' reaction was what she must learn to expect. The counsellor had gone through this, over and over again. Not everyone would understand or be supportive. She remembered the example given – think of football – some people would stab you for wearing the wrong shirt. Ms Chivers' son was missing, presumed kidnapped so she was coping any way she could. Grief showed in lots of ways. There was no point in reacting to what someone said when they were under such stress.

A bus from the town centre edged up the hill and stopped, a group of teenage girls getting off in a fizz of giggles. Robyn wondered whether they were laughing at her until she heard a mention of *Superstar Seeker* as they crossed the road, ponytails swinging and she made a mental note to stop being so sensitive. Next to the stop, on a small patch of green was an old-fashioned cluster of phone-box, post box and bench. Without a destination, Robyn sat, contemplating the regular rows of roofs. There would be plenty of toddlers just like Ben around here. Any one of them could have wandered away for a second. The CCTV was not conclusive. The footage didn't show the moment when Ben met the woman who led him away. Robyn followed the thought: if the woman had planned to take a child, this could be just a chance encounter, Ben the unlucky one in the wrong place at the wrong time. Alternatively, the toddler had been the target for some reason and a lapse in his nanny's concentration had made the snatch easier. She reached into her handbag for a copy of the picture from the camera shop. Robyn scanned the grainy image again, sure that she was missing something. The print dress looked like the ones now heavily-reduced in every chain store. The woman's height and build were nothing unusual. She followed the outline: the woman's left hand was holding Ben's right but her right was empty – no handbag.

Her phone rang. Graham was at the car, sounding anxious to be off. Robyn hurried back, hearing the engine start as she neared the car. She opened the door.

'Bitch.' Graham accelerated hard out of the space, Robyn almost banging into his shoulder as she struggled to fasten her seat belt. Another car was waiting behind, indicator on.

'I'm getting an idea of how the rest of the interview went.'

Graham grunted. 'What? I mean the bitch who took little Benjamin.' He braked at the junction where Clyde broke off a conversation with a knot of residents and shook his head. They turned into the next cross-street.

'What did she tell you?' Robyn tried to suppress the creeping fear that she'd be no use as a detective if she couldn't interview anyone.

'Couple of possible lines of enquiry, Guv. Melissa Chivers is a lawyer, done rather well for herself, partner in a law firm with offices over in the business park. Implied it was a big thing when they appointed her, "a black woman in the dusty corridors of Derby and Rutherford".' Robyn swallowed hard as Graham mimed the speech marks, both hands off the wheel. 'She's some kind of property specialist. Not your normal conveyancing, she looks after big, commercial developments.'

Graham reached into the door pocket for chewing gum. 'But, just after you'd gone, she took a call. She advises some charity and a couple with a baby were about to be evicted so she spoke to them for ten minutes. She spent time helping a family when her own son's been taken.' He offered the packet to Robyn.

Robyn shook her head. 'No thanks. Did she give you anything relating to Ben's disappearance?'

Graham chewed, the smell of mint filling the car. 'She's working on the redevelopment of the Docks area. There's going to be a new leisure centre and shopping village, as well as the warehouses being turned into flats for trendy people, as if there are any of those around here.' They were trundling down the hill behind a bus. 'It's going for a decision soon and apparently there are heritage people angry about the development so it's possible someone might resort to desperate measures to put the application off. I followed up about the threats she'd had previously but nothing else has happened.'

They were so close to the bus, Robyn could read the graffiti in the back window. She suppressed the urge to grip the door handle. 'The woman on the CCTV didn't have anything with her, even a handbag and those dresses don't have pockets. If she hadn't gone to buy anything, it makes me think she was there for Ben. What did you find out about his father?'

Graham gunned the engine to overtake the bus as they passed through the red-bricks, then braked hard behind a learner driver. 'She clammed up a bit. First she said he didn't have a father and I asked whether she'd used a sperm bank. She got a bit huffy and said "playing God" with life was against the Bible so I asked her straight out for a list of her boyfriends.' Graham smirked. 'Let's face it, a woman with a body like hers isn't going to be lonely.'

'Have you got a name?'

'No, she refused. I did explain an absent father is one of the first lines of enquiry we need to eliminate when a child goes missing and she finally admitted the father didn't know about Ben.'

'Someone must know, or at least suspect who he is, even if the father himself doesn't.' Robyn wished she had some water. 'Did you get the impression there were any people Ms Chivers would confide in?'

'Well not Susan, that's for sure. Stupid, whiny cow.' They reached the bottom of the hill, passing through patches of light and shade from the clumsy blocks of flats between Upper Town and the Docks. A rusting Astra poked its nose out into the road, the chunky blonde driver tipping her cigarette to thank Graham for letting her out. 'Doesn't seem to think of much outside work, oh, apart from church. She's a member of some evangelical one. You remember last year, there were demonstrations outside the health centre because it was giving out birth control?'

'That turned nasty, didn't it? There were threats against some of the workers at their homes.'

'Yeah. Well, that was them. Ms Chivers seems pretty keen. When I mentioned they'd broken the law, she snapped that it was new arrivals who didn't know the rules over here. When I asked if she needed more support, she said the Lord gave her all the strength she needed. I think it's ... why she's ...' Graham tailed off, chewing faster.

'Why she wouldn't speak to me?' Robyn found her jaw clenching.

'Ah, yeah.'

A second later, Graham gave a coarse laugh. 'One good thing – I've never seen Susan shut up before.' He sobered when Robyn didn't react. 'Ms Chivers is in a state though, underneath. I reckon all the DIY stuff is just something to keep her from going mad because she's not in control. She has to do something, you know?'

Robyn tensed, watching a child Ben's age stumble towards the road. His father grabbed him just in time. 'What about her home arrangements?'

'Ms Chivers sounds a bit of a workaholic. Gillian comes six days a week to do the housekeeping and teach Ben when he's not at his school – I've got the details. She was going to ring Gillian when I left so maybe Susan can be useful for once and fill us in on the conversation.' Graham smiled, without humour.

'Why is the house to let?'

'She's about to go and spend six months working in Europe, which might turn into a permanent thing. All sounds very high-powered.'

'Any other family?' Robyn gave in and gripped the door handle as they went around the roundabout too fast.

'Mother and sister. Another area she didn't like me asking about. Her early life sounds pretty hard and she came here to get away.' Graham swung the car into the police station car park, bumping over the speed humps. 'I went up to Ben's room and I've got a toothbrush we can use for the DNA test. Far too tidy, lots of educational stuff. His clothes shouldn't be hard to track – he was wearing his school uniform.'

Robyn spotted a parking space. 'Over there. I wondered about the mention of a school rather than a nursery. What can they teach a child so young?'

'Don't know.' Graham swung the car around. 'I did ask why Ben was dressed for school in the holidays.'

'And?'

'She said his school doesn't stop for summer, because it's a missed learning opportunity.' Graham adopted a clipped imitation of Melissa. 'She also told me "wearing his uniform teaches him the value of education".'

'She didn't show much emotion, did she? Certainly not the usual bereft mother.'

Graham killed the engine. 'She's upset though, I could tell and she isn't as tough as she talks. A couple of times, when I was asking her about anything personal, she talked about how she'd had to work harder than anyone else to get where she had. Almost as if she needed to convince herself.' They got out of the car. Graham paused, leaning on the door. 'I guess she's so used to acting the hard woman, she doesn't know how to do anything else.'

They walked up the steps, Graham opening the door for Robyn with an unnecessary flourish. 'Right, I'm going to drop this off for the lab.' He waved the bag. The toothbrush was plain white, the only way you could tell it was for a child was by the size.

Robyn walked up the stairs. The CID office had been opened out. Janice was marking things on a clipboard, pointing to a corner as an extra printer was carried in. Three constables were answering calls at new desks. Behind them, a large-scale map of Meresbourne and the villages was stuck with coloured pins.

'The red ones are the credible sightings.' Ravi fished in the pot and held up one. 'Blue is for possible and yellow is unlikely. We had one woman call because her drains were blocked and she thinks some-one's dumped a body down there.'

The yellow pins spread like a rash. A pair of red pins were stuck in Willingdon village.

Robyn pointed. 'What are these, Ravi?'

'Two reports, Guv, one from a woman who said she saw a child being bundled out of a van, then a second from someone walking his dog in the same area who found a child's backpack beside a track. Lorraine's out there now. She was going around the villages with the new description of the burglar so she was nearby.'

Robyn scanned the map. 'Any more of these worth investigating?'

'We're picking up all the credible ones as part of the house-to-house searches, Guv.' Ravi tapped the map with his pen. 'The last update said teams are spreading out into Upper Town and Barton.'

Graham's phone rang. 'Lorraine.'

Robyn cleared papers from a table. 'Put her on speaker.'

'Hello, darling, just putting you on speaker so everyone can hear your beautiful voice.' Graham propped the phone against a stapler.

'Hello, Graham, everyone. Two false alarms, I'm afraid. I went to see the first caller and the more I questioned her, the more muddled she got. She's unhappy about travellers living in a field near her house and I think she's trying to get rid of them by saying they're gypsies who steal children.'

Lorraine's rich laugh boomed from the phone. 'I also don't think she appreciated a black copper turning up,'cos she demanded to see my warrant card twice before letting me in. I talked to the travellers, just one family, four adults, three kids. They'd hitched a ride from town and the youngest child threw a tantrum as he got out of the van. I believe them.'

Ravi jumped in. 'What about the backpack?'

'It was a plastic one with princesses on.'

'Damn.' Robyn rubbed her forehead. 'OK, thanks, Lorraine.'

'Do you need me back there, Guv, or can I keep going on the burglar? Now I've got something, I really want to catch this git.'

Robyn stared at the map as she considered the options: decisions in a case of child abduction would always be scrutinised, internally and externally. The media were all over this story and a missed clue or any sign the case wasn't been taken seriously and they would be howling. On the other hand, in the last three months, six old people had been threatened with violence before their homes were robbed and this was the first lead. 'If you're getting somewhere, Lorraine, carry on. We've got enough of us here.' She noticed she'd smeared foundation on her hand.

'Thanks, Guv. Anything I need to know?'

Robyn nodded to Graham.

'Not much.' Graham leaned across the table to speak. 'All Ms Chivers does is go to work or go to this "Church of Immaculate Purity" …'

A noise somewhere between a snort and a laugh blasted out of the phone.

Graham jerked backwards, then recovered. 'So ladylike. Did you want to say something, Lorraine?'

'That church is bad news. They're not just a bunch of happy-clap-pies, they're anti just about everything and believe the Bible is law. They shoved a leaflet at me in the town centre one day and then closed in, kept telling me only Jesus could help a poor woman like me when the end of days came, which I think they said was going to be last Tuesday. I thought about arresting them for blasphemy, except I'm not sure it's still on the statute book.'

Robyn managed a smile. 'Have you still got the leaflet?' Ravi pointed at his computer where he'd brought up the church's website.

'Don't worry, Lorraine, we've got details here. Let me know when you get something concrete on the burglar.' Robyn felt stiffness in her neck as she stood up. She would need that information in case her decision came into question, which it would be if Ben wasn't found soon.

Robyn stepped across to Ravi's desk and leaned closer to see the screen. Ravi pushed his chair backwards so only his fingertips were on the keyboard.

Graham retrieved his phone. 'What rubbish are they spouting, Raver?'

'Lots about hell and sin.' Ravi squinted at the Gothic font. 'OK, basically, it doesn't matter who you are, race, nationality, we're all damned and our one hope of salvation is to give ourselves up to the Lord.' He clicked to another page. 'There's a "Campaigns" section. Pictures of them outside the walk-in clinic and ...' Ravi's voice tailed off and he scrolled the page down. Robyn had already read the notice for the next campaign, picketing Saints' Row, to disrupt the climax of the Gay Pride march through Meresbourne.

Ravi scrolled down. 'Yuck.' The screen filled with a bloody picture of an aborted foetus next to a coffin. 'So they're against abortion but say those who bring death should be killed themselves. A doctor was shot in the US because he carried out abortions and they're calling his killer a saint? That makes no sense at all.'

'And they're supposed to be Christian? What about "thou shalt not kill"?' Janice fished for a pin, then shoved a yellow one into the map at Lower Markham. 'I've just had the daftest call so far. A man wanted to report he could hear a child crying. When I asked him when he'd first heard this, he said a week ago.'

She shook her head as another phone rang, glanced at her watch, then gestured to Ravi to turn on the television. The one o'clock news droned through a foiled hijack, an international treaty and the potential for drought before Ravi upped the volume.

*A toddler has gone missing from a shopping centre in Meresbourne, Kent. The child is believed to have been abducted by a woman after a chance photo showed Benjamin Chivers, aged two, being led away.*

The newsreader cut to a serious-looking reporter in the shopping centre, teenagers fooling around behind him. They ran the CCTV footage with step-by-step commentary and lingered on the image of Ben walking away with the woman, before cutting back to the reporter, who was now standing near the Riverside doors. He pointed out possible escape routes: the main road was just the other side of Victoria Park and the train station only minutes' walk along the river path. After a warning of flash photography, they cut to the press briefing. Robyn stared at the screen. She wasn't sure who the person was, standing in a tatty room in a dark suit and plain blouse. Whoever they were, they looked a lot like Roger Bailley but with odd-coloured hair, lips darker than usual and the face a different colour from the neck. That was it, she realised. Now everyone could see her. Anyone could have seen her. Becky might be looking at her now ... The thought made her feel a little sick.

Ravi pressed the remote and the picture died. No one spoke until Janice came and laid her hand on Robyn's shoulder.

'Well done, Robyn. I don't know how you stayed so calm in front of all of those cameras. I hate having to do press briefings. No fun at all. Cup of tea?'

It was easy to forget Janice was a detective, filling as she did the role of hostess, agony aunt and even matchmaker at the station. The tea came from her desk store and the mini kettle they weren't supposed to have, for never-explained safety reasons. She stepped over Robyn's handbag and put down a mug and biscuits.

Robyn wondered for a second whether there was a reason she'd been given a mug with Miss Piggy on it, then thought it wasn't worth drawing attention to. 'Thanks. Have you found something?'

Janice continued to her own desk and pulled across a pile of spiral notebooks, aligning the edges. 'When Ravi mentioned I'd been involved, the case sounded familiar and checked back.'

She patted the notebooks. 'Sure enough, I've met Ms Chivers before. Three months ago, Gillian Green hired a bloke called Dean Harper to repair a gutter. Afterwards, he claimed he'd fixed other things while he was up on the roof so demanded more money. I noted Mrs Green was scared, though more of her employer than the builder.'

Janice turned a page of the notebook. One finger twisted a wisp of hair.

'I realised why when I met Ms Chivers – she was very particular about the Ms. She'd told Harper she'd pay him for the work specified and no more. He made threats and she called the police. When we started digging, we found a number of vulnerable people who'd paid up after he'd threatened them, which means goodness knows how many more were too embarrassed to admit they'd been had. We arrested him but as the amounts were petty, the guy got off with a fine.' Janice shrugged one shoulder. 'Previous record, drunk and disorderly, driving without tax and insurance. Kidnapping seems a bit out of his league. Do you want me to follow him up?'

'Yes, please. We can't overlook anything. Good work.'

'Wasn't he the guy who asked the judge if the courthouse roof needed fixing?' Graham cracked his knuckles. 'Cocky git. Hey, Janice. Are you planning on having your birthday barbecue this year? I bet your garden's looking even better now Martin's retired.'

Janice stood up, pushing hair from her face. 'How can you even think of a party when we've got a missing boy?' She made a grab for the notebooks. One flopped to the floor, then another.

'Only asking.' Graham shook his head.

Janice ducked below the desk to gather the notebooks. When she sat up, her jaw was clenched.

'Something up, Janice?' Robyn kept her voice low so Graham couldn't hear.

Somewhere under the litter of maps and statements on her desk there was a beep. Janice took the opportunity to start a call. Robyn made a mental note to catch her in private and have a chat. It was inevitable that people would be on edge during a case like this. After piling most of the paper into her in-tray, she retrieved the phone. There was one new message.

*Dad, or whatever you are now. Got your letter. Don't know what to say. Good luck in your new life 'cos it looks like you don't want your old one any more. Becky.*

# 7

It was an effort but Robyn kept her face steady as she re-read Becky's text. The counsellor at the gender identity clinic had stated the obvious by warning Robyn her actions would 'affect those closest to her'. What made the situation worse was that the process had made her realise there was only one person on that list. Exactly how Becky would take the news had been a constant preoccupation during her long brooding towards a decision. She hadn't wanted to discuss things with her daughter until she was sure she would go through with everything. After she'd booked the time off work, it didn't feel right to disturb Becky during her university exams. Then, there was the promise of a visit and she'd justified more delay, reasoning face-to-face was the best way to explain. She'd planned the confession in detail: she and Becky, talking over glasses of wine, like adults. At the end, they'd hug. Becky might shed a few tears but would offer her 'full support' or something similar that didn't sound so much like something Fell would say. Then Becky had announced she'd got a part in a festival play and was staying up in Norwich for the summer. An attempt to explain over the phone had ended in a wordless fug so, stuck for any other option, she'd written the letter. Now everything was in the open, Robyn despised her earlier cowardice. Her jumbled thoughts on how to reach out to Becky were interrupted by someone calling.

'Guv. Guv? The search has covered the area inside of the ring road – nothing.' Graham's face was grim.

The team absorbed the news and went back to work, their heads down. Everything was normal, except her. She should be leading them to find Ben not focusing on her own family worries though the urge to speak to Becky was close to overwhelming. Nowhere in the station was truly private: if she was going to do it, she'd have to go and sit in the car while everyone was absorbed in their tasks. With need overriding guilt, Robyn slipped out of the incident room and started down the stairs.

She realised she was dawdling when a group of Uniform clattered past her down the stairs, telling stories of the drunken exploits they'd had to deal with over the weekend. Robyn murmured a general greeting: she couldn't remember any of their names. They must be wondering why she was dithering on the staircase. She knew why: she'd put all of her words into the letter. There was a good chance she'd end up in a state after a conversation with Becky and everyone would stare even more. Better to make the call from home, which would also give her a few more hours to come up with something to say. Without thinking, she ran her fingers through her hair and it flopped over one eye, her fingers now sticky with gel.

Hating her indecisiveness, Robyn sent a short text back to Becky, nails sliding on the keys, sending love and saying she would call tonight. She steeled herself to turn back up the stairs, past the second floor, thinking now was as good a time as any to update Fell. The superintendent's office on the fifth floor was not somewhere anyone entered with pleasure. On this July afternoon, it would be an ordeal.

Robyn took a moment to take a deep breath before stepping into the outer office. Tracey was on the phone and held up a finger.

There were a number of theories about how Tracey had been able to work for Fell for so long, the most popular being that her own passion for perfume had killed off her sense of smell years ago. Today's was something in a squat golden bottle with a flower cap, sitting in pride of place on the desk next to her vast handbag. Phone clamped between her shoulder and ear, Tracey sprayed some onto her wrists as she said goodbye. The professional smile turned to Robyn.

'Hello, dear. You'll be wanting to update him on the progress with this little boy. He's just finishing a call and then has ten minutes free. In the meantime, you can tell me what you've done to yourself.'

You've prepared for this, Robyn told herself. You know what to say. She had never tried telling a real person before.

Tracey filled the silent gap. 'I just want to understand why you're doing this. Ever since you did the press conference, I've been fielding calls telling me you're a freak and shouldn't be allowed on a case with a kid. I know you're not the type for silly jokes and I want to help you but I need to know what's what.'

The bra constricted her chest as Robyn took a steadying breath, tasting musk. All the arguments so convincing in front of the mirror, were melting under Tracey's defined eyes.

'It's called gender dysphoria, it's …'

'Yes, I know what it's called, I had to type the memo. And I read through all of the crap from HR's diversity file. I know what you are, not who you are and that's what I need to know.'

'I'm me, Tracey. I haven't changed.' Robyn remembered Becky's bitter words and how inadequate her explanation must have seemed.

Behind the desk, Tracey angled her head, her hair rigid in its set waves.

'I haven't changed, I don't know what else to say. I'm the same person, just trying to fix the fact I'm in the wrong body. I'm still going to enter my camera club's competitions and I'm still not going to win. I'm going to renew my Town season ticket and have a pint after they lose.' She shook her head. 'Or maybe I'm supposed to only drink white wine now, I don't know.'

The painted lines of Tracey's brows lifted, lines appearing through the foundation. Her gaze had not left Robyn's face.

'Something hasn't been right for me for, well, as long as I can remember. I've never felt comfortable in my own skin. I thought getting married would sort it out, becoming a father.' Robyn blinked, not wanting to cry. 'There was still something big missing and it was inevitable Julie and I would split up. Being a detective is the only job I've ever wanted and I thought when I got into CID, this feeling of being a fraud would stop. But no matter how many cases I solved, I still felt like I was just pretending to be someone.'

Robyn's legs were threatening not to hold her up. She shuffled around the side of the chair and sank down. The temporary relief made her dizzy: she put her head in her hands and spoke through her fingers. 'A lot of things changed in a short time. The job came up in Meresbourne, my parents died, leaving me their house and Becky went to university.' She sat back. 'It suddenly hit me, I had no responsibilities for anyone else anymore and I had space to think about me.' Now she'd started, words felt like they wanted to come out. 'I knew deep down what I wanted to do: what was difficult was admitting it to myself and deciding whether I was strong enough to make the change.' She took a breath. 'Some time ago, I began talking to doctors and then, as I got more confident, to others like me. And I decided however hard things would be, I had to go ahead because I can't think of any other way I can be myself.'

Tracey blinked once. 'Are you gay?'

Robyn was gripping the sides of the chair, feeling where the fabric seat met the wooden frame, rough to smooth.

Behind the desk, wrinkles on Tracey's cleavage appeared and disappeared as her chest rose and fell.

'It's not the same. It's hard to explain.' Robyn made an effort to relax. 'Gender and sexuality are two different things. I've got to get myself sorted out first.'

Tracey's nails tapped the desk. 'And do you fancy kiddies?'

The sickly taste in her mouth made Robyn screw up her face. She took a deep breath and wiped her mouth on the back of her hand, lipstick smearing in a livid mark. 'No. Not now, not ever.' She looked at Tracey. 'I'm just trying to get the rest of the world to see me in the same way I see myself.'

'And you picked today to start.' Tracey's face had softened.

'And I picked today.'

They looked at each other. Something beeped. Without looking, Tracey pressed a button on the keyboard and the sound stopped. They were wearing the same shade of nail varnish. She stood up. 'Remember, you need more balls to be a woman than a man ever has. I'll sort things this end, you just catch whoever took the lad. And if you'll take my advice, relax and go out for a pint with people. Or a white wine. I think everyone drinks everything these days.' Turning to the inner office, she knocked and entered without pausing. Robyn heard some low words, before Tracey reappeared and gestured she should go in.

Robyn's shoes squealed on the lino. She felt flushed and wished she'd had a chance to check her make-up. 'I wanted to give you an update on the Ben Chivers case, sir. The national media is now taking an interest.'

Fell was sitting at his desk, chin touching the tips of his steepled fingers. He gazed over Robyn's left ear.

'We are following two main lines of enquiry, sir: tracing the boy's father and also investigating whether this could be an attack on the mother, in connection with her work.'

Fell's gaze drifted to above Robyn's right ear, without ever falling on her face.

'Both of those require organisation. Have you discounted the possibility of a chance snatch?'

'No, sir. We're tracking the movements of previous offenders.'

Best never to say too much to Fell. He could spin out a single fact to a three-page report. His fingers were pressed together now, as if he were praying.

'No loose ends, Bailley.'

Robyn left the office, grateful for the fresher air of the corridor.

# 8

Robyn took her time on the way back towards the incident room. Tracey was right, as usual. That was unlikely to be the last interrogation. Everyone would be paying her more attention than before. Her and her performance. She hadn't started well, not even bringing anything back for the team after her holiday. The fact she hadn't actually been away sounded, now she thought about it, a bit feeble. She lingered on the stairs, by the second floor exit, thinking there was no time to go out for something when everyone was so busy. Diverting to the canteen, Robyn bought bags of sweets. She could sense glances, looks and whispers but when you were surrounded by people trained to observe, you couldn't expect anything else.

In the CID office, there was a purposeful buzz of low conversation and typing. Robyn put the sweets on the corner of her desk, wondered if she should announce them and decided just to let everyone get on. With Fell's implicit backing, Robyn decided better to risk the budget early than be accused of delay.

She looked up the number for her counterpart in Uniform and dialled. With the big buttons of the desk phone, she could press them with her nails, then wondered whether a woman would naturally do that.

'DI Pond.'

'Hello, Matthew. It's Robyn Bailley.'

'Ah. I heard you were back. How are you?'

She wondered what he had heard and what was behind the question, then rebuked herself for overreacting because it was such an ordinary question, just what normal people said to each other.

'Fine, thanks. And you – how's the training going?'

'Not bad, thanks though the heat is making it hard work.'

'I'm sure. How long until the race?'

'Two weeks.' Matthew paused. 'Which means we'd better find that lad before then, otherwise we won't be able to spare any officers to deal with the road closures for a cycling event.'

'The intention is to find him well before then and that's what I was calling about. I want to get vehicle check-points set up around town.'

'OK. Did you have any particular locations in mind?'

'We need to cover the routes someone leaving the shopping centre could have taken. Let's get one by the station, one on the inner ring by the Docks' roundabout road.'

'Righto. Anything else I need to know?'

'We've got nothing new at this end, Matthew. I was hoping you'd have something.'

'Nothing. We're getting public support though. It's a bit of a pain sometimes. People come to take part in the searches and bring their dog along thinking it's Lassie, then all it does is bark at the police dogs.'

Robyn grunted something close to a laugh. 'OK, thanks, Matthew. Good hunting.' She stretched back, suddenly ravenous.

'Is now a good time?' Janice was standing next to her. 'I've got the contact list Ms Chivers provided.'

'Is that it?' At the bottom of the short list were two women with different surnames at an address in north London. Robyn pointed. 'Who are these two?'

'Ms Chivers' mother and sister.' Janice grimaced. 'Convictions between them: shoplifting, possession of cannabis and breaching the peace.'

'Ah. Graham said she seemed reluctant to talk about them. And no mention of anyone who could be Ben's father. Why not, do you think? A messy break-up or could he be dead?'

'If she'd lost the father of her child, why weren't there any pictures of him around?'

'I only went into the hall and kitchen but you're right, there was nothing personal on display, not even a picture by Ben on the fridge. Oh, you wanted to tell me something earlier?' Robyn pointed to a chair. Janice sat on its edge, crossing her legs.

'Talk to me.'

'It's probably nothing ...' Janice folded her hands. '... but my first thought after I knew we were looking for Ben was that his mother had got rid of him herself.'

'What?' Robyn leant forward.

'When I visited the house about the builder, Ms Chivers acted as if Ben didn't exist.' Janice breathed out, set her jaw. 'I don't think he's physically abused but emotionally ...' She shook her head. 'Gillian Green at least seems to care for him. From what I've seen of his mother, she sees him as a lifestyle accessory, cute but I wonder if he's now getting in her way.'

'OK, tell me exactly what makes you think this.'

'It was April when I interviewed Ms Chivers about the dodgy builder. Ben was stuck inside watching some educational programme, even though it was a beautiful day. I said "hello" to him.' Janice smiled. 'Ms Chivers snapped at me for disturbing his studies. I made an excuse and went upstairs. His room was like a classroom. And the books – all weird American things with titles like

"Introducing your toddler to God" but not a single toy. He couldn't play in the garden anyway – it's been concreted over.'

Robyn heard the vitriol of a passionate gardener. She tried to remember the last time she'd seen Janice so animated.

'The one time I saw Ms Chivers actually speak to Ben was to criticise some homework he'd done. Homework! Then she had a go at Mrs Green, saying she wasn't teaching him properly.' Janice stared at the ceiling. 'He was eighteen months old.'

As he walked past, Graham dropped a piece of paper into Robyn's in-tray. Janice swung around to face him. 'Graham, do you think Ms Chivers loves her son?'

Graham rocked back on his heels. 'Steady on, Janice. What's wrong with wanting your kid to do well?'

'Because he's not being allowed a childhood and he's being sucked into that weird cult she's part of.'

Graham shrugged. 'OK, she's a bit intense, one of those, what, "tiger mothers", but she's right: a kid does better when you push them a bit.'

'And the church? All that fire and brimstone?' Janice folded her arms. 'What about that case where they found the body of a boy in the Thames, killed because his aunt thought he was possessed by evil spirits?'

A mother harming her own child: Robyn remembered tragic cases where people hadn't considered the unthinkable until it was too late. 'I agree, we need to consider all angles but what about the practicalities? We can't see much of the woman in the photograph except she's definitely white. Are you suggesting Ms Chivers could have arranged for someone to take Ben?'

Janice pursed her lips. 'I've no idea.'

Ravi's voice came from across the room. 'I watched this programme where they put hidden cameras in nurseries to show parents what happened to their kids during the day. How about this? Maybe Ms Chivers got someone to test the nanny?'

After a few seconds, Graham laughed. 'What sort of impression have you all got of Ms Chivers?'

Ravi turned back to the screen and hunkered down.

'What about the kids in the Docks sniffing glue – you want Ben to grow up like them? OK, he doesn't seem to have a father but his mother isn't exactly shirking her responsibilities.' Graham put his hands behind his head.

'All I know is we're trying to return a child to a mother who, who ...' Janice's hands flapped. She seemed to be searching for words. 'Who has very different ideas to most people of how to bring up a child and also thinks God's backing her up.'

Robyn held up her hands for quiet. 'Janice, the law is clear. If there's evidence of Ben being harmed, we can act but first we have to find him. We need to speak to everyone who knows Ms Chivers. We'll keep everything you've said in mind but for goodness sake, don't make any accusations outside this room until you have evidence.' She toyed with the list of Ms Chivers' contacts. 'We could do with much more detail on Ben's home life and Mrs Green should have had time to recover by now. Why don't you come with me, Janice, as you've met her before?'

Walking down the corridor with Janice was a series of hellos and even a smile from the desk sergeant. At the top of the steps to the car park, she turned to Robyn. 'Do you mind if we take your car? I've got Martin's van and it's not the most comfortable.'

Robyn led the way. 'What went wrong this morning? You've only had your new car, what, a few months?'

Janice called a greeting to someone crossing the car park; Robyn took the chance to fumble her key out of the handbag. 'Right, where are we going?'

'One of the tower blocks in the Docks estate. All very fitting.' Janice laughed. 'The mistress lives in Upper Town and the servant lives in the Docks. Isn't tradition wonderful?'

'My mother used to say, "From Upper Town, you always look down". She thought Upper Towners were snobs. Still, if someone had offered her a house up there, she wouldn't have hesitated.' Robyn swung the car around the roundabout.

Janice wrinkled her nose. 'I can't see why everyone thinks so much of the place. Living in all those rows with everyone on top of you, no thank you. Interesting Gillian is in one of the tower blocks though. I had her down as more of a net-curtained, thirties semi in Barton type of person.'

'True. But then people can surprise you. Look at Lorraine: she's gone the other way. She spent ages talking about buying a new flat near the clubs on the riverside, then chooses a cottage in Gaddesford with roses growing around the door.' Robyn was struck by a thought of what her faded home said about her.

They were approaching the edge of the Docks estate, cars parked on either side and passed the first of the tower blocks, once white, now mottled grey and green against the blue sky. Janice glanced out of the window. 'When these blocks were built, Martin said they were giving the finger to Upper Town.'

'They give the finger to everyone. Four stabbings this year, it feels like only a matter of time before someone gets killed. Our last community effort seemed to have no effect.'

Janice craned forward. 'We need the third block, "Convoy".'

The tyres crunched over something in the parking space. A pair of kids swooped past on bikes: Robyn stepped into a dribble of fresh saliva. A sharp breeze funnelled between the tower blocks, blowing litter between bollards. The front door was held open by a rucked mat. One wall of the entrance hall was covered in grey mailboxes, leaflets spilling out. Janice saw the stains in the lift and insisted on using the stairs to the third floor.

Gillian's door was a drab brown. While they waited, Robyn wondered how the potted lily by the door managed to survive in the dim lobby until she brushed a dusty leaf and felt plastic. The spy hole darkened. There was the scrape of bolts being drawn back and clicks from multiple locks.

Still in the cardigan and skirt she'd been wearing that morning, Gillian's hair was now back in a bun, secured by crossed pins. In the main room, she sank into the one armchair, reaching for the woollen throw covering the chair's arms.

At Gillian's gesture, Robyn lowered herself down onto a spindly chair with a thin, hand-stitched cushion. Her knees were higher than her hips and she winced as the tape between her legs tightened with protest. Fortunately, Gillian's eyes were turned to the window: they were level with the rusting roofs of the warehouses. Janice had taken a solid chair from under the small dining table and got out her notebook.

'Thank you for seeing me again, Mrs Green. This is DC Janice Warrener – you met a few months ago.' There was no reaction from Gillian, just her fingers twisting at the fringe of the throw. 'We wanted to ask a few more questions.'

'You haven't found him yet?' Gillian shuddered.

'I'm afraid not. Would you like someone with you, a neighbour maybe?' Robyn wondered if it was her appearance making Gillian uncomfortable then decided the woman must be short-sighted because she seemed to look through things rather than at them. The interview had to be handled with care to avoid losing any shred of memory.

'Mrs Green, can you think of anyone who might have a reason to take Ben?'

'No. No one.'

'Do you know who Ben's father is?'

'No.' Gillian showed no inclination to continue.

Robyn gritted her teeth. From somewhere in the building, there was the sound of a toilet flushing. 'Mrs Green, has anyone mentioned Ben's father?'

'No. Ms Chivers never speaks about him and Benjamin's too young to ask any questions.' Gillian's voice sounded weary.

'Does Ms Chivers have regular men she sees? A boyfriend,

perhaps? I'm asking these questions because the first step in an investigation is to eliminate the family.'

'I took a message for her once. A company rang with a deal to restart her subscription to something. I hadn't heard of the company so I looked it up.' Gillian gave a guilty look. 'It was a dating agency.' She pressed her lips together, then raised her chin. 'I'm supposed to take messages, I wasn't snooping.'

There was a crisp noise as Janice turned a page of her notebook. 'Of course not, Mrs Green, no one's suggesting you were.'

Thumps from the floor above rattled a cluster of photographs on the side table: Gillian stretched out to steady them. In a silver frame, a young woman wearing glasses and a skewed mortar board held up a scroll. A toddler looked into the camera with a grave expression – Ben, taken maybe six months before. Finally, there was one of Gillian herself, holding flowers, surrounded by young children.

'You were a teacher?' Robyn tried to imagine her keeping order.

Gillian's face lit up for a moment, then sagged. 'All my life.'

'So how did you end up working as a nanny?'

'Schools were changing, lots of tests and pressure. I didn't enjoy it any more. So I took the opportunity for early retirement. I thought we could use the time to travel and …' There was a hesitation. Gillian leant back against the cushion.

Robyn wondered why she hadn't already spotted the bare ring finger, despite the 'Mrs'. 'You said "we" – was there someone else?'

'I was married. Thirty-seven years. Then he left me, just after I'd retired. I don't even think there was another woman. He just didn't want to be with me anymore. My pension wasn't enough and I didn't want to go back to a school.' Gillian was rocking herself in the chair, eyes unfocused.

'How did you get the job with Ms Chivers?'

'I'd signed up to a couple of agencies, thinking I could do private tutoring. Ms Chivers wanted someone who could teach. I've been there since Benjamin was six months old.'

'Can such a young child be taught?'

'He is part of a programme for gifted children. The lessons started before he was even born, with material played when he was in the womb. Ms Chivers values education.' Gillian's voice sounded prim. 'We get packs sent through for home study, supported with spiritual and nutritional advice and he goes to school for group work.' Robyn glanced at Janice, whose expression said 'I told you so'.

'So this is Ms Chivers' way of giving Ben a good start in life?' Robyn eased her position on the chair, hearing it creak.

Gillian's face was now in shadow. She nodded, once, twice. 'You don't know how hard she had it growing up. She never complains though she often talks about how nobody ever expected anything of her, how she had to ask for homework and stay behind to learn. Now she's giving Benjamin the education she didn't have.'

Janice spoke from the window. 'And is Ben happy?'

Gillian tilted her head. 'Happy? He does his work.' She blinked. 'Sometimes he doesn't apply himself enough but he'll learn. The programme says he's getting all the training and guidance needed to be a leader.'

'Even without a father?' Janice had put down her pad. Robyn cast her a warning glance.

'He must be happy; he hasn't known anything else.' Gillian's voice was getting stronger, becoming a voice you could imagine reaching the back of a classroom. 'Just like his mother. She's so strong and she helps others. I'd only just started working for her, when my ex-husband tried to stop a payment and she sorted it all out.'

Robyn raised her voice. 'What kind of mother is Ms Chivers?'

'Ms Chivers knows what she's doing. She's got a career and she earns enough to bring up a baby on her own. And the programme does wonders. I wish more parents kept up discipline like her, it'd make life much easier for teachers.'

'And you do a lot for her?'

'To help Ms Chivers, I do everything around the house, the chores …' Gillian paused, the shadows on her face deepening.

Robyn shifted her weight as her leg was beginning to cramp. 'And Ms Chivers works hard?'

'She works long hours and goes to seminars in the evenings, then there's church and voluntary work at weekends. I feed and bathe Benjamin and put him to bed.'

'What are you going to do when Ms Chivers moves to Switzerland?'

'I'm hoping to go with her. I've never been there.'

'It's not decided yet, even though she's going in a month?' Robyn and Janice exchanged a glance.

'No. She asked me how I'd cope when I didn't speak German.' Gillian sounded defensive for the first time. 'If I don't go, I don't know what she'll do.'

'Gillian, please think. Where do you think Ms Chivers met Ben's father? This could be critical.'

'I've wondered myself.' Gillian quickly touched each hairpin. 'I can't imagine where she'd meet someone good enough for her. I don't know.'

Robyn decided it was safest to agree. 'Neither do we and we have to find out. You're sure Ms Chivers never mentions anyone? Are you aware of any payments Ms Chivers receives or people who give Ben presents?'

'Nothing.' Gillian dabbed at her nose with the tissue.

Robyn had wondered how to phrase the next question without setting off too many emotions. 'Do you think Ms Chivers planned to be a mother on her own?'

'Well I didn't know her then.' There was a small flap of the spotted hands. 'Ms Chivers always seems to have everything under control.'

'And does she love Benjamin?'

Janice looked up from her notebook waiting for an answer but the question seemed to puzzle Gillian. After a moment, she reached down to her handbag and rummaged before pulling out a car key. 'Ms Chivers bought a brand new car for me to use when I'm driving Benjamin when she decided my car wasn't safe enough in a crash.' She closed the bag before setting it on the carpet. 'And she bought me the mobile so she always knew where he was …'

'Has Ben wandered off before?' Robyn hadn't got what she wanted but needed to keep Gillian talking.

'Never. We usually go to the shopping centre on Mondays and I think he finds it a bit overwhelming because he goes out so little, apart from school.'

A gull screamed outside the window. 'We're aware of the recent dispute you had with a builder. Might Ms Chivers have any other enemies?'

Gillian answered without pausing. 'No.'

'What makes you so certain?'

'Because she helps everyone. Unless …' Gillian tightened her grip on the throw. 'I hear about the cases she deals with for the advice centre – some of the things those landlords try to do is appalling. Maybe one of them?'

A clock chimed the half hour. Robyn swallowed. Ben had been missing for eight hours. Feeling her legs cramping, Robyn stood up, grateful to stretch her muscles. 'Thank you, Mrs Green. I know this must be hard for you. If you think of anything, however small, please call us – time is important.'

Gillian remained in the chair, face turned towards the picture of Ben.

'Oh, by the way, have you spoken to Ms Chivers today?'

'Yes. She phoned to ask me when I was bringing round the dry-cleaning.'

# 9

Janice had been silent as they left and sat in the passenger seat worrying at a mark on her trousers.

'So?' Robyn pulled out into the traffic. 'What did you think?'

'Gillian's position seems pretty precarious and she's obviously worried about losing her job. With Ben gone, Ms Chivers can't go to Switzerland.' Janice's voice didn't have its usual warmth.

'Come on.' Robyn glanced at Janice, who was staring straight ahead. 'Can you imagine Gillian kidnapping anyone? And the pharmacist's statement confirms she was in the shop when Ben vanished.'

They were back on the ring road before Robyn ended the silence. 'I suppose Gillian could have introduced Ben to a friend and sent her to take Ben. What do you think?'

'I'll check it out. I can't see Gillian hurting Ben – she's more of a mother to him than Ms Chivers.'

'Everybody has their own ways of managing stress. Gillian thinks she's a good person, even though Ms Chivers does sound like a pushy parent. The landlord angle sounds worth following up. We didn't get much else new, though.'

'There was the dating agency. I'll see whether Ms Chivers met – oh.' Janice broke off and sneezed.

'Bless you. Can you also check with Graham, see whether he's spoken to Ms Chivers' mother and sister? They don't seem a close family ...' There was a snort from the passenger seat. '... but we need to check everything.'

Janice made a fuss of getting a tissue out of her handbag. 'I wonder whether Ms Chivers bought Gillian a new car because she loves Ben or because she's just protecting her investment.' She blew her nose.

'Oh hell, I forgot about the roadblocks.' Robyn slowed the car, dreading how long it would take them to get through the queue of traffic in front.

Janice's phone rang. She took the call, with a quick look towards Robyn. 'Hello, love. No. Is everything all right? Yes, OK.' The phone went back into her bag and she folded her hands in her lap. Robyn turned up the air-conditioning.

'How's Martin enjoying retirement?'

'He's fine, thank you.'

They moved forward. Robyn opened the window as a red-faced constable in a stab vest approached, holding out a leaflet with Ben's picture. Robyn tried to remember the officer's name.

Janice leaned over from the passenger seat. 'Hello, Donna. Got anything?'

'Hello, Janice, ah, DI Bailley. Nothing on the boy, just a few minor offences.'

'How's your boy doing at the new nursery, Donna?'

'Better, thanks, Janice. Best get on with this queue. Everyone's being pretty good though, they all want the lad found.'

As Robyn parked at the station, Graham's Vauxhall pulled in beside them. He looked pleased with himself and started talking as

Robyn was still struggling to free her handbag strap from the gear lever.

'I've got something. The development at the Docks Ms Chivers is working on – you know who owned the warehouses before the current owner? The Dearmans.'

The three of them walked together across the car park. There was no hint of the temperature dropping, even as the low sun cast long shadows across the pitted tarmac.

'Guv, this could be big.' Graham wiped his forehead with a handkerchief. 'There was a time when the Dearmans were involved in every crime in Meresbourne somehow or another.'

Robyn nodded for Graham to continue.

'Kenny Prentiss got made DI because he spent his whole career locking up the Dearman family and their crew. One of his last gigs was to put Gabriel, Eddie Dearman's son and heir, away for ten years for multiple counts of assault, fraud and general nastiness. So then baby of the family, Micky, took over from his father and things changed a bit.'

Janice nudged Robyn. 'All this was about a year before you came back to Meresbourne.'

Graham grunted at the interruption but held the main door open. 'Yeah. Things calmed down a lot with Micky in charge, because he was more like his grandfather, Old Man Dearman, who called himself a "businessman".' He mimed tipping a cap.

'Now Gabriel was always Eddie Dearman's blue-eyed boy because they were both thugs. But Micky was clever, didn't want to go into the beating-up business and I think his grandfather funded him early on. When the Council sold land in the Docks, Micky bought a couple of warehouses, started holding raves. Probably kept his old man happy by giving him a quiet place to do people over or store things out of sight.'

Reaching the stairs, they all turned for the canteen. Graham kept talking. 'The problem came when Micky thought there would be easy money in property development. He gets a local consortium together and puts in a big application for a new casino and club. So when, after lots of wrangling, the planning application gets turned down, young Micky's lost a pile.'

He paused, letting this sink in.

'How long have the Dearmans been in Meresbourne?' Robyn had read multiple files on the Dearmans but there had been no crimes she was aware of in the last two years.

'Since the Norman Conquest, if you believe them. That's why they think they own the place. Maybe we should put them on the "Marvellous Meresbourne" heritage trail – number six, Croft's Jewellery, scene of a Dearman hold-up ...' Graham laughed at his own joke.

Robyn bought a selection of buns for the team, even though they appeared a bit stale. They walked to the lift. Janice turned to Graham. 'So how does this link to Ben?'

Graham began holding up the fingers of his free hand. 'One, if Micky was forced to sell the warehouse at a low price, then he's going to want to make the loss up now the site's expected to get planning permission. Two, if the owners aren't around, who's involved and local?' He didn't wait for an answer. 'Our Ms Chivers. Three, Micky doesn't have fancy lawyers – if he wants to persuade someone to do something, he goes back to the old ways. Four, she's off abroad soon, they have to act fast.' Graham held up four fingers, then swore as he spilt his tea.

Janice held out a tissue to Graham, taking his cup.

'Taking a child would be a big departure from their previous work.' Robyn pushed the button for the lift. 'And if Ben had been kidnapped to get a cut from the land sale, why hasn't a demand been made?'

Graham was mopping his fingers and didn't seem to hear the question.

'Where did you get all this?' Robyn stepped into the lift.

'If you buy a man a pint after his horse lost, it's amazing what he'll tell you.' Graham sounded smug.

'How reliable do you think he is?' Robyn wondered whether sweat was showing through her blouse and if she dared take her jacket off. The second floor corridor was stifling with unmoved air.

Back in the incident room, Robyn called the team together for the six o'clock news. Ben was still only a line in the national news but the local report seemed to be enjoying the drama. A long bulletin covered the press conference and shots of search teams in the park, before cutting to a dim room. A lean man, captioned as Reverend Lewis declared his church was praying for Benjamin's safe return to their sister Melissa. The camera panned around a circle of people on plastic chairs, their heads bowed. The reporter then appeared live, standing outside the shopping centre on the footbridge over the muddy trickle of the river Gadd. 'No one knows where Ben is now.' He paused dramatically. 'And, as the day passes, time may be running out.'

Robyn turned off the television. 'I hate the way everything gets dramatised. OK, everyone, let's review what we know.'

The team clustered around the evidence board to go through leads. Robyn listened, trying to maintain a distance and avoid getting bogged down in details. The investigation seemed to be going by the book – the team was working together well; everyone was now paying attention to Ravi as he summarised information coming in through social media. Robyn didn't notice she was spinning a pencil in circles around her fingers until it dropped to the desk with a clatter. They had plenty of lines of enquiry but not one she could point to and say there was the strand she could follow to Ben. She forced herself to confront the fact that it might be her that had changed and she was too busy focusing on herself to see anything else. As she picked up the pencil, she noticed one of her nails had a chip in the polish. She'd have to redo them tonight, assuming she even got home tonight. And she had to call Becky.

There was an expectant pause. In the background, a phone rang. Robyn realised Ravi had sat down and the team were waiting for her. She stood, conscious of being pinned between the team's rapt stares and Ben's steady gaze from the board behind which seemed to reproach her for not paying attention. She shoved her own problems to the back of her mind.

'Right. It's nearly ten hours since Ben was taken. These next few hours are critical because we have no sightings and no leads. We need to fix that.' Robyn paused, making sure everyone acknowledged this. 'Four lines of enquiry. Number one: we still don't know who Ben's father is. He could have found out about Ben and arranged a female accomplice to take him. Number two: Melissa Chivers' work is linked to a controversial planning application in the Docks area and Ben may have been taken in connection with this. Three, direct attacks on Ms Chivers. We know a builder made threats when she stood up to him and a landlord may have a grudge because of her voluntary work defending tenants. Finally, we have a couple of known sex offenders in the area.' Robyn became conscious of Janice's gaze. 'Oh and it's worth keeping in mind Ms Chivers hasn't reacted in the usual way to a child's disappearance, which may mean something or nothing. We haven't got a lot to go on so we'll have to do this the old-fashioned way and be detectives. I want an update from all of you in an hour.'

As the team returned to work, Robyn loitered by her desk, restless, feeling she was missing something. The calls were still coming in with unhelpful suggestions, the constables bringing over notes to be recorded. Janice stood before the map holding a yellow pin.

'I'm going to have to put a Post-it note in the sea to represent calls saying Ben's abroad. It's from someone in Glasgow whose sister in Melbourne "saw" Ben an hour ago. She thought she'd better call "just in case".'

They looked at each other, then both smiled. Janice dropped the note into a bin. Robyn glanced at her watch. It was new, a woman's watch, smaller than her old one; she had to look closer to see the numbers.

'Janice, it's time you went. You shouldn't even have been here today. Go and enjoy what's left of your birthday.'

'Well, I've had enough of them, they're nothing special any more. We didn't have anything planned.' She became serious. 'A case like this makes you worry for your own kids, even though they're all grown up. Is your Becky coming down this summer?'

Breathing in before she spoke, Robyn made an effort to sound relaxed. 'No, she's staying up at uni for the holidays because she's got a part in some summer play. I guess that counts as a job for an English student.'

'You've got to let them find their own way.' Janice gave the cluster of photographs on the corner of her desk a fond smile. 'At least my Simon seems settled now. Abi's finished her gap year after her degree and has signed up for an MA, which just sounds like an excuse to keep being a student. Josh is supposed to be job-hunting now he's finished his degree but he's in Cornwall camping with his mates at the moment doing goodness-knows-what.'

'I'll tell you what to do with your tall, dark handsome son, Janice. Lock him up until he's thirty, otherwise you'll be a grandmother before you know it.' Lorraine had walked in and was standing beside them.

'Not something to joke about.' Janice folded her arms. 'Fortunately, for an anxious mother anyway, the poor lad had his heart broken when he was eighteen and he's more interested in sport and music. Anyway, assuming he's passed his exams, he should now have a law degree so I've told him he's got to get himself out of trouble from now on.'

'Right.' The chatter about normal things was a momentary relief but Robyn was conscious they had made no progress and, beside her, Lorraine was fizzing with energy.

'Guv, have you got a couple of minutes to talk about the break-ins? I may have something.' Lorraine perched on the corner of the desk, one leg swinging, even before Robyn nodded.

'All six burglaries have had a common approach. An elderly person has opened the door and someone barges past them, grabbing cash and small valuables, leaving before the victim recovers enough to call for help. In Pickley, on Friday, we finally had a witness who saw someone running away. I thought the sighting was useless at first as she didn't see his face until I thought about her description of the clothes. She said he was all in black, long-sleeved and skin-tight as if he was wearing a wetsuit.'

She pulled a piece of paper from her bag.

'This is the report of an incident in May, before these burglaries started. You know the Gaddesford bank holiday festival: arts, crafts, music, all sorts? I was there, with the band, we were playing a set in the marquee. Anyway, all the artists in the village put on exhibitions and open their studios to anyone who wants to come in. So, on Tuesday, when an artist reported cash and some other bits missing, there wasn't a lot we could do as the whole village had tramped through their home the day before.'

Robyn's attention was caught by Graham holding his hand up for quiet, his mobile to his ear.

'Guv? You want me to come back?' Lorraine was drumming a rhythm on the desk.

'Sorry, Lorraine, carry on. So what makes you think this earlier theft is connected, when it appeared to be opportunistic?'

'I think he was warming up, testing a method ...'

Graham interrupted, phone held up. 'Guv, the search teams need to know the priorities for tomorrow so they can get the overtime budget approved.'

With a shrug of acceptance, Lorraine strolled back to her desk. Robyn scanned the map – Ravi had shaded the areas already searched. The choice now was to devote resources tomorrow to the Docks or the villages. As Graham talked cricket into the phone, Robyn ran her fingers over the map, seeking inspiration.

'The Docks.' She turned to face Graham. 'Search all the warehouses. There's a lot of waste ground and places to hide. Volunteer teams are already out in the villages. I think Ben's close and we can check out the potential link to Ms Chivers' work.'

Graham was grinning as he passed on the instructions. She would have to have a word with him as she didn't want him to be thinking they were chasing the Dearmans. Robyn turned towards Lorraine when Janice gave a cry of triumph. 'Here we are. June fifth. Anonymous tip-off: something hidden in warehouse B at the Docks. Man's voice, distorted, no background sounds, no number, nothing to follow-up. We can check this out as well.'

'Warehouse B?' Graham checked his own notes. 'That's the one Ms Chivers did the planning for.'

Robyn breathed a silent thanks. She'd never trusted detectives who claimed they acted on hunches but sometimes she was pushed to know why she made certain decisions.

Ravi hunched over his computer. 'I've got the Docks up on Google Earth. Which one's B?'

Graham leaned closer. 'Pull back a bit. It's the second one in from the estuary mouth.' The screen showed the dark rectangles of the warehouses between the pale squares of tower blocks and the grey curve of the river. 'Right, now go in. No, there, there. According to the *Gazette*, it's going to be a posh hotel with river views.'

Ravi zoomed in. 'Why would posh people want to stay in Meresbourne?'

Graham laughed. 'Apparently, Meresbourne is going to have a "leisure-led" revival, whatever one of those is. It'll never bring as many jobs as the Docks had though …'

Robyn brought her hand flat down on the desk, the bang getting everyone's attention. 'Yes, all very interesting but we need hard leads. We'll need warrants to get access to sites on the Docks – Ravi can you get those? Janice, sorry, before you go, can you get the road blocks sorted for tomorrow?'

Robyn walked across to Lorraine, who was trying to find a space in a bin. The team had been drinking a lot of coffee.

'Lorraine, I'm sorry. Carry on. So you think the Gaddesford crime is linked to the rest of the burglaries?'

Lorraine drew the file towards her again. 'Well, obviously there, he didn't need to intimidate the owner because the door was open. Still, a lot of things tally. A quick in and out and only small things taken.' She cocked her head to one side, pausing before the punchline. A trick she'd learned from Graham, thought Robyn, gesturing for her to continue. 'I reckon he's a cyclist, wearing Lycra and only taking small things like jewellery because he puts them in his bike panniers.' She smiled. 'When prompted, the Gaddesford artist remembered her neighbour had complained about a cyclist in the lane, because they kicked a cat which was rubbing itself against his bike. So, I want to check the CCTV, see whether we've got any other sightings.'

'How do you think he targets houses?' Robyn was following the logic.

'That's the big question. I think he targets the villages because there are fewer people around and he obviously likes the elderly because they'll open the door then not put up a fight.'

'Look at organisations working with the elderly, council, charities.'

'Top of my list for tomorrow, Guv. Now if I can, I've got a gig tonight?'

Of course. Lorraine's band was playing the regular Monday night jazz jam. Robyn knew, because she'd always emphasised to the team that they should have a life outside the police.

Robyn glanced at her watch: seven-fifteen. If tonight had been a regular night, she'd be getting ready to go the Meresbourne Town testimonial match for the departing manager. Lorraine was hovering, her bag slung over her shoulder: Robyn nodded acceptance.

Janice stood up, holding up her phone. 'I've got a call for you, Robyn – it's Khalid, the new media guy. He wants a word.'

'OK, put him through, then you go home.'

A map was covering her phone, so it was three rings before Robyn answered it.

'Good evening, Robyn. How are you?'

The line crackled. She used the pause to dredge her memory for the one occasion she'd met Khalid Guler, a couple of months before, when he'd been introduced at one of Fell's senior team meetings when Roger had been deputising because DCI Golding was off sick again Khalid had embarked on something called a "cross-silo listening programme". She hadn't stayed because she was busy with a case and Carl Golding had only been off for a week. There was no telling how long he would be off for this time.

'Fine, thanks. And you?'

Khalid's voice drifted in and out mixed with traffic noise.

'… seminar in London … current exposure … multi-channel … leverage …' Ravi waved and left. Janice was still straightening the items on her desk.

The wail of a siren cut through the fractured speech, followed by a beep as the line went dead. Matthew appeared in the doorway, already changed into his cycling kit. Robyn pointed to her phone, trying Khalid's number. Her call back went straight to voicemail.

Graham and Matthew were talking in low voices.

'Anything?' There was no hope in the question: Robyn knew she would have been told of anything important.

'Discarded syringes and a stash of empty handbags in Victoria Park, presumably stolen. A rough-sleeper whacked a Police Community Support Officer with a "Clean up after your dog" sign because she woke him up. Not serious but she's gone to the hospital for a tetanus booster.' Matthew scratched his five o'clock shadow and Robyn fought the urge to check her own chin. 'The check-points on the main road found four untaxed cars, two with no insurance: all makes up the numbers.' His smile was a workmanlike expression, not touching his eyes.

Robyn sighed, appreciating the attempt at lightening the mood, just not able to share it. 'What about the house-to-house searches?'

Matthew tapped his foot. 'One of our dogs sniffed out cannabis in someone's locker at the shopping centre.'

'Doesn't get us any closer to Ben, though.' She worried at a ridge of skin by a fingernail. 'What could we have missed so far?' The media

71

would ask about every aspect of the investigation – that must be why Khalid was calling.

'Now it's getting dark, the search teams will be standing down for the night.' Matthew was shifting his weight from foot to foot, his cycle shoes making an odd noise on the lino.

There was a pause. Robyn thought through the twelve hours since Ben had gone. If he had managed to escape or been dumped, the darkness would hold its own terrors for a toddler without his mother. And if someone was with him – there was another set of possibilities she didn't want to start thinking about.

Matthew put his hand on the door. 'We've had search teams all over the place, every news channel's showing the kid's picture. I don't think there's anything more we can do tonight. The teams will start again at first light.' He left, pulling the door behind him, the catch shutting with a snap.

Robyn stood up, seeing Janice at her desk with a pile of statements in front of her. 'Go home, Janice. Thank you so much for coming in but there's nothing more we can do today and we all need to get some rest.'

He could be anywhere by now.' Janice pushed her hair back from her face and sighed.

Her look of defeat echoed Robyn's thoughts. She knew it was up to her to lift everyone out of this. 'Right, tomorrow. Graham, you lead the Dock search and Janice, with him – you two know the area best. I've got to speak to our press team first thing ...'

Graham sniffed, miming yack-yack.

'... and I want to have another word with Ms Chivers. Now, good-night.' Robyn picked up the map of the Docks.

Graham's face was neutral. 'You sure that's a good idea, Guv?'

'I'm leading this case and she's the mother of the missing boy. Why shouldn't I speak to her?'

'Come on, Janice, let's get you out of here.' Graham picked up Janice's bag and started for the door.

The door swung shut behind them. The debris of a day lay scattered around the office. Somewhere, there was a small boy, away from home. Robyn forced herself to think. If the kidnapper had planned the snatch, they would have prepared somewhere to take Ben, bought nappies and food. Unless his welfare was irrelevant and he was already dead. Her phone rang.

'DI Bailley. Oh hello, Susan.'

She had to hold the phone at arm's length until the torrent of bitterness slowed. By the time Robyn dared to listen, she picked up Susan was not getting on well with Ms Chivers.

Robyn decided not to risk sympathy on a professional sympathiser. 'OK. Are there any more details you can give me on the family?'

'This woman is an utter control freak.' Susan's voice reached another pitch – Robyn put the phone on speaker and lowered the volume. 'I guess it all helped her to get where she is but I've never seen anything like it. Gillian came over just after four – she was terrified, which I suppose is understandable. Ms Chivers was spookily calm and the first thing she asked about were the receipts from the shopping! Then she stares at them for ages, leaving Gillian in the corridor holding the bags and tells her she should have got a discount in the dry-cleaners because she put in four items.'

'Wouldn't be the first thing on my mind if my child were missing.'

Susan laughed, a harsh sound. 'I reckon Ms Chivers was very poor at some point in her life; she seems obsessed with every penny. She keeps every single receipt – there are filing cabinets full of them.'

Robyn leaned closer to the phone. 'Was Ben mentioned at all?'

'It was as if she was trying *not* to mention him, as if he hadn't really vanished. I think that's her way of coping.'

'Anything else I need to know?'

'The next thing she did, she told Gillian to make dinner and, tomorrow, to ring Ben's school and tell them for every day he's not there she'll be withholding the fees.'

Robyn whistled. 'Ms Chivers thinks of everything.' Jumbled noises came down the line. 'Where are you?'

'Ms Chivers told me to go. Said she didn't need me. I asked her if she wanted something to help her sleep and she threw me out.' Susan's voice was rising again.

'Are you saying she's without support?'

'No, a tall, black bloke who called himself "Reverend" something arrived earlier. They went into the front room and shut the door. I could hear some sort of singing and a smell like incense.'

Robyn reached for the button to end the call. 'OK, well, keep on top of things, Susan. Grief can sometimes strike at odd times. If we need to talk to Ms Chivers again, we'll see her at work.'

'Good luck.'

The corridors were quiet. Robyn went to the disabled loo, to have the heavy door swing shut, leaving her in darkness. Fumbling by the door, she found a cord, then she hesitated, worrying she might pull the emergency signal. Squinting in the sudden brightness, she couldn't undo the trousers' fastening, at last remembering the hook went the other way. Desperate, she yanked down the trousers and sat, facing a large mirror on the opposite wall. She wondered why anyone thought you'd want to watch yourself on the toilet. The harsh light hid nothing. There was no trace of the make-up, applied with such care and stubble showed dark against the limp blouse. Her next laser hair removal session wasn't for over a month as the sessions had to be six weeks apart. Until she'd completed the eight treatments needed, it looked like she'd have to bring a razor to work. Roger looked back at her, albeit with different-coloured hair. All of this grief and effort to get nowhere.

In the incident room, a girl in a grey tabard was picking her way around the piles of paper. Robyn reached for her handbag. It wasn't there. The perfect end for Robyn's first day.

The cleaner noticed her expression. 'You want I come back?'

'No, no, I just can't find my bag.' Robyn smiled at her and got a broad grin back.

'I help you.' Together, they scanned the cluttered room. Robyn found the bag by Janice's desk.

'But this woman's bag. I see but not thought it yours?' The girl grinned again, her blonde pigtail swinging as she bent to retrieve her cloth. 'Ah, to your wife.'

Robyn tried to laugh, feeling the beginning of a headache. She retrieved the car key from the handbag and turned to go. The girl was the same age as Becky. She turned back. 'How are you going to get home?'

The girl emptied a bin into a black sack. 'I walk. No buses at late night.'

Before she'd gone on leave, there'd been reports of a man trying to drag young women into a car as they walked home. 'Hang on.' She went to one of the cupboards and rummaged in the box they used at community engagement events. 'Here, take this. It's a personal alarm.' The girl's mouth formed into an 'O' of surprise. Robyn held the device out. 'If you meet a drunken idiot, you pull this cord and it makes an awful noise, giving you a chance to get away.' She tipped it onto the girl's palm.

'Thank you.' The girl poked the alarm with one finger.

Robyn trudged down to the car park, wondering where her daughter was. She left the car on her driveway. Some plant in a neighbouring garden was making the air thick and sweet. In the hallway, the answering machine showed '1'. She dropped her bag and hurried forward, hoping to hear Becky but got a tinny automated message offering discounts on boilers. She stabbed at the delete button.

Slumped onto the sofa, she realised how late it was. She had promised to call Becky, found her name, hesitated, then pushed the button. Better late than break a promise.

'Hello?' The voice sounded a long way away.

'Hi, sweetheart. Can we talk? Is now a good time?'

A heavy bass beat was in the background. 'Meresbourne's all over the news.' Becky paused, Robyn straining to hear over the music. 'You're all over the news as the "cop who thinks he's a woman".'

It didn't seem the right time to say anything, even if she could think of something to say.

Becky's next breath shuddered into a sob. 'So I'm left trying to answer a lot of stupid questions like "is your dad now your mum?" and I've got trolls posting horrible things on my Facebook page.'

Robyn found it hard to keep hold of the phone, her hands were shaking so much.

'So if you have something to say to me, why don't you just say it?'

'I'm so sorry, sweetheart.' She sounded feeble. 'I wanted to tell you, face-to-face when you came down …' Now she'd made it sound as if all this were Becky's fault.

'Tell me what exactly?'

'But you said you'd read my letter?'

'I read it and I didn't know what to believe. You said you wanted to tell me something. I want to hear it from you.'

The song changed in the background, the beat faster, more insistent.

'Could you please turn the music off? I can't hear you.'

There was an exasperated snort, muddled noises, then peace. 'There. Happy now?'

'Becky, I'm going to live the rest of my life as a woman.'

There was no response. Soft sounds could have been Becky shifting on the bed.

'This process will take a while. I've got to experience at least a year of being female before any sort of medical treatment can be considered. Work is being supportive about it – I just didn't expect a case like this to blow up on my first day.'

Robyn could hear Becky's quick bites of breath. 'Then I'll need hormone treatment for another year, to prepare my body for surgery.'

'Oh Christ, you're not going to …' There was a confused jumble of sound, then the line cut.

# TUESDAY 19 JULY

# 10

When the radio alarm went off at six, as usual, Robyn was already awake. The creases on the sheet reflected the anxieties of the dark hours and a glance in the bathroom mirror confirmed it had been a bad night. There was no hiding now: she'd installed a new one with a magnifying side and built-in lighting on an adjustable arm. It was justified because shaving had to be much more precise than before. The tide mark of stubble had become a symbol in Robyn's battle – something to be defeated. When, as Roger, he'd gone to a salon to have his chest, back and legs waxed, he'd taken the easy way out and agreed with the assistant's sympathetic question of whether he had a fussy new girlfriend. Now, as Robyn, she wished she'd been bolder and asked the girl for more advice. Between strokes, she inspected the results while the radio chattered about local traffic jams and confirmed the hot spell would continue.

*It's six-thirty on Tuesday the nineteenth of July and here is the news for Meresbourne and North Kent. Despite extensive searches by police and volunteers, there are no sightings of toddler Ben Chivers, who was abducted by a woman from*

*Whitecourt Shopping Centre yesterday morning. Police are urging everyone to be vigilant and to come forward if you have any information.*

A new voice cut in, smooth, measured and precise; Khalid. His calm delivery gave the impression everything was under control. There was another plea for the public to be alert and report anything suspicious, then contact details were given, with modulated pauses so everyone could take them down. He was doing a good job even though it was normally the lead police officer's job to do the media for a case. As Robyn inspected the few hangers in the wardrobe, she wondered where this left her.

She'd visited a few shops as Roger but the questioning looks from the shop assistants whenever she'd picked anything up had put her off and decided it was much easier to buy the first set of female clothes online. After measuring her bust (as she must now call it), waist and hips, there had still been questions as many sites just had sizes but without measurements. Then when the things had arrived, most were wrong in ways she hadn't imagined. The upper arms of a couple of jackets were cut too tight for her to wear and another was too short in the body. Until she could face going to a shop and trying something on, she only had two work outfits. Although she'd made the effort to hang up yesterday's suit, it was still a creased rag. The thin lining was a mess of sharp ridges darkened by dried sweat. She threw it down on the bed frustrated at its flimsiness. She knew that there would need to be another press conference so everything she did would be on show, unless someone higher-up had decided things would be better with Khalid, who probably never had anything out of place. Well, she reasoned, if he could keep the media off her back so she could get her job done, she wasn't going to complain.

Giving up on the rumpled suit, she pulled on the other, still struggling with the trouser fastening. Robyn remembered the counsellor's matter-of-fact statement about what she'd need to do to demonstrate she was living as a woman. Make-up and skirts – they insisted on skirts. The first time she'd tried wearing one, the cool freedom was wonderful in the heat and she'd bought a couple for home. For work, she'd stuck with practical trouser suits, like all of the women in her team.

To offset the grey suit and plain blouse, she chose a bright necklace, a jumble of coloured blocks. These trousers had pockets, tiny little decorative things that might just hold a tissue. After a frantic look around, she realised she'd left her phone in the handbag, abandoned in the front room after speaking to Becky. Clearly, she wasn't a proper woman yet, or at least one of those who seemed to treat handbags like extensions of themselves. She resolved to buy a belt holster for the phone.

There was a missed call and three text messages. As she put the kettle on, she read the first text: *Hello, Robyn. I hope you're OK after what must have been a stressful day. I was wondering whether you could do me a favour sometime and take my Martin out for a drink to cheer him up as he's finding retirement a bit dull. Let me know, see you later, bye.*

Typical Janice. To show concern for you, she pointed attention another way, making you feel as if you were the one coping. Robyn was sure Martin was loving retirement. No doubt, Janice had told him Robyn needed someone to take her for a drink, to make her feel accepted. Still, you couldn't fault her for the thought.

One text from Graham confirmed there'd been no sightings of Ben overnight and the second that search warrants were in place for the warehouses. Khalid's smooth voice agreed he would see her first thing. The kettle clicked and Robyn went through the routine motions of making tea, wondering whether it was worth calling Becky. Her finger hovered over the number. Once she got to the station, everything would be focused on Ben. No, there was no point ringing now, a student wouldn't be awake yet. It might also be too soon after last night. She sent a text: *Understand why you're upset. Will call this evening.* She wondered how to sign it off, then added, *With love.*

The drive to work was an attempt to marshal all her unconnected thoughts into a plan. Now twenty-four hours had passed, the certainty Ben was nearby was fading. Life wasn't so convenient. The longer they went without a sighting, the lower the chances of Ben being alive and unharmed, or even just alive. She found herself driving faster.

The first person she saw at the police station was Janice, leafing through papers while walking down the steps to the car park.

'Morning, Janice, ready to go?'

Janice gasped, hand flying to her face before she relaxed. 'Sorry, Robyn. You made me jump. Just double-checking I've got all the paperwork. I've got through to most of the owners and we're going in.' She paused, scanning Robyn's face. 'You look tired – are you OK?'

Maybe others noticed but only Janice would say something. 'Too hot to sleep. Good luck. Keep me posted.'

Walking in through the main door, you could feel a change in the station's atmosphere. There was something in the air, a lack of energy despite the bright morning. The faces were more subdued than yesterday, the greetings in the canteen less cheery. Search teams were taking on water prior to working in the heat.

Back behind her desk with a cup of tea, Robyn dialled Khalid's number. The smooth voice answered after the first ring.

'Ah, DI Bailley, good morning. Thank you for calling me back. If you're in the office, I'll come down.'

The line cut. Robyn checked the signal, then jumped as a body stopped by her desk. Ravi stepped back, banging into the evidence board. His eyes seemed drawn to where her necklace met the blouse's lace-edged neckline.

'Morning, Ravi. Sorry, I'm expecting someone and I thought they'd arrived already. Any more news on the offenders you're tracking?'

'We can probably discount one of them, Guv. He was on the register for a relationship with a fourteen year-old girl when he was nineteen. They married as soon as she turned sixteen, five years ago. They have two kids now.' Ravi's foot started tapping an irregular rhythm. 'But the other one's more promising, a conviction for possessing indecent images of young boys and he served time. I'm waiting on a call from Newcastle to get more details.'

'Where does he live now?'

'Out in Pickley. There's a charity refurbishing and selling furniture on some old farm. It's some sort of religious-type community with accommodation in exchange for work and everyone is supposed to make sure everyone else stays straight.'

'OK, get all the details, then we can pay him a visit.'

Ravi stood up a little straighter; Robyn turned to find Khalid standing by her desk even though she hadn't heard the door open. The trimmed beard she remembered but not the force behind the deep-set eyes.

'Good morning, DI Bailley. So good of you to make time to see me. Could we find somewhere quiet?' Not wanting to miss any developments, she led Khalid to the far corner of the incident room, sheltered by evidence boards.

Forty minutes later, Khalid had probed every element of her police and personal life. He'd wanted to know how long the Bailley family had lived in Meresbourne, details of Roger's service and promotions in Bristol and even asked what his ex-wife thought of the transition. Robyn, who thought about Julie as little as possible, found her answers getting shorter. Murmurs from behind the screen told her the rest of the team had arrived and was getting down to work.

'How much more do you want? I need to be out there.'

Khalid stopped the recorder. 'This investigation is getting a lot of press and we need to be able to counter any negative accusations. The Service's positive media profile must be maintained.'

'You've got a media profile, I've got a missing child.' Robyn put her hands to her head. 'Can I get on now?'

Khalid stood up. 'You may not like it but this is police work too. I've arranged a press conference for one o'clock. You need to get a family member there to do an appeal.'

He turned and weaved his way out of the corner leaving Robyn feeling weary and in desperate need of another cup of tea. As she stood up, her foot tangled in the strap of her handbag and she cannoned into one of the evidence boards, pictures scattering to the floor.

'You all right, Guv? Bit early for the gin.' Lorraine stooped to pick up items.

Robyn picked up a picture of Melissa in a formal suit with a challenging expression, taken from her online LinkedIn profile. She needed to get through to this woman and, based on yesterday's conversation, it wouldn't be easy. 'Lorraine, I know you've got the lead you want to follow up on the burglary but I need to see Ms Chivers this morning and persuade her to do a press conference at lunchtime. Perhaps you might be more on her wavelength?'

'Are you sure, Guv? We might be similar colours on the outside but let me tell you, there's nothing a successful black woman likes less than another black woman she thinks might be doing better than her.' Lorraine grimaced. 'I'm serious, Guv. If she's as driven as Graham described, she'll want to prove she started from a worse place in the "suffering sisterhood" stakes.'

After the session with Khalid dealing with perceptions about her, Robyn had the feeling she was missing something subtle. 'I'm sorry, Lorraine, I wasn't trying to make assumptions. My conversation with Ms Chivers was cut short because, well, she doesn't want to speak to me which means I can't develop a proper impression of a person who's crucial to the case. Graham says she's distraught over Ben's loss and Janice thinks she's a heartless bully. I trust your judgements of people and I'd like your view. That's all.'

Lorraine grinned. 'Well, why didn't you say so, Guv? Give me two secs.' She focused on her computer for a moment, then snatched up something from the printer and joined Robyn in the corridor. In the car park, like Janice, Lorraine seemed to expect Robyn would drive. Robyn filed it as another difference between men and women.

'I printed off what Derby and Rutherford say about themselves, Guv.' Lorraine read from a piece of paper as they drove towards the business park. 'Founded in 1877 by men with lots of facial hair, always at the centre of Meresbourne's commercial life. Oh, here we go: "worked for the family of the renowned Victorian novelist Edmund Napier Loveless (the pen name of Faith Gregory)". Is there anything in Meresbourne not claiming some connection with Loveless?' She turned over the page. 'I've never met anyone who's read her books.'

'I did at school.' Robyn grimaced at the memory. 'We all had to. After all, she's the only thing the town is famous for, though now someone's on *Superstar Seeker*, who knows?'

'I didn't have you down as a *Superstar Seeker* fan, Guv. All sorts of things I didn't know about you.' Lorraine giggled.

Robyn's fingers tightened on the wheel for a second, before she made an effort to relax. 'Where's this office?'

If Lorraine was surprised by the tone, she didn't show it. 'Do you mean their "prestigious new office for the next generation of legal services"?' Lorraine consulted the sheet again. 'Second on the left.'

They drove past "To Let" signs, one so faded, the words were almost invisible. Robyn parked her Mondeo in a visitor's space and thought she should try and relax a bit. She couldn't keep snapping at people and expect them to remain positive. She cast around for something to say. 'They used to have that big stone building on the High Street. It's still got "Derby and Rutherford" carved onto a plaque – the ground floor is the Pet Rescue shop now.'

Lorraine heaved open the heavy glass front door. From behind an intimidating flower arrangement, a bottle-blonde receptionist interrogated them about their parking space number, pouting when they admitted not noticing. They were pointed towards a waiting area where pictures lined the walls. At one end, there were portraits of men with serious expressions standing amongst bales and crates at the Docks, their top hats suggesting it was a long time ago. In the more recent images, men in suits held large cheques in front of junior football teams and the air ambulance. The largest shot was a crowd under a banner for *Small Law Firm of the Year*. Robyn leaned closer. 'Have a look at this ...'

Lorraine scrutinised the picture. 'There's Ms Chivers.' She pointed. 'Hmm, everyone else has champagne, it looks like she's got a soft drink. Was that it?'

'No, beside her. Is that Janice's lad Josh?'

After a second, Lorraine raised her eyebrows. 'I think you're right. What he's doing there?' She looked again. 'According to the banner, it was three years ago and it must have been summer because people are in short sleeves.'

'We'll ask her. He might be able to give some inside information.'

The receptionist came out from behind the desk and held open an inner door. She led them past glass-walled meeting rooms, each with identical sideboards, round tables and four high-backed brown leather chairs. They were pointed into the third one.

'Not sure about the art.' Lorraine met the dark, dead eyes of a sculpted African woman which took up most of the sideboard. Across the room, an abstract of zebra stripes was highlighted with smears of pink. 'I can't believe she's come back to work when her son's missing.'

Melissa appeared in the corridor outside, piling files into the arms of the receptionist.

'That's why I want your opinion. Is she blocking out the trouble by focusing on normal things, or is there something more sinister?' Robyn turned to the door.

Melissa gave them a quick nod to sit down but remained standing, gripping the back of a chair. 'Why are you here?' The navy suit squared her shoulders.

'How are you, Ms Chivers?'

'Did you just come to ask me idiotic questions?' Melissa stepped closer to the chair so her body was hidden.

Robyn swallowed. She should have learned from what Susan had told her and kept it factual. 'No, Ms Chivers. We wanted to update you on the investigation and seek more information to help us find Ben.'

Melissa opened her mouth.

'Sorry, Benjamin. This is Detective Constable Mount. We tried to arrange this visit with your family liaison officer but I understand Susan is no longer with you?'

'She made inane remarks and smoked. Having her in the house was not helping the situation.'

Robyn tilted her head. 'I'm sorry, Ms Chivers. Would you like me to arrange another liaison officer?'

'I do not want anyone else in my house.'

'Of course.' If Melissa was like this all the time, it explained some of Gillian's nerves. 'To update you then, the detailed searches have finished in the town centre and we are now focusing on the Docks area. Has anyone contacted you about Benjamin since he disappeared – any calls, emails?'

Melissa's expression didn't change. 'No one, other than journalists. I should like to know where they got my number from.' She glanced at Lorraine, who sat with a straight back, echoing the sculpture's pose.

'I appreciate they're a nuisance. A liaison officer can screen phone calls and keep the media away from you.' Robyn paused while Melissa tapped her phone. 'Ms Chivers, can you think of anyone who might want to harm …'

Robyn's phone vibrated, skittering across the glass table top. With a muttered excuse, she turned away to take the call.

'Hello, Janice.'

'Robyn, the search teams have found a body.'

# 11

Robyn stood up. 'I'm sorry, Ms Chivers, excuse me.' Wind was blowing into the phone at the other end. 'Janice, hang on.' She ducked into the next meeting room, where an angular metal object on the sideboard faced a black and white photo of pylons. Her arms were covered with goose bumps. 'I was with Ms Chivers, Janice. Go ahead. Where'd you find him?'

'It's not Ben.'

'Are you sure? Have you got an identification?'

'No, but we can see it's an adult.'

Robyn slumped into one of the chairs. 'OK, where was it?'

'In warehouse B, just as the tip-off said.'

'Can you tell a cause of death? We've had deaths in the Docks before, from alcohol or drugs.' As she said it, she knew how callous she must sound: a dead tramp or a junkie, nothing to worry about. It was the sort of thing ex-DI Prentiss would have said.

'Not yet. The body's been there a while. Forensics are doing their thing now.'

'OK, I'll finish up with Ms Chivers and come down.' Robyn rubbed her arms, cold in the air-conditioning and stepped back along the corridor. Through the glass, she could see Melissa standing in a corner, staring at her phone, ignoring Lorraine's scrutiny.

Neither spoke as she entered the room. 'I'm sorry, Ms Chivers. An update from the search teams. I'm afraid there's still no news about Benjamin.'

For a second, Melissa appeared confused, one hand reaching out to the sideboard, as if for support. 'I thought you'd found something?'

Robyn wondered if this was the first time Melissa had admitted to herself the danger Ben might be in. 'They found the body of an adult in one of the warehouses at the Docks.' Lorraine raised one eyebrow.

'Who was it?' Melissa's voice was little more than a whisper.

'We don't know yet. There's no immediate indication of any connection to Benjamin's disappearance but we will of course keep you informed.'

'So where is he then?' With two quick steps, Melissa was standing in front of Robyn, almost touching.

Robyn caught a waft of Melissa's perfume. Her shoulders were back, which drew the eye down the tendons of her neck to the hints of skin visible through the lace front of her blouse. If this tactic worked on men, it wasn't working on Robyn. 'I'm afraid we don't know yet, Ms Chivers. I wanted to ask you whether you would do an appeal for information. We have the press coming to the police station at one o'clock.'

Melissa continued to stare at Robyn for a second. She took a step back. 'You want me to sob on television, to make people feel sorry for me?' She scowled. 'I shouldn't have to do this.'

Swallowing, Robyn tried to relax the tension in her jaw before she spoke. 'I know this is hard, Ms Chivers. If my daughter were missing ...'

'You have children?' The words were ground out, Melissa's face creasing. 'Someone like you is given the gift of a child?'

Lorraine half-rose from her chair. On automatic, Robyn made a calming gesture, which wasn't lost on Melissa, who smiled for the first time, a professional rearrangement of her face with no room for warmth. She opened the door.

'I will do the appeal, because, God willing, someone else will be competent. I think you had better go. Your junior seems in danger of getting upset.' She held the door open. 'I am not happy with the way this investigation is being run and will be seeking professional advice. The exit is to your left.'

Behind her back, Robyn dug her nails into her palm to keep herself calm. 'Ms Chivers, we need to know—' Melissa closed the door behind them and sat down, her back to the glass wall.

Left in the corridor, she was surprised to see Lorraine looking as close as she got to sheepish.

'Might have been my fault she lashed out, Guv. Hate to say I told you so, that was just as I expected.'

'What did you say to her when I was out of the room?'

Before Lorraine could answer, a figure appeared at the top of the corridor. Robyn found her hand being clasped by a tie-less man with sandy hair.

'Ah, officers. Mark Rutherford, senior partner. The team told me you were here and I just wanted to assure you the firm will do everything it can to support the investigation and bring Benjamin back.' He shook Lorraine's hand and began talking again, balancing the contact between them. 'I trust the investigation is going well? Right, I'm sure you are very busy.' His cologne was sharp in the chilled air. 'So good to have been able to speak to you. Good morning.'

After a further vigorous handshake each, Rutherford held out his arm towards the reception door where an older brunette smiled as she held open the door. Catching Lorraine's eye and nodding towards the woman, Robyn turned to Rutherford.

'Thank you, sir, very encouraging. It would be useful to take a few moments of your time now if it's convenient?'

'Ah, well, yes, of course.' Rutherford's positive expression didn't slip though his voice was less welcoming. 'I'm sure I have a few minutes. Come in.'

As Lorraine walked out with the receptionist, Robyn followed Rutherford into a conference room, watching Rutherford hitch up each trouser leg before sitting.

'Now, officer, what can I do for you? Derby and Rutherford is always happy to support the police ...'

No, Robyn breathed, he's surely not going to say he plays golf with someone?

'Indeed, as I was saying to Superintendent Fell at the town hall recently, a sign of a thriving community is when firms work in harmony with the police.'

Robyn tried to imagine this urbane man with the expensive after-shave lasting more than a few seconds in Fell's presence. Rutherford seemed the sort who'd despise anyone wearing a man-made fibre. His glance got to her frumpy, rubber-soled shoes and there was a definite sneer.

'Thank you, sir. I'm Detective Inspector Bailley and I'm leading the hunt for Benjamin. Your support is appreciated. I'd like to ask you about Melissa Chivers. She's going through a terrible ordeal and we want to spare her questioning as much as possible.'

'Of course, of course. How can I help?' The palms were spread upwards, gold cuff-links catching the light.

'Thank you. Can you confirm how long Melissa Chivers has worked for you?'

'Let's see, it must be almost five years.'

'Did she become partner straight away?'

Rutherford steepled his fingers. 'No, she came to us as a principal solicitor the year before my father retired. When I took sole charge of the firm as none of Derby's children wanted a role, I had the opportunity to restructure and I promoted Melissa to a partnership.'

'And this was before Ms Chivers had Ben? Have you noticed any change in her since?'

Rutherford leaned back in his chair. 'Now, inspector, how am I supposed to answer? Derby and Rutherford believes in diversity and opportunity for all. Melissa's a capable lawyer and is professional enough to manage all her responsibilities. I don't know what you are trying to get me to say.'

'Did Ms Chivers change her hours or areas of work once she had Ben?'

'I was a touch surprised when she announced she was pregnant.' Rutherford began to twist the heavy gold band on his ring finger. 'But she continued to manage her workload and was back at work full-time within two weeks of his birth. Are you aware she should be moving to Switzerland to set up a new office for us in a month's time? We have a lot of clients based in Europe with interests in UK property so she was the obvious choice. Those plans are now on hold, of course.'

'Of course. And do you have any impressions of Ms Chivers' home and family life? Did you, for example, meet her partner at any time?'

Rutherford chuckled. 'No. The days of doing business in each other's houses over canapés rather went out with my father. She does pro bono work for a charity, which is fully declared, as required and I'm aware of one criminal case resulting from the work she did on behalf of a tenant, all fully documented. Otherwise, I've never asked about her private life, any more than she's asked about mine.'

'Thank you. No, of course. I would be interested in the details of the case, to help us eliminate all possibilities regarding Ben's abduction. Was yesterday meant to be a normal day for Ms Chivers?'

'Surely, inspector, there's no suggestion Melissa's involved in her son's disappearance?'

'None at all, sir. However, we're pursuing a lead connected with work Ms Chivers is doing for properties in the Docks. Are you aware of any concerns she had?'

Rutherford's eyes stayed locked into Robyn's. 'No. As you can imagine, we vet all our clients before we agree to work with them. In this industry, a firm's reputation is everything.'

'But the company working on the Docks development is registered offshore I believe, sir?'

'Inspector, you may not have noticed in the police force but not many people in the UK have any money at the moment.' Rutherford's face creased with amusement. 'The firm's a legitimate company, which happens to be registered outside the UK. For this type of property deal, the market is international. Now, is there anything else?'

Robyn caught a hint of irritation in his voice. She held his gaze. 'Are you aware of any threats or complaints against Melissa Chivers?'

'None.' He jabbed his finger into the desk for emphasis. 'We deal in commercial property, land and shipping. We do not have a criminal practice and we do not associate with criminals. If anyone had a complaint against Melissa, they would contact me as senior partner or the Law Society. I've never had any complaints because Melissa's a first-rate lawyer with a strong sense of integrity. Now, if you'll excuse me, I have a client meeting.' He stood up.

Robyn took her time rising. 'Just one more question, sir; does your firm do any work for a local family called Dearman?'

'Unless you have a specific legal reason for these enquiries, I cannot breach client confidentiality. I'm sorry to have been of so little help, inspector.' He opened the door and gestured to the corridor. 'I will arrange for the details of the case to be sent over and I trust the rest of the investigation goes better.'

The original receptionist was waiting, swivelling from one heel to the other. To see what would happen, Robyn gave her a cheery smile, which wasn't returned. In reception, Lorraine was lounging on one of the low sofas, reading the *Gazette*. Ben's face stared out from the front page.

# 12

The chilled air was replaced by grimy heat and a smell of diesel as they left the office. Back in the car, Lorraine stretched in the seat.

'So are we going down to look at this body, Guv?'

Robyn swung the car out of the space. 'I need to check the necessary is underway but it doesn't sound as if the death is recent. Finding Ben is the priority.' That covered either him or his body.

'Of course.' Lorraine grinned. 'Well, I don't know how you got on, Guv, but the older receptionist, Cathy, had a lot to get off her chest. On reception, she sees everything.'

'But nobody pays her any attention?'

'Exactly. She seemed glad to have someone take an interest and had plenty to say, like when Ms Chivers announced she was pregnant it wasn't long after Christmas so she speculated whether the turkey baster got used a lot.'

They both laughed. Robyn checked the mirror before turning. The bags under her eyes were highlighted by a smudge of mascara. She told herself to focus on the road and listen to what Lorraine was saying.

'Now, take Mark Rutherford. Cathy's worked for the firm for thirty years so, to her, he isn't the real Mr Rutherford – she preferred his father. Since young Mark has taken over, he's been bringing things "up to date", which also means Cathy spends lots of time training up replacement receptionists, who all seem to be blonde.'

Robyn decided the route through town should be clear at this time of day. 'Rutherford's interesting. His promised co-operation was selective.'

'Sounds like there's a lot you didn't get told, Guv. From my chat, there are a number of female, ex-employees with a grudge against Rutherford.'

They stopped at a zebra crossing, a boy of Ben's age toddling across his hand gripped by an older woman. 'Maybe Rutherford put pressure on Ms Chivers? He tried to come across all enlightened new man but if he'd just made her a partner and she gets pregnant, wouldn't he feel stupid?'

Lorraine snorted. 'I believe that's why we women have equality legislation to support us. Ma'am.'

Robyn gathered her thoughts. The first was that she was an idiot. 'Lorraine, I'm sorry.' She banged the steering wheel in frustration. 'There's so much happening at the moment, I'm not thinking about what I'm saying.'

They were stuck behind a battered Volvo, parked a foot from the kerb outside a newsagent with its hazard lights on. A pot-bellied man in a Meresbourne Town away strip took a bite from an ice-cream as he got into the driver's seat.

'Can I get him, Guv? Can I? I could do with boosting my statistics.' Lorraine grabbed the door handle.

'If you've got any spare time, you can run the registration and see if he's got tax and insurance. But don't be too harsh on him – do you know how many Town supporters bother to travel to away games?'

Lorraine giggled as the car in front belched smoke and jerked away. They turned onto the main road running the length of the docks. In one of its regular articles on anti-social behaviour, the half mile of straight road had been nicknamed 'Dock Drag' by the *Gazette*.

Robyn eased the car over the speed bumps, ears pitched for any scrape. 'These new humps are ridiculous. You'd think the speed cameras would be enough.'

'First you stop me arresting a traffic offender, now, you're saying we shouldn't prevent kids from racing stolen cars. They just laughed at the speed cameras. You're going soft, Guv.'

'What did you say to Ms Chivers while I was out of the room?' Robyn wasn't in the mood. 'Come on. When I came back, the atmosphere was hostile. What did you say to her?'

'I asked her why she'd had a child in the first place if she cared so little about finding him that she wouldn't tell us his father's name.' Lorraine's voice was flat.

'Ah. And what did Ms Chivers say?'

'She sucked herself in tight and told me I was unnatural if I didn't want kids as it's our duty to give children to God.'

'And then what?' Robyn was imagining the potential call to Fell.

'And then I asked her for the name of Ben's father.'

'How did she react?'

'Oh, she got all huffy but some of what I said got through. She insisted there was no possibility the father knew about Ben. I must have looked sceptical because she added, even if he did know, he wouldn't be interested. Then you came back.' Lorraine rubbed her nose. 'I can see what both Graham and Janice mean, though. I think Chivers loves Ben but it's on her terms. She'd kill for him if he were threatened but she won't do anything to risk softening him. She's invested too much to raise a weakling.'

Robyn wrinkled her nose. 'Janice said a similar thing. What I'd like to know is whether Ms Chivers planned to get pregnant in the first place?'

They approached a cluster of police vehicles. As the car bumped onto the kerb, Lorraine stretched back against her seat belt, staring upwards.

'I think, for all her ambition, biology kicked in and Chivers realised she was thirty-five without a baby. It became one of those things where you want something so much it takes over and you can't think about anything else because whatever you try to do all ends up coming back to this one thing. Does that make any sense?'

It was a good summary of most of Robyn's life. 'I understand.'

'So Chivers decided she wanted a child and she's used to getting what she wants. The only question is, who was good enough to be the father?'

Robyn's seatbelt slipped through her too-long fingernails and clattered back. 'Exactly what we need to find out.'

Together, they walked across uneven concrete towards the warehouse. On the security fence, a locked padlock hung from a chopped chain. Halfway up the dark brick wall, a buddleia bush sprouted from a crack. One of the doors under the stone arches had been broken open. Inside, the air became harder to breathe. Dust floated through the beams of the mobile lamps, settling on clothes and equipment. Camera flashes cut through the murk. Robyn and Lorraine followed the trodden path across the debris-strewn floor to where Graham stood next to an untidy pile of corrugated roofing sheets. Drifts of dust swirled up with every step.

'Afternoon. We've got a new doc.' Graham seemed miffed his network hadn't told him beforehand. 'Because Doc Drummond's getting on a bit, he's going to stick to lab work now so we've got a new lad.' He pointed to a deep recess in the floor. 'He's down there with the body.'

Over the hum of the spotlights and relentless clicking from the camera, Robyn could just hear muttering from the pit. 'How many entrances to this place?'

'Loads, Guv. The Docks area is one big rat-run, another reason the Dearmans liked it. The security fencing's recent, something the new owners put in.' He paused. 'When did you come back to work in Meresbourne – two years ago? Must have been around then.'

The little light filtering through the algae-covered skylights gave everything a green cast. Peering into the pit, Robyn tried to make sense of the shapes and realised they were bones, a skeleton, veiled in dust.

'We should have brought Raver.' Graham pulled at one of the iron sheets, testing the weight. 'This would be his first murder and corpse wouldn't upset his delicate tum-tum.'

In the pit, a large, white shape shook itself. There was something alien about its appearance until the suit's hood was pushed back and the mask removed.

'Alright? You the coppers? I'm Dr Kelly Shepherd. Thanks for getting me a cracker for my first case.' The accent was Australian, a cheery voice sounding too loud in the sombre warehouse.

'Not a lot I can tell you from this now, I'm afraid. There's no soft tissue left at all. Been dead at least eighteen months, probably longer for complete decomposition to have occurred, though I'm used to a dryer climate so I want to get Dr Drummond's opinion. From the pelvis and the clothing traces, it's a woman.'

'Anything on cause of death?' Graham shoved his hands into his pockets.

'Well, there is one thing.' Dr Shepherd pointed to one of the larger lumps. 'The skull has been damaged which could be blunt force trauma. Of course, it's possible she was struck by something falling from the roof or she fell into the pit and knocked herself out.' He pointed to the corrugated sheets, piled at the side of the hole. 'Except, these roofing sheets were arranged over the body to hide it.'

Graham gestured around the emptiness. 'It's a perfect spot – quiet, out-of-the-way. Can you tell whether she was killed here, or just dumped?'

'No idea and not sure if I'll be able to.' Dust flew from the bodysuit as Kelly began packing instruments. 'Unlikely we'll be able to isolate anything in this mess.'

The dust was getting into Robyn's throat making her mouth feel gritty. 'How long before you can give us more details?'

Kelly pushed himself up on his arms from the pit as if from a swimming pool. 'A couple of days at least. OK, get these bagged up.'

The crew climbed down into the pit and began probing, handing up clear plastic bags of evidence. Lorraine intercepted a bag containing a shred of cloth. 'This shade of blue was everywhere a few winters ago. Wonder if we can find a label?'

Robyn leaned over to Graham. 'Have you found anything relating to Ben?'

'Nothing yet. The search teams are still working.'

Robyn glanced at her watch. 'Bugger, I've got to go. The press appeal is in forty-five minutes. Lorraine, are you coming?' She waved to Graham and walked back into the sunshine, mopping her face with a tissue, which came away stained with foundation. Outside the tape line, Janice was in discussion with a man in a hi-vis vest, open over a row of pens in the breast pocket of his shirt. He gestured towards the warehouse, then pointed at his clipboard.

Janice touched a hand to her temple, swaying backwards on her heels. 'Hello, Robyn. This is Mr Butterworth from the security company. He'd like to speak to the *man* in charge.'

'Yes, I need to know when you will be clear of the site. This is most inconvenient, not to mention the damage you're doing. I demand to know why no attempt was made to contact us.' Butterworth had a nasal voice. Robyn tried to focus on his face, finding her attention drawn back each time to a livid boil on the man's neck.

'Mr Butterworth does not accept I tried four times to get through ...'

'Most unlikely as we have a twenty-four-hour operation, where all calls are answered within five rings ...'

'How wonderful for you to have such absolute certainties, Mr Butterworth.' Robyn stepped to within a pace of the man, squaring her shoulders so her jacket fell open. 'The police don't have such luxuries. As I'm sure you can appreciate, when a body is found in suspicious circumstances, we have to carry out a full investigation.'

It was questionable whether Butterworth had heard anything she'd said. He was staring at the outline of Robyn's bra visible through her blouse in the strong sunlight. The gaze darted up to the necklace, then down the arms taking in the plum-coloured nails. Finally, he reached Robyn's crotch and then jerked away, to gawp at Janice. The man's mouth was opening without sound, his body leaning away, the clipboard now in a defensive position, held like a breast-plate under his crossed arms. Robyn leaned closer.

'Now, Mr Butterworth, it's good you're here as we need to know a lot more about the owners and their activities. Perhaps you could give my colleague the benefit of your experience?'

The man swallowed and nodded as Janice tapped her clipboard. Robyn continued towards her car. Confronting him had been unprofessional: she excused herself as having used up today's ration of control on Ms Chivers.

Lorraine slammed her door. 'There are some tossers in the world. Are you going to give this case to Ravi, Guv? As Graham said, it would be his first murder.'

'I'm not going to give it to anyone. If they've been in there for a couple of years, they can wait a couple more days.' She sensed Lorraine turning to her but kept her eyes on the road. 'I know somebody's waiting for them somewhere but we've got a choice between a dry pile of bones and a living toddler. What do you think we should do?'

# 13

The station's conference room was packed. Robyn lined up her papers to give herself another second before she had to answer, yet again, that they were 'following a number of promising leads but no arrest was imminent.' To her left, Melissa sat rigid in the camera flashes. She'd rejected the statement Khalid had prepared for her and read her own, invoking God's help and emphasising how gifted Ben was. Robyn noted a few of the journalists raising eyebrows.

Click, flash, click, flash. Khalid pointed at a young man Robyn hadn't seen before. 'Go ahead, Danny.'

'How's Ben's father taking his disappearance?'

Melissa's face closed up. She turned to Khalid and said something Robyn couldn't hear. Khalid nodded, then addressed the reporter. 'Benjamin's father is not involved in his life. We'll take two more questions, yes?'

'Is the father one of the leads you're following up?' This was addressed to Robyn.

Her papers were already in a neat pile so she couldn't even buy a second there. 'We're keeping an open mind at this stage.'

'Final question.' A number of hands went up. Khalid pointed. 'Yes, Marcus.'

'Why is his father no longer involved in his life?'

Khalid held up a finger. 'As I'm sure you appreciate, we can't answer and I ask you to respect the family's privacy at this difficult time ...'

There was a clamour of further questions, the word 'father' being repeated. Melissa was gripping the edge of the table. Robyn leant towards her. 'There's a lot of interest in this, unfortunately.'

'You did this deliberately, didn't you?' Melissa took a deep breath. 'I wouldn't answer your questions so you put me in front of this pack of animals to force me.'

Before Robyn could speak, Melissa stood up. The voices died away.

'You wonder why I don't like to talk about Benjamin's father. It's because he's dead – dead before he even met his son. So there you are. Now please find my boy.'

It was easier to clear the room than Robyn feared. She wanted to understand why Ms Chivers had kept back something so fundamental until now. Khalid checked a message and he announced the recording of the press-conference was already on YouTube.

Robyn had a craving for tea. 'Ms Chivers, thank you for coming. We do need to talk about what you just said regarding Benjamin's father. Perhaps we could go down to the canteen?'

Melissa picked up her briefcase. 'I am going to the Ladies.'

Khalid waited until the door closed. 'So she hadn't mentioned about the father being dead until now?'

'No. And what's odd, she's contradicting something she told us before. I wonder why.' Robyn rolled her neck, hearing it click. 'How do you think it went?'

'The bit about the dead dad will get a lot of space, because people love a tragedy. Whether these things help or not, the public expect them now. Is there anything coming up you need to announce?'

Robyn shook her head. 'Afraid not. I hope Ms Chivers is all right – she's been a while in the loo.'

'Better go and check. If there's a journalist, she might be cornered.'

Robyn pulled open the door to the ladies' toilet. Both cubicles were empty – there was no one there. The disabled loo opposite was empty too. She backed out into the corridor.

'Bugger her.'

Khalid leaned out. 'What's up?'

'She's left. Ms Chivers has gone.'

'Gone? Do you think she's headed down to the canteen?'

'I'll check but I doubt it.' Robyn shook her head. 'Why doesn't she want to talk to us?'

She tried to define the expression on Khalid's face while she waited for the lift. He'd been chatting to Melissa before the briefing and seemed to be getting along, one professional to another. She knew it was futile but she comforted herself the trip to the canteen was necessary, even if the cup of tea and Mars bar she picked up weren't. The desk sergeant confirmed Melissa had left a few minutes before and had overheard her on the phone confirming she would be able to meet a client as planned.

Back in the incident room, Ravi was staring at his screen. The picture had frozen showing Robyn with her mouth open and her too-big hands. She'd finished the chocolate in the lift: in need of more energy, she raided Janice's desk for biscuits.

Getting dressed, Robyn had thought how much her blouse suited her. On camera, the pattern was garish. 'It's not worth watching, Ravi. The only interesting bit is the last minute.' Robyn blew on her tea. 'Ms Chivers told the world Ben's father is dead then walked out.'

Ravi winced. 'Where is she now?'

'Gone back to work.'

'Seriously?' Ravi leant back in his chair, then, to Robyn's relief, closed the video. She let go of a long breath. Things could have been much worse. Just before they'd sat down, Khalid had nudged her because one of her blouse's buttons was undone, exposing her utilitarian sports bra.

Robyn checked the contact list.

'Good afternoon, Derby and Rutherford.'

'Good afternoon, Melissa Chivers, please.'

'Can I take a message?'

'I really need to speak to her. It's DI Bailley.'

'I'm sorry, Ms Chivers is in meetings all afternoon and cannot be disturbed. I'll tell her you called.'

Robyn was left holding the phone. After another minute of trying to organise her thoughts, she gave up and decided to make another trip to the canteen, listening to her messages on the way.

The first was from Graham. *Guv, still in the warehouse. Found something interesting in another pit, SOCO boys doing their stuff. Call you later.*

The second was from Tracey; Fell wanted to see her this afternoon and could offer slots at two thirty or four fifteen. Robyn sighed and stopped on the stairs. Potentially, she could be seeing Fell in half an hour. She quickened her pace to the canteen.

As she walked back into the incident room, Ravi leaped forward. 'Guv, Guv ...' Robyn stopped, her necklace chinking.

Ravi recoiled, his notebook falling to the floor as he groped for a corner of the desk. Robyn wondered what had happened to make him so nervous and debated whether to ask him. She was getting sick of pussyfooting around these things but decided it was better to give him a chance to calm down. She took her time over adding sugar to the tea, had a half-hearted skim through her emails and stabilised the contents of her in-tray so it didn't topple over. She forced herself to smile, to make sure it appeared in her voice. 'Ready, Ravi?'

Ravi slid into the chair beside Robyn but stayed on its far side. 'I've spoken to Newcastle, Guv. There was a lot on the sex-offender, Parkes, not on the system. He worked for the local authority as a general maintenance bloke. According to his colleagues, he often went to the older residents' houses out of hours to do jobs for them. One time, a resident had her six year-old grandson visiting. Parkes was caught with the boy in his van and he was charged with attempted abduction of a minor then somehow, he managed to convince the boy's granny he was letting the boy play at driving.' Ravi smacked his head with his hand. 'Yeah, right. After they'd arrested Parkes, they did a routine search of his house and found images of kids on his computer. DI Rainer from Newcastle said he was gobsmacked when the family wouldn't press charges when it was obvious the man was a risk.'

Ravi ran out of breath, carried by his enthusiasm to the front of his chair, the scuffed tips of his shoes nearly touching Robyn's. 'Can we go out and get him, Guv?'

'Good work, Ravi. Does he have any female associates?'

Ravi's face fell. He pulled back in the chair, turning over the page of notes as if there would be help on the other side.

'He lived with his mother in Newcastle – she died just a few months before the offence.'

'So no wife or girlfriend? OK, get some more details about this charity. I want to know who runs it, who else is there and whether we've had any trouble with them in the past, then we'll go out and interview him.'

'Right, Guv.' Ravi dashed back to his desk. Robyn gritted her teeth and called Tracey, taking her time over dialling. She was glad to just hear the engaged tone and typed a quick email accepting the later slot. The door swung open, Graham holding it for Janice.

'What a place. Feel like I've spent the morning in the Sahara.' Graham took off his jacket, traces of dust from the warehouse drifting in the sunlight. Janice put down her bag and reached for her unofficial kettle.

Robyn stood up, still restless. 'Afternoon. What progress?'

Graham stretched showing yellow stains under his arms. 'Did you get my message?'

'Yes, but you didn't mention anything linked to Ben.'

'No. We found a load of packaging though, six pallets, wrapping and tarpaulin.'

'So what makes you think anything's illegal? It's a warehouse, people unpack things.' Robyn didn't try very hard to keep the sarcasm out of her voice. She knew Fell's likely reaction to the additional search costs for a false alarm would be predictable and unprintable.

Graham smirked. 'Because the packaging was for drugs. One of the technicians was from Maidstone and he said it was identical to what was used on a shipment they raided in their patch a couple of months ago. Someone's got a nice little smuggling operation going.'

Robyn sat down. 'OK, that's more interesting. Do you think the body and the drugs are connected?'

'Not sure. Same placing, in a maintenance pit with a bit of covering. We've been promised an update by tomorrow.'

Janice handed Graham a mug before catching Robyn's longing look. With a mock sigh, she went back outside to refill the kettle. Three cups in quick succession. Robyn would have to be careful; not everywhere had a disabled loo and people might get funny about her using the ladies' toilet.

'Fine, notify whoever's handling the investigation at Maidstone. We can't get distracted from finding Ben …'

The door opened as Janice returned. She plugged in the kettle and settled down at her desk.

Robyn stepped over to her. 'Thanks, Janice. Are you OK?' She took the opportunity to look at the family picture on Janice's desk which confirmed it had been Josh in the image at Derby and Rutherford.

'Fine thanks, Robyn.' Janice wrinkled her lips. 'Just a bit of a headache from the dust. I …'

'Here we are, Guv.' Ravi held a piece of paper up in front of her. 'Jack Parkes stays at St Oswald's, Chalk Pit Farm, Pickley. Guess who's a trustee? Old Man Dearman.'

Graham stuck his head around his monitor to listen.

'From their website, funding comes from prison charities and a couple of churches. If the Dearmans are involved though, things have got to be dodgy.' Ravi sounded triumphant.

Robyn scanned the paper. It was a good excuse to delay the appointment with Fell. 'OK, let's go. Come on, Ravi.' She grabbed her handbag and started for the door. 'Janice, we'll talk when I get back.'

# 14

Robyn started the car. Ravi lowered himself into the passenger seat, leaning into the door, keeping a big gap between them.

'Right, this place is on the edge of Pickley, yes?' There was nothing to be gained by noticing his discomfort. 'And they work with ex-offenders. What else did you find out?'

Ravi's face screwed up as he recited. 'St Oswald's, founded fifteen years ago, run by a bloke called Paddy Hall, previous for robbery and assault. Sentenced to ten years, found God in prison and was out in four.'

They drove past the football stadium. Next week, she'd buy her season ticket. A new strip had just been announced: she'd have to see if the club did replica shirts in a women's fit. An approaching car flashed its headlights as they started down the Pickley road.

'What the hell? We didn't place a roadblock here, did we?' An officer was signalling for cars to turn around. Robyn wound down her window.

'You'll have to turn around. Hello, ah, ma'am.' The constable she'd last seen in Upper Town bent to the window. 'Hi, Ravi. Sorry, ma'am, the road is closed for safety checks because a lorry hit Pickley Bridge.'

'OK, thanks, Clyde.' Robyn gave thanks for remembering his name. 'Damn. We'll have to go back through Barton.'

'I've got a new mapping app on my phone, Guv, I'll see if there's a quicker way.' Ravi pressed some buttons. 'Yes. Turn right here.'

After crossing the river, they followed a series of narrowing roads, until they turned into a lane only wide enough for a single car, tufts of yellowed grass between the wheel-tracks.

'Are you sure this is right?' The high hedges blocked visibility and a bramble scraped the wing as they squeezed past a pair of hikers. She'd only seen one passing place and had visions of tractors around every bend.

'Don't panic, Guv. A bit further along here we take a lane on the left. Signal's bad though.'

'Whatever you do, don't leave us stranded.'

Ravi shifted in his seat. 'The turning should be here, Guv. Yes, now go left.'

The lane met a road at a right-angle bend. Robyn nosed the car back onto two-lane tarmac, the main road they could have taken.

'We're nearly there. Just coming up on the left.'

On the next bend, a faded sign had been hammered into the verge. Robyn slowed the car. The dense hedgerows gave way to scrubby trees in front of a tin shed, where a painted 'St Oswald's Furniture' sign competed with rust. A telegraph pole had a chair and table nailed to it, six foot off the ground.

The car bumped down a driveway between two Nissen huts, dust rising from the wheels. They parked next to an old Transit, hand-painted with graffiti images of a figure in biker gear and sunglasses, holding a hammer and saw, a golden halo at a rakish angle.

Ravi noted down the number plate. 'Cool artwork.'

In the building nearest the road, the double doors were open, painted furniture on display. At the far end, a caravan was propped up on blocks. Washing lines stretched between the caravan and the nearest building, filled with faded check shirts and jeans. On a separate rotary dryer hung patterned skirts, printed blouses and a bright, flowery dress.

'Can I 'elp you?' The voice had equal parts question and challenge.

Robyn had to shade her eyes to see the man standing on the steps of the caravan. His broad shoulders strained a white t-shirt, head seeming too small. 'Paddy Hall? I'm DI Bailley and this is DC Sharma. We need to talk to you for a moment.'

The man folded his thick arms. 'If we must.' He passed back into the caravan, turning sideways to fit his shoulders through the door.

Climbing the metal steps, Robyn and Ravi edged into the smoky fug. The caravan was a shell with two mismatched desks jammed in the centre, Hall glowering from behind the one nearest the door. The only other chair looked like a sale reject, covered with multiple shades of wood stain and missing a spindle. Robyn sat, lumps in the cushion pushing at the strapping between her legs, making her wish she had remained standing. Behind her, there were creaks from the plastic wall as Ravi leant back.

'Mr Hall, we're here to talk to you about one of your residents, Jack Parkes. How long has he been with you?'

Hall occupied himself with shuffling papers on the desk into a loose pile. Robyn recognised the attempt to buy time. The smoke from his roll-up wound up past a carved wooden crucifix. It was an impressive piece of work, Christ's agony captured in full detail, the straining tendons shown in curves of wood grain.

'Mr Hall?'

Hall's fingers were stained with paint and nicotine as he gave the papers another prod.

'Mr Hall, we'd like to know how long Jack Parkes has been with you at St Oswald's.'

'Six months. What d'ye think 'e's done then?'

Robyn noted the tone; part defiance, part resignation. 'We're investigating the disappearance of a toddler from Meresbourne yesterday. This is a routine enquiry.' There were little creaks and scuffles as Ravi fidgeted behind her.

'You're 'ere because you think Jack done something.' Hall leaned forward, the blue of old tattoos visible under the sleeves.

Ravi spoke before Robyn could answer. 'Mr Hall, do you know the record of the ex-prisoners you take on before they come to stay here?'

'No. We don't ask and they don't tell. It's 'ard enough when you come out of prison and people just expects you to step into your old clothes before they chuck you out without asking if you've got somewhere to sleep.'

Robyn's elbow dug into Ravi's leg.

Hall glared into the space between them. 'No one cares about prisoners when they're let out. Anyone can apply to come and, if we've got a space, we'll take'em, long as they're not on anything.'

A couple more questions, Robyn thought, get him used to talking. 'Do people tend to stay with you long?'

Hall deepened a scratch in the desk with a fingernail. 'Depends. We give'em a trade. Most sets out for themselves as once you've got a record, no one won't give you a chance. There's nobody comes 'ere that doesn't want to just leave all the crap behind them.'

'It's a good site. How did you get set up?'

'Some local people bought the farm and equipment. Now, we make money with what we sell.' Hall looked at Ravi and his expression changed. 'And the rest gets donated, before you start thinking.'

Robyn kept her face pleasant. 'Thank you, Mr Hall. Could we speak to Jack Parkes now?'

With a long sigh, Hall manoeuvred himself from behind the desk. 'When you see'im – just think, maybe'e's not so different to you. People judge what they see by what they expect to see.' He stumped down the steps. Robyn shifted on the chair, her trouser leg catching on a rough patch of wood.

'Is it safe – him going on his own?' Ravi sounded worried.

Robyn craned her neck around. 'Even if he does warn Parkes, he can't get far.'

Ravi kicked a cupboard. 'We knew all of this stuff already. Why didn't you ask him about the Dearmans?'

There was a low exchange on the steps, before a man slid through the doorway and took Hall's chair. Despite the heat, his denim shirt was buttoned up at the collar and wrists, the visible skin pallid. Hall remained on the top step, filling the doorway and blocking most of the light.

'Mr Parkes, thank you for talking to us. I'm DI Bailley and this is DC Sharma. These are routine enquiries. We'd like to know where you were yesterday between eight and nine am.'

From across the yard, the sound of a power-tool rose then fell. A closer buzzing came from an insect trapped under a blind. Hall tossed his tobacco packet onto the table. Parkes began rolling a cigarette. A scabbed cut ran across the base of his left thumb.

Robyn felt squashed between Ravi's presence behind and the desk pressing against her stomach. 'What happened to your hand?'

Parkes finished rolling a cigarette, placed it on the edge of the desk and began making another. 'Lathe here is a bit more powerful than the ones I've used before.'

Robyn nodded once, wondering how a voice so deep could come from such a slim frame. 'Can you tell us where you were yesterday morning?'

The tip of Parkes' tongue ran along the edge of the paper. He gave the second cigarette to Hall, who produced a battered lighter. The noise of the power-tool rose again. Robyn had to lean forward to catch his words, wincing as the desk pressed her bra's underwire against her ribcage.

'… in the van.'

Ravi grabbed the back of her chair. The tool's whine came to a pitch, then slackened. 'I'm sorry?'

Smoke dribbled from Parkes' nose. 'Was out in the van.'

'Where did you go?'

Something flew through the cigarette smoke, buzzing up towards the mouldy ceiling.

'To pick up some donations from Upper Markham.'

'And you were doing this between eight and nine?' Robyn had to stop to cough. 'Wouldn't it have been easier to wait until the morning traffic had died down?'

Parkes shrugged. 'The lady wanted the stuff picked up before she left for work.'

'We'll need her name and address please. Was anyone else with you?'

'Maggie. I picked her up on the way back.'

Ravi couldn't keep quiet any longer. 'Who's Maggie?'

In the doorway, Hall dropped the remains of his cigarette. 'Maggie does the books and the orders. She'elps us out a couple of days a week.'

Slowly, Robyn thought, slowly. 'And where does Maggie live?'

'By Meresbourne station.'

Ravi leant forward. 'So to pick her up, you'd have driven close to the Riverside entrance to Whitecourt Shopping Centre?' He pulled out the picture of Ben. 'Did you or Maggie see this toddler yesterday morning?'

Parkes hadn't changed position but his fingers tightened on the cigarette. The end fell to the desk, glowing red for a second before it went out. He glared at Hall, lips drained of the little colour they had. 'You didn't tell me they were trying to set me up.'

Hall waited until a drill whined to silence. 'Because you'd have set yourself up, Jack. I didn't want you clamming up and seeming as if you'd something to 'ide.' He twisted his shoulders, stepping into the caravan, taking up most of the free space. ''E's told you where he was

113

and Maggie can confirm it. Maybe you'll believe 'er because she's a Christian lady.'

Robyn found herself tensing as she turned to meet Hall's glare. 'Thank you, Mr Hall, we'll need her full name and address. Can you show us the van?'

The yard shimmered in a heat haze of sticky air. A man was taking in the washing. 'Radio says a storm this afternoon.'

Robyn watched him. 'I thought it was just men here – whose clothes are on the dryer?'

A gobbet of spittle landed at her feet. The man picked up the laundry basket and slouched off.

Hall's nostrils flared as he rooted in his pockets for the van keys. 'They're Maggie's. 'Er washing machine broke and she needed some stuff done. She 'elps us, we 'elp 'er.' He kicked at a stone in the dust. 'Jack was back here by nine-fifteen with Maggie and a load of furniture so I don't see 'ow 'e could have taken your kid.' One spatulate finger pointed to Robyn's chest for emphasis. 'Even if 'e wanted to. Which 'e don't.'

# 15

Hall flung open the back door of the painted van. Ravi already had his phone out to call for a forensic team. Robyn scanned the crammed space and saw spiders' webs between the clutter, concluding the load had not been touched since the previous day and they would need more evidence. Hall watched them go, face flat.

'What more do you want, Guv?'

'I really want to know about this Maggie woman and why she was washing her flowery dress – visit her as soon as possible. He said she's a Christian: check out her church and whether she knows Ms Chivers. Then check the woman in Upper Markham and where he went afterwards: the paint job should make the van easy to track on CCTV.'

Ravi was leaning into the door, as far away from Robyn as he could get.

'Anything on your mind, Ravi?'

Another buzz from Ravi's phone. He stared at the screen.

'Talk to me.'

Ravi swallowed. 'Do you know what people are saying about you?'

At last. They might be about to get to the root of this. 'I can guess.'

'I don't mean around the station, I mean on social media.' Ravi held up his phone. 'There's loads of stuff about you.'

'And I bet most of it's pretty unpleasant. Exactly why I don't use any sites.' Robyn was amazed by how easy she found it to lie now: Roger had always been awful at those little social fibs that help interactions go smoothly. She'd been active online as Robyn and other names for over a year. What had started as a quest for information had become the discovery of a community.

'Don't you care?'

'People have their opinions and that's fine. I'm not asking everyone to agree with me, just to let me live my own life.'

'But what about when what you do affects other people?'

There were echoes of Becky's anger. 'What's up, Ravi?'

A lorry went past as Ravi muttered something.

'Speak up. We haven't got time to faff around, we've got a job to do. Tell me what the problem is.' Robyn could hear the impatience in her voice.

'Guv, I'm getting people telling me I shouldn't work with you, because you're a ...' He tailed off, gazing into the footwell.

Robyn wanted to be angry but tried not to let it show in her voice. 'People. What people?'

'At the temple.'

Goodness knows what Ravi had told everyone. Robyn's attention was jerked back to the road by a learner scooter weaving out in front of her. Beside her, Ravi's rounded shoulders reminded her of early days in her own career when Prentiss, or one of his crew, had questioned her suitability as an officer. She took a deep breath.

'Ravi, you joined the police. Our job brings us into contact with some of the worst people in the world. When I interviewed you for the fast-track programme, you told me how you went against your parents' wishes when you joined up because it was something you believed in.' She risked a glance across to see Ravi with his head in his hands. 'So, if you consider I'm worse than the people we spend our time locking up, then maybe you shouldn't work with me. But I hope you will, because you've got the potential to go a long way.'

They crossed Pickley Bridge, now covered in orange netting, the Gadd below bright green with algae. Robyn's phone sounded a series of missed call alerts.

'Could you check my phone? It's in the bag on the back seat.'

Ravi lifted the bag's strap between two fingers, as if it were something unsavoury. Fumbling with the heavy clasp, he dived into the bag, sending the make-up pouch, pen, notebook, mints, penknife, teabags and, to Robyn's surprise, a clothes peg, flying. 'Blimey, Guv. Oh, here it is.'

He pulled out the phone. 'What's the code? Right. Five missed calls, three from Tracey. Uh-oh. One from Janice, one from someone called Becky. Shall I listen to the voicemails?'

Three calls from Tracey was never going to mean good news. And Becky – she couldn't risk it. 'No, thanks. We'll be back in a few minutes.'

Ravi made a vain attempt to repack the handbag. 'Honestly, Guv. Do you need all this crap?'

They pulled into the station. Robyn didn't answer. Her stomach was tightening with the anticipation of a real bollocking. Ravi had his seat belt off and opened the door before the engine was off.

Robyn felt the snub but now wasn't the time to deal with it. 'Ravi.'

At least he looked back at her.

'You go on – follow up on those leads and can you ask Janice to have a look at the church and its congregation? We haven't investigated them yet. I'll listen to these and then see Tracey.'

'Right, Guv.' You couldn't miss the relief in Ravi's voice.

Robyn leaned against the car and listened to the most recent voicemail, *Change of plan. Get back and see Fell now.* With Tracey's tone, 'now' meant an hour ago. She made her way across the car park, the phone jammed to her ear.

Becky's message was over so soon, she had to replay it: *OK, call me*. Robyn allowed herself a moment of pleasure. Then the wretched handbag wouldn't shut as she pulled open the front door and there were amused glances in the lobby as her make-up pouch and hair-brush tumbled to the floor. Unable to face the five flights of stairs to Fell's office, she pushed the button for the lift. As she waited, she scanned the noticeboard, the usual rubbish, a caravan for sale, a quiz night happening the previous week. Then her name: Fell's memo to the team. Beside the phrase *Roger will be returning in a different gender role*, someone had drawn an axe chopping at a penis with little sprays of blood.

She waited until the lift doors closed, before leaning her face against the wall of the lift and shutting her eyes. She stayed slumped until the lift slowed, when she focused on her fuzzy reflection in the steel walls and replaced the vanished lipstick, irritated that the stuff only lasted a couple of hours, even though it was sold as making you 'all-day kissable'.

Tracey was on the phone; her hair was set to curve around the receiver. She covered the phone with her hand. 'Go straight in – he's got ten minutes before the start of the press conference at three.'

Robyn tapped on the door, wondering why they were doing another press conference. As she walked in, sunshine lanced through slits in the blind lighting up the large silver trophy for 'Division of the Year' on Fell's desk. Khalid stood by one of the open windows. There was the distant sound of traffic on the ring road but no relief from the temperature or the smell.

'Where are we, Bailley?' Fell sat in his black uniform jacket. 'Almost thirty-six hours have passed since a boy was kidnapped and we appear to have made no progress. We have the national media's attention at a time when the command structure in Kent is being reviewed.' He paused. 'Do you have any sightings of the boy?'

'None confirmed, sir.'

'Do you have any leads?'

'Yes, sir. We have a previous sex offender who was in the area at the time of the disappearance. There were also recent threats against the family and we're investigating whether there's a link to the mother's work. As part of the search we've also found a body and evidence of a drugs shipment in the Docks this morning, though we don't believe either are connected to Ben's disappearance.'

Fell made a grating sound in the back of his throat. 'Are there any credible leads?'

Robyn had been asking herself the same thing as she watched the team at work. They were all so busy and purposeful but was anything they were doing making any difference? The air smelled of old leather and rotting vegetation. She'd only been in there five minutes and it felt like an hour.

'Yes, sir.'

'Do you believe Ben is still alive?'

It would be so easy to say yes for some momentary relief. She had no evidence either way. 'I don't know, sir.'

This time, the noise in Fell's throat was more like a growl. 'Given, as part of our "Open Policing" strategy,' he threw a guarded glance at Khalid, 'I have to face the national press in a few minutes and I would like to know exactly what you do know, Bailley. Have we got any identification of the woman in the flowery dress?'

'Not yet, sir.'

By the window, Khalid was concentrating on the waste-paper basket.

The lines on Fell's forehead deepened. 'Why not? Are you going to say you haven't got enough resources? Or are you not focused?'

Robyn's stomach tightened. 'More resources are always useful, sir.'

'And with those resources, I would suggest the investigation needs to focus on the basic facts.'

'Yes, sir.'

Khalid coughed from the doorway. 'The journalists will be here. I'll stall them for a couple of minutes.'

Fell reached for his cap and brushed at a speck of dust, reminding Robyn of the warehouse. 'When will we know who the woman is?'

She had to prove she was still able to deliver. 'Tomorrow, sir.'

'Very well.' Fell met her eyes for a second, before his gaze returned to the wall. 'And I want some definite progress on the burglaries. I did my quarterly update to community stakeholders yesterday and there is a climate of fear amongst the borough's older residents.' He marched out without closing the door. The outer door opened and the soft scuffle of Fell's brogues and the tap of Tracey's heels receded. Tomorrow …

# 16

'Listen up, everyone.' Robyn stood in the centre of the incident room and waited for quiet. 'I've just committed to Fell that we'll identify who the woman in the dress is by tomorrow.'

'What were you thinking of? How could you be so stupid?' Janice was on her feet. She took in a sharp breath. 'I meant the team doesn't need extra pressure, Robyn. We're all doing our best here.'

Their eyes met. Janice's lips were pressed together, bloodless.

Coming from Janice, the criticism stung. Robyn felt the team's eyes on her as she walked to the board and pointed to the photo of Ben. 'This boy has been missing for close to thirty-six hours and we've got nothing. However hard we're trying, it's not getting us anywhere so we need to do better.'

Janice half-shrugged and slumped into her chair.

'I'm always happy to hear concerns but nothing changes the job we've got to do.' Robyn's voice sounded too loud as if she was trying to convince herself. 'We start by concentrating on two things. Who is the woman and how did she get away? Questions?' Robyn's stomach rumbled. She hoped no one had noticed.

Ravi's hand shot up – 'It could be Maggie Gorton. We know she lives nearby.'

'Yes. We need to know where she is. And we should be able to track the St Oswald's van on CCTV to confirm Parkes' movements.' She turned to Lorraine. 'Forget the burglaries for the moment. Ms Chivers is hiding something about Ben's father. We need to know who he is, or was.' She tapped the grainy picture from the shopping centre. 'We've got Ben's DNA to check for potential matches.'

What she was asking them to do was all so obvious. She'd allowed herself to get lost in details. 'Graham, we haven't had any demands for ransom so let's leave the Dearmans out of this for the moment. Go and re-interview all of the people in the nearby shops. Someone must have seen the woman.'

Graham scowled, then nodded.

'Janice, Ravi, we need to close off some loose ends. Find the builder and eliminate him, then follow up the voluntary work, the church and Ben's school. Oh and keep in touch with Uniform about the searches. I want a briefing from all of you at six.' Janice stared ahead for a moment then shook her shoulders and pulled the keyboard towards her.

Robyn watched the team return to their desks. Now she'd set them working, she should be thinking of the next steps, seeing the pattern but kept wondering when she'd get a chance to call Becky. One finger hovered over her contacts; the chip on the nail had got bigger. Graham knocked on her desk, grinning.

'Before I start on the woman – I know who left the tip-off for the warehouse.'

Robyn pushed the phone away. Janice was hovering as well.

'Graham, this isn't about Ben. We can't keep getting distracted.'

'OK, OK. Don't you want to guess?'

Robyn sighed. When Graham got like this, he was infuriating. 'No. Who gave the tip-off?'

Her phone shrilled: Tracey. 'Hell, I'd better get this.'

Tracey's voice cut across her greeting. 'Can you come up to the conference room now?'

'What's the problem?'

'Just get up here. Fell needs you to answer questions.'

Robyn walked up to the fifth floor, giving herself time to run over potential questions. She hoped the sudden feeling of light-headedness was just down to lack of lunch.

As Robyn slid into the conference room, Fell was in full flow, statistics bouncing off the walls, comparing local rates of something to national averages. No one was writing anything down. Although she'd tried to be discreet, Robyn sensed a stir of interest. Khalid rose from his seat at the front and, taking Robyn by the arm, steered her back outside again.

'Thanks for coming up. The journalists want to talk to you.'

'About what? Because if questions aren't about the investigation, I'm not answering them.' Robyn folded her arms.

'Robyn …' It was the first time she'd seen Khalid struggling for words. 'There have been questions about whether you're a suitable person to be in charge.'

'I thought you'd prepared for all this? Do you really mean Fell isn't willing to confirm it?'

'This is a high-profile case and it's attracting a lot of publicity. We must manage in the best way for the Service.' Khalid pulled the door open so the audience in the conference room could see Robyn.

Robyn didn't take the chair Khalid gestured at. If she sat, she would be smaller; standing, she could feel at least an illusion of being in control, though there was the question of what to do with her hands. She settled for holding them behind her, which also pulled her shoulders back, making her feel more confident. The room was fuller than usual. She didn't see Ady at first because he was staring down at his phone.

Fell cleared his throat. 'As I said, the investigation is being led by

123

Detective Inspector Bailley, an experienced officer. You may ask DI Bailley questions now.'

Robyn registered the lack of a pronoun first, then that Fell had not limited questions to the investigation. There was a flurry of hands going up, then a strident voice cut through the babble from an unfamiliar woman in thick-rimmed glasses.

'Liz Trew, *Daily Journal*. DI Bailley, has your personal life affected the investigation in any way?'

Fell's feet scuffed at the floor. Khalid's finger swept across the screen of his tablet and hung, poised.

Whatever happened, she mustn't show any sign of hesitation. 'No.' Robyn paused, letting her gaze sweep the room. 'I'm a career police officer, a detective for nearly twenty years and I'm approaching this case exactly as I have all the cases I've worked on.'

There was a low buzz of comment. The journalist hadn't written anything down. 'Can you truly say nothing is different?'

Robyn nodded. She was getting the sense she had in an interview, when something shocking was about to come to the surface. 'Any case involving a child will always get the highest priority and we are doing all we can to find Ben.'

The journalist's face was in shadow. 'But how do suspects react, being questioned by a detective in drag?'

There were gasps around the room. Robyn had a sudden rush of grim exhilaration and decided to tell the woman exactly what she thought of her but Khalid had jumped to his feet. 'Ladies and gentlemen, we are here to talk about the investigation into Benjamin Chivers' disappearance. Who has the next question, please? Yes, Colin.'

The balding veteran from the regional paper seemed surprised to be chosen. Robyn bit back what she had been about to say and sank onto a seat, conscious of how close she'd been to losing her temper.

'Can you tell us …?' Colin broke off when Liz Trew spoke over him.

'So you're not prepared to consider the people you may be offending?'

'I'm afraid we only have time for two questions per person.' Khalid turned away from Trew, pointing at Colin. 'Before we started, Colin asked me whether this crime would mean a review of the planned closures of the remaining village police stations.'

Fell embarked on what promised to be a long answer. Robyn tried to sit still, knowing attention could turn back to her any moment. Tracey, in the front row, tapped the jewelled face of her watch several times until Fell noticed.

'And we have to conclude, ladies and gentlemen. Thank you for coming to our Open Policing Session. I hope you found it useful.' Khalid held up a sheet of paper. 'Ah, yes, I have been asked to remind you about the feedback forms by the exit and we'd be grateful for all your ...'

Robyn was already through the door. Seeing the HR Business Partner waiting for the lift, she diverted to the stairs. Down, rubber soles squeaking as she turned each flight, keeping going past the second floor, until she pushed through the back door into the car park. She got her phone out, then stared at it. The secrecy of the last few months had meant she'd kept herself to herself: she had no idea who to call. The muggy air was hotter than the corridor, dark clouds banking overhead. A steady flow of the early shift were heading to their cars, home to forget another day. Robyn returned a few nods, one 'hello'. It emphasised how few people she really knew in the station.

Sick of missing calls, she'd put the phone's volume up to maximum. Now, the ring was so loud, she jumped. She fumbled the phone to her ear and managed a hello, before Ady appeared around a corner of the building.

'Afternoon.' He slipped his own phone into a pocket. 'You dashed out of the briefing so I thought I'd give you a call. I could hear your phone ring from the front entrance.'

He held out his hand. Robyn paused for a second. In the years since they were at school together, they'd only ever shaken hands on some sort of milestone. The last time, the occasion had been their first meeting in nearly twenty years, when Ady had interviewed Roger as Meresbourne's newly-appointed DI. Robyn's hand met Ady's, feeling his calluses. 'You've been getting a lot of tennis in.'

Ady smiled and kept on smiling. The handshake was going on for too long. When Robyn relaxed her grip, Ady seemed to focus and shoved his hand into his pocket. His lips opened a few times before he spoke. 'That must have been ...' He searched for words. 'Christ, Fell's a pompous prat and the woman from the *Journal*'s a grade-one bitch. It's what she does with everyone, finds a weak spot and pokes it for a reaction.' He shrugged. 'Liz Trew has set herself up as this moral crusader against the "tide of filth threatening to engulf our peaceful society", something along those lines. She's always ...'

Robyn's hands balled into fists. 'The way you've said it, I'm more of a problem than whoever took Ben.'

Ady folded his arms. 'No and no, that wasn't what I meant. I wanted to call you to, well, see if you were OK, maybe go for the beer we always talk about. Now ...' He uncrossed his arms, palms up. 'I don't know what I can say.'

Robyn was silent as he turned to go. There was the sinking feeling of a bad mistake. She touched his arm. 'I'm sorry, Ady.' The right words wouldn't come. 'I just seem to be making a real mess of this and upsetting everyone.'

There was a pause. Ady's lips creased. 'I can't say I understand, because I don't but whatever you do, don't go away thinking we're all like her.' He turned back towards her. 'If you do want to tell your story, then we'll do it properly, present it from your side. We could run a series, get some decent pictures ...'

'Until we find Ben, nothing else really matters, does it?'

Ady shrugged. 'I guess not. Hey, if you need anything, give me a call, OK?'

'Thanks.' Robyn smiled.

'Well, see you.' Ady started towards the visitor's car park. The sun went behind a cloud.

An idea flashed into Robyn's mind. 'Ady! Before you go – the Gaddesford festival in May – have you got any pictures?'

Ady turned back, his eyes lifting as he thought. 'Ah, yeah, probably. Yes, we did a colour supplement covering the weekend.' He inclined his head. 'Thought you'd have been out there taking some pictures yourself.' He stroked his chin. 'Hang on, this isn't a plan to enter our pictures into one of your photo competitions, is it?'

Robyn held up her hands. 'OK, you've got me.' They both smiled, deep creases showing in Ady's tanned face. 'No, this is for an investigation. Could you give me the photographer's details?'

'Sure. I'll get them when I get back to the office. What's your email?'

'You've got my email.'

'Oh, I thought it would have changed, given … well, OK, I've got it then. I hope if you get something useful, you'll let me in a bit earlier.' Ady held out his hand again, then pulled back. Robyn watched him walk back to his car. The email address would go onto a long list of things to be changed. Everything would have to wait until they found Ben. No parent, even one as icy as Melissa Chivers, should be deprived of their child. She turned towards the steps to the station then decided she would call Becky now, otherwise she might never get the opportunity. She went to sit in her car.

The sky had darkened but the cockpit was stifling. Robyn propped the phone up on the hot dashboard, to see Becky's picture as she spoke to her. The phone was answered on the second ring.

'Hello.'

'Hello, Becky, thanks for picking up. Am I disturbing you?'

'You mean other than by announcing to the world you think you're a woman, no, you're not disturbing me at all.'

'Becky …'

'Yes? What do you want to say to me?'

There were a lot of things she wanted to say. They all sounded stupid. 'I'm very proud to be your father and I'll never stop being your father. That's it.'

One fat drop of water hit the windscreen.

'That's it?' There was a new note in Becky's voice, more puzzled than sarcastic.

'That's it. And I'm sorry for the letter too. I thought if I could see you in person I could tell you. I'd tried to tell you a couple of times over the phone and ended up chickening out. So I wrote to you because I had to tell you and didn't know what else to do.'

The rain was heavier now. Becky made a noise Robyn hoped was a laugh. 'I'd worked out you were trying to tell me something. I guessed you were getting married again.'

Thunder sounded overhead. Robyn leant back against the headrest. 'No. Nothing so simple.'

'I can't hear you. What's happening at your end?'

Rain was hammering on the roof. 'A storm.' She paused. 'I'm going to go now. Could we speak again soon?'

'Can't hear you.'

'Bye, sweetheart.'

She wasn't sure whether there was a response.

# 17

A ragged edge of cloud marked the end of the deluge: the rain lost its insistent rhythm, slackened and dribbled to a stop. Robyn's thumb hovered over the redial button for a long time before she loosened her grip on the phone. Weak sunlight crept across the car park: the car windows were steaming up. She stretched back in the seat then, to give herself a purpose for staying put, switched the radio on for the five o'clock news.

*A new witness has come forward in the hunt for missing Meresbourne toddler, Benjamin Chivers. After his mother appealed for his safe return, a witness at Whitecourt Shopping Centre says he saw the child being taken.*

The reporter cut to a new voice with a thick accent.

*I finish my work and saw a woman pick up this kid. But it was OK, you know, like they were together.*

Robyn flung open the car door and splashed back to the station. She ran up the stairs to the second floor, the damp hems of her trousers flapping.

The radio in the incident room was off. Robyn raised her voice.

'We need to get down to the shopping centre. There's a witness, an employee, who saw the woman take Ben. He's just given an interview to North Kent FM.'

Janice's eyes widened. 'Why didn't he get picked up during the shop-to-shop searches?'

'Something to ask Phil. Assuming he's credible, we'll bring him back and use his description to make up an E-FIT of the woman's face. We could then run a reconstruction tomorrow morning. Janice, can you organise everything? We'll need Gillian Green.' Robyn paused. 'Well, come on then. Graham, with me.' And she intended to find out why Graham wasn't already at the shopping centre, as asked.

As they reached the top of the steps to the car park, Graham already had his keys out. 'I'm parked over there.' Too tired to argue, Robyn followed, picking her way around the puddles under blue sky. Graham pulled away, not even waiting for Robyn to fasten her seat belt, slipping into half a gap in front of a bus.

'So, the tip-off …'

'Go on then, who and how did you find out?' Robyn's right foot stiffened against an imaginary brake pedal.

Graham waited for a bicycle, fingers tapping. 'Micky Dearman.'

'No way!' Her laugh was closer to a snort. 'Micky is about as likely to help the police as I am to win Miss World.' She was embarrassed to see spit on the dashboard.

Graham's jaw clenched, while Robyn forced herself to calm down. After all, she'd upset enough people for one day. 'Are you sure?'

Graham tapped on the steering wheel. 'I've been speaking to a source of mine who was round at the Dearmans' place recently and the warehouses were mentioned. There was a lot of talk about what could be done to stop the council granting planning permission.'

'So why should Micky Dearman ring us?'

Graham adopted the tone he used when doing schools' visits. 'Because Micky wants to buy the warehouse back as cheaply as possible.'

'Still seems unlikely.' Robyn risked a glance across.

'Well, he wouldn't have made the call himself – he'd have got someone to do it for him.' Graham raised his eyebrows.

'But it's incredibly risky for Micky. The Dearmans would be putting themselves in the frame for the girl's death, when it's not going to hold up the development for more than a few weeks. It doesn't sound worth it.'

Diving through a gap, Graham parked again in the loading bay. 'It's nearly closing time. Come on.' He led the way towards the access passage. Robyn watched him for a few steps and followed. Graham shoved his hands in his pockets. 'I don't think the Dearmans killed a woman though. Not their style.'

'No.' Robyn nodded agreement. 'Are you saying they didn't know the body was there? Or, did someone tip us off about the drugs shipment and the body is just a coincidence?'

'Micky's got manners. He wouldn't want someone to kill a girl and get away with it.'

Robyn glanced at Graham: he didn't look as if he was joking. The concourse was almost empty, the first shutters coming down. Near the pharmacy, a man in baggy combat shorts was marking out the floor with masking tape.

Robyn nodded for Graham to continue on. 'Excuse me. What's happening here?'

The man tore off a strip of tape with his teeth and stuck it to the floor before reaching for a plan. 'Promotion for the college tomorrow. A load of stands.'

'When do they get taken down?'

The man traced a line on a plan. 'Tomorrow night.' He stretched his measuring tape almost across Robyn's feet.

Robyn stepped back. This ruled out a reconstruction tomorrow but it had been wishful thinking to imagine they could organise one so quickly. What was more worrying was that no one in the team had spoken up to say so.

Graham was sitting in a corner of the staff room with a slight youth with headphones around his neck. His glance towards Robyn became a long appraisal until he smiled, lines appearing around his eyes, ageing him.

'Guv, this is Jaime Restrepo.' Robyn cleared faded magazines and sat down. She shifted an inch back on the sofa, feeling Jaime's gaze like a physical force. Graham leant forward, the chair grating as its legs shifted. 'Jaime works dusk and dawn shifts, finishing at eight o'clock which meant he was on his way out when he saw Ben and gone before we arrived.'

Robyn had to fight a sudden urge to run her fingers through her hair. 'Jaime, can you tell us what you saw yesterday morning?'

'I told it on the radio. I finish here, start to go to college. Not many people so I see the little boy.' Jaime's long fingers were twisting through the headphone cable.

'Was there anyone with him?' Graham pulled out his notebook.

Jaime's face lifted and met Robyn's. There was too much knowledge to hold the gaze more than a second.

Graham coughed. 'Was anyone with the boy?'

'No. Then kids turn up and boy was in middle. Before I do anything, woman in dress call his name, pick him up ...'

'Where was the woman before?' Graham poised, pen above paper.

'I no see.' The deep brown eyes stroked across Robyn again.

'And then?' Graham raised his voice.

'Boy was quiet, think everything OK. Woman talking to him.'

She was getting used to being stared at but this level of scrutiny felt far more intimate. Robyn told herself she couldn't afford to be distracted. 'Can you describe the woman?'

'She wear sunglasses, big ones. Over her face.' He mimed the size of the lenses. 'Mostly ordinary. Like an aunt or granny.'

The information is there, don't push, keep him talking. 'Where are you from, Jaime?'

'Venezuela. I have to leave.'

'Why?'

Jaime ran a hand through his hair, pushing it back. His left ear had an ugly rip where part had been slashed away. 'I'm gay.' He let the hair flop back. 'Some people think is no good.'

Robyn tried to think of something to say and was glad when her phone buzzed. She nodded back to Graham, who began a question. Robyn stared at the message from Tracey. *Meeting with Fell 2pm tomorrow, no excuses.* A bald man appeared in the doorway, directing a stream of Spanish at Jaime.

'I got to go. My supervisor.' Jaime stood, turned so his back was towards Robyn, legs pressed together as he bent to retrieve a grey boiler suit. He lifted one leg and began to pull the suit on over his tight jeans.

'We need you to come to the station with us to complete an E FIT of the woman you saw.' She would have to get Graham to lead the session because the prospect of being in a small interview room with Jaime's intense gaze was not something she wanted to deal with.

The boy stopped, overalls halfway up. 'I can no go. Days, I go to college, nights and mornings, I work here.'

The supervisor tapped his watch. Robyn took two steps towards him, smiling into his anger.

'We are taking Jaime with us because he needs to give evidence.' The glare had turned into a sneer. 'And if I find he's in any trouble when he gets back, I'll charge you with obstructing the police.'

As they walked past the half-built stands, Graham took his hands out of his pockets. 'So, it's an older woman. We're narrowing it down.'

Behind them there was the scuff of Jaime's feet. He had his music back on.

# 18

'Hi, Khalid, we're on our way back to the station with a witness who saw the snatch and can give us a description.' Robyn ignored Graham, who'd made it clear he thought involving the Communications team was pointless.

'Great news. How long do you think it'll take?'

'Hard to say. Could be a couple of hours.'

'OK. I'll let the media know so they give it space. If we can get it out by ten pm, we should meet the newspapers' deadlines, then have a press conference in the morning. You OK to front it?'

The car jerked forward as Graham accelerated. There was a gasp from the back seat.

Standing in front of the press wasn't an attractive thought but she wasn't going to admit it. 'Of course, bye.'

They drove into the station car park.

'Jaime, DS Catt will take you through the E-FIT.' Robyn opened her door.

'Righto, this way.' If Graham was thinking anything was odd, he didn't show it as he shepherded Jaime across the car park.

Robyn watched them go, feeling purposeless. She felt more useful when she got to the incident room. Ravi leapt up with an eager expression.

'I've got a photo of Gorton.' He pointed to the board. 'It's a few years old, from a school where she taught. She's retired now but she's got a criminal record for assaulting a police officer on a picket line. She's also disappeared. Neighbours haven't seen her since Monday afternoon and her car's gone.' He ran out of breath.

'Good work, Ravi. We've got the witness from the shopping centre in an interview room. See whether he recognises Gorton.'

Unpinning the photo from the board, Ravi dashed out.

'Right, the reconstruction. Janice, how are you getting on?' Robyn paused. 'OK, where's Janice?' It was worrying she again hadn't noticed Janice wasn't there.

'She went up to London, Guv, to see Ms Chivers' relatives. Asked me to mention this.' Lorraine stretched across her desk and held up a plastic wallet filled with printed sheets. 'Janice was looking into Ms Chivers' church. It's part of some "global network of faith".' She shook her head. 'They really are barking. Like, they say families are supposed to have lots of kids to keep the faith strong but then they shouldn't vaccinate them because God created everything perfect and that's enough.' She frowned. 'But get this. They believe that if they do something against the law of man, it's OK as long as it's for God's purposes. That means, it's fine for them to obstruct clinics and harass anyone trying to go in. And she spoke to someone in the US who was able to look up that preacher of theirs, the Reverend Lewis – he was arrested for attempted murder in the States for running over a doctor with his car.'

Robyn took the file. 'Interesting but if Ms Chivers is a member of the church, I couldn't see them harming one of their own, can you? What about Ben's father?'

Lorraine shuffled one set of papers to the side and pulled over another pile. 'Right. Ben was born in September. Her church doesn't allow IVF treatment because it's "playing God", which means Ben was conceived the old-fashioned way.' She grinned, reminding Robyn of Graham. 'So, Chivers got together with the father around Christmas-time, three years ago. We know she was signed up to at least one dating agency.' Lorraine pointed to a print-out. 'I've contacted the company. It's one where you're not allowed in unless you're a rocket scientist or a brain surgeon. They remember Chivers being pickier about the health and qualifications of potential matches than looks. She also specifically requested a white partner.' Lorraine tapped Melissa's picture. 'The question is why? It meant she reduced her choice and the dating agency told me a couple of potential matches turned her down. They didn't say so but I'm guessing it was because she was black. Why make such a fuss unless it was really important? Either way, she only met two men in the year she was a member and requested no further contact after the first meetings. Then, she let her membership lapse many months before Ben was conceived. So I think she found herself a baby-father somewhere else.'

'Work?' Robyn leaned back in her chair. 'Or church?'

'Exactly, one of those two. After all, she doesn't seem to have much else and seems too concerned about good genes to pick someone up in a nightclub. I reckon she found someone at work, because the church's congregation is more likely to be couples and they wouldn't approve of adultery. Plus, I can see her going for someone with lots of qualifications, like a lawyer.'

'Rutherford, do you think?'

Lorraine chewed her lip. 'I don't think so. From what I've seen, the gentleman prefers blondes. He wouldn't be able to get rid of Ms Chivers easily, either. No, someone else.'

Robyn crossed her legs, feeling the strain in the taping and uncrossed them. 'But, if the father works with Ms Chivers, how would he not know she was pregnant? A client, perhaps?'

The door opened. Ravi and Graham appeared, shoulders drooping. There was no need to ask whether Jaime had recognised Maggie Gorton.

Graham threw himself into a chair. Ravi filled the blank space on the board with the new E-FIT. Robyn and Lorraine moved closer.

'That could be anybody.' Lorraine spoke for both of them.

'Our boy was happy with it. He described the bloody dress better than the woman and he wouldn't commit about Maggie Gorton. Said it could have been her.' Graham flicked an elastic band which hit the image between the eyes. 'But it might not be.'

'Well, it's the best we've got and it will make tomorrow's papers.' Robyn raised her voice. 'We have to find this woman. Ravi, find Gorton, check her friends, family and get a warrant to search St Oswald's.'

'I'll see if anyone recognises this picture or Gorton at Derby and Rutherford when I get the staff and client lists first thing tomorrow.' Lorraine sat down.

'All this makes me wonder about Rutherford. He's hiding something.' Robyn stared at the ceiling, trying to organise her thoughts.

'Too right, Guv.' Graham leaned back in his chair. 'My source said Rutherford's father and old man Dearman go way back.'

'Something to remember in case Rutherford reminds me again he knows Fell.' Robyn clapped her hands. 'Right – we need to make sure everything is ready for the reconstruction.'

'Unless we find him before then.' Ravi spoke for all of them.

No one wanted to be the first to leave. At seven-thirty, Robyn ordered pizzas, remembering to take advantage of 'Two for One Tuesday'. She reread statements from the shopping centre's staff, chin on her hand, feeling stubble. At eight-thirty, Ravi took a call and blushed, bending to muffle his words. When he came off the phone, Graham threw a ball of paper at him. 'Has your mummy got dinner ready, Raver? Can we all come?'

For Robyn, it looked like a sign enough was enough and she held up her hand before Ravi could reply. 'OK, I think we call it a day. Thank you everyone, we've made some progress. Now it's time to go home. Oh, one bit of good news. Fell has promised us more resources tomorrow.'

As she pulled out of the car park, the confused mess of impressions in her mind became the dull certainty of no milk at home. She was in the wrong lane of the roundabout for the superstore on the ring road and the prospect of navigating miles of aisles was not enticing. She turned into the mid-sized store on the Barton Road. The car park was nearly empty – she'd be able to slip in and out.

After the soft twilight, the spotlights at the entrance seemed too harsh to light a few ragged bunches of flowers. Squinting, she stopped in front of the depleted newspaper stand to get her bearings.

Someone walked into her from behind. 'Watch out!'

Robyn muttered an apology without turning round. She tried to think: milk, bread, soup: did she need loo roll? And beer. She'd drunk the house dry while she'd been off, a combination of celebration and Dutch courage. She decided it was easiest to just go up and down and take what she needed.

A minute later, glancing up, she became aware that a knot of people were staring at her. There was no shame in their scrutiny; Robyn looked at them, they looked at her. Things were balanced in her arms because she hadn't thought she'd need a basket. By resting the loaf against a padded breast, she could free one hand to pick up what was in front of her, showing she'd meant to stop here all along. It was rice pudding – just the sort of comfort food she fancied but shouldn't eat if she wanted to fit into a size fourteen dress. The group kept up their scrutiny, all their jaws chomping gum. An older woman with home-made tattoos pointed at her. 'You're the policeman off the telly.'

Robyn stood her ground, the groceries clutched like a shield.

'The one hunting for the little boy.' The group began talking amongst themselves, praising Ben's cuteness and describing what they would like to do to the person who'd taken him. Robyn relaxed. There seemed to be no need for her to say anything, just stand and be talked at.

'Are you getting your bollocks chopped off?' This voice was different, harsher; Robyn thought this came from the one with the vest-top straps sunk between rolls of flesh. 'Like on Jeremy Kyle,' another voice added. The tone was curious.

Robyn smiled, while she thought of something to say. The tannoy asked Sandra to take a call on line two and gave her a few extra seconds. 'Yes, I'm the detective hunting for Ben. Were any of you shopping yesterday morning? Did you see anything?'

There was a collective intake of breath and a pause in the chewing. Robyn guessed being asked, in public, to help the police was not something they felt comfortable with. She smiled again. 'Well, if you do think of anything, we'd be grateful. Good night.'

The urge to escape was paramount, stronger even than the desire for a drink. She got to the checkout without further comment, though her skin prickled, all the way to the car and home.

There was no post in the dark hallway, only a message on the answering machine. *'Hello, ah, hello. This is Keith from Camera Club. We've seen you on the news and guessed, ah, you won't be able to do your talk at the meeting tomorrow. Val has stepped in and is going to talk about her landscape work. Perhaps you can do yours when you're a bit less busy. Bye.*

Camera Club. She'd been supposed to run a session for Camera Club tomorrow night. The talk was ready, prepared during her time off, as an antidote to the more serious steps towards her transition. For her first talk to the club since she'd joined, she was going to talk about portraits and how to capture the inner essence of someone, which fitted with introducing herself as Robyn rather than Roger. Another chance missed.

The pizza seemed like a long time ago so a soup bowl joined the previous night's washing up on the counter. Installing a dishwasher was one of the many things she needed to do to the house because everything still reflected her parents and the fussy décor they'd put up in the enthusiasm of new retirement. She'd got round to replacing the soppy watercolour landscapes and nautical scenes with prints of her own photographs, including, in pride of place above the fireplace, the one commended in the Kent Print Cup. The other change was the new bed bought for the master bedroom: you couldn't sleep on the bed where your mother had died. Roger's childhood room was now where junk was kept. It was becoming a habit to just throw something in there and say she would deal with it later.

She was in the bathroom when the phone rang and the answering machine kicked in downstairs before she could get to it.

*Hello, leave a message after the beep.*

'Hello?'

'What the hell do you think you're doing, Roger?'

Robyn let her neck go slack. She'd last spoken to Julie six months ago, when they had agreed how they were going to fund a car for Becky. It had been a civilised conversation between two concerned parents. The voice now at the end of the phone sounded near hysterical.

'Hello, Julie.' She slumped onto the bed.

'You bastard, you're doing all of this to get at me, aren't you?' Robyn held the phone away from her ear. 'Well you've got no rights, stop this. Stop this now.'

'Julie, this has nothing to do with you.'

The voice at the other end rose to a shriek. 'Nothing to do with me? You're reifying the gender binary I've spent my whole career trying to break down and you say this has nothing to do with me?'

Robyn couldn't help laughing. 'I've no idea what you're talking about. We've been divorced for seventeen years. Other than Becky, there's no reason anyone would make a connection between us …'

'But everyone—'

Robyn kept talking. 'Unless you've been complaining about me, in which case, I can't say I've got any sympathy.' Merciful silence

140

from the other end. 'I don't think we have anything to talk about, Julie.'

'You're not a fit father for Becky, you never were. I'll stop you seeing her.'

Robyn was gripping the phone, trying to contain her fear. 'Becky's an adult and can make her own decisions. It's up to her.' She tried to sound confident.

'Well I've spoken to her and she's disgusted with you. You sicken her, you—'

After she'd put down the phone, Robyn unplugged it.

# WEDNESDAY 20 JULY

# 19

A drunken brawl inside the Quiksilva nightclub, involving Meresbourne Town's expensive, newly-signed striker was top story on the local radio as Robyn drove into work, trying to clear Julie's accusations from her mind. Wednesday was the Home feature in the *Gazette* and the billboards advertised *Ways to keep your child safe*. It made her wonder whether she did deserve any kind of relationship with Becky.

The incident room's purposeful hum was a relief. In half an hour, she'd be briefing journalists with the E-FIT and began scribbling notes. A quiet tap made her glance up. Janice was on the phone; Ravi engrossed in watching CCTV. Lorraine and Graham were debating whether or not the Dearmans would ever co-operate with the police. Thinking she had imagined the noise, Robyn returned to her notes.

A moment later, there were two thumps as if someone was trying to break down the door with a blunt instrument. After a second where everyone stopped what they were doing, Ravi rose and opened the door. His head dropped: the person in the doorway didn't even reach his shoulder. Graham craned his neck. 'Morning, Chloe. So you're the new resource are you?'

Chloe took small steps into the room. 'Morning. I'm joining the investigation.' She stood, her feet pointing together. 'Hope that's OK.'

Robyn walked over. 'Welcome, Chloe. Good to have you on the team.' They shook hands. 'Everyone, Chloe organised the first response at the shopping centre, even though she was off duty.' Robyn paused to make sure this had been noted.

Chloe gave a shy smile. Her hair was flat today, her tiny frame lost in a boxy jacket, like a child in a new school uniform.

'I'll let the team introduce themselves. Ravi, can you brief Chloe on everything so far?'

The portable air-conditioner whirred into life then died a few seconds later. In the sudden quiet, Chloe's voice just reached her. 'But what do I call DI Bailley?'

Lorraine swung her bag to her shoulder, just missing Chloe's head. 'I'm off to the lawyers, Guv, to get the staff and client lists. When I spoke to the HR woman there yesterday, she came over all legal and went to check with Rutherford. I'd rather go down there and make sure they deliver.'

'OK. Can you also chase up the details on this housing case led by Ms Chivers?' Robyn sat back at her desk, the multiple strands of her bracelet rattling on her wrist. Every time she used the mouse, they got in the way. The matching necklace tickled and the clasp rubbed at her over-shaved skin. She'd chosen her brightest set of jewellery for this morning to give her confidence to face the press. Glancing at her watch, she had time to nip to the loo before the briefing. Stepping into the corridor, Robyn turned at the sound of her name. Khalid was hurrying towards her.

'Robyn, I'm glad I caught you. We've decided to issue the E-FIT without a briefing.' The handkerchief in his breast pocket was crooked, not its usual perfect triangle.

'Why? I thought your strategy was always to get in front of the press when we could?'

A crease darkened between Khalid's precise eyebrows. 'Have you seen the *Journal* this morning?' He rubbed his forehead, as if trying to erase the lines.

'No. You mean that journalist from yesterday?'

'Coming through –'scuse.' Two men in paint-stained overalls were pushing a trolley covered with tins and ladders. Robyn and Khalid flattened themselves against the wall.

'Come on, we'll talk in the canteen.'

Robyn realised something was missing. 'You'll have to buy the teas, I haven't got my bag.'

They sat in one corner, Khalid scrutinised the table top, scrubbing a couple of areas with a napkin, before passing over a copy of the *Daily Journal*. Robin scanned the front page, which screamed about deaths from the heatwave. Khalid tapped the banner headline at the top of the page: *Latest barmy police fad.*

Robyn spread out the paper. Opposite an ad for anti-wrinkle cream, a picture of Liz Trew in a leather cat suit and heels ran the full height of the page, a speech bubble coming from her scarlet mouth: *Trew's Truth: Daring to say what everyone's thinking.* The picture must have been taken some years ago, Robyn decided; the woman at the briefing wouldn't have fitted into the outfit. She didn't bother to read the article: certain phrases had been picked out in pink, italicised text between the main paragraphs, for those who liked their outrage in bite-sized chunks. *Diversity gone mad; Investigation going nowhere; Dressing-up more important than finding a child.*

There was a waft of chamomile as Khalid fished out his teabag. A drip hit the newspaper.

Robyn made an effort to relax her shoulders, to sound calm. 'OK, she's done a hatchet job. Why cancel the briefing?'

Khalid took a sip of tea. 'Because you're becoming the story. Everything you do on this case will be judged by what you're wearing.'

Robyn focused on where the blouse rubbed around her armpit; something real, keeping her grounded. 'So are *you* ...' she stressed the word, '... telling me *Fell* ...' again the emphasis, '... has taken me off the case?'

'Off the case? No, of course not. Did you think ... oh. No.' Khalid put both hands flat on the table. 'All I meant was we change the approach to the media.'

'So no more "Open Policing Strategy"?' Robyn failed to keep the sarcasm from her voice.

Khalid made an unnecessary fuss of stirring his tea.

She couldn't afford to add Khalid to the list of people she'd managed to upset. 'I'm sorry for making your job harder. All I want to do is get on with things. It seems the more we try with the press, the less they help us.'

Khalid made a clicking noise in his teeth and began refolding the newspaper. 'They will help us, they are helping us but people can get facts anywhere so columnists like Trew and their opinions are what sells papers now.'

They both drank. A party of searchers, who must have been out since first light, crowded the counter ordering coffee and bacon sandwiches. The talk was of the football transfer market, which meant they'd found nothing.

'I'm sure Ben's alive.' Robyn searched for the right words. 'Unfortunately, I don't know where he is.'

'We can't put a hunch in a press release.' Khalid pushed back his chair, causing a wail from the lino. 'I'll do what I can, of course I will.' He shrugged. 'Just find Ben. If you do, no-one's going to care what you dress like.' Without waiting for an answer, he walked out.

Whether she was listening to herself more now or something about her really had changed, Robyn wondered whether she'd always sounded so weak and vague. She walked towards the exit, dropping her cup into a bin.

A bellow of laughter rose from the searchers. 'And so after she'd got herself covered up, she only went and complained it was our fault because Willingdon doesn't get enough regular patrols.' Robyn glanced towards the group: a young constable with red hair was telling the story. She remembered him: an applicant for the fast-track who hadn't impressed her so she'd given the vacant place in the CID team to Ravi. Jeremy, his name was Jeremy. As Robyn reached the door, her name was just distinguishable in the racket of more laughter.

# 20

Robyn trudged back to the incident room, at a loss for what to do next. She'd spent a long time thinking about how to manage the press briefing and no time on planning what to say to Fell. Whatever else happened, she mustn't allow her nerves to infect the team. She stared into the artificial eyes of the E-FIT in the centre of the board. It was an unremarkable face, an everywoman no one would look twice at. Derby and Rutherford had put up a reward for information leading to Ben's safe return. The phones rang and rang.

The team were taking calls as fast as they could. Ravi read one out: *I saw her in the supermarket yesterday – she was buying cherry tomatoes.* He laughed. No one else raised their head.

Chloe was hanging back until Robyn beckoned her forward. 'I thought this one was worth checking but now ...'

This one at least had a name: *I know it's Miss Fletcher at school – she teaches History but she does PE too and she stares at us when we're changing for gym.* 'OK, Chloe. What do you think?'

'I thought it sounded bad but now I'm thinking if someone was interested in teenage girls, they wouldn't snatch a male toddler.' Chloe blinked a couple of times, toes turning inwards.

'Good.' Robyn nodded, then held up her hand as Chloe began crumpling the paper. 'When all of this has finished, then follow it up. Trust your judgement.' Chloe nodded and scurried back to her desk.

A new map had been put up to show the calls. Green pins for those worth following up, white for potentials, chosen because they were the remaining colours left in the pot. Two names had come up twice. One, a known shoplifter, had been pictured in the local paper the week before. The woman was banned from the shopping centre, her photo up in the staff room so even though there was a passing resemblance to the E-FIT, it seemed unlikely no one had recognised her. The other was more interesting. Anonymous callers named the same woman who lived in Willingdon village. One noticed shopping being delivered for the first time, including what she thought were nappies, even though there were no children in the house. The other had heard strange cries in the night.

Robyn put the notes in front of Janice. 'Can you follow this one up? Of all the villages, I guess Willingdon is the best place to hide someone because it's isolated. These callers must be neighbours because they know the person's habits.' She dropped her voice. 'Are you OK, Janice? I haven't even asked whether you got anything from London.'

'Oh, Robyn, it was horrible. Ms Chivers' sister is living with her mother because she broke up with her latest boyfriend.' Janice shook her head. 'Three children, all by different fathers and no man in the place, all the kids running around with no control or attention, unless they break something.'

'Don't say you're starting to have some sympathy for what Ms Chivers was trying to do for Ben?'

'They haven't seen Ms Chivers for years – weren't interested.' Janice's voice was thoughtful. 'When I told them she had a child, they laughed and were amazed Little Miss Perfect would ever let a man touch her.'

'Sounds like a dead end.'

'Not quite. I showed them a photo of Ben and they weren't surprised Ms Chivers had got herself a white baby, saw it as another way of showing she thought herself better than them. It did come out she's a carrier of sickle-cell anaemia so picking a white partner was a good way to make certain it wouldn't be passed on to her child.'

'Sounds plausible. What did you pick up on the volunteering?'

Ravi leant across Janice, slapping a printed picture down. 'Here, Guv. I've watched the footage from the traffic cameras and found this car making an illegal turn out of the centre's loading bay at eight forty-four. We can see the driver's sunglasses and there's a shape in the back which could be Ben.'

'Good work, Ravi. Can you see the number plate?'

'Too blurred, Guv. I've tried everything.' Ravi produced another picture, a mass of pixelated squares. 'The car's so dirty, this is all I can get. We're looking for a new shape Fiat, in white, cream or silver. I've been through all of the CCTV again and there's one more sighting, at the next roundabout where they must have turned onto the residential roads with no cameras.'

Janice inspected the picture. 'Are you sure about this? Ben was wearing red which would show dark in black-and-white, not light.'

Ravi's voice flattened. 'It looks like a child in a car seat.'

Janice shook her head. 'It could be or it could be a big bag. Or it could even be a jacket hung up. Did you spot the St Oswald's van?'

'The van passed the station at eight twenty-five. I couldn't find anything else until eight forty-eight when the van appears on the inner ring road again. It takes the Pickley road, then I lose them.' Ravi kicked his filing cabinet.

The door banged open as Lorraine bowled in, bag swinging from one hand, coffee cup in the other with a large iced bun wedged into her mouth. Dropping the bag, she cleared her desk with a sweep, sending papers to the floor, then deposited the cup and bun with rather more care.

'You were a while. I hope you got something.'

Lorraine was chewing and pointed to her mouth.

Robyn turned back to Ravi. 'OK, track down the owners of similar cars in a twenty mile radius and visit all of them and I need a progress report before I see Fell this afternoon. And where are we with that warrant?'

Ravi grimaced. 'I'll chase them up, Guv.' He sidled back to his desk.

Lorraine finished chewing and swallowed. 'Sorry, Guv, I'm starving. I got the stuff from Derby and Rutherford, after a lot of grumbling. Then as I was leaving their offices, I met Cathy, the receptionist, taking documents to the Post Office and offered her a lift.' Lorraine took a deep breath. 'She likes a chat does Cathy.'

'So what else did you get?'

Lorraine took another bite and made an attempt to wipe her fingers before getting her notebook out of her bag. 'She opened up a bit, once she was out of the office. There are a whole load of things Rutherford didn't talk about. For a start, they haven't got a lot of work on and Cathy has noticed people coming in who might not be up to the usual client standard.' She saw Robyn's mouth opening and continued. 'I did ask her about the Dearmans. She didn't recognise the name, though she says more and more meetings are happening out of the office, which is new. Mark Rutherford also runs the firm like his personal toy-box. She told me staff have left because the firm gets them to do ridiculous things.'

'Like what?'

'Well, aside from Rutherford wanting too many one-to-ones, girls have been told to dress up and drape themselves over potential clients.'

Robyn's attention was wandering despite Lorraine's excitement. 'What's this got to do with Ben?'

'I'm getting there, Guv. Seems as soon as Chivers was made a partner, she became a bit of a diva too. Apparently, she started demanding people bring things to her house and ...' Lorraine paused for effect '... she once insisted a receptionist cleaned her office, shifting files and boxes, even though the girl was pregnant.' Lorraine crammed the last of the bun into her mouth and carried on, still chewing. 'The next week, the girl lost the baby – what better motive can there be for wanting to snatch Melissa's child?'

'When did this happen?' Robyn asked, the pencil flicking around her fingers.

'November last year. I've got the girl's details. We're talking about the receptionist before the current one.'

'She may find the reality of looking after a child harder than she thought.' Janice sounded anxious.

Ravi's forehead was wrinkled in concentration. 'But ...' Faces turned to him. 'But the description the cleaner gave us said an older woman, perhaps Ben's grandmother?'

'Did anyone recognise the E-FIT?'

Lorraine snorted. 'No but all I know is it's a damn good motive and it's the first link to a woman we've had.' She folded her arms.

'Apart from Maggie Gorton.' Ravi stood up.

Robyn cut across the raised voices. 'We can't miss any leads. Ben's been gone over forty-eight hours now. Are there any more clues to Ben's father?'

Lorraine fished in her bag. 'I've got the list of employees here on the payroll records. When I asked for as close to Christmas as possible, there was a choice of the tenth of December because they ran payroll early or the twenty-eighth of January. I got both and a list of the main projects Chivers was working on. The client records seem a bit of a shambles, which is interesting.'

Lorraine laid the sheets out and Robyn craned forward, Chloe squeezing in beside her. The staff list for December was annotated with ticks and crosses. Lorraine dabbed at the crumbs left on the desk. 'I got Cathy's opinion on likely men.' She pointed at the marks. 'Crosses are those men Cathy thought stood no chance – too old, ugly or stupid.'

Janice shook her head, face screwed up in disgust.

'Leaving two, including Rutherford.' Lorraine laughed. 'I think Cathy dislikes him so much, she believes the worst of him.'

'Who's this other one, James Kinnister?' Robyn pointed. 'Does he still work there?'

Lorraine reached again into her bag and pulled out a company brochure, corner folded down on a page of pictures. She tapped a photo of a handsome dark-haired man. 'He was poached by another firm so he only appears on the December sheet as he had to do gardening leave.'

'So if this man no longer worked there – Ms Chivers said the father didn't know about Ben!' Faces turned to Chloe and she subsided.

Robyn smiled encouragement. 'It certainly sounds plausible. OK, Chloe, find Kinnister. Good work, Lorraine.' She was about to tell Lorraine she had a spot of white icing on her cheek, when the door opened.

The tall figure of Dr Shepherd appeared, casual in a polo shirt and long beige shorts showing toned calves. 'Hey. I was passing and thought I'd drop off the initial pathology report and see where you guys hang out.' With two long strides, he was at Lorraine's desk. 'Can I use your computer?' Digging into his pocket, he produced a memory stick and leaned on the edge of the desk, one ankle resting on the other knee.

His easy confidence was borderline irritating, Robyn decided. 'This is a nice surprise, Dr Shepherd. As you can see it's not glamorous but we manage. What have you got for us?'

'Call me Kelly. I can give you some more details, though I've still got some specialist tests going on the bones.' Dr Shepherd reached around Lorraine to the mouse. 'I also wanted to show you these.'

Blurred black and white images filled the screen. Robyn squinted, until the shape became recognisable as a skull. With a quick check to make sure everyone was watching, Dr Shepherd pointed to the screen with a pen.

'When a body has lost all its soft tissue, there are things I can't tell; for example, if they were poisoned or suffocated, because there'll be no evidence on the bones. Even a stabbing or a strangulation might cause death without marking the skeleton. But fortunately, this killer decided to hit the victim a number of times, giving us a clear cause of death.'

The choice of words made Robyn wince. Graham also seemed fidgety, while the rest of the team stared at the screen.

On the next image, patches were highlighted in a searing green. 'There were three, possibly four, hard blows to the front of the skull.' He turned back to the team, cheery smile showing white teeth, one at a crooked angle. 'So you've got someone who needed to make sure this girl was dead.'

'But did they want this particular girl dead or did they want to just kill?' Lorraine leant forward to study the screen, cheek close to Kelly's.

'Can you tell if there was any sexual motive?' Robyn's voice was dry.

Kelly leant back, folding his arms. 'I can't. Any traces, semen, blood, bruising, would have vanished a long time ago. We're still ana-lysing the clothing pieces and you'll get a full report in the next couple of days.'

He reached into his satchel, pulling out a dirty shoe in a plastic bag.

'And, this was found by your lot near to the door. Size seven, a woman's shoe and the body's female too.' He glanced at Robyn. 'What's interesting is when you compare this left shoe to the remains of the right one from the pit. It appears as if some chemical agent was poured over the body to speed up decomposition.'

Chloe took the bag and began studying the shoe, her nose touching the plastic.

'One other thing, the warehouse is dry with little organic matter, soil or plants to narrow down the date of death.' Kelly paused, scratched his leg. 'My assessment is the body must have been there a minimum of two years to reach this level of decomposition but a maximum is harder to pin down. Sorry I can't be more precise.' He inclined his head. 'Did you know you've got paint on your face?'

It took a second for Lorraine to realise he was speaking to her. She ducked her head, rubbing at her cheek.

Kelly grinned. 'Other side.' Lorraine smeared the icing into a tear drop.

Robyn cleared her throat. 'Thank you, Dr Shepherd, Kelly. It's good to have you on the team and we'll await your full report …' The team weren't listening. Graham and Ravi were laughing, Janice passed Lorraine a tissue, glancing at Kelly with disapproval or appraisal.

'Well, see you.'

The door closed behind him. 'Smug git.' Lorraine raised an eyebrow to Janice, who nodded.

'But quite a good-looking git.' Chloe might have been speaking to herself.

# 21

Janice switched on the television at one-thirty for the local news. Ben was the top story. The reporter described the progress of the searches in the villages, the airfield, the nature reserve. Everywhere, the pictures showed lines of people in hi-vis tops walking shoulder-to-shoulder, staring at the ground. The report cut to a mousy woman in front of the Citizens Advice Bureau, who talked about the marvellous legal support Melissa Chivers gave them.

Half an hour to go until Robyn was due to see Fell. 'Any news on the getaway car, Ravi?'

'There are thirty-two registered vehicles within an area of twenty miles. So far, I've made contact with four of the owners …'

Robyn banged the desk. 'We need to go faster. Split them between you and Janice and get through them today. Any you don't get an answer from, visit them. At the moment, given the rubbish we seem to be getting from the E-FIT, it's the best lead we've got.' Everyone was busy yet she still had nothing to say to Fell and couldn't keep her promise.

'Guv, I'm going to Lower Markham to see the ex-receptionist.' Lorraine was already halfway through the door.

'Are you all right, Robyn?' Janice was perched on the corner of her desk, her eyes wrinkled in concern. Robyn was angry with herself for letting the team know she was worried. She prodded at the papers in her in-tray, the sheets spilling onto the desk. 'Sometimes it feels like all I'm good for is signing things.'

'We're doing everything we can. There are never any guarantees, are there? We might never find Ben.' Coming from anyone but Janice, it would have sounded callous.

It was possible a decision had already been made and Fell wanted a meeting just to tell her the case was being assigned to the larger team at Maidstone. One of the constables called Janice back to the phone. There was a scent of vanilla: Chloe was standing by her desk.

She held out Lorraine's lists of names. 'I've got an address for Kinnister, Guv and I've noticed something else. He's just got a divorce finalised – do you think it means something?'

Robyn's first thought was she didn't want to follow another half-theory – they had been too distracted already but she didn't want to criticise Chloe for trying on her first day. Before she could respond, Lorraine charged back into the room. 'Guv, the burglar's hit another property and this time he's put the owner in hospital.'

Robyn stood up so fast, her chair shot backwards, hitting the wall. 'What did he do?'

'Knocked out an old lady.'

Robyn tasted the familiar cocktail of emotions; revulsion, then a surge of adrenalin, followed by a cold desire to get whoever had done this. 'Sure it's the same man? We've had intimidation before but not violence.'

Lorraine nodded. 'I'm sure, Guv. Another Gaddesford house, another pensioner.'

'Is the victim in any state to talk to us?'

Lorraine shook her head. 'She's an elderly lady. There's another witness, her friend who called it in. Scene of Crime are at the house now.'

'Get down there, Lorraine. Where's Graham?' This would need two people.

'He said he was going to get an update from the search teams.' Janice took a neat bite of a home-made sandwich.

Robyn hesitated for a second. They were finally making progress but the team needed more time to follow through on the new leads. She shouldn't have made the stupid promise to Fell yesterday, so an excuse to postpone the meeting was welcome. Then when she did see him, she might be able to give him an answer. 'Right, change of plan. Chloe, let Graham know about Kinnister when he gets back. Janice, can you go out and see this girl from Derby and Rutherford? Let's go, Lorraine. Oh and Janice …' Robyn tried not to sound guilty, 'could you please call Tracey and tell her I won't be able to see Fell as planned?'

She collided with Phil in the doorway, who stepped back, brushing down the front of his uniform. 'Sorry, ma'am. Is Graham here?'

Robyn kept on walking. 'I thought he was with you?'

Phil's lips twitched. 'I thought I was meeting him here.' He turned away, then realised Robyn was following him down the corridor. In the lobby, he loitered, waiting until Robyn and Lorraine turned for the stairs before he pressed the button for the lift.

At the top of the external steps, Robyn pulled up, realising her car had been blocked in by the painters' van.

'Typical.'

'We'll take mine, Guv.' Lorraine pointed to the other end of the row.

As the engine started, there was a blast of music before Lorraine turned the stereo down. Robyn turned it back up. 'This is good – who's playing?'

'It's us.' There was pride in Lorraine's voice. 'My band. It's so easy to make and issue your own recordings now. We even made the download charts for one exciting week.'

'Impressive. I don't suppose you do anything for a Luddite, like CDs?'

'We're talking about a new album so, maybe.' Lorraine glanced across. 'How's this whole thing going?'

Robyn swallowed, guessing she didn't mean the case. 'Fine, thanks.' The safe response. A soaring clarinet solo started the next song, Lorraine's unvarnished nails playing the notes on the steering wheel. Robyn remembered her own chipped nails. 'Actually, no. Better. Good. Really good.'

Lorraine glanced over. 'Good.' She indicated, moving into the outer lane. 'I'm glad. Because things must be ... must be grim at the moment.'

She turned into the street leading to the hospital and swore at the traffic.

Robyn searched for a topic. 'I should be in a meeting with Fell now and you know what he's like ...' Robyn stopped, confused because Lorraine was laughing.

'What's so funny?'

Lorraine's laughter subsided. 'Sorry, Guv.' She pulled herself together. 'I know just what Fell's like. Did you know he's a jazz fan? He often comes to the club. Someone suggested campaigning to get the smoking ban lifted on nights when he came, to hide the smell ...' Lorraine giggled again.

A siren sounded behind them. Lorraine checked her mirror. 'It's about time they built a new access road to the hospital.' She twisted the wheel to manoeuvre onto a driveway as an ambulance drove past.

Robyn found her fingers tapping to the song's rhythm. 'So Fell likes jazz? Explains a lot.' Lorraine pulled a face. 'But we do need a new road. Maybe the council can get the Dearmans to contribute. They must be responsible for a fair amount of the people needing hospital treatment ...'

'You sound like Graham, Guv. Always blaming the Dearmans.'

Robyn tensed. 'Who are we going to see?' Conversation was safer if she stuck to cases.

Nipping in front of a truck, Lorraine turned into the hospital. Robyn found herself grabbing the door handle.

'Sorry, Guv, otherwise we would have been sitting there for ages. We're seeing Mrs Jarvis, the victim and Mrs Whittaker, the victim's friend. Now where the hell do I park?'

For want of a parking space, Lorraine squeezed the car between two waste containers. As they opened the doors, a traffic warden was in front of them.

Lorraine sighed. 'He must love his job.'

The man loomed over the bonnet, wheezing. 'You … can't … park … here … without … a ticket.' Stretched around his gut was a utility belt with an array of pouches. He peered from the warrant card Robyn was holding up to her face and back again. 'What's your name then?'

'Detective Inspector Robyn Bailley. We're investigating a violent robbery and need to interview a witness.'

The man showed yellow teeth: it was hard to tell if he was smiling or scowling. 'Your card's not valid. It says "Roger Bailley" but you say you're Robyn Bailley.'

'Oh for crying out loud. Here.' Lorraine shoved her warrant card forward. The man subjected Lorraine to the same scrutiny before stepping aside. He made a fuss of taking a photograph of the car.

Robyn watched him as he lumbered away. 'I didn't think people could be so petty. Still, I'd best get my warrant card updated.'

Lorraine locked the car. 'And your driving licence. And your passport. And what about your bank account?'

'Yes, thank you. I know.' Robyn felt her nose itch. 'I was going to do the deed poll first, then it's easier. I was just waiting for …' She tailed off as they approached the hospital's entrance.

Lorraine stepped aside to let a wheelchair pass. 'What were you waiting for?'

Robyn paused. She wasn't going to admit she hadn't got a clue and was able to cut off any further conversation by approaching the reception desk to find out where to go.

They were outside again within a few minutes. To Robyn's frustration, they couldn't see Mrs Jarvis because she was in surgery and Mrs Whittaker had discharged herself. They got back into the car. Robyn hated being a passenger, her thoughts started wandering and she couldn't stop herself questioning her every action. As a way to stop any more probing from Lorraine, she rang Janice.

'Hello, Robyn. I was just about to call you. I've got something on the landlord Ms Chivers took to court.'

'Oh, yes What had he done?'

Janice laughed, sounding less strained than she had before. 'Not a he, a she. A woman called Jaqueline McManus, aged fifty, who was convicted and had to pay a big fine.'

'Where's McManus now?'

'Her business is registered to an address in Maidstone so I'm on my way there now.'

'Good work, Janice, keep me posted.'

They passed the Gaddesford village sign. 'Sounded good, Guv.'

'Yes, a woman of the right age with a grudge against Ms Chivers.'

Lorraine slowed the car. 'Where do you want to go first, Guv? The witness or the crime scene?'

Lost in a moment of hope that they were getting closer to Ben, Robyn pulled herself back to the burglary. 'Let's talk to the witness first. The scene of crime team will be busy at the victim's house, no point in getting in their way.'

Lorraine slowed the car. 'OK. The two houses are on opposite sides of the village, it'll be quicker to park in the centre and walk out to both.' As they pulled into the village square, the butcher had already closed for the half-day and the fancy-goods shop was pulling down its blinds. Outside the Lion and Flag, men without shirts drank lager.

'Your local?'

Lorraine grimaced. 'No way. They don't even do live music in there. Right, we're crossing the road, Guv.' After a couple of hundred yards, the single-width brick pavement outside the Georgian houses changed to a wider, paved path. They kept going, the houses becoming more modern as they moved towards the village's edge. 'I think it's sweet there's still a police house here in Gaddesford.' She pointed to the shabby sixties' house. 'If I were based there, I could walk to work in five minutes.'

They reached a crescent of bungalows, each with a garage and neat front garden. Lorraine paused at the gate of 'Spinnaker' and pointed across the road, to where a small, cream Fiat was parked outside 'Buntings'. 'Wonder whether this one is on Ravi's list? We can visit them while we're here.'

They crossed the road and Lorraine rang the doorbell. The car had big sprays of mud behind each wheel. Lorraine pushed the bell again. Somewhere inside, a dog barked.

Robyn scraped at the thick dirt. 'It's been driven off-road, which is odd for a small car.' She squinted through the window. In the back, a stained child's car seat was half-covered by a blanket.

Lorraine peered past her. 'I hadn't considered the kidnapper could already have kids of their own. Maybe a boy died and they've taken Ben to replace him?' She noted the number plate. 'I'll text Ravi.'

'Interesting theory.' Robyn started back across the road. 'Except I still don't believe it was a chance snatch. Why was Ben targeted?'

In 'Spinnaker', they sat at the square table in the kitchen while Mrs Whittaker brewed tea. 'Well it's very good of you to come to see me when you must be so busy ...' She began a stream of small talk which, by the time she sat down, had covered the hot weather, the traffic, the appalling upkeep of St Leonard's square and the high numbers of greenfly, which she suspected were caused by the hot weather.

The whole monologue had circled around and appeared to be about to start again. Robyn gritted her teeth: she had to get something

164

of value from this interview; the phone at her belt had vibrated a couple of times and Fell would need to see progress to justify missing his meeting. Mrs Whittaker finally came to the table but her tweed-covered bottom had only just touched the patchwork cushion before she bobbed up again to fetch napkins.

Lorraine lost patience first. 'Mrs Whittaker, we need to talk about …' She stopped, uncertain, as Robyn held up her hand where Mrs Whittaker couldn't see. The tea had been made the proper way and Robyn made a noise of appreciation. In response, Mrs Whittaker held out a plate with three types of biscuit. Robyn took her time choosing, rattling her bracelet as she decided. Mrs Whittaker reached into an embroidered pouch and slipped on some glasses. She gasped as she focused on Robyn's face; for the first time, they had her full attention.

'Please tell us what happened today.' Robyn smiled at Mrs Whittaker, who took off her glasses.

Once she'd started, Mrs Whittaker seemed keen to tell the story and get them out of her house. During the interview, Robyn compared how she had been treated by Melissa to Mrs Whittaker's reaction and had to conclude she was scaring the old woman. She hadn't expected to generate fear and made sure she kept the questions short. As they left, the door was shut before they'd left the top step.

Robyn made a point of closing the gate and checking the catch. 'I think Mrs Whittaker is frightened so I didn't want to rush her. What did you get?'

Lorraine sounded like a child reciting a lesson. 'Every Wednesday, little Mrs Whittaker and little Mrs Jarvis go to book club, then afternoon tea with their friends, which is quite the highlight of their week, though some recent book choices are not quite suitable for respectable people–'

'Lorraine – this isn't the time.' Robyn could feel the phone vibrating again and ignored it. They were walking back to the village's centre.

'Sorry, Guv. OK, Mrs W normally picks up Mrs J at one-thirty but arrived early. As she was walking up the path, a man, all in black, burst out of the house and ran past her to the street. He was carrying something metal, possibly a wrench and he threatened her as he passed. Inside, Mrs Jarvis was unconscious in the kitchen.'

In the square, the bunting was still up from the festival, the edges frayed. 'Telling us what?'

'It's all too close to home.' There was a catch in Lorraine's voice. 'The first burglary was on Priory Street, over there ...' she pointed, '... the third was half a mile away on the Pickley Road and now another one. I thought a village would be quiet. Do you think he lives here?'

They were walking in single file on the narrow brick pavement. 'Risky to operate somewhere you might be recognised but he does do his homework and seems to know who lives alone.' Around the next bend, houses gave way to fields on one side. 'The best way to stop worrying is to catch him.'

A small crowd of villagers stood behind blue and white tape at the top of a lane. Ducking underneath, Robyn and Lorraine approached the end cottage, pink with a thatched roof. A scene of crime officer came outside, stretching his arms and taking a deep breath. Robyn had a vision of how tight it would be inside. 'Lorraine. I'm going to stay out here and call Ms Chivers about the reconstruction.'

Lorraine nodded and had to duck as she went through the front door.

*This is the voicemail box for Melissa Chivers of Derby and Rutherford. Leave a concise message after the tone.* 'Ms Chivers, this is DI Bailley. I wanted to confirm we'll be running a reconstruction of Ben's disappearance at the shopping centre tomorrow from eight am. Please call me if you would like further details.'

Enjoying the escape, Robyn idled in the sun, dealing with messages: Tracey made clear her disappointment that she'd ducked out of Fell's meeting and Ravi was so excited he was unintelligible. After the third replay, she picked up that one of the small Fiats belonged to Maggie Gorton and her number plate had been picked up by a traffic camera near Gatwick Airport on Monday afternoon.

Lorraine appeared in the doorway. 'Got something, Guv?'

The crowd was watching them. 'Maybe. Let's go.' They ducked under the tape and walked up towards the main road until they were clear of the spectators. 'Anything interesting?'

'A couple of things. No signs of a break in, the victim must have opened the door to her attacker. I couldn't see a tool box anywhere: conclusion, he must have brought the weapon with him. And another thing.' They waited while a tractor rumbled past before crossing the road. 'He upended her jewellery box and took trinkets yet left her father's war medals which were on top. Then he went to the kitchen and emptied one storage jar. Nothing else. Mrs Whittaker said she didn't think Mrs Jarvis had anything special but in the front room there are some Wedgwood figures. The most valuable stuff, he didn't touch.'

'Do you think he was on drugs and looking for food?'

They reached the car. Lorraine waved to someone across the square. 'Unlikely he'd choose a jar marked "Flour", Guv, when there was one marked "Biscuits" right next to it. He must have known there was something in that particular jar.'

Robyn's phone buzzed again with a text from Tracey. She tried to focus on what Lorraine was telling her but she couldn't escape that she'd promised Fell answers by today. There had been no sensible reason for accepting, she should have just refused to be held to a deadline she'd no chance of meeting. Roger would have had answers. He'd have dealt with this case as he did everything; without fuss or drama. She stared at the roof of the car, trying to find a reason why Robyn couldn't find Ben.

Lorraine turned the stereo on again. Approaching town, the traffic ground to a halt in road works, a bitter smell of tarmac hanging in the air. A group of teenagers loitered past them.

'Hello, gorgeous!' Robyn jumped. A lad's face was pressed up to the car window, drool on the dust in the window. 'You're so horny, I'd like to stick my cock–'

Lorraine pressed hard on the horn. Though the traffic-lights were green for them, a car was still blocking the single lane. More horns sounded from behind. The lads had already lost interest.

'Bet you're not in too much of a hurry to get back and see Fell, are you?' Lorraine glanced at Robyn, then away, her face settling into a more serious expression.

The car in front of them moved and Lorraine eased the car forward. The stench of bitumen lingered all the way back to the police station.

As they went under the car park barrier at the police station, Graham drove out past them, cigarette already on the go. Robyn wound down her window.

'Got a whisper on the drugs, Guv.' He accelerated away before Robyn could ask why he wasn't following up on Ben. She didn't have time to think about it because they were able to slot straight into a parking space. It was time to see Fell.

# 22

After a brief catch-up with the team, 'good lucks' in their eyes, Robyn dawdled towards Fell's office. Tracey was squeezed into a bright fuchsia top, the perfume chosen to match, shrill floral notes with hints of bleach. 'Where have you been?'

'Sorry, Tracey. Someone was supposed to ring you to let you know. I've only just picked up your messages – there's no signal in Gaddesford.'

Tracey glared at her. 'Please don't break a nail on my behalf, DI Bailey. Go and tell the superintendent.'

Fell stood by the window. Robyn remained standing, filtering the thick air and scanning the mass of papers on the desk, including two mauve HR files.

Robyn swallowed. 'Thank you for getting us Chloe, sir. She's hit the ground running.' The part of her brain that listened wondered why, when talking to Fell, she always lapsed into cliches.

Fell cleared his throat. Robyn braced herself. She must be used to the room now because all she could smell was her own sweat through the thin blouse, no trace of the lavender body spray she'd used this morning.

'Bailey, I am disappointed by your progress so far. I don't know whether this is to do with your mind being distracted by your – personal situation – but this case is not being run to your usual standard.' Fell's voice was little more than a rumble.

She reasoned it wouldn't matter whether she said 'Yes' or 'No' at this point, as long as it was in the right tone.

'Yes, sir.'

Fell moved to the desk, sat down and shifted papers. Now Robyn could see one of the HR files was hers, 'Roger' crossed out in thick black pen. Someone had written 'File closed – now Robyn Bailey' underneath. The other file, in Robyn's name, was already almost as thick as the original.

'Although you have only been back in Meresbourne for two years, you have over twenty years of excellent service, Bailey.' Fell opened the newer file. 'It is therefore disappointing I now have to deal with a complaint against you.' He selected a sheet and began to scan it.

Robyn tried to swallow down the lump in her throat. 'What's it about, sir?'

'It has two parts. Concerns have been raised firstly about your general fitness to handle the Ben Chivers case and secondly, your specific conduct towards a witness. This complaint came in yesterday. I am confident, with immediate action on your part, we can resolve it locally, without having to involve the Independent Police Complaints Commission.' Fell glanced over the top of the page.

Robyn tried to ignore a sudden sick feeling. Melissa had taken part in the appeal yesterday, in the conference room just up the corridor. She had a vision of how far Melissa would get if she tried to bully Tracey and couldn't help smiling.

'I suggest you take this seriously, Bailey.' The sheet of paper crumpled in Fell's grip.

Robyn stood up straighter. 'Sorry, sir. May I know more details about the complaint? What particular aspects of my conduct were not appropriate?'

Fell put down the sheet then took a long time pouring water from a jug into a glass and taking a sip. Robyn waited.

A drop of water hung from the end of Fell's moustache. He picked up the sheet. The water droplet quivered. Fell made a noise in the back of his throat and put the paper down again. 'There is an objection to you working on a case involving children and people with a strong faith.'

Robyn counted to ten, digging a nail into her palm with each count. 'Thank you, sir, for clarifying. Of course I'm disappointed we haven't found Ben yet but the investigation is following the set procedures for this type of case. And as I can't have any contact with the child until I find him, I don't see how there's an issue.'

Fell's eyebrows came together.

Robyn's mouth was dry. 'Yesterday, for the first time, Ms Chivers stated Ben's father was dead. She still refuses to identify him and I admit I've been pressing her about this because it's crucial to the enquiry. It was inevitable the media would ask because it makes a better story.'

Fell raised his eyes to the ceiling.

Robyn bit her lip. 'As for upsetting Ms Chivers, I don't understand why the public can discriminate against me if my colleagues aren't allowed to?'

Fell's palm crashed to the desk. 'Bailley, your attitude is not helpful. The force is supporting you in your, ah, endeavours but I will not allow investigations to be compromised. I want an update from you every four hours and make sure a member of your team handles contact with Ms Chivers in future. I do not expect to receive further complaints.'

'Yes, sir.'

# 23

As Robyn left the office, the stifling combination of sweat and perfume was replaced by a reek of paint. Two decorators had started work by the lift, stained sheets rucked across the carpet. Robyn stepped across with caution.

'Cheer up, love, might never happen.' The painter was grinning, his tanned face a series of lines and wrinkles.

Robyn kept walking, passing a second painter leaning on a ladder, whistling. The note died away as she passed. Robyn pressed the button for the lift, then heard a whispered conversation start up between the decorators and decided she would take the stairs.

On a landing, she stopped, leaning back against the wall. She held the rail, one foot dangling over the edge of a step. Above her, the whistling restarted. Thoughts refused to organise themselves in her mind – outside, she watched a gull landing on a street light, two pigeons scattering to make room. Below, voices echoed, cut off as a door closed. Robyn sighed and turned down the stairs.

The incident room was quieter than she expected until Chloe

bustled over. She'd got hold of a clipboard. 'Guv, I've been talking to the TV people about the reconstruction tomorrow ...' then stopped as Robyn frowned.

'A bit unfair to dump this on you.'

'I don't mind, Guv, in fact I asked.' Chloe smiled. 'I know what the TV people need – there's got to be some use for a media studies qualification, after all.'

Graham chuckled. Robyn managed a small smile.

'I was thinking, if I could go down to the shopping centre now, Guv, to make notes for the TV people on where they need to go?' Her eyes were bright.

Robyn stood up. She needed to be doing something constructive. 'Good idea. I'll come with you.'

'Hang on, Guv, how did the meeting go with Fell?' Graham was half out of his chair.

Robyn stopped for a moment. 'We keep going.' She walked out.

The van had moved and Robyn wanted the simple focus of driving to stop her brooding. During the journey to town, Chloe read and re-read the reconstruction summary. Robyn parked in the shoppers' car park and led Chloe through the grubby swing doors into the central rotunda, where the college's display stands were being taken apart.

Chloe held the clipboard across her body as a youth gawped at Robyn. 'What are you after, Guv?'

'Something.' Robyn stopped. 'At five past eight, Gillian and Ben left their car and walked in, the route we just came. They turned up towards Northbank.'

Chloe fell into step beside her.

'They stopped at the health food shop.' In the window, a slogan advertised something herbal: *Every woman has natural beauty within her*. The glassy-eyed woman in the picture wasn't anyone Robyn would aspire to be. 'Then the dry cleaner's.'

Chloe was staring up the concourse. 'Guv! Then they went to pick up the shoes.' She pointed at the cobbler's beside the Northbank entrance. 'They were right by the High Street and the doors were open. If someone wanted to snatch Ben, they could have been away in seconds.'

Robyn nodded. 'Exactly. But there are lots of CCTV cameras out there. I think whoever we're dealing with took steps not to be caught on camera. Gillian said she comes here regularly to do a similar set of chores. Someone knew her routine and planned.'

They turned down the slope. Robyn stopped outside the pharmacy, sitting on the nearest of the benches. 'Gillian had her route: up one side, down the other, then home for vitamins and lessons.'

Chloe sat beside her. 'How did the snatcher know Ben would wander off?'

The stone bench was cold through the thin material of her trousers. Robyn pulled from her bag the picture taken outside the camera shop, gazing at the blurry figures. Leaving Chloe, she strolled down, unable to resist peering into the window to see whether the second-hand Hasselblad she coveted was still on sale. Chloe, left on the bench, was like an abandoned child herself. Robyn checked the photo, then the scene in front of her. 'Chloe – could you go and stand over there?'

Chloe trotted across the aisle. Robyn held the picture up and gestured. 'More to the right, nearer the shops.'

Someone in a suit, hurrying to the station, swore as he swerved around her. Robyn imagined herself seeing the scene through a lens. A step to the right and the shop-fronts on the far side aligned with the photograph.

'OK, face as if you're going to the car park.' Chloe turned and was now almost side on: if she'd been holding Ben's right hand, he would have been on her far side, probably hidden. In the picture, the figures had their backs to the camera.

'Now as if you're going down to Riverside.' Chloe turned and stood almost face-on. Robyn checked the picture again. 'OK, now turn your back on me.'

They were attracting attention now, a group of girls giggled. Chloe obeyed, casting a glance back over her shoulder. Robyn fixed the scene in her mind, then crossed the aisle.

'You've got something, Guv?'

Robyn held up the picture. 'We are where they were.' She pointed ahead. 'Look.'

Chloe scanned from the curtain shop to the fashion boutique. 'What?'

Robyn pointed again, to the gap between the shops. A few yards away, painted to match the wall, was the staff door to the loading bay. Robyn and Chloe slipped through the door into a corridor of flickering fluorescent tubes. There didn't appear to be any CCTV cameras. At the end of the corridor, through a set of double doors and they were in the loading bay, traffic passing outside.

'This was the way she came.' Chloe shook her head. 'So easy. A second to grab Ben, a few steps to the service door, then down here and away.'

Robyn nodded. 'She must have parked on the access slip road, then drove out the same way, making the U-turn Ravi spotted.'

'I don't remember seeing this area on the CCTV footage we've watched. I'll check.'

Robyn's phone rang. She took a couple of steps away. 'Hello.'

'Hi, Ro … Robyn, it's Ady. Can you talk?'

'Go ahead.'

'The burglary today – it's a big story, the first time someone has been hurt and, well, there isn't anything new about Ben and we're running this front page. I know you were in Gaddesford today, what's happening?'

Robyn watched Chloe as she studied tyre tracks on the grubby concrete. 'I'm sorry, Ady, I can't give you anything. Have you spoken to Khalid?'

There was resignation in Ady's voice. 'He's just given the usual flannel about pursuing all lines of enquiry. Did you get the link by the way?'

Robyn grimaced. 'Haven't checked, I'm afraid. As soon as we have anything, I'll call you.' She tucked the phone into her bag and watched Chloe, who was peering under a workbench.

'OK? Shall we?'

'Hang on, Guv: there's something here.' Chloe fumbled in her pocket for a glove, then reached down into a box of dirty rags. She lifted up something by one corner, holding it at arm's length. It unfurled, a child's sweatshirt, red with blotchy stains.

Robyn reached for her phone again.

Chloe's face lost the little colour it had. 'What do you think those marks are, Guv?'

While technicians examined the loading bay, Robyn and Chloe interviewed the maintenance team in the staff room.

'This is what it's all about, isn't it, Guv? Being a detective?' Chloe tucked her notebook into her bag.

Robyn rubbed her eyes. She had been standing yards away from the sweatshirt less than an hour after Ben went missing. She'd even asked Phil about the search and then had just accepted his answer without checking. Maybe this was trying to tell her something about her own instincts. They walked back towards the car park.

'Every investigation has its ups and downs. Most of the time you gather hundreds of tiny bits of information, ploughing through lots of rubbish before you find something important. Or, something you were certain of turns out to be wrong, like we now know the kidnapper changed Ben's appearance before they left the shopping centre.'

They settled into the car. 'So always speak up, Chloe, because you may realise something's important when no one else does.' Robyn comforted herself that this was one area where she could say she was unlike the former DI, Kenny Prentiss, who had loved mocking his juniors' ideas.

'Thanks, Guv. I find it a bit difficult sometimes. Either you know what you're trying to say and it doesn't come out right, or you're sure of something and someone asks you a question and suddenly, you're not so sure any more.'

Robyn chuckled, without humour. 'Unfortunately, that feeling doesn't go away. You're uncertain most of the time.' She hoped she was sounding experienced rather than cynical.

'I suppose nothing's ever certain, is it?' Chloe ran her fingers through her hair. 'At least when you're on the beat, it's easy – someone puts a problem in front of you and you sort it. With this, you're trying to solve something you can't see.'

Robyn drove into the police station car park. 'Well, keep doing what you're doing. And don't be afraid to say what you think.' She paused to let a car pull out, her mind pulling together strands. She should park in the free space and go and see Matthew and let him know what a poor job Phil had made of the search on Monday. Or, she could accept she was no longer up to the job and go home, get into bed and hope the world would go away. Robyn drove past the empty space and up to the base of the steps.

'Good work, Chloe. Can you let everyone know I'm going to see Gillian Green again? I want to talk to her about tomorrow.'

'Oh. Right, OK, Guv.' Chloe got out, turning at the top of the steps with a brief wave, before walking into the station.

Robyn let the engine idle as she dialled Gillian's number. There was no answer at her flat or from her mobile, meaning she was probably at Ms Chivers' house. Seeing her there would mean going against Fell's direct order but there was a void of information there that needed to be filled. And she wanted to see Ms Chivers' reaction when she heard about the sweatshirt, perhaps as a test of Janice's theory. Robyn turned her car towards Upper Town.

# 24

Upper Town was quiet apart from an occasional dog walker. Each lamppost had a yellow ribbon or a picture of Ben. Robyn rang Ms Chivers' doorbell, a single, sharp sound. She thought a shadow moved behind the Venetian blinds. After a few seconds, she rang again. This time there were steps and the door opened.

'Hello, Mrs Green. I understand your precautions. May I come in?' The scented air in the hallway was immediately oppressive.

Gillian stepped back to let Robyn pass. 'Ms Chivers isn't here. She's still at work.'

Robyn tried to avoid smiling. 'I wanted to see you, Mrs Green, to make sure you were prepared for the reconstruction tomorrow.'

They stood in the hallway, until Robyn gestured towards the kitchen. 'Perhaps we could sit down?'

Gillian led the way, immediately picking up a tea towel. The kitchen was sombre, spotlights off, the garden in deep shadow. Robyn attempted to perch on one of the white stools, then stopped, one leg crooked, struggling to keep her face neutral as she realised she'd pulled away a corner of the tape around her groin. She slid off, leaving the seat spinning.

Fortunately, Gillian was hanging a glass on a rack. Robyn decided to stand. 'Mrs Green, have my colleagues taken you through what we are asking you to do tomorrow?'

'I must be at the shopping centre for seven-thirty and then will have to do everything I did on Monday.' Gillian sniffed. 'As if I had Benjamin with me.'

'Yes. Did my colleague mention we would like you to wear the same clothes?'

'They were very insistent about it. I suppose there will be another little boy?' Gillian reached for the next glass.

'Yes, we are trying to make everything as similar as possible to prompt people's recollections. Can you recall anything else that might be relevant?'

Gillian put the glass away and reached for a long-bladed knife.

When it became clear that Gillian had no intention of answering, Robyn tried another tack. 'I'm glad to see you're still working for Ms Chivers.'

Gillian was stroking the blade through the tea towel, down, turn, up. 'I do a lot of things for her.'

Robyn shifted her weight to lean on the counter. 'We're still no closer to identifying Ben's father, or even whether he's alive or dead. Is there anything else you can tell me?'

Gillian slid the knife into a block and reached again to the draining rack. 'I don't know.' She turned to face Robyn. 'I really don't. She's so certain about everything and with her faith, she just doesn't seem to need anyone else.' Each item was wiped twice before she reached for the next. 'I sometimes see other kids with their fathers and wonder what's going to happen to Ben when he gets bigger.'

There was a click of locks, the solid sound of the front door shutting, then brisk heels along the tiles. Melissa Chivers appeared in the kitchen, switching on the lights, then freezing for a second when she saw Robyn. 'What are you doing here? I gave instructions.'

Robyn blinked in the brightness. 'Good evening, Ms Chivers. I came to speak to Mrs Green to finalise details before the reconstruction tomorrow and to let you know about a recent development in the investigation.' Melissa frowned at the misaligned stool, turning the seat back to face the counter, before putting down her briefcase and handbag. 'Have you found him?'

'Not yet, I'm sorry.' Against the white stool, Robyn could see the red, picked skin down the edge of Melissa's fingernails. Robyn took half a step forward. Melissa retreated around the corner of the breakfast bar, pausing, before covering the movement by picking up a glass, reaching into the fridge for mineral water. She stopped, inspected the glass and put it on the draining board with a thump.

'This glass is dirty. Check the others.'

Gillian's eyes shut for a second, before she filled a fresh glass and gave it to Melissa who glared at her before transferring the look to Robyn. 'Whatever it is, get on with it. I have a contract to read this evening.'

'Thank you. I wanted to let you know we've found the sweatshirt Benjamin was wearing when he was taken.'

Gillian gasped. Apart from a slight tensing of her jaw, Melissa remained still.

Robyn kept her eyes fixed on Ms Chivers. 'The sweatshirt was in the shopping centre's loading bay. Our scientific teams are looking at it now.'

Melissa banged the glass down onto the counter. 'What chance is there of finding my son when you missed something so obvious?'

Gillian hurried forward and placed a coaster under the glass.

Robyn rolled back on her heels. 'I appreciate you're upset Ms Chivers, which is why I thought it was important to tell you in person. You also gave new information about Ben's father during the appeal.'

'If you believe a woman took Benjamin, why are you so concerned about his father?'

Biting back her urge to swear, Robyn kept her face as bland as possible. 'Stranger-abduction is, thankfully, rare. The family is always the first place we check in these cases. The woman could be someone connected with the father.'

'Why would Benjamin go to a stranger?' In the corner, Gillian seemed to be talking to herself.

There were definite shadows under Melissa's eyes but her lips were pressed hard together. Robyn could almost pity her for wanting to keep up the strong façade.

'One other area I wanted to ask you about, Ms Chivers. You led a successful case against a landlord, a Mrs McManus ...'

'I got rid of her.' Melissa blinked. 'I got her struck off from the National Landlords Association. She went to Spain.'

'Unfortunately, it appears she didn't stay gone. Has she made contact with you?'

Melissa blinked a couple of times, then crossed the kitchen and slid onto one of the bar stools, dipping her head. She clasped her hands together and her lips moved without sound. Clicking her teeth, Gillian went back to drying-up. The cutlery was finished before Melissa raised her head.

'Why are you still here?'

'Ms Chivers, your refusal to answer questions is making it much harder for me to find your son.'

Melissa's hands balled into fists. 'Don't you understand? I don't want you to find him. God is taking care of him, wherever he is but I don't want him polluted by you.'

Robyn took a deep breath, to make sure her voice was even. It was amazing how little the woman was disturbing her now. She'd complained to Fell, there was nothing else she could do. She would find Ben, regardless.

'Very well, Ms Chivers. Goodnight, Mrs Green, see you tomorrow.'

In the car, Robyn scrolled through the radio stations until she got something loud, turning up the volume until her thoughts were swamped. Back at the station, she pulled in next to the decorator's van.

Climbing the stairs to the incident room, she ran through the loose ends she needed to follow up. When she opened the door, the usual hum was missing. She headed to her desk then changed her mind, moving to the evidence board and giving it a couple of sharp raps to get everyone's attention. 'Right, there are things I need to know.' Heads went up. 'Who was following up the ex-receptionist?'

'Janice.' Chloe swung her chair round. 'She visited the address from the company's files but the girl's gone so I'm trying to track her. Janice is following up the Willingdon lead from the E-FIT now.'

'OK, what about Ben's teachers?'

Graham held up a bundle of statements. 'We've interviewed all of them and they're all the same, earnest, keen to help, with no motive for taking Ben and alibis for Monday morning.'

Robyn swore. 'What are we missing here? What about Kinnister?'

'Er, sorry, Guv.' Chloe looked up through her fringe. 'I haven't been able to get hold of him yet but I'm keeping trying.'

Robyn banged her desk. 'We are getting nowhere. There is a toddler out there. Where's Gorton? Go back over everything, what about other landlords? We have missed something.' She pulled over the file of the shop-to-shop interviews and started to review them. Each time the phone rang, she flinched, expecting a summons upstairs. One by one, the team left for home. With the room quiet, Robyn jumped when the door banged open.

The young cleaner smiled as she put down a bin bag. 'Thank you for alarm. Understand now. Make me safe.'

'You're welcome. It's important women look after themselves.'

The girl cocked her head to one side. 'You a woman?'

Robyn made a half-hearted attempt to push the papers together. 'Yes. I'm a woman.' Whatever she'd been searching for in the statements, she hadn't found it.

'But you is real woman?' The girl was still smiling but her expression was puzzled.

Robyn tapped her head. 'Up here I'm a real woman. The rest, I'm trying. Good night.'

On the way out, Robyn tried to pin down what was wrong with the case and what was wrong with her. The car park was almost empty now, just the late shift. She frowned. Where she'd parked, at the end of a row, there was now a white car. Getting nearer, she could see it wasn't all white, there were streaks and patches of blue. Someone had poured a can of white paint over her Mondeo. On the driver's door there was a scrawled word: 'Tranny'.

Robyn choked back a sob and forced herself to think like a police officer. First question: when had the crime occurred? She dipped a finger in the paint: tacky which meant it had been applied not long after she got back. The paint must have been grabbed from the decorator's van. Although most likely that the person came from the station, they could have sneaked through the barrier when it was open. That seemed a better option than one of her colleagues hating her that much.

She notified the desk and managed to get hold of a pool car. On the way home, Robyn stopped at a convenience store, picked up a four-pack of beer and a bottle of brandy. At the counter, the young assistant scanned the items.

'Have you got some ID for me?'

Robyn began paying attention. 'Sorry?'

'I need some ID because you're buying alcohol.'

'I'm forty-four.'

The assistant pointed to a sign behind the till – *No ID = no alcohol & no tobacco*. There was a picture of a policeman making a stop sign.

Robyn sighed and opened her bag. A queue was forming. She had her warrant card and a driving licence, both still with Roger's name. The assistant was waiting, face neutral. The prospect of being called out on the names was too depressing. 'I'll leave it.'

'Whatever.' The assistant grunted, shoving the bottles to one side. 'Next.'

Robyn drove straight home. In the back of the dresser she found half a bottle of cooking sherry, probably decades old and drank it to the dregs. She went to bed. There was nothing else to do. Lying in the darkness, she rolled into a ball, squeezing her knees against her flat chest. She'd lain like this before in the dark hours, wondering what to do. Then it had seemed enough to be brave once, make the change and everything would fall into place. Tears began to run onto the pillow. A twinge of cramp flared in her calf. Stretching, she turned and reached for the phone on the bedside table. She guessed her voice wouldn't hold out so tried to get the feelings across in a text.

*Becky, please talk to me. I knew this would be hard but if you're not there, it's impossible and there's no point to anything. Dad.*

# THURSDAY 21 JULY

# 25

At seven-fifteen in the morning, Robyn and Graham paced Whitecourt Shopping Centre looking for anything not matching the photos from Monday. Commuters on their way to the station tutted as they dodged the official filming team with their piles of gear and freelance photographers jostling for the best spots. Outside shops, staff chatted in their last moments of freedom, as shutters rattled up. The centre's manager picked her way about the floor in a tight black suit and platform heels.

'One thing's not right – the place is a lot cleaner today. Reckon the manager wanted it to look its best for the cameras.' Graham pointed to a figure pulling litter out of a flower feature. 'There's Jaime, Guv.'

'Good. Can you make sure he's positioned where he was on Monday?' Robyn kept moving, looking for Melissa Chivers. The pharmacist bustled out of his shop: Robyn had a nasty suspicion he wouldn't want to stick to what he was supposed to do. On one of the stone benches, Gillian sat hunched in olive and brown. Next to her, Donna – the PC from the road block – stood out, wearing a garish, flowered dress instead of her uniform, a lad that must have been her son on her lap.

Robyn laid a hand on her shoulder. 'Thanks for doing this.' The dress looked a size too small: Donna's muscular shape wouldn't match the image.

'No problem, ma'am.' Donna grinned. 'Saves another shift on traffic and a morning's nursery fees.'

'Robyn.' Khalid beckoned her over to talk to a man wearing a battered leather jacket. 'Morning. This is DI Bailley who's leading the investigation, as I've told you.' The glance between the two men was just momentary before Khalid continued. 'Robyn, this is Connor Grayson, director for Crimewatch.'

They shook hands, Connor glancing at Robyn's outfit; plain blouse with a high neckline, slim silver chain, discreet make-up. He nodded with what Robyn hoped was acceptance.

Khalid was gesturing towards the crew. 'For the appeal, they want a bit more background and to shoot some scenes of the lead-up to the snatch. We'll be starting with your plea for information.' He seemed to enjoy Robyn's surprised stare and continued. 'Fell's orders. To hell with Liz Trew and the *Journal*.' Connor turned back to his team and began issuing directions. Khalid dropped his voice. 'Once this is over, we could do with sorting out the burglaries.' He unfolded the *Meresbourne and North Kent Gazette* from his folder. Dominating the front page was a picture of an elderly woman swathed in bandages, under a headline *New Burglary Horror by Ady Clarke*. 'I thought you knew this guy?'

Robyn was saved from answering by a wail cutting across the chatter. Donna's son was refusing to put on Ben's red sweatshirt. Across the aisle, the stage-school kids playing the teenagers were loitering in a very convincing way, even though filming hadn't started yet.

'Guv – two minutes.' Chloe held the clipboard up for Gillian, who nodded once and took the bags Chloe gave her.

Connor raised his voice. 'Places people. We start with the kidnapper sighting the boy.'

The manager was swaying on her heels. 'We must have this finished as soon as possible. We're losing trade.' She stopped, realising she was being filmed. 'You can't film me. This is private property.' Her face was pinched into angry creases. Robyn took the opportunity to slide away.

From somewhere, there was a sound of singing, rising above the piped pop music. A procession of people in white robes, walked two by two from Northbank. The man at their head wore a purple sash around his waist and clasped a book. His bass voice could be felt as a vibration in the air. Robyn recognised Reverend Lewis from the TV interview. Beside him, carrying a lily, was Melissa.

The procession halted, the song continuing for a few more seconds, notes chasing each other to the roof. Somewhere, in the scrum of camera men, someone began to applaud, hushed by his neighbour.

Robyn weaved through the crowd. 'Ms Chivers, thank you for joining us. I'll ask one of my officers to accompany you, in case you have any questions.'

Reverend Lewis laid his hand on Melissa's shoulder, holding up his bible. 'She has no need of you; the Lord is with her.'

Robyn thought of Ben and swallowed a number of responses. 'Very well, Ms Chivers, whatever you feel most comfortable with.'

Connor arrived beside her. 'This is the mother?'

Robyn nodded.

'Hi, I'm the director. The choir's an interesting set up – we can make a good sequence and segue it into the interview with you. Should get great coverage.' Connor consulted his clipboard. 'We have the make-up team here ...'

'We sing for the Lord, not for television. And she won't be speaking to you.' Reverend Lewis emphasised the point by jabbing the bible into Connor's chest.

'In which case could I ask you to stand to the side as we are about to start filming?' Connor turned. 'This way, DI Bailley.'

As Robyn followed, Reverend Lewis's velvet voice carried above the crowd. 'You see, my brothers and sisters? When the unclean shall walk among us, we are truly in the end of days.' A low ripple of agreement passed through the group.

Cutting across the whispers, Robyn heard Graham's voice 'Ms Chivers – we've been in contact with Mr James Kinnister.' Melissa's reply was inaudible.

Someone touched Robyn's arm.

'Guv, it's your introduction.' Chloe stepped back.

Everyone focused on her. Roger had done these briefings lots of times which meant Robyn could do them too. She remembered how Ms Chivers stood when she exuded a feminine authority and turned a little to the side so that she no longer faced the camera head on, putting one foot half a pace in front of the other. That felt more natural. She took a deep breath. 'Three days ago, little Ben, Benjamin Chivers, was taken from this shopping centre by an unknown woman. He has not been seen since and we are here to get him back. Please think about anything you may have seen or heard. Even the most trivial information, a tiny change in someone's behaviour, could be what leads us to Benjamin.' She kept her focus steady, the camera's green light still shining. Chloe, standing with the camera man, gave Robyn a thumbs up.

'Cut. OK.' Connor raised his voice. 'Scene one places, everyone.'

Robyn shuffled sideways to stand next to Janice, who was holding her handbag in front of her. 'Are you OK?'

'Fine.' Janice appeared to make an effort to relax, swinging the bag to one shoulder. 'Oh, I checked out the Willingdon lead from the E-FIT – it's very sad. The woman's husband has dementia and she's determined to care for him at home. The neighbours didn't see nappies, they were incontinence pads.'

'Damn. By the way, I meant to ask you. I saw your Josh in a picture at Derby and Rutherford. Why was that?'

Janice's hand flew to her mouth. 'My God, I'd forgotten all about that. He did work experience there the summer before he went to uni.' She cocked her head on one side. 'If I remember, he found it really dull because all he was doing was photocopying. They didn't let him anywhere near the partners or the clients.'

In front of them, the TV crew checked clipboards and spread out. Someone was lecturing Donna on her role. 'Scene one: we need a shot of you when you start tracking the child. Keep it natural please.'

There was a loud ring from Robyn's waist. The producer glared in her direction. 'All phones should be on silent when we're shooting.'

Stepping away from the filming area, Robyn fished out the phone. 'Hi, Ravi.' The line was terrible, not helped by Ravi's rush of words. 'Slow down. I can't hear you.' Janice joined her. The line crackled and cut out. 'Bugger. Ravi's got something.' She willed the signal bars to increase from zero.

There was a call for silence. The assistant director positioned Donna just outside the pharmacy. 'This is the scene where you first see the child.'

Janice shook her head. 'We need some new leads because we're not going to get anything from this – Donna's been put in completely the wrong place.'

Robyn looked at Janice who was still looking at Donna. Her phone shrilled. Robyn stabbed at the screen to silence it.

'Ravi.'

'Guv, are you there? I've finally got the warrant for St Oswald's. Shall we get the search teams out?'

Robyn shut her eyes, making noises seem louder: the crew's chatter, pop music, Ravi's voice. 'Guv?'

Conscious that Janice's eyes were now fixed on her, Robyn looked ahead. Donna lured her son out of the shop by holding out a sweet. Once he was in the middle of the aisle, she retreated, leaving him standing in a patch of empty floor, gazing at the multitude around him. Without the promised sweet, he began to wail as the stage-school teenagers swept past him. 'Cut.' Connor pulled off his earphones. 'Can you stop him crying?'

'Guv! What do you want us to do?'

As Robyn stared through the scene in front of her, strands were starting to come together in her mind. Decision made, she turned back to Janice, whose handbag was back across her body. 'Ravi. I want you to call Janice right away and go through all the details with her.' She cut off the spluttering from the other end. 'Right, Janice. You heard what I said. Ravi's got himself into a state and needs to talk to someone with a clear head. Check he's done all that's necessary, get the details. And make sure they finish everything here.' The boy was still crying. 'I'll speak to you later.'

Janice looked as if she wanted to say something but Robyn turned and pushed through the crowd, scanning for Jaime. She stopped by the centre's manager who stood glowering at the bystanders, the choir and the crew.

'Where's Jaime Restrepo gone?'

The manager scowled. 'Who?'

'The cleaner. He was here.'

The woman wrinkled her nose. 'Someone spilled a drink at the Riverside entrance.'

Robyn stared into the bony face for a moment, then spoke, keeping her anger under control. 'You sent the only witness to the abduction away during the reconstruction. Why?'

The manager put her hands on her hips. 'I'm responsible for the safety of everyone in this centre. If someone slipped, we could get sued.'

'And where is he now?'

'If he's finished his shift, I expect he's left.'

In the corner of Robyn's vision, the Reverend Lewis raised his arm. The choir began a peal of sound and the camera swung to capture them. Without waiting for an answer, the manager stalked across to remonstrate, leaving Robyn outside a jewellery store.

Disgusted, Robyn turned her back on them all, gazing into the shop window. There was no escape, the glass reflected the filming. She ran through her impressions one more time. From the reflection, she saw the producer placing Gillian and the security guard for the next shot.

'Can't afford those on a police salary unless you're doing a paper round as well.' Graham had appeared beside her, pointing at a string of pearls sitting in a velvet case in the centre of the window.

The choir swelled to a crescendo, then stopped. Connor shouted something. Robyn let out a long breath. A little patch of steam appeared on the window.

'Guv?' There was concern in Graham's voice.

With an effort, Robyn stood up straight. 'There's something I have to check.' There was no point in trying to explain, she just needed to get moving. She turned. 'Right, I need you to get the team organised. When you get back, Ravi should support Lorraine with the burglaries and you and Chloe start reviewing missing persons' lists – I want a name for the young woman in the warehouse by tomorrow. And get Janice to, to ...'

'You sure you're OK, Guv? Don't you want to hear what Ms Chivers said about Kinnister?'

'No. Not now. I don't think he's taken Ben.' Graham rolled back on his heels, frowning. Robyn jabbed her finger down for emphasis. 'Just get on with it, Graham.'

Robyn squared her shoulders and turned away. Graham started to say something but she kept walking and the comment was lost behind the heavy swing doors to the car park. Stamping up the stairs wasn't enough and she slammed the car door. At the car park exit, she forced the car into the line of traffic, ignoring hoots of protest. She'd lost her temper with the team, something she swore she'd never do. It didn't matter what they thought of her at this moment anyway, if her idea was correct.

# 26

Robyn put her foot down as she passed the last houses on the edge of town, frustrated by the pool car's lack of power. Now the idea was planted, previously unconnected impressions were coming together and she needed to know as soon as possible whether she was right or not. Around the next corner, she had to brake hard when a harvester trundled out of a field. The next couple of miles were a frustrating crawl until the machine lumbered into a farmyard. She accelerated, crunching the gears until she passed shop-fronts and realised she was heading into Lower Markham village and had gone too far. As she did a U-turn, her phone beeped. After a quick check to make sure no one was watching, she scanned the message from Graham. *All finished here. Where are you Guv?*

Robyn threw the phone back onto the seat and retraced her route, forcing herself to slow down, earning a hoot from the car behind her, repeated when she stopped to peer up at a sign, half-covered with ivy. Waving an apology, she backed up and turned into the single-track lane. Around a couple of bends, she recognised the heavy wooden gates, even though her only visit had been a year ago. She left the car in a passing-place and walked back to the house.

In the driveway, a small car sat under a tarpaulin. Robyn lifted a corner and peered inside the off-white Fiat. In the back was a clean child-seat. Robyn slipped through the side gate taking care not to let the catch make a noise. The path led past a vegetable garden, bean canes groaning under the weight of produce. She stopped at the corner of the house and peered around. The garden was empty apart from a blackbird hopping across the lawn. Moving on, she risked a glance into the open patio doors, conscious of a dog curled in the doorway. Inside, a man rolled a shiny, blue ball towards a toddler who ran forward, tripping on his own feet. The man bent down and stood the boy up. The boy tried to kick and fell again, this time with a whimper of protest. The man took the child's hand and stood him on the sofa.

Robyn stepped into the open doorway. The man had his back to her but Ben pointed. Martin Warrener jerked around to see Robyn standing behind him.

'Hello, Martin.'

As he stood up, Martin's jaw tensed. He took a step forward, his fists clenching.

"Are you …?' Martin's lip curled back. 'Janice told me about you.'

'Janice doesn't know I'm here. She didn't tell me you had Ben.' Robyn held her ground as Martin took another half step forward, his shoulders going back.

Behind him, Ben wobbled on the sofa and Robyn's instinct made her step forward. Martin dropped his shoulder and drove forward, shoving her backwards. She hit the wall, her arm grabbing an edge for support. The bookcase tilted, photo frames crashing into each other, then the shattering of glass as one hit the floor. Robyn staggered, trying to stand up, taking a shuddering breath. Martin stepped towards her, snarling. Behind him, on the edge of the sofa, Ben wobbled. Still unable to speak, Robyn pointed. Martin glowered at her before turning, then his face softened as he scooped Ben up and sank onto the sofa. Nestled in his lap, Ben played with the pocket of his check shirt.

Robyn pulled up the nearest chair. In all of the pictures she'd seen of Ben, she'd never seen him smiling.

'How did you know?' Martin jiggled his knee, making Ben giggle.

Robyn coughed and took a deep breath. 'A lot of little things, like why the most sociable officer on the team wasn't having her usual birthday barbecue at her secluded village house? Then something Janice said at the reconstruction confirmed it. She said the snatcher had been put in the wrong place, something there's no way she could have known. Even though I couldn't understand why she would be involved, I had to check. But I keep asking why?'

Ben made one, two tries to pull at Martin's beard without managing to hold on. 'Ganda.'

'He must go back to his mother.' Robyn wondered why this next step no longer seemed so clear.

Martin kissed the top of Ben's head and set him down, watching him toddle away to curl up beside the dog. 'You can't give Ben back.' He stood up, fists clenching again. 'She may be his mother but she's not a fit one.'

Somewhere, a door opened. Janice appeared in the doorway and ran to Martin who folded her into his arms. They stood locked together, ignoring Robyn. No one knew she was here. She could just walk out and pretend this had never happened. She found herself half standing up, then subsided back into the chair. The terrier raised its head, scratched with one back leg. Robyn glanced at her watch; she'd have to account for every minute of this time.

Still in each other's arms, Martin and Janice were talking, voices too low to be overheard.

With a giggle, Ben threw the ball, which bounced through the open door and into the garden. The child followed it, beginning to climb down the step. Glad of the distraction, Robyn reached him in a couple of strides, swinging him to her hip as she'd seen women do.

'Hello, Ben.' The little boy's fists were balled, his body tense as he slid down. Robyn tightened her arm and bounced him up and down, waiting for him to relax. 'We've all been wondering where you were. Everyone will be happy we've found you.'

There was still a hint of tears. Robyn did her best impersonation of Fell, jutting out her chin and wrinkling her nose and there was a little giggle. 'You're not going to cry, are you? Are you?' She pulled another face and was rewarded with a chuckle. A hand stretched out and touched her face. Jiggling Ben, Robyn turned to see Janice and Martin still pressed together but both watching her.

'Janice – I need to make the call. The longer I leave calling this in, the worse things will get for everyone.'

Martin glowered at her, his arms still tight around Janice.

'We don't have long, you need to tell me everything.' The whispered conversation began again. 'I'll do what I can, Janice. You know I will.'

'Why should we trust him?' Martin didn't bother to drop his voice.

Janice's reply to Martin was inaudible. She held his eyes for a second, then broke away and walked to Robyn. She nodded once, then held out her arms for Ben, who stretched out to her. Robyn handed him over and went into the garden, sinking onto a patio chair. She kept the call to Fell as short as possible, distracted by Ben's laughter.

When she returned to the lounge, Ben was curled on the floor drinking from a beaker while Janice and Martin sat on the sofa, their hands clasped. Robyn pulled the chair across until she was directly in front of them. 'Now we talk about what you're going to say and do because we have less than fifteen minutes.'

# 27

Robyn felt the noon sun prickle on her nose as she watched an ambulance disappear around the bend in the lane. Ben's excitement at going in a vehicle with blue lights turned into fretful wails when Janice and Martin were not allowed to go with him. Janice was still staring up the road until Matthew murmured something in her ear and indicated his car. There was another pause when he opened the back door for her, before she settled herself beside Martin.

Matthew shut the door and walked over to Robyn, rubbing the back of his neck.

'I'm taking Janice to Gaddesford Police House – Fell wants to keep this discreet. Martin's going to the regular cells. Are you ... going back?' His expression was a mixture of pity and distaste.

Out of words, Robyn nodded. She knew what he was trying to say: was she going to do the paperwork, to make it official, or was there still a chance to change things? She'd wished the station would stop talking about her transition: it was a dull irony that arresting a member of her own team was probably the only thing she could have done to make that wish come true. 'Thanks for doing this, Matthew. I'm glad you came. This was very hard for Janice.'

Matthew's eyebrows went up. He looked as if he were about to say something, then turned and got into his car. She held up a hand as they drove past – no one responded.

Robyn locked up the house as Janice had asked, struggling to find space in her handbag for the keys. Halfway back to her car, she stopped and went back into Janice's garden, scooping up the blue ball from a flowerbed. She sat down on a patio chair to make two more calls.

'Melissa Chivers.' The phone was answered on the first ring.

The ball slipped through Robyn's fingers and rolled away. 'Ms Chivers, it's DI Bailley.'

'Why are you ignoring my requests? I have made it clear I do not want you to contact me.'

'I wanted to tell you we've found Ben – Benjamin. He's safe and appears to have been well-treated but he's having a medical to be sure.'

There was a pause at the other end of the line. 'Why has it taken so long? Where has he been?'

She shut her eyes for a second. Her response had to be neutral. 'I'm afraid I can't tell you at this moment. We must secure all the evidence …'

'Gillian will collect him.' The line was cut.

Robyn strode to the edge of the patio and spat into a flowerbed, to trying to clear the bitter taste from her mouth. She retrieved the ball, checked the back door and had to exchange pleasantries with a neighbour who'd arrived to take the dog and wanted to ask a lot of questions. Robyn managed to keep smiling as she confirmed, yes, Martin and Janice had gone without notice and no, she didn't know how long they'd be away for. She was edging away, then realised the woman expected the blue ball. She took another step back. 'Oh, this isn't the dog's ball. It's mine – my dog's, I mean. He's in the car. Thanks for coming.' It hadn't sounded convincing.

Robyn escaped into the lane. Before opening the boot, she glanced over her shoulder – the neighbour was nowhere in sight. She tossed in the blue ball and rearranged the borrowed tarpaulin to cover all of the clothes and toys Janice had bought for Ben. At least she'd had the sense to pay cash for them.

There was another call to make: the most important thing. She scrolled through her contacts, then selected the number Janice had saved into her phone. The call went straight to voicemail. She tried it again, this time leaving her number.

She took a deep breath, slotted the phone into the cradle and started the engine. Torn between wanting a last few minutes of peace and needing to know the worst, she switched to the local radio station, hoping Khalid had things under control and she wouldn't hear a voice announce the breaking news as she drove back to town.

Immune now to the desk sergeant's looks, she took the lift to the fifth floor, glancing up the corridor to make sure there was no sign of Fell, before slipping into Khalid's office.

Khalid saw her and clamped his phone between his shoulder and ear, thrusting over a piece of paper, still warm from the printer. Robyn took the sheet and scanned the two paragraphs of black text. She was finding it hard to focus but one phrase jumped out: *full, independent review of the investigation*. The bitter taste was back in her mouth.

'Yes, there will be a briefing on the Ben Chivers case at three o'clock. OK, thanks.' He placed the phone into a carved wooden stand on the desk.

'Well, you heard. Fell will be doing a press briefing and we'll be issuing this at the same time.' He turned on the desk fan; corners of the paper flapped in the breeze. 'You need to be there. We won't be publicising the fact a serving officer was involved.' His fingers pulled at the tip of his goatee. 'With something like this, it's normally best just to be upfront and then let the storm blow over.' He traced the shaved edge of his beard, finding something not quite in line and worried at the hair with a manicured nail. 'However, in this case, we'll wait a little. Someone from Professional Standards is on their way. The plan is, we get everyone feeling good about Ben being safe, then release the details of the charges when everyone's moved on.'

Robyn sighed. 'Will it work?'

Khalid shrugged. 'You got any better ideas? And everything must stay confidential.'

Robyn sat back. 'I've got to tell the team. They'll be asking what's happened to Janice and if I don't tell them, well, they're detectives, they'll go and find out.'

'If you have to.' The dark crease reappeared on Khalid's forehead. 'Oh, just so you know, Fell has already been asking what took you so long before you called in.'

'Janice and Martin were trying to get hold of their children so they heard the news from them first.' Robyn's eyes met Khalid's.

Khalid's face didn't relax. 'And if they hadn't been caught, just when exactly were they planning to tell them?'

Robyn tapped the press release. 'That's the whole point, they didn't plan anything. We need to make sure that fact is made clear.'

'No. It stays as it is.'

'Why?' Robyn stood up, pacing the small office. 'Well, why?'

'Because we don't know it's true. It's just what you want to be true.' Khalid let the words hang between them for a second.

Robyn stared ahead. She'd chosen this way but she could help Janice more if she didn't allow herself to be compromised. 'OK, I'll be here.'

'No one should make any comments, just refer them to me.' Khalid winced as his phone rang. 'Tell the team if you have to, just remember, whatever we do, write or say, we are going to get crucified at some point.'

The incident room was the usual mass of paper, now with pictures from the reconstruction up on the boards. Robyn stood in the doorway. 'Right, everyone out. We're going to the meeting room.'

A phone started ringing. Robyn held up her hand to stop anyone from answering it. 'Leave the phones. Come on.' She sounded harsher than she'd intended.

Robyn held the door open. Graham was the last out and fell into step beside her. 'The reconstruction hasn't brought any sensible calls, so, as you said, we've focused on the body and the burglary. The scene-of-crime details from the latest break-in should be here this afternoon.'

Robyn wished Graham would shut up. She was trying to put into words what needed to be said. All the meeting rooms were occupied apart from the smallest. Ravi offered Robyn the fourth chair.

'Sit down.' Robyn stood, back against the wall. 'I took you out because I have some bad news.' She took a deep breath.

'Ben's dead?' Ravi was on the edge of his seat.

'No. He's getting a check-up from a doctor.' There were sharp intakes of breath. 'It should be a formality because when I found him, he looked well cared-for.'

Four startled faces were fixed on her.

Robyn had to focus on the wall. 'I found Ben at Janice's house. Janice took Ben.' Silence, one, two, three, then a rush of noise. Graham swore. Lorraine laughed, a hysterical, unbelieving noise.

'But why, Guv? Why would Janice ever do something so mad?' Chloe seemed calmer than the others, perhaps because she knew Janice least.

The wall behind her was solid support: Robyn was glad of it. 'Because Janice is Ben's grandmother.'

She didn't wait for the gasps and swearing to stop, just talked over it and the team quietened. 'Janice's son, Josh, met Melissa Chivers during summer work experience at Derby and Rutherford, three years ago. Janice told me this morning she remembers Josh spent almost no time at home the following Christmas. He admitted he was with Ms Chivers, saying she was helping him with his studies. When Janice went to Ms Chivers' house to follow up on the dodgy builder, she met Ben.'

Robyn held up the picture of Josh from Janice's desk, then the picture of Ben. Someone whistled. 'Janice spotted the resemblance ...'

Graham interrupted, shaking his head. 'But, Guv, why did she take him? Why risk her pension? If he's her grandson, why didn't she apply for access?'

Robyn tried to keep her voice even. 'Although Janice believed Ben was being abused by his mother, she couldn't do anything formal about Ben before she'd confirmed the paternity through a DNA test.'

Graham's voice was too loud in the tight room. 'Are you telling us Janice planned this? She'd know she'd never get away with keeping him, surely?'

There didn't seem to be enough air. 'Janice told me.' Robyn stopped. 'And I believe her, all of this was chance and things, well, escalated before she knew what was happening.' She paused, letting this sink in. 'Janice was browsing in the shopping centre first thing and saw Ben on his own, apparently abandoned. She said instinct took over ...' The sentence tailed off as the door opened and an HR assistant stuck her bleached head around the door.

'Hello, are you like going to be long? It's just like I've got this room booked for an interview?'

Hoping the girl didn't notice the team's expressions, Robyn managed to smile. 'Just finishing up.' Through the glass panel in the door, she could see the HR Business Partner frowning. 'As I said, Janice felt she had to protect Ben from what she thought was the cult's brainwashing ...'

'What will happen to her?' Lorraine leant forward, gripping the edge of the table.

'I don't know. I've got to go and interview Martin.' The mood in the room had gone from disbelief to anger. 'Professional Standards are on the way. She will almost certainly have to retire. But there are things we all have to do. Not talk to anyone – let Khalid handle the press. Fell's statement won't identify Janice. The best thing we can do now is catch the burglar and find whoever killed the girl.'

As motivational speeches went, she'd done better. No one had questioned what she had done yet, though that was sure to come. There was a sharp knock on the door.

'Come on.' Robyn tried to make her voice more positive. 'Let's get back to the incident room, get on with things.'

The team straggled from the meeting room into the lift, not speaking. When the doors opened at the second floor, Robyn hung back. 'OK, I should be back after the press conference and I want updates on the body and the burglary then please.'

Robyn pressed the button for the basement. She bought two cups of tea, then waited in an interview room. Martin said nothing as he was led in and didn't respond to Robyn's greeting or the tea.

They both waited until the custody sergeant left.

'What have you done with Janice?'

'She's in Gaddesford. We're trying to minimise publicity. We won't be releasing any details about her until ...' She realised she was whispering and made an effort to speak in a normal voice. '... until the independent inspector has decided on charges.'

Martin ground his teeth.

Robyn raised her voice to cover the horrible noise. 'I'm not allowed to see her. Do you understand? This is out of my hands now.'

'Where's Josh? When is he coming home?'

'I've left him a couple of messages ...'

'You're going to ask me why we didn't go to the authorities. Well, this is why.' Martin was shouting now, face flushing. 'Because you're useless.' He kicked the table, causing his untouched tea to teeter and tip over.

Robyn fumbled with her bag, finding tissues. Tea began to drip to the floor. A face flashed in the window as the custody sergeant checked on them. She gave up trying to mop the desk and reached for the recording button. The face vanished from the window. 'You have to work with me, Martin ...'

She started the recorder. The cameras would capture the expression of dislike on Martin's face which was what she wanted. 'Interview on twenty-first July at two thirty-four pm. Present DI Robyn Bailley and Martin Warrener.' She went through the caution. 'Mr Warrener, could you confirm whether you require a lawyer?' She had to sound crisp and professional: no possibility for any leniency. Martin jerked his head once.

'For the recording, Mr Warrener has declined a lawyer. The reason you have been arrested is because I found Ben Chivers at your house this morning. We believe he's been there since Monday morning after he was taken from Whitecourt Shopping Centre by your wife. Can you tell me why you were keeping him?'

Martin was gazing at the far wall, eyes unfocused.

Robyn held her breath. The room was getting stuffy.

'We were keeping him because we believed he'd be abused if he were returned to his mother.'

Robyn let the air go in a rush, steadying herself before the next question. 'Why did you believe Ben was being abused?'

'Because he wasn't being allowed a childhood. His mother was indoctrinating him into a cult.'

'And how did you know this?'

'Janice had to visit Ben's mother's house. She described what Ben was made to do. Then we found out the way the church treats children, the brainwashing and the beatings. They're poisonous.' Martin rolled up the sleeves of his shirt.

'When did you realise Ben was your grandson?'

'About three ...'

Robyn coughed, breathed, coughed again. She'd caught Martin's eye.

'Three days ago. I found out when Janice brought him home.'

'Why didn't you approach the authorities?'

Martin ran his fingers through what remained of his hair.

Robyn let the pause lengthen. 'Why didn't you tell someone, Martin?'

The man slumped, shoulders sagging. 'Because we've got no rights. If the bitch didn't even tell Josh he had a son, who would believe us? Janice explained even the DNA test wouldn't help because she shouldn't have taken the item from the house.' His voice faltered. 'Ben needed to be saved from that woman ...' His eyes were moistening.

Robyn's phone vibrated with a text from Tracey: *Press conf starts in 15 – where are you?*

Martin was crying now, silent tears running into his beard.

'Interview terminated at fourteen fifty.' She stopped the recording. 'I'm sorry, Martin ...' Robyn stood up, to give herself another second to find the right words, then just shook her head. 'I've got a press conference now.' Of all the excuses. 'I'm sorry.'

As she left, the custody sergeant brought in a glass of water and rolled his eyes at the pool of tea. Robyn took the nearest exit for a few seconds of fresh air before the briefing. She'd never seen the car park so crowded. A PC was having to squeeze a suspect between the lanes: there was a scrape as the handcuffs grazed a mirror.

Robyn walked through the front door of the station. The lobby was full, people crowded around the lift. One, dressed like a roadie in black shorts and t-shirt was carrying a TV camera slung over his shoulder. If she took the stairs, she'd be a panting wreck by the fifth floor. As she hesitated, a glance from a young man with a styled beard turned into a double-take.

'Inspector Bailley? I'm Danny from South East Media.' The camera swung to face her.

'It's so good we've run into you. Can you confirm you're about to uncover a paedophile ring suspected of kidnapping Ben Chivers?'

The others brushed past her into the lift. Robyn kept her face neutral. She got a glimpse of her own image reflected in the camera lens: her hair was a windswept mess.

'I'm sorry, ah, Danny. I can't make any comment before the briefing. Now I have to get up there.' She squeezed into the last space in the lift, people shifting to make room for her. The doors started to close, then stopped as Danny eased himself in beside her. She had to wriggle backwards as Danny edged closer to let the doors close, the others muttering as they shuffled together.

'Now, Inspector Bailley, what has been the most difficult aspect of this investigation?' Danny managed to wriggle one arm from his side to emphasise words with little jabs of his fingers.

'I can't comment. The briefing starts in five minutes.' They all shuffled to let someone out at the third floor. Danny refused to step out, as if he feared not being allowed back in. The doors closed again.

'Well, if you can't talk about the investigation, how does it feel being a woman?'

A voice came from behind Robyn. 'How you think? Do much work but not much thank you, like all women.'

The doors opened at the fifth floor, where the hallway was crowded with reporters. Robyn pushed past Danny while she had the chance, then swung around to see who'd spoken for her. The young cleaner was carrying a bucket towards Fell's office, a blonde ponytail swinging above the shapeless grey uniform.

'Thank you.' Robyn called to her retreating back, hoping she'd heard over the crowd. Filtering along the corridor Robyn made it into the meeting room, past Khalid and Tracey who were taking names, to where Fell shuffled notes, his face in deep shadow. On the hour, Khalid stood and welcomed the group. Most of the audience were staring at phones or tablets, giving their faces a blue tinge. Fell's sweat had an extra sour tang.

'Sir.'

Robyn kept her voice low so that no one in the audience could overhear. 'Remember, for the world, this is good news. We found Ben. He's OK. We need to sound pleased, sir.'

Fell shook his head and moved to the lectern.

# 28

An hour later, Tracey read out numbers. 'Sixty-two attendees; forty-six questions. Why aren't we releasing a name, why haven't we caught the burglar and what brand of make-up does DI Bailley wear? I'll type everything up.' Her shoulders slumped, looking like Robyn felt. Then she clicked her tongue, straightened and opened the large diary she'd been using as a rest, addressing Fell. 'On we go. You've got a meeting with the County Financial Controller in ten minutes for the quarterly budget review.' She gave a bleak smile. 'Though he sent a text to say he'll be late because he couldn't find a parking space.'

Fell took off his cap and ran stubby fingers through his hair. 'Thank you, Tracey, I shall be there.' Tracey wiggled to the door, tugging her skirt down. A hint of sunshine gleamed while the door was open. Fell turned to Robyn. 'Well, Bailley, where do we go from here? Do we have enough to charge Chivers with obstruction?'

Before Robyn could reply, Khalid cut in. 'Whether we have or not, we need to think what the point would be. Chivers would just say she was distressed and not thinking straight. We'd be accused of bullying.'

Fell put his cap on. 'And I suppose she has plenty of friends in the legal profession.'

Khalid drew a tissue from a packet and wiped his hands. 'We are absolutely sure on this, aren't we?' Robyn was grateful for the 'we'. 'I mean, there's no doubt of the relationship?'

Robyn reflected she'd been an idiot to think this wouldn't come up. 'No doubt. Janice had a DNA test done. She picked up something of Ben's when she visited Ms Chivers during a routine enquiry. She showed me the report – the lab confirmed paternity.'

An indignant Fell leant forward.

'She got the test done by a private clinic, sir.'

Fell sat back in his chair, his expression unchanged. 'How can the lad not know he was a father? You're not telling me a nineteen year-old boy doesn't know the facts of life? What did he think was going to happen?'

'I don't think he thought about much, sir. For him, it was a holiday dream.' Robyn rubbed her forehead.

Fell grunted. 'This student fling is going to cost me an officer.'

The ventilators were beginning to make some headway against the muggy air, until Fell stood up. 'When the inspector from Professional Standards arrives, I expect full co-operation. I must go and deal with the budgets. Guler, please try and keep all of this under control. Bailley, I want a progress report on the burglaries first thing tomorrow.'

As the door closed behind him, Khalid slumped back in his chair. 'It would be nice to have some good news.'

'I'll do my best. You can imagine how this has hit the team and now there'll be an investigation blaming them for not noticing what Janice was up to.'

'It's not just your team.' Khalid pressed fingers into his temples. 'It's the whole station. Janice has been mother hen for everyone at some point. When I joined, she went out of her way to make me welcome and introduce me to people. All the things HR are supposed to do and don't.' Khalid began to collect discarded copies of the press release.

'Need a hand?'

'No.' Khalid stopped and turned back to Robyn. 'Couldn't you have "found" Ben in a hedge or something? Did you have to do all of this?'

The question hung in the air. The station would let her know exactly what they thought of her, this was just the start of it. Khalid was considering her, his hands full of loose paper.

Robyn's voice was quiet. 'Secrets come out, Khalid. They always do. From the moment I realised, I hoped to be wrong. When I watched Martin playing with Ben, I wished I could leave them together.'

'But you didn't.' Khalid crumpled the paper he was holding.

'No, I didn't. Because what good would it have done? Would Janice and Martin have just quietly let Ben go back to his mother?'

Muttering something under his breath, Khalid crushed the remains of the papers into a ball and stalked to the door.

'You said Janice helped you when you started? Well when I was an eighteen year-old recruit, she was with me when I made my first arrest and saved me from really screwing up on more occasions than I can remember. She knows what she did is wrong and there's no other way.'

Khalid tossed the paper towards the bin, the ball bouncing on the rim and rolling across the floor. 'Well, as you're such a good detective, why don't you just catch the burglar? Oh and haven't you got a murderer as well? Either would do.'

There was a gentle knock and a constable stuck her head around the door. 'Ma'am? There's a lady for you in reception, a Mrs Green.'

'Thanks.' She turned to Khalid. 'I'd better get down there.'

Khalid screwed up his face.

In reception, Gillian Green sat perched on the edge of one of the plastic chairs, leaning away from the girl on the next seat who tapped a phone with tattooed fingers. As Robyn entered, Gillian stood up checking her hairpins.

'Hello, Mrs Green, we're all delighted Ben's safe and well. Please come through.'

Gillian bit her lip. 'Is he ...' Her eyes held an appeal.

'He's fine.' Better than when you had him, Robyn wanted to add.

Gillian swallowed. 'Who took him?'

'I'm afraid I can't tell you. We need to complete the case first.'

The interview room door opened. Ben cooed and wriggled out from the arms of a constable. Gillian met him in an awkward hug halfway across the room before she stood him up on a seat, exclaiming at the mismatched clothes. 'You gave me such a fright. Where have you been?'

As Ben stretched for her neck again, she stepped back, pulling a set of baby reins from her handbag. 'Now, I've got to get you home because you almost lost me my job. And you've got to wear these, to make sure you don't run away again.'

'I'll come back with you, Mrs Green, to make sure there are no problems with journalists. I'd also like to speak to Ms Chivers.' Robyn held the door open.

The constable bent to hug Ben as he struggled against the unfamiliar restraint. Gillian pulled him back after a second, appearing anxious to be gone. 'Come along. We've got to get you home.'

Ben began to whimper.

Outside, Robyn held the door open for Gillian. She stared for a second, open-mouthed in the camera flashes, then grabbed Ben and hurried to her car. Robyn kept pace, shielding her as much as possible. There was a perverse enjoyment in not being the one the photographers wanted to see.

Once on the road, Robyn kept glancing to the rear view mirror to check for anyone following. Journalists wanting to get to the house first would have an easy job as Gillian was a cautious driver. From the ring road, she indicated right towards the business park and Melissa's office. Robyn was pleasantly surprised until Gillian sailed past the turning, indicator still on. Robyn followed the blinking light for a mile before Gillian's car turned left, towards Upper Town.

At the top of the hill, Robyn abandoned her car across a driveway, hurried to the house then had to loiter at the gate, scanning the street until Gillian appeared.

'Can you take him while I get my keys?' Gillian shoved Ben into Robyn's arms and opened her handbag.

Robyn hitched Ben up and smiled into the small face. 'Going home. Yes, going home.'

Ben's nose was inches from hers. 'Ganda.'

'No, not Granddad; Mummy.' Ben screwed his fists into his eyes and started to sob.

Gillian froze, door open, one foot on the step. 'What did you say?'

To soothe Ben, Robyn jiggled him, the way Martin had done. When Gillian didn't move, Robyn raised her voice. 'Mrs Green, I suggest we get inside, in case any journalists are nearby.'

With a fearful look up the street, Gillian turned and headed for the kitchen.

Robyn followed, carrying a weepy Ben against her shoulder. 'Where's Ms Chivers?'

'She'll be in a meeting until at least six. She sent me a text. I've got to do a protein-rich evening meal and make sure Benjamin gets his supplements.' Gillian put her bag down on the counter and reached into a cupboard, pulling out a series of tubs. 'He'll need his nutrients, there's no knowing what he's been eating.' She began mixing powders with a measure of thick, green liquid from a bottle in the fridge. 'So here are vitamins and kelp extract and you've got everything you need to become a big, strong boy.' The sloppy mixture was transferred into a beaker. She pointed to one of the stools and Robyn deposited Ben, who wriggled and jerked, coming close to falling as he twisted his body away from the bottle, green goo spilling down his front.

'Now what has got into you?' Gillian swept a cloth over his face.

'Do you need anything else, Mrs Green?' Robyn moved to the door.

'Why did he say "Granddad"? Does he have another family?' Gillian wrung out the cloth, knuckles white.

Robyn smiled to soften the words. 'Again, I'm afraid I can't tell you.' She continued before Gillian could speak. 'Oh, I forgot, he was given a ball.' She bent to Ben. 'Your blue ball. Shall I fetch the ball for you? Shall I?' She nodded to Gillian. 'It's just in the car.'

'A ball?' Gillian blinked several times, before her face closed in on itself. 'No, we couldn't have a ball here. A ball is not educational.' She bit her lip. 'Ms Chivers was so kind and kept my job open for me. I have to make sure I do everything she expects.'

'It's a ball. Kids like balls.' Robyn's nails were digging into her palms.

'No, it's out of the question.' Gillian turned to Ben. 'Now, you need to be in your school uniform for when your mother gets home because she'll want to see you've started your studies again, won't she?'

Gillian marched Ben upstairs. From the hallway, Robyn caught a shadow crossing the glass of the front door. A couple of quick steps and she opened it. Pressed up against the front window was a man with a camera, who took a picture of Robyn then ran for the gate. Robyn's phone rang. The display flashed up "Josh".

She turned back into the house. 'Mrs Green? I have to go now. There are journalists outside so I'll get someone from Family Liaison round.' The satisfaction she was both doing her duty and would be annoying Melissa Chivers didn't last long. She closed the front door and answered her phone.

'Hello, Josh, it's DI Bailley from Meresbourne police station. I work with your mother and she gave me your number.'

'Right. Yeah, Dad left a message, said I had to call you. What's going on? He's not answering his phone?'

Robyn set off back to the car, scanning the road for the photographer. 'Your father asked me to call you as he couldn't tell you himself. Are you in a place where you can talk?' There was chatter in the background.

'Yeah. What's happening?'

'You need to come home to Meresbourne as soon as possible.' Robyn reached her car.

'Has something happened to Mum?' His voice rose. 'Keep it down, guys.'

Robyn slid into the driver's seat. Better to get straight to it. 'Have you seen the news about a toddler disappearing in Meresbourne?'

A figure appeared outside the car window, mouthing something. Laughter came through the phone, then a faint voice. 'You're breaking up. What did you say?'

'Josh have you seen the news about Meresbourne?' The knocking on the window was becoming more insistent.

'Can't hear you, bro.'

The red-faced man opened the car door. 'Do you realise you're blocking my driveway?'

'Can't hear you.'

'I'm sorry about the obstruction, sir, I'll be gone in a few minutes.'

'You've got to go now. I need to pick up my wife.'

'What's going on, mate?'

'Josh, have you seen the news about Meresbourne?'

'You move this car or I'll call the police.'

'Sir, I suggest you take a less aggressive attitude.'

'Who's being aggressive? You told me to ring you.'

'Don't tell me what to do. You're the one parked where you shouldn't be.'

There appeared to be a space on the other side of the road. Robyn started the engine.

'Driving with a phone is illegal you know. I'm going to call the police.'

'Sir, I am a police officer.' Robyn reached for her warrant card, before remembering it was still in Roger's name. 'Josh, sorry, I've got to call you back in a couple of minutes.'

'Well if you're the police, why don't you do something useful, like stop lunatics on mountain bikes riding on the pavement and nearly knocking people over?'

Robyn closed the window and left the angry little man in sole charge of his driveway. From the other side of the road, she called Josh. The phone rang for a long time.

'You. What's going on?'

'Josh, I'm sorry about …'

'You're having a laugh.'

'Josh, have you seen the news?'

'Yeah, right, I'm in Cornwall on a beach, I'm watching the news all day.'

'Josh, I'm afraid it's bad news. You need to come back to Meresbourne because your parents have been arrested.'

'Bullshit. I don't believe you.'

'They took a toddler from a shopping centre.'

'No way. Mum's a copper.'

'I'm sorry, Josh, it's true. I found the child at their house this morning.'

'Yeah, right. I don't know what kind of sick pervert you are but you are talking bullshit.'

The car from across the road nosed out, the man gesturing at Robyn as he passed. 'Josh. The child is your son. Melissa Chivers had your child.'

'What the …'

A series of thumps, then no sound from the line.

'Josh? Josh, are you still there?' Robyn checked the phone, full signal. 'Josh?'

'Yeah, I just had to get outside. What …' Josh broke off.

'You had a relationship with Melissa Chivers in December, three years ago, yes?'

215

'I didn't think she'd tell anyone.' Josh mumbling as if he were talking to himself.

'She didn't tell anyone but your mother worked it out. His name's Ben. He was born nine months after your relationship.'

'She was like all over me for two weeks, then blanked me.' Josh's voice was rising.

'And your parents hadn't told you she'd had your child?'

'No!'

Robyn found herself tapping the door frame. 'But now everyone is going to know and your parents need help. You need to come back to Meresbourne as soon as you can.'

'You know I'm in Cornwall? I got a lift down. We're not coming back for another week.'

She began tapping the dashboard because it made a louder noise. 'Well, can you get a train?' There was no answer again. 'Josh, your parents need you.'

Someone yelled in the background. Josh answered them; Robyn couldn't catch the words. 'Like, I've got to think about this ...'

Robyn gripped the phone tighter, trying to keep him on the line. 'Josh, you'll get journalists calling you – don't answer any questions.' He'd hung up.

She thumped the passenger seat, the sleeve of the blouse protesting at the unusual movement. She wanted to do something. A large part of her wanted to go to Derby and Rutherford, march into whichever over-designed icebox Melissa Chivers was in and tell her she didn't deserve Ben back. A wild thought was to find a number for Liz Trew at the *Journal* but the small practical voice at the back of her mind, who sounded a lot like Roger, told her Trew and Chivers would probably get on like a house on fire. Another part wanted to meet Ady in a pub and tell him all about Ms Chivers and her odd views. Apart from the pub bit, the idea wasn't such a bad one. She checked her contacts.

'Ady Clarke.'

'Hi, Ady, it's Robyn. How are you?'

'Robyn? Oh, Robyn! Hi. Yes, I'm fine, thanks, fine. And you?'

'Fine. I owe you a favour. I know you're going to be busy with Ben's discovery but if you want another angle, you might want to check out Melissa Chivers' church and links to crimes in the States.'

'Thanks.' There was surprise in Ady's voice. 'Why are you telling me this? Are you saying someone from the church took Ben?'

Robyn leaned back, trying to stretch the tension out of her neck. 'Let's just say, they have some extreme ideas about raising children.'

'OK, thanks, I'll look into it. Why don't I buy you that drink and we can—'

'I've got to go.' Cutting off Ady's voice, Robyn started the engine.

# 29

Robyn drove back to the police station without putting the radio on until the pool car's unfamiliar noises became too distracting. The one o'clock local news featured Khalid, giving wise words about child safety.

In the incident room, the team huddled in one corner. There didn't seem to be a lot of work going on. The only person at a screen was Ravi, reading out tweets. 'Ouch. Don't want ones like this. *Bitch shud get hunged for taking a kiddie.*'

Robyn put down her handbag.

Ravi pointed at the screen. 'Finally, a good one. *Little Ben safe & no one harmed him. Nothing else important.*'

The door opened. The team sat up straighter when they realised it was Fell. Behind him, a man in a pale grey suit stooped to pass through the doorway. Robyn stood and waited for the introduction. With Professional Standards carrying out an investigation in the station, there would now be someone who would attract more attention than her.

Fell cleared his throat. 'DI Lance Farnham of the Professional Standards team, DI Robyn Bailley.'

Robyn shook Lance's bony hand.

From the doorway, Fell glanced around. 'I will leave you to it, DI Farnham. Please let Tracey know if there is anything you require.' He lowered his voice. 'Bailley, do you know where Josh Warrener is now?'

'He's in Cornwall. I got through to him about half an hour ago and told him the facts. He was shocked. He didn't know about Ben and said he needed time to think. I warned him not to speak to journalists.'

Fell nodded. 'I am meeting the PCC for the rest of the morning. Please keep me updated.'

Robyn introduced the team and Lance shook each hand with the same solemn courtesy and minimal words. When it was Graham's turn, Robyn thought she saw a slight narrowing of Lance's eyes, gone in a second. Graham gave no indication he recognised Lance and Robyn filed it as a question for another day, settling herself to complete her statement.

'DI Bailley? Are you free now?' At least Lance had the courtesy to frame it as a question Robyn thought as they stepped together into the lift. She could see his distorted reflection in the steel doors; his lips were pursed to whistle, though no sound emerged. Her stomach rumbled; she hoped the noise of the lift disguised it.

As they passed the canteen, the smell of food made Robyn's stomach protest again. 'Where are we going?'

Lance led her out into the car park. 'I need you to be present when I interview DC Warrener. My car's over there.'

Robyn stopped for a second, then hurried down the steps to keep up. 'You might have let me know.' She hadn't expected this to happen and needed to find out how much Lance suspected: the interview would be a test for her as well as Janice.

Lance didn't appear to be listening. The driver's seat was as far back as it could go: he probably wouldn't fit into most cars. The interior was spotless, a sat-nav on the dashboard.

Lance clicked his phone into its holder. 'I've listened to your interview with Martin Warrener.' He took his time releasing the handbrake. 'Do you really believe he wasn't aware beforehand?'

Robyn stiffened, choosing her words with care. 'I know Janice. She's always thinking of others. I think it's likely she didn't say anything because she'd checked and found out Josh's paternity wasn't recorded, meaning there'd be nothing they could do. She wanted to tell Josh face-to-face, then before she could do that, she met Ben by chance.' She paused. Lance was still an unknown quantity and so she needed to be careful.

There was no immediate reaction. Lance was pre-occupied with manoeuvring the car out of the car park.

'Can you direct me?'

Robyn wondered why Lance needed directions when he had a sat-nav, then noticed the red light on the phone. If Lance was recording the conversation, the sat-nav's interruptions would disturb the playback. 'Yes, of course. Take the third exit from the roundabout, where the bus is going.'

'Tell me about your relationship with DC Warrener.' Lance wasn't looking at her but, if there was a sound recorder in the car, why not a camera too? Robyn made an effort to relax her shoulders, hands loose in her lap.

'Janice has reported to me since I took the DI role in Meresbourne two years ago. She's a meticulous officer, always very supportive of her colleagues. You need to be in the right-hand lane.'

'I understand your relationship is very close.'

At least there was no innuendo in the tone. Robyn looked across but Lance's gaze stayed on the road. She coughed. 'I've known Janice since I started on the force.'

'Describe how DC Warrener conducted herself during this investigation.' Lance slowed, allowing a car to pull in front of them.

Robyn calculated how far she could protest. The more she wound Lance up, the worse the outcome could be for Janice. They were still waiting to get onto the roundabout. Opportunities came and went. Behind them, someone hooted. Lance waited until the road was clear before edging forward and taking the Gaddesford turn.

Robyn made her decision. 'DI Farnham, I don't appreciate you treating me like an idiot or recording me without warning. I know why you're here and I'm happy to answer all your questions. You don't have to try to trick me.'

Lance's fingers tightened on the wheel. 'I just wonder how you could have missed this happening right under your nose.'

After what felt like a long time in silence, they pulled into the driveway of the police house in Gaddesford. As they got out of the car, Robyn tried a more conversational tack. 'I was here only yesterday – a burglary around the corner. Do you do regular investigation work as well?'

Lance pulled boxes from the boot. 'Why did you attend a routine crime scene when you had a missing child?'

It wasn't clear whether he didn't do small talk or whether she had offended him. Robyn gritted her teeth, then forced herself to relax. 'Because this was the seventh incident in a series with escalating violence. It's a priority for the superintendent.'

Lance set off up the path, laden with equipment, then stood at the door, unable to do anything until Robyn reached around him and pressed the bell.

Phil opened the door without a greeting. He pointed them towards the hard chairs in the front room which had been set up as a basic office. A copy of the *Daily Journal* was open at the puzzles' page; a Sudoku half-completed.

Robyn made brief introductions. There was a clatter on the stairs and Janice came in, her smile fading when she saw Lance. She had made an effort: even her hair was under control, tucked into an Alice band. Robyn nodded to her: just one colleague greeting another.

Phil sat behind the desk, glowering. 'We are honoured, ma'am. This station normally opens only on Tuesdays and every other Saturday. And now a DI and a PS turn up.' He pronounced it 'piss', nose wrinkling, as if there were a bad smell.

Robyn had hoped for an ally. Phil's presence wouldn't help. 'We appreciate your time, Phil.' The lines on Phil's forehead deepened.

Lance stepped forward. 'We need an interview room: where is it?'

Phil pointed. 'Upstairs. The room away from the road is quietest. Need a hand, sir?'

Hoping for a chance to speak to Janice, Robyn hung back until Lance spoke from the foot of the stairs.

'DI Bailley – if you could come with me, please?'

As Robyn followed Lance, she caught a look of contempt suggesting that Matthew had passed on her dissatisfaction about his team not finding the sweatshirt. Robyn registered it but anything she said now would draw unnecessary attention to Janice's actions. She walked upstairs behind Lance, then watched as he set up and tested his equipment. She went to the toilet and returned to find Phil in conversation with Lance about cricket.

'Ask DC Warrener to step up.' Phil nodded and started downstairs, without protest.

Janice slipped in and sat down, making a reflex movement to tuck a strand of hair behind her ear.

Lance finished setting up the recorder. 'Interview commencing sixteen forty-eight on twenty-first of July. Present, DI Bailley, DI Farnham and DC Warrener, who is the subject of the investigation.' He cautioned her. Janice's lips moved in time with his.

'DC Warrener, to confirm for the tape, you have chosen not to have a lawyer present?' Lance clicked the end of his ballpoint.

'Please call me Janice.' She sounded hesitant.

'Do you require a lawyer?'

'No.'

'I require access to your house.'

222

Robyn ran through yesterday's frantic race to remove the
and clothes. She reviewed whether they'd left any cupboard
anything that might show they'd been searching.

'My house. Oh, yes.' Janice blinked.

Confident they'd covered everything, Robyn leant forward. 'I ha
the keys, I can take you there.' She hoped she sounded relaxed and
professional.

'Tell me what happened on Monday morning.' Lance's attention
had shifted back to Janice.

A slight flush showed on Janice's throat. 'Martin said I could
choose my birthday present so on Monday – Monday was my birthday
– Martin, oh, Martin's my husband.' Janice stopped, trying to smile.
'Sorry, I'm not used to being on this side. Shall I start again?'

'Just the facts, please.' Lance's pen was poised over a page, blank
except for an underlined title.

Janice gave a dry cough. 'I went to the shopping centre on Monday
because I had a day off for my birthday. We were going out for lunch
later so I'd dressed up a bit.' She paused for a second. 'My husband
had asked what I wanted for my present and I'd set my heart on some
pearls. We'd agreed I'd go and choose because Martin hates shopping, then he'd buy them when his pension came in, at the end of the
month. Not very romantic maybe but we've been married twenty-
eight years and I suppose it's lucky we're still speaking at all.'

Robyn smiled, encouraged Janice could still attempt a joke.

Lance didn't. He stroked the pen.

'Because I wasn't actually going to buy anything, I didn't have my
bag with me.' Janice stopped again.

Robyn dug into her bag and found a pencil. It was a relief to be able
to flick it around her fingers.

Lance sniffed. 'Go on.'

'Yes, of course. I was outside the jeweller's when I saw a toddler
being attacked by a group of teenagers.' All of Janice's throat was
flushed a dull red.

as being attacked?'

nodded. 'When I turned around, I saw all these youths
ing around a toddler. I didn't know it was Ben.'

obyn shifted her chair into a position where she'd be able to see
at Lance wrote.

'Go on.'

'So I panicked. I ran over and picked the boy up and got him away
from them.' Janice paused again, eyes fixed on Lance's pad.

Robyn concentrated on keeping her breathing natural and her
expression neutral. Everything she'd seen so far about Lance suggested he wouldn't welcome someone else asking questions. She
might be on this side of the desk but she was a suspect.

'And then?'

'Well, this is where I suppose everything will sound stupid. I'd just
got the letter with the DNA results to tell me I had a grandson and
there he was in front of me. When I was sure he was all right, I went
to find a guard because I didn't have my phone with me. I thought the
obvious place to look would be the security corridor.'

Lance made the first marks on his pad. Robyn glanced over but the
page had just the lines and curves of shorthand.

'There was no one around.' Janice paused. 'So because I knew
where Ben lived, I thought I'd take him home.'

'To his home or to your home?'

Janice raised her eyes. 'To his home.'

'How did you intend to get him home?'

Robyn's teeth were jammed together, toes curling in her shoes. She
had just remembered the brand-new car seat, still sitting in Janice's
car, on her driveway.

There was a knock at the door.

Grateful for the interruption, Robyn stood up before Lance could
say anything. She walked to the door opening it enough to see out.

'Thought you should know, there's a journalist outside.' Phil was
craning his neck to try and see in.

'Thanks for the warning. Can you give Khalid Guler a call?'

'If you say so. Ma'am.'

'Just let him know, thanks, Phil.' Robyn shut the door and returned to her seat. Lance was checking something on his phone. Janice's eyes met hers. She mouthed 'car seat' and hoped it had got through, covering the movement with a cough. Lance looked up then transferred his attention back to Janice.

'I'd just bought a car seat.' Janice's eyes were very bright. 'I've started baby-sitting for Donna in Uniform and because she works shifts, it's easier for me to pick her lad up.'

Outside, Phil's feet banged down the uncarpeted stairs. Robyn watched Lance, his fingers tapping the pen, tendons flickering in his lean arms.

Dropping his eyes, Lance made another series of marks. 'If you were taking him to his home, why did you hide his sweatshirt?'

'I didn't.'

'You didn't?' Lance made another quick mark on the page.

Janice took a quick breath. 'No, he did it himself. I didn't notice until we got to the car. He'd looked so hot and uncomfortable, I'm not surprised he wanted to get rid of it.'

'Go on.'

'When I saw how much he wanted to get rid of the school sweat-shirt, I remembered what I'd seen at his house. 'ow he was mis-treated.' Janice set her jaw. 'How he was abused.' She breathed in. 'I wanted to protect him. I didn't think what I was doing, it was instinct.'

'During a routine visit, three months ago, you say you observed a child being abused.' Lance paused. 'What did you do about it at the time?'

Robyn was dreading Janice's answer. Part of her admired Lance's technique, part of her wanted to scream.

'I took the material for a DNA test. Without that, I didn't believe there was anything I could do.' Janice's voice was little more than a whisper. 'The law wouldn't recognise an offence as there were no apparent physical problems. I thought we might be able to get access to Ben if we could prove we were his family.' She stuck her chin out. 'It's not Martin's fault, he didn't know. I made him help me.'

Lance folded his arms. 'You didn't tell your husband he had a grandson? For the record, you are saying he found out when you arrived home with the child?'

Janice nodded. 'Until the DNA was confirmed, there was no point: I might have been all wrong.' She stared down at her hands. 'When he saw Ben, he said we should report it until I told him about the abuse. We're going to apply for formal custody. I know I've been stupid and everything's been done the wrong way, of course it's wrong but I did all this to keep him safe.' The last words came in a choking rush.

'DC Warrener, do you expect me to believe any of this?' Lance put the pen down with a sharp rap. 'You're in the shopping centre, wearing sunglasses covering your face and just happen to find your grandson. Despite being a police officer for nearly thirty years, you claim you panicked. You then kept him at your house for four days, during which time you worked on the investigation into his disappearance.'

There was nothing Robyn could do. She sat still, concentrating on keeping her own face calm and her breathing steady. Outside the room, there were the sounds of footsteps on the stairs.

'As a minimum, we have charges of withholding information, dereliction of duty and unbecoming conduct, before we even start on the abduction.'

'I know what I did was stupid. But I did this for Ben. If you could ask him, he'd tell you where he wants to be.'

'Interview concluded at seventeen fourteen. DC Warrener, you remain under caution and may not leave here without my permission.' He stood up.

Janice turned towards Robyn, her face creased into panic. 'Where's Martin? Is he all right? When's Josh coming back?' She clutched the edge of the table. 'Robyn, tell me everyone's all right?'

Ignoring Lance's questioning gaze, Robyn reached across the table. 'I spoke to Martin earlier, Janice. He's fine. Worried about you, of course.' Janice's fingers were cold under hers. 'I've also spoken to Josh.' Janice's face lit up. 'He's confused and said he needed some time to think.'

'Is he coming home?'

'Not yet. He needed some time.' Janice pulled her hand away. Robyn wanted to say something but Lance was holding the door open. She left the room, hearing the door close behind her.

Phil was drinking tea in the office.

'What did Khalid say?' Robyn knew he was trying to wind her up and was annoyed with herself for letting him succeed.

'Couldn't get through.' Phil shrugged.

Lance's steps sounded on the stair. Robyn spoke quickly 'You messed up. Don't push it.' The harshness in her voice caught her by surprise.

Phil's mouth twitched. He took another mouthful of tea before answering. 'Oh I'm sorry, ma'am. I didn't realise you were so sensitive. Is it your time of the month?'

Lance appeared in the doorway.

'We shall discuss this back at the station.' Robyn turned her back on Phil and spoke to Lance. 'The journalist is still outside. We don't want anything to draw attention to the activity here. Can we wait a bit before we leave?'

Lance made his way to the window and peered through the blinds, without caring if he were seen. 'He's leaving.' The scooter buzzed away, in the direction of the Markhams.

More to avoid being left alone with Phil, Robyn grabbed some of Lance's equipment and took it out to the car. As she fastened her seat belt, Lance reached for the sat-nav.

If they turned right, they would be going back to the station. Left meant he was going to inspect Janice's house. Lance clipped the sat-nav into its cradle. *Turn left.* The journey passed in silence. When they

227

got to the house, Lance peered under the tarpaulin at the new car seat then waited for Robyn to unlock the house and deactivate the burglar alarm. She excused herself and went upstairs to the bathroom, risking a quick glance into Josh's room at the top of the stairs as she passed. Lance was on the landing when she came out.

'Why didn't you use the toilet downstairs?'

Every response had to be consistent. 'Is there one? I'd forgotten. I've only been in the house once apart from yesterday and that was a year ago.'

'Where did they keep the boy?'

She could have so easily told him. 'I don't know. Ben is Josh's son so maybe in his room?' She pointed at the animal letters spelling 'Joshua', hoping he didn't see her gripping the bathroom door handle.

Lance turned into the room. Inside, the single bed was made up with Batman covers. He opened a wardrobe. Robyn moved to get a better view. The clothes were faded and sized for a child bigger than Ben.

'This matches what he was wearing when I found him. I guess these are their children's old clothes they had in the loft.'

'You should not be here, DI Bailley. I am the investigating officer.'

To be safe, Robyn left the house and stood in the porch, trying to follow Lance's movements from the faint sounds within.

'Oh hello. It's you. I heard the alarm being deactivated so I thought I should check it out.' Janice's neighbour walked up the drive, with Janice's terrier and a Labradoodle on leads. 'Janice and Martin not back yet?'

'No, I'm afraid not. Thanks for checking up.'

'While I'm here, I wanted to look for Morrison's tablets. Janice said he needed something for his joints. Mind if I ...?'

She held out the leads to Robyn who took them without thinking. The woman walked through the front door, the terrier straining to go with her until his lead slipped out of Robyn's hand and the dog dashed into the house. Following him into the kitchen, Robyn retrieved Morrison and watched the woman opening cupboards.

'DI Bailley. What is going on?'

'This lady is a neighbour. She came for the dog's pills.' There didn't seem any point in trying to explain it further.

'Here they are.' The woman held up a packet. 'I'll leave you to whatever you're doing. Give my best to Janice.' She took the leads from Robyn, casting a searching glance up to Lance as he stood aside to let her pass.

Lance turned without comment and walked out. Robyn locked up and joined him in the car. She would no doubt have to account for her behaviour at some point, the question was whether the interrogation would come sooner or later.

'Where will you be for the rest of the afternoon?'

'I'll be in the incident room.' She knew he wanted to keep her on edge, rather than give the certainty of a definite time.

'Let me know before you go anywhere.'

*In one hundred yards, turn left.* The rest of the journey passed in silence.

When they reached the police station, Lance marched across the car park without a word. Robyn was in no mood to pander to him and let him go. He reached the top of the steps and swiped his pass across the door sensor. As she ambled across, he was tugging at the door without success.

Robyn climbed the steps at an even pace. 'Here, let me.' The door clicked open.

By the lift, Lance called over his shoulder. 'I'm going to see Fell now.' He started up the stairs, taking them two at a time.

Wanting to stretch her legs, Robyn decided to walk up. A few steps above her, Lance spun around. Robyn's face was level with his flies. 'You briefed her then?'

229

A cleaner appeared at the turn of the stairs, putting a bucket down with a clank. She stroked a mop along the landing, stray drops of water flying down.

Robyn took a grip on the bannister. 'DI Farnham, I do have other cases. Please let me know when my formal interview will be.' She called up the stairs. 'We'll get out of your way. DI Farnham? After you.' Lance strode up the stairs. Robyn let out a long breath and watched his departing back before turning downstairs for the canteen.

The incident room was already reverting to its usual layout, the additional tables gone, extra chairs stacked in a corner. Lorraine, Ravi, Graham and Chloe were clustered in front of the television, watching the news. Robyn caught a glimpse of herself on screen and turned away.

The evidence boards bristled with paper. Robyn began removing items, until she uncovered the map showing the burglaries, each marked with a pin and label summarising what had been stolen, all in Janice's tiny handwriting.

When she'd cleared one board, she started on the other and put up the pictures taken from the warehouse and images of the damaged skull. The news turned to an unexploded bomb somewhere and Ravi switched off the TV. Robyn didn't turn to the team until she'd finished. Everyone was watching her.

'Right. You all had things to follow up. I don't mind which of you goes first.'

Everyone suddenly seemed to have something else to do. She looked from one to the other: Ravi appeared engrossed by the blank TV screen; Graham had buried his nose in a report; Lorraine rummaged in her handbag. Only Chloe faced her, looking uncomfortable, feet swinging above the floor.

Robyn was getting impatient with everyone's passivity. 'OK, fine, we'll start with the burglary. Ravi, can you get this map updated, please? The latest job isn't shown or the first one in May. Lorraine, have you spoken to the victim?'

'I checked with the hospital, Guv. Mrs Jarvis is still too frail for visitors. We've already got the outline forensic report but unfortunately, there were no prints and the village only has CCTV in the main square so no pictures.'

'Pictures.' A faint memory surfaced. Robyn's inbox was full of hundreds of unread emails, all screaming their importance. She scanned through them, searching for anything from Ady. 'Got it.' The message had a link to a photo library and a login. She tried the link. 'OK, why doesn't the password work?'

'Here, let me, Guv.' Ravi leant over and tapped into the keyboard. The screen opened to a list of events. 'Right, sort events by date. May: Gaddesford festival – here we are, Guv, seventy-one pictures.'

'Thanks, Ravi. OK, check those. If Lorraine's right and this was the first crime, then our man could be pictured here. Look for a cyclist in black Lycra.'

Robyn turned to Graham. 'Have you got the full autopsy report?'

Graham held up a document. 'I'll say one thing for the new doc, he's to the point. Not like Doc Drummond and his 'venture to suggest'. This one tells you things you need to know in ten pages without too many long words.'

Robyn sat, knowing Graham would be more communicative with the audience on him. 'Let's have it then.'

Graham held the report at arm's length. 'First, the bad news. She's not on the DNA register but definitely female so at least that's fifty percent of the population eliminated.' He glanced around.

No one said anything. The thought entering Robyn's head would be what a similar test would say about her.

He turned a page. 'OK, age eighteen to twenty-four, because something unpronounceable hasn't fused and some other bone has done. The doc's confident the murderer used a hammer because the holes in the skull had clean edges. Listen to this though. He found another wound to the side of the head, which he says must have been the first blow.' Graham checked again to make sure they were all listening. 'That means the killer didn't need to be strong because the first blow would have stunned the victim and she'd probably have been lying on the floor when she was hit in the face.'

He turned the page. 'Here's something else new: the skeleton had reduced bone density and the most likely cause is the girl suffered from anorexia as a teenager.' He put the report down. 'Another nasty note. After the body was dumped in the maintenance pit, caustic soda was used to rot the flesh and clothes.' There was a squeak as Chloe shifted in her chair.

The memory of the dust from the warehouse made Robyn swallow. 'What about a date of death?'

Graham flicked to the last page. 'He can't be precise about it because of the chemicals. Between two and five years.' He cracked one knuckle, then the next. 'He say any one of the blows to the face was hard enough to kill. Someone wanted this girl wiped off the earth.'

Robyn tapped the photo on the board. 'Thanks, Graham. I think you're right, this isn't a random attack because someone went to a lot of trouble to dispose of her. So our priority is to identify this woman and find out who hated her enough to do this.'

'Yeah!' Ravi banged the table.

Robyn permitted herself a sliver of hope. With a purpose, the team would keep going, so she needed to keep them occupied. If they blamed her for Janice, they were doing a good job of hiding their feelings. She glanced at her watch: it was already nearly half past six. Without thinking, she clapped her hands.

'Listen up, everyone. We've all been working hard. I know this hasn't been an easy time so let's go and have a drink and welcome Chloe to the team. I'm buying.'

Smiling, Chloe got up. She was the only one. A phone rang and Ravi stretched out to answer it. The one-sided conversation seemed loud because no one else was speaking.

Her optimism draining, Robyn waited. 'Well?'

Graham was unfolding a paper clip. 'Nice idea. But it seems wrong to go out ...' He tailed off.

'We can't go out without Janice.' Lorraine blinked. 'What will happen to her?'

'I don't know. Fell wants everything done by the book which means DI Farnham is leading this investigation. It's not my decision. I'm sorry.'

No one seemed keen to be the first to say anything until Lorraine checked her watch and screeched she was late for a band rehearsal.

Ravi got to his feet, muttering something about hockey training.

Graham grabbed his jacket from the back of his chair. 'Sorry, Guv.'

Robyn watched them go. That had been her first attempt at a team social and, with hindsight, she'd misjudged their mood. She began gathering her own things. An early night would be good. She could try and have a decent conversation with Becky, if it wasn't too soon. On the way to the door, Robyn stopped beside Chloe, who had sat back down and was going through the missing persons' list. 'We'll have a drink for you another day. You must have something to do this evening too?'

'Not much, Guv.' Chloe wasn't as cheerful as usual. 'I'm new around here and I still don't know too many people.' Her left hand clenched, then relaxed. 'And my ambition has always been to become a detective ...'

Robyn was relieved nothing was being taken personally. 'Well, you've made a good start. Do you still want a drink? It's been one of those weeks where I could really do with one.'

# FRIDAY 22 JULY

# 30

Whether it had been the couple of pints, the fish and chips picked up on the way home or just the joy of talking to someone who hadn't yet become cynical, Robyn slept better than she expected and started Friday early. A text from the garage said respraying the Mondeo would take a week, meaning she had more time to dispose of the things from Janice's house before she handed the pool car back. She strolled down to the canteen with Graham for a cup of tea, chatting about the Dockers' chances for the new season. She allowed herself a hint of optimism that things would somehow work out for the best.

Back in the incident room, Khalid manoeuvred through the door sideways, carrying a pile of newspapers which he dumped on Robyn's desk. On top, the *Daily Journal* devoted their front page to a picture of Ben, taken outside the police station, under the headline: *Safe*. At the bottom of the page, an inset picture of her had the caption: *Trans cop's painted lips are sealed on snatcher's identity.*

Robyn gestured at the pile. 'Is any of this worth reading?'

Khalid shrugged. 'Most papers have understood why we can't release a name yet so instead, we have lots of theories as to where Ben was. Now we need something bad to happen somewhere else to distract everyone.'

Robyn studied his face to see if he were joking: it was fifty-fifty.

'There is one thing though.' Shuffling through the sheets, Khalid pulled out the *Gazette*, turning to an inside page. 'After all the usual bits about finding Ben, there's a bit of a hatchet job on Ms Chivers' church and some of their more extreme views. There's some really nasty things they do to kids to convince them that hell is real and punishments that sound like exorcisms to me. I don't think they would have dared run this if Ben were still missing.'

Their phones rang simultaneously. Khalid grimaced. 'I've got to go.' He turned and set off up the corridor, passing Lorraine walking in.

Robyn gritted her teeth as she pressed the button. 'Morning, Tracey, how are you?'

'Well, thanks. You?' Her voice was brisk.

'Arrived and had my first cup of tea.'

'Lucky you. You might have got me one. Well, good thing you're awake, because the superintendent wants everything with Professional Standards wrapped up today. He's got a meeting with the chief this afternoon so he needs to know what charges will be brought.'

Robyn bit her lower lip. She had to stop doing that if she wanted the lipstick to last more than five minutes. 'OK, Tracey, thanks for letting me know. Bye.' She stared at the phone for a moment, wondering whether she should try to call Josh again.

The team seemed to be all putting on brave faces, until Lance arrived. Robyn showed him to Janice's desk since it was the tidiest: paper filed into plastic wallets by subject and notebooks sorted by date. Lance raised the chair to its maximum, his feet now flat on the floor with two inches of white calf showing above grey socks. In response to the offer of tea, he accepted hot water then rummaged in his rucksack and produced teabags of some herbal variety with a humid, green scent. He'd acquired a lot of paper which seemed to hold his attention, the team quiet around him.

When Susan from Family Liaison's name appeared on her phone, Robyn hesitated and let it go to voicemail.

*You'll never guess what the crazy bitch has done now. I refused to go back there so Laura got assigned. She said Gillian opened the door nearly in tears, then calls for Ms Chivers and the woman wouldn't even let her in the house! Apparently, she's moving to Switzerland in a week. Good riddance, I say. Bye.*

She controlled her urge to kick something. Somehow, she would have to tell Janice. She fidgeted at her desk for a few minutes, keeping an eye on Lance, anticipating a request for an interview, then wondered whether this apparent indifference was a tactic. If she allowed his presence to get to her, then it would worry the team. She needed to keep them and herself busy. 'Chloe, where are we with the missing persons list?'

Chloe jumped. 'Nearly finished, Guv. I've been through the list for women reported missing between two and five years ago. There's a lot of them, even if you take out anyone over twenty-five. But I think we can cut the list further.' Chloe seemed pleased with herself. 'When Graham said I should work on the murder, I popped into the shoe shop after we'd finished yesterday – just for the investigation, you understand.' She grinned. 'The undamaged shoe had a label with a code on it and I asked an assistant if they could find it on the system.' She held up the evidence bag, pointing at a dirty white square on the shoe's sole. 'Well, they couldn't in the store because they just have current stock so I got a number for Head Office. This design was shipped to stores in mid-November, three years ago.' Chloe glanced at her notes. 'So, I think our girl went missing between then and Christmas, because by Boxing Day, the shoes were in the sale and the labels marked with reduced prices. I'm just running a check now on how many women were reported missing in those six weeks.'

She looked to Graham, who gave her a quick nod. 'Right, here we go. In those six weeks, there were just two women in the right age band reported missing. I'll get their records up now.'

'Good work, Chloe. How come no one else picked that up?' Robyn looked around.

Chloe's smile drained away leaving two bright red spots colouring her cheeks. Beside her, Graham put down his cup so hard, tea slopped onto the desk.

Robyn replayed what she'd just said: Roger had rarely spoken out or courted controversy. From the looks around the room, she risked losing the team with such tactless remarks. She was in danger of becoming Prentiss, praising favourites, needling and nit-picking the rest in front of everyone. Just to add to the humiliation, Lance was probably taking all of this down to use against her later.

She held up her hands – everyone needed to see how sorry she was. 'And I'm counting myself – I know I've missed things – we've just got to keep focused now.' Graham was folding a piece of paper over and over. Someone coughed.

Robyn swore under her breath. All she could do now was keep going. 'So, Chloe, show us the two you've found.'

The team straggled over and gathered round Chloe's screen which showed a picture of a red-headed girl, plump face nestled into the fur of a retriever.

'Emma Caddy, fifteen, went missing from Upper Markham on Friday seventeenth of December, the last day of term. Her mother thought Emma had a sleepover after school.' Chloe took a sip of water. 'She helped Emma pack a rucksack and a sleeping bag then dropped her off at the school gates and that was the last time she was seen. On Saturday, the mother went to pick her up but the girl she was supposed to be staying with said Emma hadn't been at school on the Friday and there hadn't been a party. School friends said Emma was scared about failing her mock GCSEs. Conclusion, she had run away.'

'She was fifteen.' Robyn shook her head. 'Whether she planned it or not, she was a child.'

'Sorry, Guv. Just reading out the notes here.' Chloe's lips pulled together for a second and Robyn wondered whether she should try to explain there were a lot of cases like this on the system, where Kenny Prentiss, or one of his crew, decided a case was too hard and just dropped it. Graham was staring into the screen, his face a blank, tension showing in the rigid set of his jaw.

'I'm sorry, Chloe. Carry on.'

'That's all there is on this one, Guv.'

'I didn't work on this case.' Graham spoke in a rush.

There was silence for a moment. Ravi leant forward, frowning. 'Didn't the doctor suggest the girl in the warehouse was anorexic? Doesn't look likely with her.'

Robyn looked at the screen then at Graham, one second, two. She nodded. 'Agreed.' Graham's face relaxed. Robyn turned back to Chloe. 'OK, who's the other one?'

On the screen, a slim woman with badly-dyed hair stood by a fountain, squinting in bright sunlight. The image must have been scanned from a larger photograph as there was a jagged edge as if someone else had been removed.

Chloe scanned her notes. 'This is probably Turkey. This girl went on holiday just before she went missing.' She cleared her throat. 'Tania Shipford, twenty-two.' She scrolled down the page. 'A few more notes on this one. The last confirmed sighting was at Gatwick Airport when Tania was recorded re-entering the country through passport control on the twenty-fifth of November. She wasn't reported missing until the fourth of December, though. When questioned, her boyfriend claimed they'd had a row on holiday, she'd moved out on the twenty-sixth and he said he didn't even know she was missing.'

Robyn leant forward. 'Sounds interesting. What else?'

Chloe skimmed the pages. 'Boyfriend didn't have an alibi for the weekend after they flew back. When we searched the flat, a lot of her things were still there.' She turned to Graham. 'It says you worked on this one – what happened?'

Graham scratched the back of his neck. 'We couldn't find Tania. We found some stolen stuff in the boyfriend's flat and got him sent down for a few months but we couldn't find anything to pin her disappearance on him.' Chloe was pointing at the screen, mouth open.

Graham sighed. 'Oh, I know it's clear now when you've got everything in front of you. At the time, we were getting information through in tiny pieces.'

'You think her boyfriend murdered her?' Chloe winced as Graham cracked his knuckles.

'I'm sure he did.' Graham changed hands. 'He's a nasty piece of work, a cheap hire if you want someone beaten up. He's not the brightest and his story didn't stand up. There were lots of little things, like if Tania left of her own accord, why didn't she take her asthma inhaler?'

Chloe asked the question Robyn had wanted to ask. 'So why did the investigation stop?'

There was silence. Graham raised his head, saw everyone was staring at him and took a deep breath. 'Tania had a bit of history. She'd started as an escort, ended up on the streets.' He was talking to the wall. 'Her drugs counsellor reported her missing when she missed a second appointment. She didn't have any family to keep pushing it, another case came up and we were short of resources and this got dropped.' He shrugged. 'I wanted to pursue it but Kenny, DI Prentiss, gave me a direct order to leave it.'

Chloe squared her shoulders as if she was about to start a fight: the anger coming from Lorraine was colder. 'So would your precious Kenny Prentiss have told you to leave it if Tania had been a "normal" girl?'

Graham's shoulders hunched forward. 'You only worked for him for six months when he was about to retire. You didn't see what he could be like …'

242

Robyn waved to get everyone's attention and nodded to where Lance sat. He seemed absorbed in papers but she didn't want the team to forget he was there or what he was there to do. 'Right, everyone.' She raised her voice, wanting to put an end to the bickering. 'Stuff happened. What matters is what we do now and the priority is putting away a violent burglar and finding a name for a murdered girl.'

'So Tania could be our ...' Chloe paused. 'Body.'

Robyn nodded. 'A good possibility. Do we have her DNA on file to confirm her identity?' Out of the corner of her eye, she saw Lance stand up.

'I'll look, Guv.' Chloe turned to her screen then jumped as Lance loomed over her monitor. 'Ah, hello. Would you like another cup of tea, sir?'

'I'll be interviewing you first. You don't need to bring anything.' Lance tucked a pen into the breast pocket of his shirt.

Robyn tried to catch Chloe's eye, trying to convey without words there was nothing to worry about. Lance had done exactly what she would have done. If you start the investigation with the person with the least experience, there was the lowest chance of misplaced loyalties getting in the way of evidence.

'A bit odd, isn't it, Guv?' Lorraine watched the door swing shut. 'I mean, interviewing Chloe first, when she's been here all of two days.'

'We'll all need to go through the process. DI Farnham will have his plan and if we want to avoid more of this ...' Robyn gestured at the pile of unread newspapers, '... everything must be reviewed. Meanwhile ...'

'Gotcha!' Ravi punched the air, before spinning his chair round and round. 'Guv, I've got the burglar.' He dashed to the printer and held up a picture. 'Look who's here, mingling with the crowd.' He pointed at a man, casual in cords and a polo shirt, snapped inspecting antiques on a stall. 'There's Roderick Dearman. He was at the Gaddesford festival.'

'Uncle Roddy, well, well.' Graham lumbered over and inspected the picture. 'That's him all right. Liked his antiques did Roddy – last time we questioned him, his house was full of them. Good spot.' He punched Ravi on the shoulder.

Robyn moved to the screen, peering at the picture. 'Does he really ride a bike?'

'More of a Jaguar type I thought but once a criminal, always a criminal.' Graham laughed. 'Even though Roddy's getting on a bit, he could still push a pensioner out of the way. Used to be a bit rough when he was younger. One time he was arrested he needed four constables to hold him down ...'

Robyn held up her hands. 'We'll need more than that picture to go on before we can talk to him. Any sign of cyclists, Ravi?' A closing of his eyebrows made her aware this wasn't helping him feel more relaxed around her.

'Just kids. The pictures are mainly stallholders and shots of acts on the stage.' There was boredom in Ravi's voice. He turned his screen to show Robyn, flicking through a series of pictures of people holding the tools of their trade in front of various stalls. He stopped on a shot of a couple in 1960's dress standing in front of a display of vintage clothes, the effect rather spoilt by the man's heavily tattooed arms.

With a soft wumph, the contents of Robyn's in-tray slid down across the desk. She'd been ignoring paperwork and decided she could leave it no longer. Top of the pile was Graham's mileage log. After a quick check, she signed at the bottom. Her new signature was her full name, the letters curlier than before. As part of her transition, she'd spent a long time coming up with the new signature because it seemed an important symbol, something representing another step in the change. By the sixth piece of paper, she was already bored and the careful tracing had regressed to the old scrawled initials. Chloe slipped back into the office and went to sit by Graham.

Somewhere under the paper, her phone rang. She fumbled it into her hands. 'Hello, Josh.'

'Yeah, hi.'

'Josh, are you OK?'

'Yeah. I've been watching the news. He's everywhere. Does anyone know he's my son?'

'Not yet.' Robyn tapped her pen on the desk. 'I hope you haven't spoken to any journalists?'

'No and if they speak to me, I'll tell them where to get off.'

Robyn raised her voice. 'Josh, if anyone from the press rings you, pretend it's a wrong number, then let Khalid Guler, our media guy, know. I'll text you his number. He's got this under control.'

'Are they going to say things about me or Mum and Dad?' There was a hint of fear in Josh's voice. 'What are they going to do?'

'Josh. JOSH. Calm down. You need to get back here as soon as possible.' Robyn realised she was standing up.

'Yeah, there's a night bus from Newquay getting into Victoria coach station tomorrow morning.'

'Great. I'll come and pick you up from London. Try not to talk to anyone in the meantime.'

'Why are you picking me up? What's happened to Mum and Dad?'

Lance dropped back into Janice's chair. Robyn lowered her voice. 'They're still in custody.'

There was a mumble from the other end, then the line went dead. Robyn let out a snort of frustration. She couldn't let Janice know so there would be no one for Josh to talk to, apart from his friends and social media and the story would be certain to come out. She sent Josh a text confirming arrangements and reminding him to keep everything quiet. The best thing she could do was to get on with her job, which meant getting back to the paperwork. She reached for the next sheet and two slid to the desk. Underneath a memo about the decorators was a page printed from an internet site, the story of man who'd picked up a woman for sex, then murdered her when he realised 'she' was in fact a 'he'. Bits were underlined in red, in case the message needed to be any more obvious.

Covering the page with a form, Robyn swallowed, not wanting to show any concern. If someone had put this into her tray to upset her, then it was someone with access to the CID room. They could be in the room now, waiting for her reaction. Her pulse was high but she was determined she wouldn't give anyone watching her the satisfaction of knowing she was upset. The insults were childish: chick with a dick, pervert. She screwed up the paper and dropped it into the bin. The only thing that bothered her was wondering whether the person that put it there was the same one that had vandalised her car.

Graham groaned. He was making some point to Chloe, his finger jabbing the desk. She was slumping in her chair.

'What's the matter with you two?' A distraction was welcome.

'Tania had broken her arm six months before she disappeared.' Graham held up the autopsy report. 'The doctor doesn't mention anything about bone injuries in his report. It's not her.'

# 31

'Bugger.' Robyn tapped on the desk. Since her nails had been longer, they gave a satisfying, crisp noise. 'So if the body isn't Tania, either the dates are wrong …' She caught Chloe's grimace. 'Don't worry Chloe – it's not a criticism of you. You had a good idea, it just didn't work out. Most don't. The other possibility is she's not on the missing person's list.'

Chloe didn't quite manage a smile. 'So if the person isn't on the list, how do we find her, Guv?'

'We start by checking a month or so either side – the shop may have been wrong about the dates the shoes were stocked, or they missed being marked up for the sale. If we get nothing there, we'll have to do things the old-fashioned way and try to identify her from her dental profile. That's what being a detective's like, Chloe – having to visit every dentist in Meresbourne and the villages …'

'Couldn't we just email them all the scan?'

Robyn couldn't stop herself laughing. Chloe looked blank. Graham was also chuckling, his laugh turning into a cough. 'You young people …' He adopted a passable imitation of Fell's conference drone. 'Statistics show eighty-nine point two percent of recruits to the police force in the last five years don't know they're born.'

Behind his screen, Ravi chortled.

'DC Sharma? You're next please.' Lance was standing next to his desk. Ravi froze, then shut his mouth and he followed Lance out of the room.

'Ah, he's going for those who've been in the team the least time.' Graham's lips pressed together for a second. 'So you'll be next, Guv, then Lorraine and maybe he'll get to me by Tuesday.'

Lorraine walked to the door. 'Guv, there's a vintage and craft fair in Lower Markham tomorrow, just like the one in Gaddesford. I was thinking of checking it out – what do you think?'

Robyn nodded, pleased with the thought of action. 'Good idea. I'll come along. I'm picking up Josh in the morning from Victoria coach station and will drop him at Janice's. Meet me by the Air Force memorial at eleven o'clock and make sure you've got the full list of the stolen property.'

Over in the corner, Robyn heard Chloe saying to Graham, 'But if the body isn't Tania Shipford, then we need to find her as well …' Graham's reply was inaudible. Robyn settled down to the paperwork again.

When Ravi returned from his interview with Lance, Robyn glanced at her watch. Given it was nearly one thirty, she felt justified in having a break, even though there were still emails to answer. 'I'm going down to the canteen, would anyone like anything?'

Chloe declined. Ravi was unwrapping the lavish package he got from home each day, the smell of spices confirming lunch was over-due. Graham stood up. 'I'll come with you.'

As they stepped out, Graham scanned up and down the corridor. 'Guv, it's about these interviews …'

Lance appeared from the stairwell. 'DI Bailley, I'd like to speak to you now.'

Graham was already halfway through the incident room door.

She and Lance took the lift to the basement. Neither spoke. They sat facing each other in the interview room. Robyn shifted on the hard seat. Lance hadn't switched on the recorder.

'Fell needs–' 'The investigation is–'

They both stopped and looked at each other. After you.' Robyn sat back.

'I need to give a conclusion to Fell in the next hour. The facts of the case aren't up for debate – DC Warrener took the child.' Lance paused, waiting for a reaction. 'The two questions are whether she planned to take him and whether the investigation was flawed.' Lance tapped the table. 'I need to give Fell my assessment of whether something stopped you seeing what was going on under your nose.'

The wrong response here could ruin her career as well as Janice's. It would help no one if she allowed herself to be provoked. Robyn smiled, hoped the expression didn't seem too forced. 'I've been asking myself the same question.' She had to keep calm. 'I've been a detective a long time. I don't believe I've treated this case differently from any other. Ms Chivers is a lady whose controversial views polarise opinions. Janice's concerns didn't stand out because they were shared by other members of the team. Ms Chivers' complaint about me was not relating to the investigation but because, well, she thinks I'm …' She coughed, started again. 'Ms Chivers does not believe gender realignment should be allowed.' Lance marked his pad.

Robyn found herself flicking a pen and made a conscious effort to stop. 'As soon as I had a suspicion, I acted. I could have warned Janice to hide Ben before I went to her house. But I didn't.'

'That would be more believable if you had told someone where you were going and hadn't waited almost an hour before reporting it.' Lance was watching her without blinking.

'Janice and Martin were trying to get in touch with their son.'

'We'll see.' In the corridor, someone was yelling. 'Is their son coming back?'

Robyn nodded. 'I'm picking him up tomorrow morning.'

'OK. Well, we can grant bail for the husband by then. He won't go anywhere.'

'Thanks.'

The yelling sounded again from further down the corridor. Footsteps pounded past.

'You admitted you lacked focus.' Lance shuffled in his seat.

'Do you think …?' Robyn shook her head. 'Do you really think I'm not aware of the comments and criticism about me?'

Lance stood up, now towering over her.

'Do you know what I got today?' Robyn stood and stepped in front of Lance. 'Someone put a note in my in-tray suggesting I'll get beaten up. To be clear, the in-tray on my desk in the incident room. Earlier this week, someone trashed my car in the car park downstairs. So it's someone in this station. I think I'm focusing pretty well, considering.'

Lance folded his arms across his chest. 'I have to see Fell.'

'Do you want me to come with you?'

'No. I believe you have other cases.' Lance stepped around her and let himself out.

Robyn kicked the table leg once, twice. The second time hurt. She'd forgotten women's shoes weren't as sturdy as men's.

Her phone rang. 'Hello, Graham.'

Graham's voice was taut. 'Guv, Janice has been named on TV.'

She kicked the table again. 'Bugger. How?' A beep on the line. 'Graham, Khalid's trying to get hold of me. Must be the same thing.' She switched lines. 'Khalid.'

'The media know it's Janice.'

'Graham just told me.'

There was a hard edge to Khalid's voice she hadn't heard before. 'Can you come up? We'll need to see Fell.'

Robyn limped to the lift. On the fifth floor, the new paint was bright in the sunshine, the smell still strong. Khalid was watching something on his tablet. He saw Robyn and turned the screen to her. A dark-haired woman was talking into the camera, in front of Janice's house.

'That's Janice's neighbour. I spoke to her yesterday when she came to fetch the dog. Either she spotted Ben at some point, or recognised me from the TV and put two and two together.'

Khalid silenced the tablet. 'Now everyone'll be trying to find out where Janice is.'

'Didn't Phil tell you there was a journalist outside Gaddesford police house yesterday when I was there with DI Farnham?'

Khalid rolled his eyes. 'No. Better and better. OK, we need to get a statement out sharpish. Has matey-boy made his decision yet?'

'DI Farnham's with Fell at the moment.'

Khalid stood up. 'OK, let's go and give them the good news.'

Tracey scanned their faces as they walked in. Without asking what they wanted, she stood and knocked on the inner door. Fell held his hands steepled in front of him. Lance sat folded in the guest chair. Khalid cleared his throat. 'I'm sorry to interrupt, superintendent. We have a problem: the media have got hold of Janice's name.'

'How did this get out?' Fell tugged his moustache.

'Janice's neighbour identified her.' Khalid paused. 'There was no leak from anyone within the police station.'

'We are in a position to action the second part of the media strategy.' Fell cleared his throat. 'Farnham, would you summarise your findings?'

Lance gathered himself. 'DC Warrener will be charged with parental abduction and dereliction of duty. Mr Warrener will be charged with concealing evidence.'

Robyn tried not to appear pleased. It was better than she'd dared hope but would still mean a prison sentence. Her mouth was dry.

'And on the other matter?' There was no change in Fell's tone.

Lance coughed, crossing then uncrossing his legs. 'I've concluded DI Bailley's personal situation didn't have a material effect on the investigation. In relation to the additional allegation of bringing the

251

force into disrepute, although the approaches adopted can be unconventional, I see no evidence to support it.'

Someone in the station had made a formal complaint about her. The room was hot but Robyn now found it overwhelming. Lights flashed in front of her eyes; maybe it was just the flickering sunshine through the blinds. She had to bend her knees to stabilise herself. Beside her, Khalid mouthed something, concern in his eyes. Robyn nodded to him and concentrated on staying upright. Neither Fell nor Lance seemed to have noticed.

'So, Guler, prepare details for me to meet the media. Do we need a press briefing?'

Khalid pulled a sheet of paper from his folder. 'I've prepared a draft statement already and I think speed is important here.' He glanced at his phone. 'If you're happy with this, we could give people an hour to get here and organise a briefing for three o'clock.'

Fell brushed his moustache with the tip of a finger. 'That seems reasonable. Bailley, you had better let Ms Chivers know. I want you to be there when I give the statement.' He turned to Lance. 'Thank you for your input, DI Farnham. I shall await your formal report.'

Robyn walked as far as the lift with Lance. 'Do you want help with any of your equipment?'

'No, thank you, DI Bailley.' Lance pushed the button for the basement.

Robyn got out at the second floor. In the CID office, the team relaxed when they realised it was her. Robyn remained standing. 'DI Farnham has made his decision. It's the minimum charge we could expect. Because the news has leaked, there's going to be a press briefing in an hour. I suggest you all go home before then, because the media will be chasing everyone for stories.'

'Will DI Farnham be leaving?' Graham was trying too hard to sound casual.

'I don't know. He was reporting on an internal complaint about me.' Graham gasped. 'Fell seemed satisfied so I've got to meet the media with him.' Robyn sat down trying to catch her breath in the stuffy room. The earlier wooziness was returning and she wanted to be alone.

'Someone complained about you? From here, in the station?'

'Yes. Bringing the police force into disrepute.'

Graham laughed, a full belly-laugh. 'Sorry, Guv. You disreputable? A bit like charging Snow White with scrumping apples.'

Ravi stuck his head around his screen. 'Guv, I've been doing a bit of digging on the woman who shopped Janice ...'

'No, Ravi. Whatever it is, no.' She sighed. 'We've got the best we could hope for. Good work everyone, now bugger off. Have a good weekend.'

She kept her head down, signing more forms, until everyone had gone. Lorraine stopped at her desk on the way out. 'I've got the list of stolen property for tomorrow. I'll see you in Lower Markham for the fair at eleven.'

Ten minutes before the press briefing and she needed to find a mirror. 'Thanks, Lorraine. See you there.'

In the lobby, Matthew stood with six of his officers.

Khalid looked up at the CCTV screen. 'There's more of a crowd than I thought.' He scanned the officers. 'Was no one else available?' His quick steps were unlike his usual measured paces.

With the officers clearing a path, they walked out to face the media. Robyn was closer than she'd like to be to Fell, pressed in by camera lenses and microphones. Questions were being screamed out from all directions.

'What part did Janice play in the investigation?' 'Is anyone going to be sacked?' 'Were any other officers involved?'

Khalid had to call for calm three times before it was quiet enough for Fell to read the prepared statement. There were continuous interruptions: Liz Trew from the *Journal* was leaning over someone's shoulder to see. 'Are you going to bring in some proper coppers now?'

The shouts started up again the second Fell finished the statement.

'Are you going to resign?' 'Has Ben taken part in church rituals?'

'Ladies and Gentlemen.' Khalid's call was drowned in the clamour.

'QUIET.' Matthew's roar flattened the hubbub.

Khalid took advantage of the second's lull. 'Ladies and gentlemen, a full, independent investigation is underway and, until that is concluded, it is not appropriate for us to answer any questions. Thank you for your time.'

They turned to leave, with officers linking arms against the scrum as it tried to move with them. Fell led them across the lobby until they were out of sight of the front doors. 'What now, Guler?'

Khalid sighed. 'Now we let the story die down because there's nothing more to say. I've issued Janice's record including the commendations. Fell sighed. 'Has Ms Chivers got a liaison officer with her?'

It took Robyn a second to realise he was speaking to her. 'She's turned one down, sir.'

'I am surprised by that, particularly with the level of interest in her.' Fell straightened. 'I expect you to keep on top of things, Guler. Bailley, you are late with a briefing on the burglaries. I expect it first thing on Monday.' He crossed to the lift.

Khalid watched Fell go, then turned to Robyn, as if he was about to say something.

Fell called across the lobby, 'Guler, I need details of who will be at this community event this evening.'

Robyn turned to Matthew. 'Have you thought about trying out for the role of Town Crier?'

Matthew smiled. 'When you coach junior football, being able to yell loudly is about the only skill you really need.' His face became more serious. 'I spoke to Phil about the missing sweatshirt ...'

'I know. It's not hard to tell when Phil's pissed off with you, is it?'

Matthew shook his head. 'You want me to have another word with him?'

That was the appropriate way, what Roger would have done. Feeling a sudden rush of energy, Robyn laughed. 'Thanks but don't worry. I'll deal with him.'

There was a moment of silence as a frown flitted across Matthew's face. 'Well, if you're sure. OK, bye then.'

Left alone, Robyn glanced towards the front door, where reporters were still milling around. This should be as bad as it got. If Lance had finished his review, there would be no more questions asked and her role would stay a secret. She began climbing the stairs back to her desk. It was always a bad idea to take work problems home: if she was going to think about who'd put the article in her in-tray, she'd do it at work. In the peace of the empty incident room, she considered the facts. Because of the scale of the investigation, more people than usual had been in and out. The pile was larger because she hadn't kept up with the paperwork. Compared to the car damage, this wasn't worth getting worked up over; most rookies had silly messages or pictures stuck on their lockers at some point. Someone was just trying to be funny. Someone in the station. Someone who was supposed to be a colleague.

The clock showed four o'clock. Robyn had lasted a week at work. There was nothing to stop her going home now and shutting the door on the world. Friday evenings were normally the time for a good film and some wine: she could go to the supermarket as they didn't ask for ID when buying alcohol. On the way to the door, she noticed the autopsy report in the muddle on Graham's desk and asked herself why the girl had gone to the warehouse. She wondered if part of the reason she was still thinking about the case was because she wanted to make up for time lost in her own uncertainties.

Back at her desk, Robyn re-read the comments about the first blow. Dr Shepherd's conclusion suggested the attacker had struck from behind, to stun rather than kill. Robyn let her eyes drift out of focus, trying to picture the scene. There must have been two people and the girl trusted the other person enough to turn her back on them. If she'd met someone in the clubs and wanted a quick shag, there were closer places than the warehouse. Even as somewhere to take drugs, there were dry, secluded places in the Docks without the dust. It was reasonable to suppose 'they', the girl and her killer, had arrived by car because the warehouse was at least fifteen minutes' walk from the town centre. The girl might have been killed elsewhere and dumped but for some reason, the idea didn't feel right and she tried to work out why.

A shouted goodbye in the corridor brought Robyn back to the present at ten to six. Of all of the scenes she'd played out in her head, the one she kept coming back to was the girl being alive as she entered the warehouse. Although quiet, the Docks were overlooked and had some CCTV: carrying a body around would be risky unless it was an unplanned attack, which didn't fit with the body being hidden. No, she must have been alive.

Mind clear at last, she walked down to her car. Two civilian workers in the car park broke off their conversation as she passed, faces hardening. Behind her, she heard them carry on what they were saying, including something sounding like 'Janice'. She picked up a Chinese takeaway on the way home and collapsed on the sofa, enjoying the sick feeling from simple gluttony and the pre-supplied laughter from a TV comedy. When the smell from the residue got too much, she ran the water for washing up. The sleeves of her blouse wouldn't stay rolled up and were quickly soaked.

She switched on her computer and checked the time Josh's coach arrived, then swore – she hadn't realised it was quite so early. It was tempting to log on to a couple of her online profiles and see what other trans-women thought of Robyn so far. There would be a risk she could end up getting sucked into the mix of praise, pity and polemics filling these sites. Bed was the simpler option. She was on her way upstairs, when the phone rang.

'Hello?'

Her first reaction was delight at Becky's voice then worry about what she might be about to say. 'Mum rang me yesterday in a right strop about you.'

'Oh?' Robyn hoped she sounded casual, rather than terrified at the prospect of Becky siding with Julie.

'She was so cross, she could hardly speak. Seems like you've not just upset her, you've insulted the whole sisterhood.'

'The counsellors warned me about this. I don't understand why wanting to be a woman is an insult to women – you'd think it would be the ultimate compliment.' Robyn was encouraged by a giggle from the other end. 'Do you think she's going to write an academic paper about me?'

The laughter faded. 'Mum's having a bit of a hard time at the moment. I think the university is cutting back on budgets for Women's Studies and, well, she and Richard are going through a bit of a rough patch.'

Robyn switched the phone from one ear to the other. 'Ah. Nothing serious I hope. After all, they have been married, what, fifteen years now?'

Becky sighed. 'Richard got made redundant last month and now he's home all day and there's a bit of what Mum called "reversal of gender roles" with her having to pay the mortgage and I don't think she likes it.'

'Oh, dear. Well, if there is anything you need, sweetheart, call me, OK? As I said, I'm still your dad.' There was a brief pause.

'So, what am I supposed to call you now?'

'You can call me Robyn.'

'I'm not calling you by name, that's creepy.'

'I just thought as you're an adult now, you wouldn't want to call me "Dad" anymore.'

'Don't make this any weirder than it already is. You keep saying I'm the only person in the world who can call you Dad so I'm going to keep doing it.' There was a pause. 'Unless there's something else you need to tell me?'

Robyn laughed. Becky could joke with her. 'You don't need to worry there.'

'Good. Well, I do need to think about this a bit more. I'll call you in a few days.'

'OK. How's your play coming?'

'Good, thanks, except I die at the beginning of the second act which is a bit depressing to do over and over again. OK, I'll call you. Bye, Dad.'

'Bye, sweetheart.'

Robyn prepared for the morning, unable to shake a vision of Becky lying still and dead with everyone staring and her far away, unable to help.

At ten o'clock, she put the television on for the evening news, then muted the volume, letting the pictures tell the story. A shot of Gillian carrying Ben to her car. A shot of Janice's house, an interview with the neighbour. Robyn, Fell and Khalid at the press briefing, all of them hemmed in behind a crush of bodies. A picture of Josh, taken from Facebook. Finally, an unknown man, standing under a 'Families Need Fathers' banner. Robyn turned up the volume.

*... condone what's been done but this is what happens when there's an attempt to exclude fathers from a child's life.*

She went to bed.

# SATURDAY 23 JULY

# 32

Robyn was awake before the alarm, even though it was set earlier than usual. Getting dressed was simple, the feminine equivalent of what she'd always worn at weekends but she lost precious minutes trying to choose a belt. She hadn't bothered buying belts, assuming they were all the same, until she found the loops on the new jeans were too narrow. After trying another belt and having the same problem, she gave up and picked a longer t-shirt to cover her waist. She didn't have time to make up her face, her lips feeling rough without the lipstick.

She caught up time on the clear roads into London, clutch slipping a couple of times as she got used to the heels on the new ankle boots. Next time, she'd have to bring some flats to drive in. She made herself up in an empty taxi rank at Victoria Coach Station, surprising herself by how much a part of her revelled in being so open.

Her phone rang. 'Morning, Josh.'

'Hi. Where are you?'

Robyn got out of the car. New arrivals streamed out, lugging bags, one boy even carrying a surfboard. A tall youth appeared, recognisable from the picture on Janice's desk. She waved. Josh crossed the road then stopped a few yards away, shuffling backwards. One bag slid to the tarmac.

'Sorry, I thought you were my lift.' He wrestled the stray bag back onto his shoulder and started back towards the station.

Robyn stepped out from behind the car. 'Josh. I'm DI Bailley. I'm here to pick you up.'

She reached for the bag, which was about to slip off Josh's shoulder again. Josh pulled back from her outstretched hand. Under the tan, his face was puffy, eyes bloodshot. 'You're Roger Bailley?'

A large group in matching yellow baseball caps and rucksacks surged across the road behind them, chattering in some other language.

Robyn nodded. 'Or, I used to be, until last Monday. I'm Robyn now.' It was the first time she'd actually said the words.

Josh swayed to rebalance the bag. He didn't seem to have heard. A latecomer ran to catch up with the yellow group.

Robyn raised her voice. 'I was Roger Bailley. Now I'm Robyn.' She'd meant to sound positive and had ended up sounding loud.

Josh rubbed at his stubble. 'And you're Mum's boss?'

'Yes, I'm a detective inspector.'

Josh opened his mouth once then closed it again. As he swallowed, he lingered on the bulges in Robyn's t-shirt, then stared into the ground. 'Mum and Dad are in trouble, aren't they?'

Robyn nodded. 'Yes, they're in trouble. I'm trying to help them.' She stepped back and put her hand on the boot, before remembering the things from Janice's house. She opened a rear door. 'Josh?'

Josh shuffled forward, keeping his bag in front of him. Robyn thought now wasn't the time to upset him and got into the car. Josh loaded his bags, then opened the passenger door, hesitating before sliding in. He shoved buds into his ears, curling his body away from Robyn. She gave up on any idea of conversation and put the radio on. They were out of range of the local station so she switched to Radio Four and let the voices drown the dull beat just audible from his headphones.

*It's seven o'clock on BBC Radio Four and this is the Today programme. The headlines this morning: there are questions over why it took four days to discover that a missing toddler had been taken by a police officer ...*

Robyn switched to Radio Two. At half-past seven, she pulled into a service station. Josh was snoring in a steady rhythm. She'd planned to have breakfast in the café, then considered Josh's probable embarrassment if they were to walk in together. She glanced over. He appeared to be fast asleep so she left him in the car.

When she got back, Robyn left the door open, letting in air and the sound of the motorway. Josh murmured, turned his head but didn't wake. Robyn wondered whether she should touch him. Pulling back, she switched the radio on, turning up the volume. 'Josh, I've got you a bacon roll.' She held it close to his face.

A breath turned into a sniff. Josh stirred, opening his eyes. He focused on Robyn and bit his lip.

Robyn held out the food.

Josh accepted the roll. 'Did you get ketchup?'

Robyn dug in her own bag. 'Here. You dozed off. Rough journey?'

Josh balanced the roll and ripped open the sauce.

'Are you OK?' Robyn winced for the upholstery as the sticky sachet teetered on Josh's knee. 'I know this must all be a shock for you.'

'I just can't believe he's really my son.' Josh added three sugars to his tea.

'There's no doubt.' Robyn blew on her own tea. 'Your mother checked his DNA against yours.'

'What's going to happen now?'

'At the moment, your parents are in custody for taking Ben. I hope your father will be released on bail this morning ...'

'So they're getting out?'

Being realistic wasn't pleasant. 'Only temporarily. There will be a trial, I'm afraid. As a police officer, the chances of your mother avoiding prison are minimal.'

There were small sounds, which could have been sobs. Robyn turned away, gazing out of the window, watching a patrol car park and the officers stroll into McDonald's.

'How come nobody told me?'

'You aren't named on Ben's birth certificate and, as far as I know, Melissa Chivers has never mentioned your name to anyone.'

'Bitch.' Josh slapped the door panel.

Robyn took her chance. 'What did she do to you?' Josh's new hatred might make him forget his discomfort at sitting next to her.

Josh was squashing the sandwich wrapping into a tight ball. 'I worked with her, at D&R, my last summer before uni. The stuff I got to do was pretty dull until Melissa started asking for me to join her client meetings so I got to see how all the property side works, which was really interesting. Then, on my last day, she asked me if I wanted to sleep with her.'

Robyn stared at him. 'Melissa Chivers propositioned you?'

'Yeah, just came out with it, like in some film. So, I mean, who wouldn't?' Josh glanced at Robyn and blushed. 'But I was seeing a girl, we were getting serious so I said no.'

'Then what happened?'

'I was glad I was off to uni. It would have been seriously awkward.' Josh stretched for his rucksack and pulled out a phone. 'When I came down to see Lacey the first weekend though, Melissa got dead huffy–'

'Sorry, who's Lacey?'

'This girl I was seeing. Worked on reception at Derby and Rutherford. When I went to uni, we saw each other every weekend.'

A siren wailed past on the motorway. 'Go on.'

'Once Melissa found out, she was seriously mean to Lacey. But then, a week before term ended for Christmas, I get a text from Lacey to say she's dumping me.'

The policemen strode out of MacDonald's carrying bags, then drove away without touching their food. Josh twisted the festival bands looped around his wrist. 'Anyway, I got back and went to the office to talk to Lacey, because she wasn't answering her phone. I just like, wanted to find out why she'd ended it. I met Cathy at the office and she told me Lacey had walked out. Then Melissa turned up and told me Lacey had been two-timing me.'

Josh took a gulp of air. 'Oh, can I charge my phone? The battery died.' He plugged a cable into the USB socket. 'I was a bit pissed off, like. My first term at uni and I'd stayed faithful and come down to see her and she'd just gone. So when Melissa asked me again, I went back to her place, because I was like, angry and she was pretty sexy in those suits of hers.'

His last words were drowned by a series of beeps from his phone as missed calls and messages racked up. Robyn kept her gaze on his face. 'What happened?'

Josh stared at the screen, then threw the phone down. 'Everyone knows it's my baby.'

'What happened when you went to Melissa's house, Josh?'

'Well, you know, she got me inside and just said we should go to bed.' Josh was staring into the footwell. 'And so it started. I had to go home, because Mum and Dad were expecting me but Melissa told me to come the next day and then every day for the holidays. I asked a couple of times if we could go out somewhere because all we did was stay in bed.' He was blushing again. 'She was different from the office, really filthy. And she told me she was on the pill too.'

Robyn sipped at the last of the tepid tea. 'What happened when you went back to uni?'

Josh laughed. 'She blanked me. Didn't answer her phone or reply to email. I tried calling the office, even though she said not to and she wouldn't take my calls. Then, well, I discovered what I'd been missing at uni by coming back every weekend.'

'And did you ever hear from Lacey again?'

Josh leant back against the rest. 'No. Is there any more food?'

Robyn made a show of checking, even though she knew the answer. 'Sorry, all gone.'

Josh stretched, then pushed open the door. 'I'm going to get something else and I need the loo.' He swung himself out of the car and pushed the door to, before stopping. 'Hey – you want anything?'

Robyn smiled at how the gesture reminded her of Janice. 'No, thanks.'

Josh jogged across the car park, muscles flexing on his tanned calves.

Robyn retrieved her handbag from the back seat. Its squat blackness felt too formal against the blue jeans – maybe she needed a weekend handbag. The prospect of having to transfer stuff between bags wasn't enticing, given how long she'd taken to organise this one. She tucked the spare napkins into a pocket, dislodging the picture of Ben. Now she'd seen both of them, the resemblance was striking: Ben's straight nose came from Josh and there was something similar in the shape of the ears.

The door was wrenched open and Josh threw himself back into the seat. 'Dad just rang. He's been let out on bail. Can we get home now?' He stretched out his hand for the photo, pulling his knees up to his chin, staring at the boy's face. 'I saw it on my phone but didn't think he looked like me. Now …'

Robyn steered the car out onto the slip road. On the other side, the traffic was stacked back, stationary. Josh was silent, still holding the photo, his phone buzzing every few seconds. They pulled off the M2, passing an oast-house, then took the Markham road, fields visible between the hedges.

At the entrance to the lane leading to Janice's house, a horse and two ponies trotted across the road. Robyn had to jam on her brakes,

Josh's bags thumping into their seats. One of the ponies skittered backwards, a chubby girl flapping the reins. A woman on the chestnut horse yelled commands until the girl got her pony to the verge. A bigger girl on a white pony gave Robyn the finger as she eased the car forward. Outside Janice's house the gates were still closed, a couple of cars parked hard against them. One of the drivers raised his head.

'Bugger.' Robyn accelerated. 'Journalists. Josh, is there a back way into your place?' Around the next bend she slowed, checking the mirror for anyone following them. 'Josh?' For a second, Robyn wondered whether the lad had fallen asleep again because he was curled into a tight ball but the sun glinted on tears on his cheeks. 'Is there a way we can get into your garden without going through the front gate?'

She stopped out of sight of the house. For want of something to do, Robyn reached into the back seat for her handbag, hoping her mobile had a signal.

The phone rang, then went to an answering machine. 'Hello, Martin. It's Robyn Bailley. I'm outside in the lane with Josh …'

'Yes.' The phone had been picked up.

'Hello, Martin. I understand your caution.' In the passenger seat, Josh lifted his head. 'Has your house got a back gate? There are journalists at the front and I don't want Josh to have to face them.'

There was a grunt. 'He used to get over the side wall by climbing the pear tree. First track on the left.'

'But how will I get over?'

Martin grunted again. 'You won't. Thank you for picking him up, just throw his bags over.'

'Martin, I'm trying to help you.' Robyn realised she was talking to herself. She took time putting her phone away and fastening the bag, before speaking.

'Your father's suggestion is you avoid the journalists by climbing a tree to get over the wall.'

Josh's mouth opened, then he laughed. 'The pear tree? I haven't climbed it for, like, years.' He paused, the smile fading. 'Mum isn't there, is she? When's she coming home?'

Robyn gazed up at the roof of the car. 'Not for a while, I'm afraid. Now, where's this lane?'

They drove on, then Josh pointed out a rough track, a high wall on the left. Around a tight bend, a pear tree laden with fruit grew on the verge. Josh opened the door before the car had stopped. Robyn reached into her bag. 'I need to give you the house keys back. Are you going to be OK getting over there?'

Josh reached for a branch. 'I'm not sure this'll bear my weight anymore.' He pointed to the wall. 'Dad's put the ladder up on the other side. If you give me a hand-up, I can climb down.'

A car passed the end of the lane. Robyn got out of the car, thinking if a journalist were to spot them here, it would be worse than if they'd gone in the front way. She opened the door, pulling out Josh's bags. 'OK, if you get up there, I'll pass you the bags.' She stood against the wall and cupped her hands for Josh to step on. He pushed upwards, his weight transferring to her. When he stretched to grab a branch, his t-shirt rode up and the bare skin of his stomach was an inch from her face, giving hints of a night's sweat and salt. Now his bare leg was brushing her cheek as he lifted one knee to her shoulder and she could feel each soft hair tickling her ear. A sudden fear he was over-balancing was her excuse for grasping his calf. There was a final push as he shifted his weight to his arms, then Josh was on the wall, swinging his leg over and onto the ladder. Robyn leant back onto the wall while the tingling in her skin subsided.

'Are you going to pass the bags up then?'

Robyn pushed herself off the wall and grabbed the first bag, hoisting it up to Josh. Their fingers brushed as he took the handle from her. It was just an accident. The second, heavier bag needed to be hoisted from underneath so there was no repetition.

'Well, thanks.'

Robyn's mouth was dry. She hoped he couldn't hear the tremor in her voice. 'Call me before you do anything, OK? And don't talk to the press. You saw them in the lane, they'll try anything to get to you. If you need advice, call me.'

There was a hint of a smile then a voice sounded in the garden and Josh dropped out of sight.

# 33

Robyn got back into the car. After several long minutes while her pulse returned to normal, she faced herself in the rear view mirror, assessing herself as she would a suspect. There was definite guilt written in the flush high on the cheeks but a hint of something else. Her body had responded the way a woman's would. She told herself it was shocking she could act in that way towards a boy young enough to be her own child and the son of a fellow officer as well, though the only regret she could find was that the moment hadn't lasted longer. The corners of her mouth were turning up, emphasised by the brighter lipstick she'd picked for the weekend.

It seemed important to do a good job on her make-up but it took longer because her hands weren't steady, making the thought of reversing down the lane too nerve-wracking. While inching the car around between the wall on one side and a ditch, she saw two men, walking up the track towards her. They could have been hikers, if one of them hadn't had a professional-looking camera. Robyn saw them speed up as they got closer.

'DI Bailley? DI Bailley, can you give us a comment on the case?'

Accelerating, Robyn swung the car around them, skirted the edge of the ditch and got away. On the lane, more cars were now loitering around the gates, the journalists peering at their screens. She kept going to the junction and turned out before someone decided to follow her. At the bottom of Markham Hill, her phone rang and she pulled into car park of The Airfield pub.

She'd been expecting to see Lorraine's name, given they were meeting in fifteen minutes, but the number was unfamiliar. 'DI Bailley.'

'It's DI Farnham. I've decided we can release DC Warrener tomorrow. She remains suspended from duty and a condition of bail is neither of them can approach Ben Chivers.'

'Thank you.' Robyn gritted her teeth, then relaxed. 'I appreciate what you've done.'

'I'll send Fell my report on Monday. Goodbye.'

The line went dead. Maybe it was a combination of her previous behaviour now combined with relief but Robyn found herself laughing. A tattooed guy getting out of a pimped pick-up truck gave her a look that reminded her of Martin's hostility. It was easier to send a text to Josh to let him know the good news. The thought that journalists now had another reason to besiege the house sobered her. She turned back onto the road. At the next junction, ignoring the fluorescent 'Grand Antiques Fayre' signs pointing towards the grey façade of Markham Hall at the top of the hill, she turned towards the centre of Lower Markham and took the first parking space available.

Tinny music drifted across from her left, where the tops of fairground rides could be seen over the rooftops. She was walking towards the sound of light jazz, when someone made an unintelligible tannoy announcement. In the High Street, craft stalls had been set up along both sides, browsers crowding around them. The only clear space was in front of the war memorial where two couples in 1940s clothes were waltzing, the music coming from speakers on a small stage. Robyn spotted Lorraine talking to a man unpacking a van. Avoiding the dancers, she crossed towards Lorraine, then stopped, conscious she might be interrupting something. Extracting herself from the flow of people, she moved to a shop doorway in the shade to send Lorraine a text. A minute later, Lorraine glanced down and said something to the man before kissing him on the cheek. He waved, then stepped up onto the stage and began moving instruments. Lorraine made her way through the crowd.

'Morning, Guv. Don't think I've ever seen this place so busy.'

'These crowds might be a problem if anything kicks off. Have you got the stolen property list?'

Lorraine's look was sceptical. 'Here's a copy for you, Guv. We've only got pictures of two items as most were trinkets.' She held out two images: a woman sitting at a tea table wearing a cameo brooch and a man in a stiff, hired suit wearing a jade tie pin. 'By the way, what do you expect to kick off?'

'This burglar's getting more violent. If we get close to him, he may attack. We just have to keep our eyes open for any cyclists in black Lycra.' Robyn went to mop her brow and remembered the make-up. 'Right, let's go. By the way, for today, best if you call me Robyn.'

Lorraine giggled. 'OK, I'll try. But I've just got used to calling you "Guv". If I do, we'll have to pretend it's short for Guinevere or something.'

They stepped forward onto the pavement and began shuffling along with the crowd. Robyn recognised several stalls from the Gaddesford festival: she turned to point them out to Lorraine. There was no answer. Lorraine had stopped beside an antiques stall and was fingering a set of fire-irons. There had been no antiques on the stolen property list so she'd either spotted something else or was doing a bit of personal shopping. Rather than fight her way back, Robyn shaded her eyes to study the crowd. All around were men and women wearing vintage costumes, their hair teased into a range of styles. A woman with a peroxide beehive chatted to a couple as they admired mini-dresses that hung from a stall like bunting. Beside them, a man dressed like Eddie Cochrane looked hot in a leather jacket with the sleeves pushed up. The couple moved on and Robyn edged closer to the stall, drawn by the displays of costume jewellery.

"'Elp you?' The man looked her up and down, folding his thick arms across his chest, the shapes of his tattoos distorting as they were squeezed together.

She'd seen him before somewhere. He must have been in the Gaddesford pictures. 'Ooh, aren't these beautiful? May I?'

The hard set of his jaw showed what he thought about the camp inflection in her voice. 'Go ahead.'

Robyn fastened a bracelet on the third attempt. It was too tight, the rough underside scratching at the soft skin of her inner wrist. Now she had to get it off.

The beehive woman peered under the stall. 'Damn, I thought it was here. Dean, when you're done there, can you get the blue box out of the van?' The man grunted.

Her nails kept slipping on the tiny clasp because her eyes were drawn to the man's arms. His name was Dean and she'd seen the tattoos before in the file of the builder who'd threatened Ms Chivers. He was still watching her. At some point, she was going to have to admit she couldn't unfasten the bracelet. There was no sign of Lorraine.

'Could you help me?' Robyn held out her arm, thinking hard. If this man wanted to hide his identity, he'd have to hide his arms too.

'Are you takin' the piss?' Dean was shifting from foot to foot like a boxer until she smiled at him, which seemed to make him stand stiffer.

'No. I can't get it off – the clasp has jammed.' She remembered the burglar knew exactly who lived in each property and where items were, as if he'd been there before and had seen where money was kept.

'I'll get Cindy.'

'Thanks. By the way, it's Dean Harper, isn't it? Didn't you do some building work recently for a neighbour of mine in Gaddesford? Mrs Jarvis, in Hollyhock Cottage? I need some work done myself.'

Dean folded his arms again. 'Yeah. Fixed some guttering for her. What do you need done? Oy, Cindy, give us a hand here.'

Cindy laid a hand on his arm. 'Calm down. What's the problem?'

'I'm sorry, I can't get this off.' Robyn held out her arm.

Tutting, the woman unfastened the clasp in a second. Robyn rubbed her wrist.

'Thanks. Have you got a card?'

'Nah.' He looked to Cindy. 'We got any paper?'

Cindy gave Robyn a quick smile. 'If you can hang on just a second, I've got some other things which might be in bigger sizes.' She turned to Dean. 'In the van, the blue box has my notepad and the new jewellery I was pricing yesterday.'

Dean squeezed sideways between the stalls. Robyn inspected the other items, fingering a pendant.

'Where do you get all these lovely things from?' Robyn upped the camp. It seemed to work better with the woman as her smile was warmer.

'My boyfriend.' Cindy jerked her head to where Dean had been. 'He works in house clearance and saw all this stuff going to waste so he kept it for me. Amazing the things people get rid of, isn't it?'

'You're lucky. He's got a good eye.'

Robyn sensed him behind her as a cloud of his cigarette smoke dispersed around her face. She turned. 'I understand it's you who finds all of this jewellery. I'm looking for something in particular, a cameo brooch. Have you got anything like that?'

The woman smiled again. 'Ooh, now we've got just the thing – it's in this box somewhere.' She took the box from Dean and began hunting through it.

Behind her, Dean's fists clenched. 'Cindy, leave it.'

'Here it is.' She ignored Dean and held out a gold-edged terracotta disc with a Roman lady's head picked out in white. 'It isn't it darling? We can let you have that for seventy-five pounds.'

Robyn took the brooch, turning it in her hand. 'It's lovely but I'll leave it.'

'Well, we could drop by five pounds but no more. There's real gold around the rim.'

Dean moved forward, shoulders pushing back.

'No, I'll leave it because I believe it's stolen …' She had enough of a reflex to swing away, lessening the impact of Dean's punch but there was still a horrible crunch against her jaw and a sharp pain as a tooth pierced her tongue. She was sent sprawling backwards into something soft, before half bouncing, half stumbling forward when her shoulder hit metal and she was able to get a grip. She hung on to the lamp post, waiting for the fiery heat on the left side of her face to calm. Somewhere, someone was screaming. Nails scratched at her hands: she tightened her fingers on the brooch. Something jostled her. There were more screams. She opened her right eye as far as it would go and got a sight of Cindy's spotted dress and a white, bulging mass.

'Thief! You've got my brooch.'

'You nearly knocked me over.'

The strain of keeping her eye open was too much. Robyn moved her body behind the post for a second's relief. Time to stop all of this. With difficulty, she got her left hand into her bag for her warrant card. 'Police. I suggest you all calm down. I have reason to believe some items on this stall are stolen property.' She blinked to clear her vision. Standing next to Cindy was an obese man in a bulging white t-shirt. There was no sign of Dean.

'Guv? You OK?' Lorraine pushed her way through the circle of people.

'Fine, Lorraine. The suspect's made a run for it. Can you secure the stall?'

'You're doing nothing of the sort, this is my living, get off.' The woman grabbed Lorraine's arm.

Lorraine shook herself free and reached for her mobile. 'Unit requesting backup, officer down, suspect fled, repeat, officer down …'

'You nearly knocked me over. I don't believe you're a real police officer. Real police officers aren't made up like clowns.' From somewhere in the chins, the obese man had a wheezy, childlike voice. He prodded Robyn's chest again.

Robyn pushed herself upright. 'Would you like me to prove I'm a real policeman by taking you to the station? You're causing an obstruction in more ways than one. The only problem is, I'm not sure I've got a cell big enough for you.'

'This is police brutality.' The man wobbled backwards a couple of steps, stopped by the crowd.

'He's got my stuff.' The woman made another grab at Robyn's wrist.

A handcuff clicked. Lorraine spun the woman around and clipped the other cuff, securing her to one of the stall's uprights. 'It isn't your stuff. It's ours until we check where it's come from. Now, unless you want to be on the same assault charge as your boyfriend, you're going to tell me everything I want to know.'

'You bitch. You can't do this.'

Over the woman's protests, Robyn thought she could hear sirens in the distance. A crowd was still watching them. She found herself slumping against the lamp post and straightened up. Yes, definitely sirens and getting closer.

'Stop looking through there.'

'Calm down.' Lorraine continued rummaging through the box. 'Now what's this?' She held up a tie pin set with a large green stone. 'This looks familiar.' She looked over the crowd. 'Ah, at last.'

Voices were coming closer. The crowd parted, the obese man taking the chance to lumber away. Donna and Clyde stepped into the circle, taking the scene in.

'Good to see you. We need to get an alert out for a Dean Harper, he's got a record and everything on this stall needs securing …' Robyn hoped she sounded more coherent than she felt. A sudden thought crossed her mind, one question that might still be asked.

Donna leant towards her. 'Are you all right, ma'am? I'll get an ambulance.'

'No, no, we need to get this done.' In the background, the woman was still shrieking. 'Donna, I hear Janice is picking up your son after nursery. That's good teamwork.'

Donna opened her mouth, then closed it again.

'You look really rough, Guv. I can finish up here.' Lorraine was now standing next to Donna. 'Guv, let's get you patched up.'

Donna took Robyn's arm. 'Let me help you get sat down, ma'am.' She dropped her voice. 'What are you talking about?'

Lorraine looked round. 'Sorry, Donna, I need you. The St John's Ambulance can do that.'

A lad in a cap and uniform who looked no older than twelve was waiting. Robyn tried to smile at Donna before she started clearing the stall then refused the offer of the boy's arm. She made it to a bench in the shade where her eye was bathed. Water went up her nose, making her sneeze. When she wiped her face, the tissue came away streaked with the make-up she'd reapplied so carefully. A nasty, sick, queasy feeling was building and by the time Lorraine came over to tell her the stall and van were secured, Robyn was happy to go along with the suggestion for Clyde to drive her home. He'd been gallant to the point of irritating, even offering to walk her up the path. Robyn had waited by the gate until he'd driven off.

A sharp flare of pain made her snap her eyes open, followed by a second pulse reminding her that her left eye was swollen almost shut. The right side of her face had corrugations from the cushion: she must have fallen asleep on the sofa. The team would be out there, searching for Harper and she should be with them. Swinging her feet to the floor made her dizzy and she dropped her head between her knees until it passed.

Feeling redundant, Robyn made tea and scavenged through the fridge then, unable to settle, picked up her phone and skimmed through her contacts. Without pausing to think whether this was a good idea, she pressed the green button.

Becky's phone was answered on the second ring. 'Hello?'

'Hello, sweetheart. It's Dad. Something happened today and I needed to hear your voice.'

'What happened? Are you OK?'

'We were tracking a burglar and he punched me in the face. Nothing serious, I've got a fine black eye.'

'Wow. Take care of yourself. What's going on at the moment? Nothing ever happens in Meresbourne.' There was a pause, a friendly one, without pressure to fill it.

'I'm not keeping you from going out?'

'Not tonight, Dad. Been rehearsing all day and we've just ordered some pizzas.'

'I'd like to see this play. Come and support you. When is it again?'

'Oh? Well we're just doing two performances.' There was a new note in Becky's voice. 'I think Mum's coming. To both, I mean. So maybe not.'

'Ah, right.' Robyn could blame the tears on her cheek from the earlier damage. 'It's probably best I don't meet your mother. Well, perhaps you could get someone to take a picture of you – the last one I've got of you is in your prom dress.'

Becky laughed. It sounded like a release. 'Well, one of the guys will be recording it. You can watch the whole thing on DVD.'

'Great. Send me a copy.' The pause this time felt as if someone should fill it. 'Becky, will you be coming down this summer? Or could I come up and see you?' She started counting the bouquets on the wallpaper: yellow flowers, blue ribbon; white flowers, pink ribbon; blue flowers, red …

'Dad.'

Pink flowers, white ribbon; Yellow flowers …

'What are you going to look like?'

Robyn tried to make her voice relaxed. 'I'm going to look like me. Like I'm supposed to look.'

'You mean in a dress, don't you?'

'I will be Robyn, yes.'

The hesitation became a pause, lengthening into a silence, until there was a burst of chatter at the other end. 'Dad, the pizzas are here. I'll come down and see you after the play, OK? The beginning of September.'

Robyn resolved to be grateful for what she had. 'OK, sweetheart. I'll be here. Bye.' She sat back on the sofa. She had had a conversation with her daughter and felt a sense of achievement. White flowers, pink ribbon; yellow flowers, blue ribbon. Her mother had thought it was a good idea to have flowers on the wallpaper and fruit on the carpet. Where a channel had worn in the doorway, the woven cherries were stained brown, like rot. It felt dark inside already because the heavy flounces on the curtain rail blocked most of the light, though when she closed the curtains, they didn't quite meet in the middle. Then, there was the ugly, dark furniture which took up too much space. The vast dresser couldn't be moved because it hid the bare strip where the special-offer wallpaper had run out. She wondered why none of this had bothered her until now.

Reaching behind the dresser, Robyn ran her fingers over the wall, finding the wallpaper's edge and probed with a fingernail until there was enough to get hold of. She tugged. There was brief resistance, then a soft ripping noise as the old paste gave up. Getting a good grip, she pulled hard and the sheet came away from the wall, shreds of paper and paste settling on the carpet. One of the china dogs cluttering the dresser teetered and fell. She kicked the shards under a coffee table and went for the next sheet, picking at the edge until a harder flake of glue snapped a nail. Jaw set, Robyn searched in the toolbox for a scraper and began again.

# SUNDAY 24 JULY

# 34

The kettle was pre-filled to ensure the first tea of the morning took as little time to make as possible. While it was brewing, Robyn contemplated the devastation in the lounge. She'd started piling rubbish in one corner, then decided there was more satisfaction in just ripping the wallpaper off, leaving everything where it fell. With the pale plaster exposed, the room already seemed bigger and lighter, the furniture darker and uglier. She began to plan a day's decorating before her thoughts fixed with a sudden clarity on Melissa Chivers and the need to tell her about Janice's imminent release. To be professional, she would have to do it face to face or at least by phone. As the pot steamed, she decided to visit because a part of her wanted to see Ms Chivers squirm when Josh was mentioned. She was certain she'd be criticised whatever she did but if Ms Chivers wanted to complain again, let it be about too much concern for her welfare rather than too little.

After giving the tea a final stir she had to stand at the counter. There was nowhere to sit in the kitchen because of the vast freezer her mother insisted be kept fully stocked, even in the last days of her final illness when she'd been incapable of cooking. Now there were just a couple of packets of frozen vegetables at the bottom of the huge chest. Robyn blinked to clear her sore eyes. If she got rid of the freezer, she could put a table at the end of the kitchen and have breakfast overlooking the garden. As the toast popped, Robyn found herself whistling.

Make-up was a problem. The left side of her face was a swollen mess of yellow and red. It would be impossible to even try to cover it up. She settled for just some foundation and lipstick, wincing as she rubbed the tender skin. Choosing a suit meant wearing the last of her blouses: she wondered whether she could get away without ironing any of them.

On the way to Upper Town, Robyn pulled into the recycling centre. The things from Janice's went into the 'general waste' skip, mixed up with torn wallpaper. Next went a bag of ancient ornaments from the lounge. One smashed, ripping the first bag, the bright sleeve of a boy's t-shirt poking out. She emptied the wallpaper from the third bag over it. Behind her a queue of people waited with more junk to go on top. Relieved, Robyn brushed dust from her suit and hurried back to the car. She double-checked the boot: it was empty, apart from the blue ball. Everything was now covered, except Janice herself. She didn't know that Ben's move to Switzerland had been brought forward and that might push her to do something else stupid. The rest of the journey continued to erode her good mood. Under an overcast sky, a series of four-by-fours going down the hill seemed to be trying to drive everyone else off the road. There were no reporters visible outside Ms Chivers' house but also no sign of her Lexus. Robyn rang the bell and waited on the doorstep. Another ring and she walked back up the path to survey the house. Outside on the pavement a woman in a thin tracksuit swore at something on the ground. The clouds had closed in now, the sky a uniform grey.

'Excuse me.' Robyn wasn't prepared for the woman to whip out a phone and hold it up, thumb on the keypad, tugging a miniature Schnauzer to heel.

'We've had enough of your sort around here, I'm calling the police.'

Robyn reached for her warrant card keeping her eyes on the woman's face and reminding herself never to wear that much foundation.

'Please don't worry, madam. I am a police officer.' She opened the gate and stepped onto the pavement, waiting for the reaction.

The dog sniffed Robyn's trousers. The woman tugged the lead and took the warrant card. As she squinted down, the skin around her nose wrinkled though her forehead didn't.

'Oh, you're the transsexual policeman. Are people beating you up? Aren't we a bit more advanced than that? I thought you were a journalist. We've had so many and they're so intrusive.'

Robyn gave a professional smile. 'I understand what a nuisance they are.'

Tucked under the woman's arm was a copy of the *Sunday Journal*. Whatever the headline was, the first word was *SCANDAL*. Robyn couldn't see the picture – the article might be about her. She scolded herself for being paranoid. 'I was hoping to see Melissa Chivers about some loose ends we need to tie up. She's not at home – do you have any idea where she may be?'

'It's Sunday.' The woman shivered. 'She'll be at church.'

Robyn sighed. Of course she would be. 'Thank you.' She stepped away, to find the woman moving with her.

'Is it true, she seduced this teenager?' For the first time, the woman leaned forward. The dog, ignored, tugged at the lead.

'I'm sorry, I can't comment on an ongoing case. Good morning.' Robyn turned without looking, nearly knocking a paper-boy off his bike. She hurried back to the car as the first drops of rain hit the windscreen.

The drive back into town was full of stops and starts to avoid more four-by-fours, now all coming up the hill. The rain was a steady deluge, thunder rumbling in the distance. At the bottom of the hill, Robyn crossed the roundabout towards the town centre, into a street lined with cars taking advantage of the free parking. A woman in a t-shirt ran to a car. Robyn let her pull out, then tucked the Mondeo into the slot outside a shuttered shoe-shop. Its doorway was spattered with vomit.

Robyn got her umbrella out of the boot, wishing she'd brought a coat. She followed the street into Market Square. The stalls were huddled under tarpaulins: no one seemed to be browsing. Crossing the empty plaza, she stepped through The Cut into St Leonard's Square then turned into Saints' Row. At least here, the overhang of the medieval buildings gave some protection from the rain. The address for the Church of Immaculate Purity was on the second floor of one of the bland, seventies office blocks in Commercial Square.

Halfway down the Row, a mauve number '6' denoted a stop on the 'Marvellous Meresbourne' tourist trail. The stock image of Edmund Napier Loveless glared down from a board on the front of her old house, severe in her high-necked Victorian dress. A man with a shock of white hair strode out, pulling on a tweed cap as he glared at the sky.

A woman joined him tucking a gift-shop purchase into a large shoulder bag. 'I don't know why you bothered coming, I know you're not interested in her writing …' They continued up the street towards Saints' Fountain.

'You spent over an hour in there – the woman pretended to be a man and wrote, what, three books?'

'She had to because women weren't allowed to express themselves and still aren't …'

'Big Issue?' A man in a red tabard over a worn fleece jacket held out a magazine. The couple ignored him and Saints' Fountain, walking on and turning right towards the High Street. The vendor's attention shifted to Robyn. 'Big Issue, this week's Big Issue?'

Robyn felt a pang of guilt but rationalised she was in a hurry. She turned left, stepping over dropped kebabs and into Commercial Square. Fifteen minutes later, she'd gone the full circuit of the square, checking each shuttered door and was back where she'd started, at the fountain.

Robyn closed her umbrella and walked across to the Big Issue vendor. 'Hi.' The man smiled, reaching for a magazine. 'Do you know the Church of Immaculate Purity?'

The vendor frowned. One stubby finger scratched a scab on his neck. 'You sure you're not after the shrine to Saints Sergius and Bacchus? Number 7 on the tourist trail. It's right here.' He pointed past the fountain to a worn stone carving, almost obscured by the coloured ribbons tied into the protective grille.

Robyn, cold in her suit, shivered at the rip in the man's fleece. 'Thanks. It's the church I need. I'm meeting someone.'

The man offered the magazine to a party of students straggling out of the museum. They flowed passed him without acknowledgement and regrouped on his other side. He turned back to Robyn.

'Building on the corner over there. Tried to convert me once. Only went in with them because I thought I'd get a cup of tea.'

'Thanks. I guess you must see everything around here.' Robyn wondered if her presence was putting off purchasers.

'Yeah. I watch them go in there not long after I arrive Sundays and some days in the week too and they're in there 'til after I go but no one buys a copy of the magazine.'

Robyn blinked and reached for her bag. 'Oh yes, I'll take one please.'

The magazine was too big for her handbag so she had to hold it as she walked over to the building he'd pointed out. None of the buzzers were for the church. She looked back, feeling helpless. The vendor gestured to one side. An anonymous passage cluttered with rubbish bins ran between two buildings. Robyn waved back to the vendor and stepped forward, wrinkling her nose at the conflicting smells of cleaning fluid and urine. Whoever was behind the door at the end seemed to have taken recent steps to conceal their identity. A clean, white square of paint marked where a sign had been removed and the door bristled with shiny-looking locks. An obvious security camera swung to point at her, red light blinking. A small hand-drawn cross next to the entry intercom was the only clue this was the right place. She pressed the button, hearing nothing. On the road, a group headed towards the river, complaining about the wind. Here, at least, it was sheltered. She pressed the buzzer a second time. A car hooted. There was a crackle beside her. 'Who's there?'

'This is Detective Inspector Bailley. I need to speak to Melissa Chivers and I understand she's here. May I come in?'

There was no answer, just a continuous red blink from above. Somewhere, a siren sounded. She debated whether to press the buzzer again. A gull landed on the roof next door and began cleaning its feathers in the soft drizzle.

'DI Bailley, why are you still harassing me?'

The sudden speech had made Robyn jump. She took a second to make sure her own voice was level. 'Ms Chivers, I have some information for you. May I come in?'

'No. This is a place of God. We would need to purify it after your entry.'

A drop of rain went down Robyn's back. There was no room to put the umbrella up. 'I'd prefer to discuss this with you.'

'What is it?'

'Ms Chivers …'

'DI Bailley, I resent this constant intrusion and your persecution of my faith. What do you need to tell me?'

Robyn counted to ten. 'Ms Chivers, I wanted to let you know the person who took Ben will be released on bail tomorrow, on condition they do not approach him.'

'I do not see that as relevant, given I will be leaving the country in less than a week. Now leave me alone.'

There was a crackle from the speaker then silence from the other end. Robyn stared at the box for a minute, then whacked the door as hard as she could with the rolled-up magazine. The gull took off, screeching.

# 35

Robyn marched back to the car, starting the engine just to get the heating on. She was wet, angry and hungry. For want of further inspiration, she turned the car towards the police station and took refuge in the canteen. The looks she sensed were no longer just curious. Now there was anger there too. She could guess what they were thinking, she'd heard snippets. *Janice was just taking care of her own flesh and blood. His mother's a fruitloop. OK, she'd been an idiot but one cop shouldn't shop another.* And it was someone who couldn't even decide what sex they were. If she had been a target before, there was now the possibility things could get rather more personal.

Robyn retreated with her lunch to the empty incident room. Hanging her wet jacket over a chair, she checked under Janice's desk and found a fan heater, then read through Lorraine's notes of the incident at Lower Markham, nodding with approval. Cindy had given a full statement, denying all knowledge of the items' history and had been released on bail. There was nothing she needed to add. She took the last bite of her roll, sat back and enjoyed the flow of warm air. With one finger she typed 'Lacey' into the computer.

In under two minutes, she'd read all the notes on Lacey Penrose's disappearance. Her parents lived in Pickley village. Robyn hesitated, then she looked at the picture of the mutilated skull and picked up her damp jacket.

The house was on the edge of Pickley, one of a row of identical executive homes: the image of safe, secure suburbia. Robyn edged past the Toyota estate in the driveway and rang the doorbell. The man who opened the door was wearing a light sweater, just like one Roger had owned. His expression was of polite disbelief, taking in her clothes and swollen eye.

'Mr Penrose? My name is DI Bailley. Do you have a few moments?'

Robyn followed the man into the main room, his family looking up from their half-eaten lunch at the other end. 'Mr Penrose: I'm sorry to disturb your lunch. I wanted to talk to you about Lacey.'

Mr Penrose didn't answer and sank onto one end of the sofa. There were noises as the others put down their cutlery, rose from the table and came to the lounge end of the room. Mrs Penrose joined her husband on the sofa, rumpled sections of the *Sunday Journal* between them. An older woman with the same prominent nose as Mr Penrose shuffled to a big recliner closest to the fireplace. A girl, maybe eighteen, had a silent argument with a younger boy, then left him at the table and curled herself into an armchair. Robyn waited until it was clear she wouldn't be offered a seat.

'Mr Penrose, I'm reopening the investigation into Lacey's disappearance as we have found some new evidence ...'

There was a clatter as the boy dropped his fork, startling a Labrador from under the table.

'A body. You found a body.' Mrs Penrose's voice wavered. She fixed her eyes on the family pictures on the mantelpiece.

Of course. This was how any normal mother would react. Robyn tried to make the bland phrases as sincere as possible. 'Yes, we've found a body …'

'So you think it's her.' The boy left the table and lurched forward; once you saw past his height, he was perhaps only fourteen. 'The skeleton in the warehouse. You think …' He tailed off, hands beginning to flap. His sister rose, put her arms around him and pulled him down into the chair with her.

Robyn jumped as something damp skimmed her hand. The dog was sniffing her: she scratched behind its ears. 'We do need to make sure the body we found isn't Lacey, using DNA. Would one of you be prepared to give a sample?'

Mr Penrose rubbed his face and nodded.

'Thank you. I've read the case notes. It was thought at the time Lacey went to Manchester to meet a new boyfriend?'

'She sent us a text message to say she was going away but then …' Mrs Penrose choked on her words. 'Then there was nothing.' The mother stopped speaking and slumped back against the cushions. The father reached across. Their hands fumbled together, settling an inch apart.

The grandmother gripped her chair's arms as she addressed Robyn. 'We've talked to her friends, officer, which is more than you ever did. Lacey already had a boyfriend and he was at university in Leeds, not Manchester.'

The Labrador was leaning its full weight against Robyn's leg, golden hairs already showing against the dark trousers. 'We now have new evidence of Lacey's actions in the week before she went missing.'

'With respect, officer, we've heard something similar before.' The grandmother sniffed. 'Just after the case was closed, we had a visit from a nice lady officer who promised us she was still investigating. She called back a month later saying she hadn't found enough to convince her superiors to reopen the case.'

The dog lost interest in Robyn and flopped onto a patch of floor. 'Can you remember the officer's name?'

'Of course.' The grandmother's thin lips were pursed with disapproval. 'It was Detective Constable Warrener. The child-snatcher.'

'We tried writing to the senior officer and got a letter saying they'd done everything they were going to and Lacey would turn up when she wanted to. That was nearly three years ago.' Mrs Penrose covered her face.

Robyn spoke over the dog's gentle snores. 'Why were you convinced she was missing?'

From behind Mrs Penrose's hands Robyn could hear fast, ragged breaths.

'We didn't hear from her on Christmas Day.' Mr Penrose gazed ahead. 'When we went to her flat in the evening, there were no decorations up. We could see through the letterbox: nothing.'

Robyn frowned for a second.

A plaintive voice came from the chair. 'We always put the decorations up on the first of December.'

'So you believe Lacey went missing before December the first, otherwise her flat would have been decorated?' Robyn saw the girl nod. 'Is there any chance she might have changed her routine?'

'No way.' The girl's face showed how stupid she thought the question had been.

Robyn leant forward. 'When was the last time any of you saw Lacey?'

The boy scrambled up and ran out of the room. There were rapid thuds as he ran upstairs then a door slammed.

'It was Luke who was the last one to see her.' The grandmother's voice was matter-of-fact. 'She took him to the cinema for his birthday.'

'The rule is, we're not allowed to mention Christmas until after Lukey's birthday.' The girl spoke as if she was talking to an idiot. 'And Lacey said to Luke on the twenty-ninth she was getting paid the day after and was going to buy decorations for her new place on the Saturday.'

'And on the Saturday, you received a text message to say she was going to Manchester. Has there been any other contact with Lacey?'

The father shook his head.

'Do you still have a copy of the message?'

The woman shuddered. 'It deleted itself. I didn't know it was the last one I would get from her.'

Mrs Penrose blew her nose. Her voice was clearer, anger making it louder. 'The officer in charge, a DI Prentiss, said this proved she'd run off with someone.'

'And he kept saying so even when we got the landlord to open her flat and all her clothes were still there.' One of Mr Penrose's feet was tapping, tapping. The dog raised its muzzle.

'Where are those clothes now?'

The mother muttered something Robyn couldn't catch.

The grandmother pointed. 'They're in the cupboard under the stairs. Lacey's old room was turned into a room for me after she left home.'

'May I look at them?'

The grandmother nodded and Robyn stepped out into the hall. From upstairs, a faint bass beat came from behind a door with a Manchester United poster. She opened the cupboard. Behind a litter of sports equipment, paint pots and a stepladder were three large cardboard boxes. After clearing a space, Robyn lifted out the first. On top was a square shape wrapped in newspaper. Robyn peeled apart the sheets, to find two photo frames. One was a family Christmas from perhaps a decade before, everyone in paper hats, a decorated tree in the background. The other was of pair of happy teenagers. The girl had long hair mussed by sea and sand and the same snub nose as her mother. One strap of her vest top had slid down a lithe arm as her fingers rested on a boy's shoulder. Robyn recognised a younger Josh, brown curls reaching his shoulders, his arm around Lacey's waist. They looked very happy.

Underneath was a pink handbag, full of clutter. Next, were layers of clothes from High Street chains, a mix of size eights and tens. Robyn reached to the bottom of the box, feeling the irregular shape of shoes. She selected one at random and noted they were size seven. Robyn pushed the box back, keeping the photo and handbag. When she returned to the lounge, the family was still sitting around the log burner, the remains of their lunch left on the table.

'Thank you, Mr and Mrs Penrose. Do you know who this is next to Lacey?' She held out the photo.

Mrs Penrose blew her nose again.

'Josh, Lacey's boyfriend.' The girl's voice was firmer.

'Did you ever meet him?'

The girl opened her mouth, her father speaking first. 'No, we never did.'

'Officer, one of the reasons Lacey left home was because of differences over a boyfriend.' The grandmother touched Lacey's picture on the mantelpiece. 'There was one horrible man we warned Lacey against. There was a row, she moved out and even after she'd split up with him she didn't bring anyone else to meet us.'

The father's shoulders slumped. 'That was the one thing the woman officer did say when she came back. Said she'd checked out Lacey's boyfriend.' He waved at the picture. 'Him. She said he couldn't have been involved because he was away studying at university. We'd have been happy to meet him.'

A clock on the mantelpiece chimed the hour. Robyn held up the handbag. 'Is this Lacey's?'

'Yeah.' The girl shuffled in the chair, shifting her feet. 'All her stuff was in there.'

The bag on Robyn's arm was heavy compared to her own. 'How did you get it?'

'Somebody found it. It was on the Monday. After the message, I was texting Lacey all weekend. She didn't come back to me, which was odd. I called her and got this bloke in Manchester who was cleaning a train.

Everyone had got off and he heard the phone ring in the bag under a seat.' The girl's voice broke and she buried her face in a cushion.

The grandmother continued. 'The train company was very kind. They sent the bag back to Euston and we picked it up. The police thought this confirmed Lacey really had wanted to leave everything behind.'

'Is the phone still in here? May I look?'

The nod took a long time to come. The phone was in the outside pocket, though no sign of a charger.

'One final question. Did Lacey have any links with Manchester? Friends or family up there?'

The girl hit the arm of the chair with a cushion. 'Are you listening? Lacey never went to Manchester. She was happy here, happy with Josh and yeah, I did meet him.' She glared around the room. 'And he seemed really nice.' She met her father's flat stare and her tone became more defensive. 'I didn't tell you because I thought you'd be cross.'

'When was this meeting?' Robyn heard a change of note in the mother's weeping. The dog sat up and shook itself.

'It was the beginning of November. Josh came down for the weekend and we went to a fireworks party.'

Robyn chose her words with care. 'Do you believe the relationship was serious?'

The girl nodded. 'Er, yeah. Why else would Josh come all the way back to see her each weekend? Everything was good. OK, Lacey didn't like her job but it paid for her own flat. Why should she go?'

Robyn nodded. 'I intend to find out. Thank you for your time and I'm sorry for what has happened. Could I take these things with me? And, Mr Penrose, if I could take a DNA sample, I'll leave you to your lunch.'

Five minutes later, as she walked out, it was just the dog accompanying her to the door. Robyn decided to take the DNA sample straight to the hospital for analysis.

Robyn was able to slot into a parking space near the hospital's main reception. There were giggles from the receptionist at the front desk when she asked for the lab and showed her warrant card. 'Take the far lifts, second floor and turn left. I'll let Glenn know you're coming.'

Robyn thanked her and followed the directions, wondering what she'd missed. When she knocked, a voice called. 'Oh. Well. Come in, why don't you?'

The man was what her mother would have called 'a nice boy'. Robyn had a sudden certainty the receptionist would now be telling everyone she'd met Glenn's girlfriend.

'Hello, I'm Robyn Bailley, police. I've got a DNA sample I need matching. It's for a murder enquiry and it's urgent so I thought I'd drop it in myself. When would you be able to—?'

The door banged open and a porter wheeled in a trolley laden with tubes and vials. 'Alright, Glenn. Got the latest batch of samples for you. Sign here.'

'I guess this isn't a good time.'

Slotting the sample into a rack, Glenn sighed. 'I'll see what I can do. Now, excuse me.'

Robyn left him to it and walked out, ignoring a knowing glance from the receptionist as she crossed the foyer. Outside the hospital, she had to squint into unexpected sunshine. She should be typing up the Penrose interview but apart from that, there wasn't a lot more she could do until the DNA link was confirmed. The Kent Print Cup was coming up and the rose garden in Victoria Park would be at its best. The thought of losing herself in taking pictures was a welcome one: she hadn't picked up her camera since the start of her transition but as she drove home to the outskirts of Barton, she noticed the 'sale' banner was up at the retail park and, giving in to another impulse, she parked at the DIY store.

An hour later, she arrived home with a neat table and stacking chairs for the kitchen and, on impulse, a fancy feeder for birds. To fit the new table by the window, she manhandled the heavy freezer into the hallway. Sweating, she started inching the heavy dresser out of the lounge, swearing as dark furniture polish stained her top. Everything in her wardrobe was new and there was nothing scruffy to wear for DIY or gardening. For a moment, she thought of going to the charity shop and buying back some of her old clothes, dismissing the idea immediately: Robyn would develop her own style. The clutter of old furniture made getting through the hallway difficult. She picked up her mobile. The phone rang for a while before she heard the wheezy voice of Paddy Hall.

'St Oswald's furniture. You're too late, we're closed now.'

'Hello, Mr Hall. This is Detective Inspector Bailley. I wanted to follow up on our meeting on Tuesday.'

'Well, what do you want? You've found the kid and 'e wasn't here.'

'No, I wanted to let you know we won't be pursuing any enquiries against Jack Parkes.'

'Well that's kind of you. Not pursuing enquiries against someone what 'asn't done nothing.'

'We had to investigate all angles, Mr Hall. But there was something else I wanted to talk to you about. I've got some furniture I'd like to donate. When can you collect it?'

Hall coughed. 'You want to give us stuff?'

'Yes.' Robyn edged her way into the front room. 'There's a dresser, a sideboard, two coffee tables and a bookcase. Do you take electrical stuff as well? There's a big chest freezer.'

'All this yours?'

'My parents' old stuff. It's all wood, walnut I think.'

'Sounds like it needs the bigger van.' Hall was sounding more eager now.

'When can you come? I'm in Barton.'

There was a thump of the phone being put down on a hard surface. Hall yelled something, then there was just his edgy breathing.

'Sorry 'bout that. A couple of the lads could get over by six tonight if you're there?'

It was almost five o'clock. 'Perfect, thanks.'

She made tea for the men who arrived to collect the furniture, watching their eyes dart to her bruised face. When the door shut behind them, she walked back into the now-huge room and spun around, arms outstretched.

Given how dizzy she felt after the first turn, the punch was still affecting her and she would have to be careful. From the sofa, she began thinking of colours. Maybe she needed a couple of magazines. The doorbell rang. Surprised, Robyn hauled herself off the sofa. On the doorstep, Clyde gave a nervous smile.

'DI Bailley, how you doing? I just heard over the radio that your man Harper has been pulled over on the M2. Looked like he was doing a runner. They're bringing him in now. Thought you'd want to know.'

'Hello, Clyde, thanks, that's great news.' She thought for a second. 'Look, could you drive me down there? I want to see him brought in.' She stopped, aware of the stains and sweat on her top. 'Give me a minute and I'll change.'


The outer door of the custody suite swung open and an officer stepped through backwards. There was an angry muttering and Harper stepped through, his shoulders ducking and twisting as he tried to avoid being touched by the officer behind him. He stopped suddenly when he saw Robyn leaning against the reception desk.

'What's that fag doing there?'

'Keep going.' The first officer looked over his shoulder. It was Jeremy, the failed fast-track candidate. 'That fag is a detective inspector.' Harper was at the counter now, the officers on the balls of their feet, watching him.

'Well I didn't know he was a copper, did I? He didn't say nothing, just came on all gay-like.'

Even with his back to her, Robyn knew Jeremy was sniggering from the shaking in his shoulders. The custody sergeant proceeded with the booking in and Harper's handcuffs were removed. Robyn wondered why she'd come. The question and answer seemed to go on for an age and the strip lights were overwhelming her good eye. Harper demanded a lawyer.

'Cell six.' The custody sergeant handed Jeremy a clipboard.

He and his colleague closed in on Harper. 'You heard the lady. Down there.'

Robyn stood at Jeremy's shoulder and moved with them along the corridor. The looks Harper and Jeremy gave her were remarkably similar. Outside the cell, Robyn faced Harper.

'Right, Dean, now we're here, I'd like to have a little chat and we could do it in the cell, just you and me. Not about what happened today, this is a little bit of history ...'

Harper jerked around. The two officers closed in.

'I'm not having a fag in my cell. I've got rights.'

Robyn stepped into Harper's eyeline. 'So tell me one thing and I'll go away. Three months ago, you tried to scam a house in Upper Town and the home owner made a complaint about you. What do you remember? You've already paid the fine, there's nothing else we can do, I just want some more details.'

Harper massaged his neck.

'That was the one I got done for. The black bitch, she was so cold. Like she's the queen or something. She was scary.' He stopped. 'Got nothing else to say until my solicitor gets here.'

Jeremy tutted, rolling his eyes to his colleague.

Robyn blinked and tried not to wince. 'OK. Good work, you two.' She turned away.

'Why thank you kindly, ma'am.' She heard it, whether Jeremy had meant her to or not. Harper sniggered.

Robyn stopped and walked back. 'If you spoke to a suspect like that, you'd be suspended.' She smiled at Jeremy. 'If you speak to me like that, I'll make sure you stay a constable. Oh look, I already have.'

As she walked down the corridor, she heard Harper's grunt of pain as he was shoved into a cell.

# MONDAY 25 JULY

# 36

Shaving her tender skin had been difficult and getting ready had taken longer than usual but having breakfast at the new table, looking out at the garden in the early light, cheered her up. Robyn lingered over her tea, watching as the first sparrow discovered the bird feeder, until she saw how late it was. It was only in the car she realised that in her haste to get out, she'd forgotten to put any jewellery on. With no school traffic, she made up time and at eight-thirty, she caught the faint chimes of St Leonard's as she crossed the police station car park. Her pass was now in the outer pocket of the handbag, no fiddling required. The desk sergeant was leaning on the counter, chewing the last of a MacDonald's breakfast.

'Morning, ma'am.'

'Good morning. Can we get this area tidied up? We shouldn't have food at the front desk, it doesn't create a good impression.'

She waited until the sergeant's 'Yes, ma'am' was followed by some actual action to remove the wrapping. She ignored the lift and took the stairs, keeping an even pace to the second floor.

The door to the incident room was propped open. Robyn stopped in the doorway. 'Morning, all. Bacon rolls all round? And egg for you, Ravi.'

She reckoned taking the lift down wasn't cheating.

As the doors opened in the lobby, Khalid was waiting. 'Morning. I was on my way to see you – that's some black eye. Are you OK?'

'I'm fine, thanks.' Robyn smiled. 'And we caught the burglar, as requested. I'm going to the canteen – join me?'

Khalid smiled in return. 'Why not? Yes, it was a good result just a shame his arrest came too late for the local paper. Never mind, more coverage tomorrow.'

'Just what you wanted.'

'Yes. Stolen jewels, a fight, an escape. All we needed was some scouts and it would have been a Boy's Own adventure.'

'Girl's Own.' Robyn held up a finger. 'Lorraine and me.'

Khalid tensed, searching her face until Robyn smiled and he relaxed. 'Well then, Girl's Own. But it should be "Lorraine and I".'

Robyn opened her mouth to protest then saw the corners of Khalid's mouth were starting to rise. 'OK, one all.' She turned to the counter. 'Four bacon and one egg roll please.'

'Do you know anything more about when Janice will be charged?' Khalid had lowered his voice but the lady behind the counter grimaced.

Wanting to get away, Robyn stopped searching for the right change and handed over a note. 'Can we talk about this upstairs?'

Khalid drew back as Robyn took the bundle of rolls, grease already leaking through the napkins. 'And you're going to eat those?'

'Well, could you carry the drinks then?'

In the lobby, the HR Business Partner pushed into the lift as the doors were closing. 'You might have held the doors open.'

'I'm sorry.' Khalid gave a charming smile. 'Your people normally do that for you.'

She sniffed and stared into her phone until they reached the second floor.

Robyn checked to make sure the lift doors had shut behind them. 'I see why you work in PR.'

'Because I speak proper.'

Stepping into the incident room, Robyn sensed a charge in the atmosphere. Ravi spoke first. 'It's her, Guv. The lab called. The skeleton is Lacey Penrose.'

Robyn's jaw set. 'I only put the sample in yesterday. Are they sure?'

'Absolutely, Guv. Lab said ninety-nine point lots percent certain the skeleton was a close relation to the sample provided.'

'Sounds like you made a bit of a hit at the hospital, Guv. The technician you spoke to yesterday was very upset when he couldn't speak to "nice DI Bailley".' Graham sniggered.

Robyn ignored him. Someone had killed a girl the same age as Becky. She was looking forward to finding them. She took a deep breath. 'Right, to work. We need to cover all aspects of Lacey Penrose's life. First, her work: Lorraine, as you got on so well with the receptionist at Derby and Rutherford, with me. It'll be a nice surprise for Ms Chivers to see us again so soon.'

Lorraine grinned and reached for her bag.

Robyn took a breath and continued. 'Ravi, Chloe, follow up on the home side. I've got these things of Lacey's from her parents' home – go through the handbag and get the lab to test everything. The last time she was with her family was the twenty-ninth of November – find when Lacey last used her bank cards, phone, anything else to help us pinpoint when she died.'

Chloe scurried to her desk and scrabbled papers into a pile.

'And, Graham, can you find out who else used warehouse B – as we suspect something illegal was going on there, find out whether Lacey was mixed up with it. We need the reason she went to the warehouse.'

One of the bacon sandwiches fell to the floor with a soft thump. Robyn jumped; she'd forgotten them. 'OK, I'll have that one. Here we go, everyone.'

'Do you want an announcement to go out?' Khalid passed over the last drink and wiped his fingers.

'The killer's had nearly three years of peace and quiet before we found the body. They can sweat for a bit. Also, we need to tell the Penroses before we do anything. I'll go as I spoke to them yesterday.' Robyn moved to the door.

'Ah, Guv?' Graham was hovering. 'What's happening about Janice?'

Robyn forced herself to keep her face neutral. 'DI Farnham has confirmed the charges. They're the lowest we could hope for and she should get bail today.' She paused. 'You all know what happens next. I'm guessing Janice will ask for a trial and let a jury decide.' She paused. The tips of Graham's ears had flooded a dull red. Robyn swung her bag to her shoulder. 'I did what I could.'

Without waiting for anyone to ask exactly what she'd done, she walked out. Only when she got to the lift did she realise she'd forgotten her tea.

# 37

Frustrated, Robyn jabbed the lift button once, twice. Up the corridor, Lorraine manoeuvred backwards out of the incident room carrying two cups. The lift arrived.

'Here you go, Guv. The bacon roll wasn't worth saving.'

'Thanks, Lorraine. Can you keep mine until we get there? I'll need it more then.'

Neither of them spoke on the journey to Pickley. Robyn parked outside the Penroses' house: the driveway was empty. She downed the barely warm tea in a couple of swallows.

'You might as well stay in the car, Lorraine. Oh and I didn't get a chance to say, good work on Saturday.'

'Thanks, Guv. Glad you're OK.' Lorraine settled into her seat with the autopsy report.

From inside the house, Robyn could hear the faint burble of a radio. She rang the doorbell. Luke poked his head around the door.

'Hello, I'm DI Bailley. We spoke on Sunday. Are either of your parents in?'

The lad was the same height as her and seemed fascinated by the bruises around her eye. 'Luke? Are your parents in?'

He dropped back into the hallway, allowing the door to swing open. 'Gran. It's the policeman from the weekend.'

Of course. She was hardly wearing any make-up and, without jewellery, in a grey trouser suit, what else could she expect?

A voice responded with something inaudible and the radio was switched off. Luke slouched into the front room. Robyn followed, closing the door behind her. The grandmother was sitting at the dining table, photos and bundles of letters spread out in front of her.

'Good morning, Mrs Penrose. May I sit down?'

The woman took off her glasses and met Robyn's eyes, without any reaction. When the contact was finally broken, she indicated a chair with a flick of her hand, passing the other over her face. Robyn had a dull certainty the woman understood why she was here and wondered whether Luke had a foreboding as well: he refused to settle, sinking onto a chair before rising to pace the floor.

'Mrs Penrose, I'm afraid I have some bad news. I wonder if we can speak in private?'

'Luke, come here.' Robyn found her own back straightening. Luke stood up and came to stand at the end of the table. 'Sit down, dear.' The tone was softer but no less commanding. 'You need to hear this.'

Surprised, Robyn cleared her throat. 'Mrs Penrose, Luke. I'm sorry to have to tell you the DNA provided confirmed it was Lacey's body in the warehouse. We have launched a murder enquiry.' She watched the faces. Luke's drained of colour, leaving his spots as livid highlights in his white face. Mrs Penrose remained impassive, reaching across the table for a picture of a family standing beside a font next to a vicar with a white bundle in his arms.

'Lacey's christening. She was such a good baby, never cried, smiled at everyone.' She picked up the photo. 'Look, Inspector. Lacey took so much after her mother.'

Robyn took the curled print. Everybody looked very happy. There was a contrast between the two Mrs Penroses: Lacey's mother was wearing a fashionable frock which now looked dated while the older woman's dress was elegant and timeless. 'I am sorry for your loss. We think she died soon after she disappeared.'

'So even if the police had investigated, they would not have found her. How convenient.'

Luke sobbed, the cry of a frightened child, burying his head in his arms.

'We believe she was killed on or around the thirtieth.' She tried to speak so that the old lady could hear and Luke couldn't. 'Luke saw her on the twenty-ninth. May I ask him some questions?'

'You must remember, he was only eleven when this happened.'

Robyn nodded.

Mrs Penrose placed the photo of Lacey in front of Luke. 'Do this for her.'

'Luke, will you help me, please?' Robyn paused, wondering if Luke could even hear her. 'Can you remember anything particular Lacey said to you when she took you to the cinema?'

There was no answer.

'For example, did she say she was worried about anything?'

'If so, she would hardly have mentioned it on Luke's birthday trip.' Mrs Penrose tapped the photo in front of Luke. 'Luke, stop crying. Lacey is gone, now we need to find who did this to her. What did she say to you?'

Luke spoke through his arms. 'There was one thing but she told me to keep it secret.'

Robyn and Mrs Penrose's eyes met in a shared moment of understanding.

'I know she said—'

'She may have meant—'

Robyn indicated for Mrs Penrose to continue.

'Luke, she may have meant it to be secret at the time but it was a long time ago and now it may help the police catch the person who killed her. What did she say?'

It was hard to make out the words. 'She said Mum and Dad were going to be surprised because she was bringing someone home for Christmas.'

'Did she say who it was?' Robyn leant forward to catch the words.

'Her boyfriend. She said I'd like him because he played sport.' The sobs joined up and became a choking gurgle. He didn't look in any state to continue.

Robyn stood up. 'Once again, Mrs Penrose, I'm sorry. What happened with this case before, will not happen again.'

Mrs Penrose bowed her head and put her hand on Luke's shoulder.

# 38

'How did she take it?' Lorraine put her seat belt on.

'About as well as you could hope for. These old ladies are tough and I think she already suspected the worst. Right, let's go and annoy Mr Mark Rutherford.' Robyn started the car.

'Anything you want me to focus on, Guv?'

'We need to know the last contact anyone from the office had with Lacey and whether she'd mentioned any plans to go away. Also, find out what people remember about Josh.'

Lorraine shifted in her seat. 'Please tell me you're not suggesting Josh ...'

'No. I'm not.' Robyn turned to Lorraine to make her point, then had to brake as the car in front stopped to turn right. 'Bugger. I don't believe Josh is involved. Like Lacey's mother, he had a strange text and Luke just said Lacey intended to introduce Josh to the family at Christmas which makes it even less likely she'd dump him.'

'Good. Just checking.' Lorraine relaxed her grip on the door handle.

A sandwich van was parked across the visitors' parking spaces at Derby and Rutherford. Workers queued in the sun, chatting. Lorraine pointed. 'There's Cathy, the receptionist. Let's see what she can tell us.'

'Right, you go and talk to her. I'll park and see who's in the office.'

Lorraine leapt out and Robyn reversed into a parking space next to the front door.

A dark grey Aston Martin surged over the speed ramp at the entrance, stopping a few yards in front of Robyn's car. The Aston's headlights flashed, followed by a curt beep on the horn. When Robyn didn't move, the driver opened his door, striding towards her. Robyn opened her window and watched as recognition dawned on Rutherford, who managed to put his features into neutral within a pace.

'DI Bailley. We didn't expect you back now Benjamin is safe. You are in my parking space.' The Aston's engine was a smooth hum in the background.

'Good morning, Mr Rutherford.' Robyn gestured towards the sandwich van. 'As you can see there aren't any visitor spaces. Something else has come up and I'd like to talk to you. Could I take a moment of your time?'

'What for?'

'I'd like to talk to you about an ex-member of your staff.'

'Please stop playing games, officer.' Sweat slicked Rutherford's hair to his forehead.

There was a grinding noise as the sandwich van started up and drove towards the exit.

Robyn smiled. 'Well, if you have time now, perhaps we could discuss this inside?'

'Oh, very well.' Rutherford turned back to his car.

Robyn ran the Mondeo the twenty yards to a visitors' space, letting the man park in his personal spot. She followed him into reception where Lorraine was leaning against the desk with Cathy, who began fussing with something behind the reception counter.

Rutherford glared at the desk. 'Cathy, why aren't there any flowers?'

Cathy muttered about calling the florist. Robyn was swept into a meeting room with a nautical theme, an anchor propped on the sideboard. She sat down, feeling a chill from the cold leather working through her clothes. 'Thank you, sir. I'd like to talk to you about Lacey Penrose.' She pushed the photo of Lacey on the beach across the desk.

Rutherford ogled the sunlit body before he spoke. 'Did she work here? No, I don't believe I remember her.'

'She worked here as a receptionist three years ago.'

'Officer, you can hardly expect me to remember every receptionist. What about her?'

'She was murdered.'

'Murdered?' He swallowed. 'This can have nothing to do with Derby and Rutherford.'

'She worked for you and her body was found in a warehouse sold through your firm. You can understand why we're curious.'

After a deep breath, Rutherford reached for the phone on the table. 'Ursula, I'm in Marine room. I need all the paperwork we have on a Lucy Penrose. She worked for us some years ago ...' He frowned as Robyn signalled.

'It's *Lacey* Penrose.'

'Did you hear, Ursula? The police are here, quick as you can.' One of his feet began tapping under the table.

Knowing she'd already irritated him, Robyn wanted to push it a bit further. She smiled. 'Perhaps while we wait for Ursula, you could tell me what you know about warehouse B at the Docks, the one Melissa Chivers is dealing with?'

The rhythm under the table speeded up. 'What is this about?'

'We're interested in the warehouse because it appears to be a hub for illegal activity. Lacey's body was found there and we also believe it was used to store drugs. We're searching for a murderer and a smuggler and wondered whether you can help us?'

Rutherford shifted in his seat, then rose and fiddled with the controller for the air-conditioning. He sat down again, face impassive. 'We are not aware of any illegal activity at the site and if anything came to our notice, we would report it to the proper authorities.' The cold air had a bitter scent of sweat.

There was a tentative tap on the glass before a short woman in a twin-set opened the door.

'Mark? I have the file you asked for.'

'Thank you, Ursula.'

The woman advanced a few more paces into the room. She held the cardboard folder by one corner, dropping it on the edge of the table. She took a step back, then stopped.

'Yes, thank you.' He watched the woman until she had closed the door and was no longer visible in the corridor, then began leafing through the file.

'Right, Lacey Penrose. Started in January three years ago. With us until, let's see, November of the same year. Work just about satisfactory, took a lot of sick leave ... oh.' Rutherford stopped.

Robyn thought he'd relaxed now they'd stopped talking about the warehouse. She wanted to keep him on edge. 'What is it?'

'We were on the point of dismissing her.' He ran his finger along a line of text. 'She'd had two warnings about the amount of sick leave she'd taken, though she provided a doctor's certificate explaining these were complications linked to an abortion. We gave her a chance and extended her probation for a further six months, only for there to be ongoing complaints of poor work.' He turned over the sheet. 'Ah, now I do remember this. She left without giving notice and we then discovered she'd committed fraud.'

'Did you contact the police?'

'No. The sum was trivial and we doubted the police would take it seriously.' Rutherford sounded sarcastic.

This was presumably his way of trying to regain control of the interview. Robyn smiled. 'All the details are in here, are they? Thank you.

I'll take this with me, giving you a receipt, of course. Now, perhaps you could tell me about the warehouse?'

'I'm afraid Melissa manages everything for the client.' He closed the file. 'Derby and Rutherford operates within all rules, regulations and legislation and is audited regularly.'

'Could you give me a list of all companies with an interest in the warehouse? Was one of them run by anyone called Dearman?' Robyn pulled Lacey's file towards her.

'No.' Rutherford pushed his chair back hard, where it teetered and fell. 'I believe we've already provided you with client lists and I don't understand the reason for this fresh enquiry. I repeat, the firm is run to the highest professional standards.'

Robyn decided to let him stew. She picked up the file and got to her feet. 'You've been a great help, sir. Thank you. I know the way out.'

# 39

Robyn pushed through the double doors into reception expecting to find Lorraine. Cathy, on the phone, pointed into the car park. As Robyn opened the outer door, she heard Cathy telling someone Mark Rutherford wasn't in the building or expected back. Lorraine was leaning on the Mondeo finishing a call.

'Great, thanks, Ravi. Bye.' She put the phone into her bag. 'All good stuff, Guv. They have finished the detailed search of the burglar's place and found a pile of cash and a black cycling outfit.' She was grinning.

Robyn grinned back. 'Great, got him.'

'Ah, you've got lipstick on your teeth, Guv.'

Robyn's pleasure at having got Rutherford where she wanted him faded. He could be laughing at her now. She counted to ten. Lorraine had been trying to help. She should say thank you. They got into the car.

'Did you get anything useful, Guv?' Lorraine sounded like someone who wanted to change the subject.

Trying not to make a performance out of it, Robyn wiped her teeth with a tissue then started the engine. 'Only Lacey's personnel file. Everything Rutherford said was bluster. Anything more from Cathy?'

Lorraine started flicking through the file. 'Seeing Rutherford made her clam up. She did tell me the firm's in a spot of bother though. There aren't any flowers because the florist hasn't been paid. Perhaps hard times have made Rutherford less fussy about clients?'

'Possibly. Could Cathy remember Lacey?'

'Vaguely. Don't forget, she's seen a lot of girls come and go. The picture jogged her memory – brunettes seem quite unusual. She couldn't remember much about Lacey apart from how she left. The first Cathy knew, Lacey didn't turn up one Monday morning and her resignation arrived in the post. Then, the company discovered Lacey had committed some sort of fraud meaning she would have been fired anyway.'

'Rutherford mentioned something. What did she do?'

Lorraine flicked through the file. 'There are a load of petty disciplinary things: God, they even confiscated her phone at one point. Sounds like school. Here we go. They found Lacey used the company's credit card to book things for herself, a train ticket and a hotel room in Manchester.'

'Interesting. When were they booked?'

Lorraine turned over another page. 'There's the disciplinary report – ah, here's the bill. The bookings were made on Thursday, the twenty-ninth of November.'

'Had Lacey said anything about resigning?'

'Apparently not, Guv, although she moaned lots to Cathy about the job. It seems receptionists are expected to do everything, like picking up partners' dry-cleaning, even babysitting their kids if needed. Then, on what turned out to be her last day, which was ...' Lorraine turned sheets in the file, '... the thirtieth of November, Cathy remembers Lacey was told to deliver some papers to one of the partner's homes

317

and she threw a tantrum because it was late on a Friday afternoon and she was supposed to be going out.'

Robyn gripped the steering wheel a little tighter. 'Could she remember which partner Lacey had to visit?'

'No – they all act like queens, apparently. There are only four of them so it shouldn't take too long to find out.' Lorraine turned over another piece of paper. 'And here's Lacey's resignation letter. One line, printed, squiggle for a signature, dated November thirtieth, stamped as received on December third.'

'What about the relationship with Josh?'

Lorraine glanced up from the file. 'Cathy says everyone knew about it. It's even noted here, under "personal notes". Cathy didn't remember too much about Josh, just he was a nice lad.'

'Does she think Lacey was faithful to Josh when he was at university?'

Lorraine shrugged. 'She couldn't remember and I believe her.'

'Shame. Still, we're narrowing the dates.' They drove into the police station.


Walking into the incident room, the first thing in her eyeline were two photos of Lacey pinned side by side: a happy girl on a beach, next to a dry skeleton lying in dust. Robyn stood at the board and called the team's attention.

'So, the last days of Lacey Penrose. On the twenty-ninth of November, she takes her brother to the cinema. On Friday the thirtieth, she goes to work as usual. She left Derby and Rutherford's office in the business park around five pm to deliver papers to a partner's home, then resigns, apparently typing and posting a letter to confirm, that evening. Her handbag is found on a train to Manchester on the Monday but the rest of her stuff is still in Meresbourne. What else do we know?'

Chloe actually put her hand up. 'She took out twenty pounds from a cash-point in the bus station at seven forty-five on Friday morning, the last time her bank card was used. In December, only the regular direct debits went out and the account went overdrawn in January as there was no salary paid in. The bank sent Lacey letters, none answered.'

Robyn nodded. 'Anyone got any activity later than the thirtieth?'

'She used her phone.' Ravi smoothed a sheet of paper in front of him. 'We were lucky: the phone company had the records on an old system. The last call was made at seventeen fifteen on the thirtieth of November. The last texts were sent the following morning, Saturday, between eight forty and eight fifty-two: one to her mother: one to Josh and one to the number she called on the Friday. Another thing: I charged up the phone but there's nothing in the memory. It looks like it's been factory reset.'

'What does that mean?' Having to ask made Robyn feel old.

Ravi held up his phone. 'If my phone is locked and I forget the code, I can only use it again by resetting it, wiping everything on the memory. It takes it back to how it came out of the factory.'

'So Lacey forgot the code to her phone? How much did she use it?'

Ravi fanned out four sheets. 'A lot. This is the week up to the thirtieth, including lots of calls and texts to Josh.' In his other hand, was a single sheet. 'This is everything since then – three texts.'

There were a couple of seconds while they all stared at the papers then everyone spoke at once.

'She died on the thirtieth'; 'Why did she go to the warehouse?'; 'Who sent the text messages?'

Robyn let the buzz die down. 'OK, our premise is something happened to Lacey on the evening of the thirtieth, even if she wasn't killed then. Ravi, find out who got the third text. Chloe, track Lacey's movements on CCTV from when she left the office and see what you can get from around the Docks area for Friday evening.'

Robyn paused for breath. Lorraine's lips were set in a hard line 'I've got the lists from Derby and Rutherford, Guv. I'll work out which partner Lacey went to see.'

Robyn turned on the television for the one o'clock news. Four Britons had died in a holiday coach crash in France which had pushed everything else aside. The local news was dominated by the story of a child attacked by a dog in Barton. Janice wasn't mentioned.

When Robyn switched the television off, Lance was sitting at Janice's desk. She wondered how long he'd been there, unnoticed. 'Hello, I didn't realise you'd be coming back.' She hadn't meant it to sound like an accusation.

'A couple of loose ends. I need to talk to you.' He stood up. 'Now. It seems I was not given all pertinent information. Why didn't you tell me Ben Chivers was about to be taken out of the country?'

Breathe, Robyn thought, easy in and out.

'Guv.' Ravi waved. 'The last person Lacey called was a girl named Gemma. I've left her a message.'

Lance was waiting, hand on the door. Robyn steeled herself: Lance could still reopen the enquiry.

'Guv!' Chloe was grinning. 'I've got something.' She pointed to her screen. 'There's no CCTV that old so I wondered what else I could find and look at this. You know the speed camera on Dock Drag? It was installed in October, three years ago. A month later, on November thirtieth, look who got caught, speeding out of the Docks.'

Over the team's comments, Robyn heard her phone ring. 'DI Bailley. Yes. What?' She had to cover her ear, there was so much chatter. 'When did this happen? OK, I'm on my way.'

Robyn clapped her hands for quiet. 'Right everyone. We've got a situation. Josh has gone to Melissa Chivers' house and she's called 999. I'm going up there – Graham, with me. The rest of you, keep following these leads and give me an update when you've got anything.' Robyn turned towards the door to find Graham already there, his back to Lance.

Robyn grabbed her bag. At the door, she stopped. 'I'm sorry, DI Farnham. I've got to go.' There was no acknowledgement. She could worry about him later.

As they reached the bottom of the steps, Graham was already jiggling his car keys. He turned left. Robyn turned right, not bothering to look back until she had reached the pool car and opened the door. 'I'm driving.' Graham, still at the bottom of the steps, was trying to put his jacket on, snagging his arm in the sleeve. Robyn edged the car forward. Graham gave up with his jacket and got in.

As they pulled onto the roundabout, Robyn switched on the siren. 'I was worried something like this might happen. Josh has had since Friday to think. The question is whether he just wants to see Ben or have it out with Ms Chivers for lying to him.'

Graham braced himself as Robyn accelerated. 'Who's up there?'

Robyn overtook a bus, before speeding around a traffic island the wrong way. 'Uniform. Josh must be on his own, as Janice and Martin can't approach Ms Chivers. At least I hope they're not there.' It would mean everything she'd done would be for nothing. She focused on driving because these were residential streets, packed with families. A mother pulled her child back from the road and the toddler watched them pass, hands over his ears.

A group of gawpers drifted out of the way as Robyn pulled up behind a police car outside Melissa Chivers' house. Clyde paced by the front door.

Graham strode up to him. 'What's happened?'

'A bit of a domestic, Graham, ma'am.' Clyde looked around at the crowds of people. 'A man's keeping two women and a baby inside.'

Robyn kept her voice low. 'Are you saying this is a hostage situation?'

'I don't know, ma'am. When I first got here, I heard some shouting. It's been quiet for about ten minutes.'

'How long has the man been in there, do you know?' 'Look!' Graham pointed to an upstairs window, where Ben could be seen peeking under the corner of a blind. The crowd saw him too and there was a ripple forward.

Robyn's phone rang. 'Make it quick, Ravi.'

'OK, Guv. I've just spoken to Gemma, Lacey's five-fifteen call. They were due to meet at six-thirty but Lacey sent a message saying she might be late because of someone called "Queen Bitch". Lacey never turned up and didn't answer calls. All Gemma got was a text from Lacey on Saturday morning saying sorry, gone away. Then, no messages, social media, nothing.'

'Thanks, Ravi, keep going.' Robyn squared her shoulders. 'Right, Clyde. Whistle up some help and get this street cleared. Graham, get Janice on the phone. We might need her to talk some sense into Josh, even if she's not allowed to be here.' Robyn waited for nods from Graham and Clyde then opened the gate. Ben's face had gone from the window.

Robyn kept her finger on the doorbell. After ten seconds, she opened the letterbox. 'Josh, it's DI Bailley. I'd like you to let me in so we can talk.' She waited. Behind her, she could hear Clyde shouting directions.

'Josh. Open the door, please.'

Graham approached, phone held to his ear. 'I've got Janice on the line. Yes, the Guv's trying to talk to Josh now.'

Robyn leant to the door again. 'Josh, I've got your mother on the phone. She wants to talk to you.'

Graham nudged Robyn. Gillian was standing at the front window. Robyn mimed pushing up the sash. Gillian disappeared, then the blind was pulled up and the window opened.

'Are you OK, Mrs Green? What's going on?'

Gillian's hair had escaped the pins. 'They're in the kitchen. He just turned up. I didn't know what to do and I let him in. He's only a boy himself ...' She became aware of the crowd, gasped and stepped back.

'Mrs Green, Gillian.' Robyn turned. 'We need to get everyone back. Graham, help Clyde.'

With the crowd further back, Robyn called again. 'Gillian. Gillian?'

It seemed like a long time before Gillian reappeared. Robyn smiled, willing Gillian to ignore the people staring 'What did Josh do when he arrived?'

Gillian murmured something '… said he was Benjamin's father.'

'Did he threaten you in any way?'

'Oh no, no. He just wanted to talk. I'd taken Benjamin upstairs first because it would be a shock for him, then we talked in the lounge. He was nice.'

'So you didn't do anything wrong. Now let me in, Mrs Green.'

Gillian blinked. 'I don't know …'

'Mrs Green. Open the door, now.' Robyn was losing patience. She hadn't heard any other sounds from inside the house but anything could be happening.

The window closed. Robyn beckoned Graham. 'When we go in, you take Ms Chivers – if she's upset, there's no telling how she might react. If I get close to her. I'll take Josh.'

Face neutral, Graham nodded.

Many, slow seconds later, a shape became visible through the panes of the front door. As the door opened, Gillian jumped back as Graham rushed past her, stopping at the doorway to the kitchen. Robyn hurried to his side, remembering the full knife block on the counter.

Melissa Chivers was perched on the furthest bar stool, black suit standing out against the white leather. On the floor, Josh sat with his back to a cupboard, arms wrapped around his knees.

Graham muttered into his phone. 'It's OK, I'll call you back.'

'Josh, it's DI Bailley. Are you OK?' Squatting down beside Josh, Robyn smelled a child-like cleanliness, mixed with a harsh note of bleach from the floor. She couldn't get any closer without touching his shaking shoulders. Behind her, Graham's questions and Melissa's complaints were blending together with the hum of the fridge. Robyn put her arm around Josh and pulled him to her. After an initial resistance, his weight rested against her chest, one shoulder squashing the padding in her bra. He shook in her arms as she rubbed his back, waiting for him to quieten. As his ragged breathing slowed, Robyn felt

Josh tense and a quick breath on her face before his body jerked backwards away from her, his head hitting the edge of the kitchen counter with a thud. Robyn stood up, feeling her knees protest.

There were three quick steps behind her. She turned to see Melissa Chivers, face set, lips pressed together.

'You should have protected me from this. I will file a complaint.'

'Ms Chivers—'

Melissa cut Graham off. 'Your colleague has been trying to persuade me this is just youthful high spirits when I have been threatened in my own home.'

Josh rubbed the back of his head, before he leaned forward again, hiding his face.

For the first time since she'd had the emergency call, Robyn felt in control of the situation. She turned to face Ms Chivers so they stood almost chest to chest: Melissa held firm, just a slight rock back on her heels hinting at discomfort. 'I quite understand, Ms Chivers. It must have been extremely distressing for you.' She smiled to emphasise the point. 'I suggest the best thing now would be for you to accompany me to the station so I can take your complaint immediately.'

Graham stared at her. 'Guv, what about—'

Robyn held up a hand. 'Thank you, sergeant. Could you get a statement from Mrs Green? I'll take Ms Chivers' statement at the station where we can give her complaint appropriate consideration.'

'Yes, ma'am.' Graham's voice was clipped.

Robyn followed Melissa into the hallway. Gillian loitered on the stairs, shrinking back when Melissa glared up at her.

'I am going to the police station to make a complaint. Prepare the evening meal, then we will be discussing your continued employment. I will not have you admitting lunatics to my house.'

Robyn opened the front door and took a step out onto the path, holding the door open so Melissa could sweep through. Clyde waited for Robyn's nod and began rolling up the blue-and-white tape. People approached to see what was going on, then fell back as there was no drama.

The woman next door was peering from her front window. Robyn gave her a cheerful wave which was not returned. 'Right, Ms Chivers. I'm presuming you'd prefer to drive yourself? Can you get out with my colleague's car parked there?'

Melissa stalked to her Lexus. Robyn dashed to her own car, slotted the phone into the cradle and began to dial.

'Graham, I know this looks a bit weird but I've got an idea. Here's what I need you to do ...'

# 40

Robyn made a point of smiling at regular intervals while she took down Melissa Chivers' statement.

'So did Josh threaten you at any point?'

'Haven't you been listening? He said he was going to tell everyone he is Benjamin's father.'

'I meant physically, Ms Chivers. Did he make any threats to harm you, Benjamin or Mrs Green?'

'Threats to my reputation are more damaging than physical ones.'

Robyn put down the pen. 'Ms Chivers, from your statement so far, Josh hasn't committed any crime.'

Melissa was silent.

Robyn sighed. 'Everything points to Josh Warrener being Ben's father. Unless you can prove otherwise, I don't think there's a case against him.'

Melissa reached into her bag and retrieved a packet of tissues.

'But while you're here, Ms Chivers, I'd like to ask you about Lacey Penrose.'

There was a pause, Melissa with the tissue half-extracted in her lap. She blinked once, bringing her hands together, crumpling the paper and plastic. 'Who?'

Robyn composed a look: sympathy and understanding. Having Ms Chivers under her control was close to being enjoyable. 'Please take your time. We're investigating the murder of Lacey Penrose. She worked as a receptionist at Derby and Rutherford about ten months before Benjamin was born.'

Melissa shuddered as Robyn pulled her own handbag onto the table, marvelling how much these little demonstrations of femininity seemed to upset Melissa. She placed the photo of Lacey and Josh on the desk.

'I don't remember her.' Melissa had focused on the image for no more than an instant.

'Please look again.' Robyn nudged the photo closer. 'I understood you worked regularly with Lacey, close enough to file complaints of poor work against her on four occasions in six months?'

'There were a lot of receptionists.'

'But only one whose body has been found in a property you were connected with. And only one who was also in a relationship with Josh Warrener.' Without a reaction from Melissa, Robyn had to keep suppressing her doubts. 'Ms Chivers, I believe you summoned Lacey Penrose to your house on the day she disappeared so you are, potentially, the last person to have seen her alive.'

'I believe you have got me here on false pretences, DI Bailley.' Melissa squared her shoulders. 'If you are accusing me of a crime, then I would like to have my lawyer present.'

Robyn sat back and smiled yet again. 'Of course, Ms Chivers. I shall let you get your representative, then we can reconvene. Interview terminated at sixteen forty-seven. DI Bailley leaving the room.'

There was a queue waiting for her in the corridor, everybody with a piece of paper. Robyn counted them off. 'Where's Graham?'

A voice from down the corridor. 'Here, Guv. It was there, just as you thought.' He thrust a leather-bound book forward. 'Also, we've got something else.' He pointed at another sheet of paper. 'Interesting eh? I'll get the details in the morning.'

Robyn smiled, the first genuine one of the afternoon. 'Thanks, Graham. What do you think made the difference?'

'I think it was Josh turning up, Guv. It sounds like he and Gillian had a good chat and she fell for his boyish charm.'

Robyn hoped it was just the heat in the corridor making her face flush. 'Good work, everyone. Well, we've got to wait for Ms Chivers' lawyer to get here – might as well have a cup of tea.'


'Interview restarting at eighteen fourteen. Present, DI Bailley, Melissa Chivers and Gerald Straker, Ms Chivers' legal representative. Ms Chivers, I will now caution you.'

Both managed to look bored as Robyn recited the caution and laid a pile of paper on the table.

'Ms Chivers, when we spoke earlier, you didn't remember Lacey Penrose. You've spoken to your lawyer and you've changed your statement. You now admit Lacey came to your house to deliver papers on your instructions at around seventeen forty-five on thirtieth November, three years ago. At her request, you then drove to a bar in Riverside, where you dropped her at around eighteen fifteen, which was the last time you saw her.' Robyn smiled at Ms Chivers. 'Am I correct?'

'Yes.' The word was bitten short.

'It is a long time ago, officer. It is perfectly understandable my client's recollection is a little hazy.' The solicitor sniffed. 'And you have also failed to explain why you are asking my client these questions.'

'We are asking Ms Chivers these questions because it's probable she was the last person to see Lacey Penrose alive.'

'Other than her killer, officer.' The solicitor pulled a handkerchief from his pocket and wiped his glasses, left lens, right lens, breath, right lens, left lens.

'Of course.' Robyn inclined her head to the solicitor, who matched the gesture in a polite harmony. 'But we've reason to believe Ms Chivers had a particular interest in Lacey Penrose.'

The solicitor put his glasses on.

'Let me put a story to you, Ms Chivers. You were desperate for a baby but your beliefs prevented you from using artificial means to conceive. You used a dating agency to try to find a suitable father and we have the agency's comments about the long list of requirements you sent them.' Robyn held up a piece of paper. 'You only met two men in the year you were a member and had no further contact after the first meetings. Then Josh Warrener started at your office. He was intelligent, healthy and handsome. But there was a problem; he began seeing someone else, Lacey Penrose.'

The solicitor muttered something to Melissa. She shook her head, one confident movement.

Robyn coughed to bring back their attention. 'Because of Lacey, Josh turned down your advances in September and they stayed together even when he was away at university.'

Ms Chivers muttered something to her solicitor, who made a note on his pad. 'My client denies she made any advances to Mr Warrener. These are the fantasies of a teenage boy.'

'Thank you for clarifying the position.'

The solicitor capped his fountain pen. Outside, there was scuffling in the corridor.

Robyn shut her eyes for a second to ease their stinging. She opened them to Melissa's contempt. 'Very well, let me continue the story. We have a witness who says Josh and Lacey were still in a relationship at the start of November and things seemed to be going well, despite the distance. Then on the first of December, without warning, he gets dumped. To add to his misery there's no explanation, just a text message. He tries to get hold of Lacey, even coming to her office to see her. While he was there, you told him Lacey had gone away to Manchester, with another man.' Robyn steepled her fingers like Fell:

it showed off her nail varnish and she enjoyed the sickened expression on Ms Chivers' face. 'It does seem a bit odd, Ms Chivers, you knowing personal details about Lacey, when you stated you had nothing to do with her?'

Ms Chivers rested her chin on her hand. 'You cannot avoid hearing office gossip.'

Robyn took a sip of water. 'Josh claims you propositioned him at your office taking advantage of his girlfriend's apparent betrayal.' The solicitor opened his mouth; Robyn kept talking. 'It doesn't really matter who said what because I believe Benjamin Chivers was conceived in the two-week relationship you had with Josh Warrener over the Christmas period.' Robyn paused. She wanted the next revelation to have impact. 'We also have the results of a DNA test saying Josh is Ben's father. Ms Chivers, do you wish to challenge those results?'

The close room was getting warmer. Robyn glanced at her watch. 'Is there anything I can offer you? Some water?'

The solicitor took off his glasses and put them in his shirt pocket. 'I think we would prefer to conclude this as quickly as possible, officer.'

Robyn inclined her head again. This time, there was no answering movement. 'As you wish. To continue: Lacey was due to meet a friend at six thirty in a Riverside bar on the Friday evening. She didn't turn up which suggests she must have been attacked between six fifteen, when you say you dropped her off and six-thirty.' Robyn picked up the top item from the pile, holding it around the edges, to avoid finger-marks. 'This picture shows Lacey's skull. She was hit with a hammer.' She pulled across another picture, showing the skull from another angle. 'The first blow, was here, to the side of her head. Now, I believe that if the killer was of a similar build to Lacey, they would want to stun the victim to make sure they couldn't fight back. Lacey was five foot, eight inches tall. How tall are you, Ms Chivers?'

Melissa sounded casual. 'As I'm sure you have already worked out, DI Bailley, I am five foot, seven, along with many other people.'

'It was a mercy she was stunned first, though.' Robyn tapped the picture, peach nail bright against the dun-coloured bone. 'The blows to the face were done while the victim was on the ground. It was a savage attack, as if the killer wanted to wipe out all trace of Lacey.' Neither Melissa nor the solicitor did more than glance down at the picture.

'Here's what I think happened.' Robyn focused on Melissa. 'Josh fitted the bill as a suitable father for your child but he turned you down.' Robyn paused, smiled. 'And he turned you down for Lacey. I understand why you got angry. A mere receptionist and someone who'd also had an abortion, a murderer according to your church …'

'Officer, is this necessary?' The solicitor sat back, folding his arms.

'Yes, sir.' Robyn turned back to Melissa. 'You needed Josh and to get him, you had to remove Lacey. At work, she had to do what you said making it easy to get her out of the office to deliver papers. Did you kill Lacey at your house?' Robyn stared at Melissa. 'No, too much of a risk. I think you drove her to the warehouse, which you knew would be secured in the next couple of days by the new owners. You thought of some excuse or another, to get Lacey inside – inspecting something perhaps – then knocked her out. Your handbag could hide a hammer.'

The cross around Melissa's neck flashed as she took quick breaths.

'This is pure speculation.' The solicitor tapped the table. 'You are accusing my client of murder. I assume this is a crude revenge for the complaint she made about your shoddy handling of her son's disappearance?'

Robyn slid over the next piece of paper. 'I'm showing Ms Chivers an extract of her work calendar for Monday the third of December, three years ago. You had a meeting with a client in Euston.'

Melissa glanced at the sheet. 'I attend a lot of meetings.'

'Of course, Ms Chivers. A coincidence though, it being the day Lacey's handbag was put on the train to Manchester, which departed from Euston station.'

The solicitor was becoming more animated. 'You are taking incidents and making connections where none exist.'

'Our job is to make connections.' Robyn lifted Lacey's handbag onto the table. 'This was a nice touch, the final proof to everyone Lacey had gone away, worth taking a risk for. Well, here it is and what's more, it has dust from the warehouse in it, hidden in the folds of the lining.' She flicked at one of the handbag's straps through the plastic. 'So how did Lacey's handbag get out of the warehouse, if Lacey didn't?'

Without waiting for a reaction, Robyn pushed across the next piece of paper.

'This is Lacey's phone bill. You'll notice the usage stopped, almost overnight. When we looked at the phone, it had been reset, meaning anyone could send messages from it. There's a record in her work file of a complaint you made against her where you confiscated her phone. I think you took it and wrote down the numbers Lacey called most often so that later, you could send false messages to them.' There was a twitch of Ms Chivers' lips, then outrage as Robyn reached for a thick, burgundy book.

'My home diary – how did you get it without my permission?' Melissa turned to her solicitor, her voice rising. 'They have taken things from my house.'

'Items taken from my client's home without a warrant may not be used as evidence.' The solicitor's voice was a low rumble of disapproval.

'You'll be reassured to know we didn't take the diary. Mrs Green gave it to us.'

The solicitor pushed his glasses down. 'Who is Mrs Green?'

'She was Benjamin's nanny. She had access to all my papers.' Robyn noted the past tense. The solicitor sat back in his chair with a snort.

Robyn opened the diary to the first week of December. 'On Saturday the first of December, you had a manicure and an appointment for someone to come and valet the car.' She turned the book around to face Melissa. 'I don't expect you to remember details; as you say, it was a long time ago. Perhaps you could explain one odd thing.' She began turning pages, pointing at dates. 'For the rest of the year, you have a manicure every fortnight. Then you book at a new salon the week after your regular session, returning to your favourite one for your regular appointment a week later. Did something happen to damage your nails?' Melissa's lips were pressed together. Robyn flicked back through the other pages. 'And another thing – this weekend was the one time your car got valeted all year. Were you trying to cover up Lacey's presence in the car?'

Neither Melissa nor her solicitor spoke.

Robyn reached for the next piece of paper. 'When we found Lacey's body, we wondered why decomposition was so complete. Then we found a chemical had been poured over her to speed up the process. Here is your credit card bill; it shows a large purchase from a DIY store the weekend before Lacey went missing.'

The solicitor pushed his chair back. 'Officer, this has gone on long enough. Unless you have anything other than this circumstantial evidence, this interview should be terminated.'

Robyn pushed across the final piece of paper. Her solicitor reached for his glasses. 'For the recording, I'm showing Ms Chivers the image from speed camera C1926, where her car was captured doing fifty-seven miles per hour out of the Docks at eighteen thirty-six pm on the thirtieth of November. I don't understand how this happened given you dropped Lacey off at eighteen fifteen?'

The solicitor finished his scrutiny of the picture. 'My client was working on properties in the Docks area. Either she had business there or she may have mistaken the time she dropped this girl off.' He fumbled with his glasses and they dropped to the table.

'With this evidence, we have a complete case against you, Ms Chivers.' Robyn paused, leaned back in her seat and smiled. 'With three other items, I believe it'll be watertight. Firstly, we have requested CCTV from Euston Station, which will show you dropping Lacey's handbag onto a train.' She let the pause stretch out, in no hurry.

'You may think no station is going to keep footage for that long and you're probably right. So we've got something from closer to home. This is the December statement for Derby and Rutherford's company credit card. It shows two items booked in the name of Lacey Penrose, a train ticket and a hotel room in Manchester.' She raised her finger: the solicitor's eyes followed it though Ms Chivers continued staring at the table. 'At the time these items were booked, Lacey was sitting in the cinema with her brother. Your company is providing us with log in records to show exactly who was in the office on the Thursday evening and I think it will show you bought these items, Ms Chivers. You ordered them, in her name, to make it appear as if she was going away.'

Robyn took a breath. She was calm, steady. 'Finally, the DIY store is finding us a breakdown of the exact purchases you made. My bet is you bought a hammer, caustic soda, protective clothing and a watering can. The watering can would be the clincher, because caustic soda needs water to start the reaction but you don't have any plants at home. Am I right? Well, it doesn't really matter, because we'll have all the details by the morning.'

Melissa Chivers swallowed once, her hands coming together, as if in prayer. 'She was a murderess. She had no right to live.'

The solicitor was protesting but Robyn wasn't listening. 'Melissa Chivers, I'm arresting you for the murder of Lacey Penrose ...'

'Nice one, Guv.' Ravi grinned at Robyn as she left the interview room. 'I've been listening in for experience. Present the evidence, bang, bang, bang, she had no chance.' He ran his hands through his hair. 'But I didn't know we'd got the lab results on the handbag already.'

'They haven't come back yet.' Robyn watched the shock turn into delighted surprise on Ravi's face. 'But, it was enough to get her to confess.'

'Graham said I should watch you and learn.' Ravi was nodding, more relaxed than she had seen him in a while.

'DI Bailley? Tracey on the line for you.' The custody sergeant held out the desk phone.

'OK. Ravi, can you let the team know? We still need as much supporting evidence as possible.' Robyn took the phone. 'Hello, Tracey.'

'Hello, I didn't realise you'd be out. Where are we?'

'We've got a confession.'

'Excellent. Hold on a mo.' The line went quiet giving Robyn a chance to think about the paperwork she needed to do.

Tracey's voice came back on. 'When you're done, can you pop up? The superintendent would like a word.'

Once the forms were complete, Robyn started up to the fifth floor, legs welcoming the walk after the confinement of the interview room. The case had to be seamless and give no possibility for further complaints which meant she could expect a grilling from Fell. Her thoughts kept coming back to Josh and Ben: this didn't feel like a victory – there were no winners.

Tracey's office was empty with a smell like rose Turkish Delight. Robyn tapped on the inner door, waiting for the brisk 'Come in'. Fell and Khalid sat at the round table, Khalid's face lit by the glow from his laptop's screen as he typed.

'So we can emphasise the concerns raised over Chivers' parenting skills …' his fingers fluttered over the keyboard, '… and make the point she excluded all family contact from her son's life …'

Robyn paused by the door. 'Sir? You asked me to come up? The paperwork's up to date on Melissa Chivers. Because of concerns about the church, Social Services are arranging a foster carer for Ben immediately.'

'Yes, thank you, Bailley. We are drafting the press release now.' Fell turned back to the paper on the desk.

'Was there something specific, sir?' Robyn shifted her weight from one foot to the other, feeling redundant.

'Oh yes, well done, Bailley. Good news on the burglar. No long-term harm from the attack, I hope?'

'No, sir. Thanks.' There was no dismissal so Robyn waited. 'Sir, will DI Farnham be revising his report on Janice?'

'We shall do what is necessary, Bailley.' This time there was a definite impatience in Fell's tone. 'Was there anything else?'

Robyn turned for the door. 'No, sir.'

Tracey was back at her desk in the outer office. The corners of her mouth turned down, little sparkles in her lip gloss catching the light. 'Oh, to let you know, I just took a message from Social Services. Someone's on their way to pick up Ben now.'

Robyn knew this had to happen. She was wondering how she was going to put this to Janice. 'Thanks, Tracey.' There was also the trip she'd have to make to see the Penroses, to bring them 'closure' and 'justice'. A couple of abstract terms wasn't the same as bringing their daughter back but it was the best she could do. The best she could do … but there was something else. 'Tracey, I've just thought of something. Got to go.'

'You look like you could use a drink,' Tracey called after her.

Robyn hurried into the incident room.

'Great interview, Guv. Ravi's just been talking me through it.'

'Thanks, Chloe.' Robyn paused in the doorway. 'I've got to get over to Upper Town. We'll go through everything in the morning.'

Too tired to find a parking space, Robyn double-parked and rang the bell of Ms Chivers' house. The door was answered by a young man in a shiny, tight suit. Robyn showed her warrant card. 'Are you the social worker?'

'Yeah. We've got foster parents set up. The nanny's just packing some stuff for the kid now.' The man was chewing gum which slid in and out of view as he spoke.

'OK, well, he might like to have this.' Robyn held out the blue ball. The man hesitated. 'This was his only toy.' The man shifted the gum to the other side of his mouth and took the ball.

Gillian came down the stairs, holding two bags, one with a school crest, full of books. She stopped, one foot poised over a step.

Robyn held the bannister. 'Mrs Green, Gillian ... I just wanted to thank you. She admitted the killing. Thank you for your help.'

Gillian sat down on the stairs, head falling into her hands.

'I think you should leave this with us now.' The young man stepped in front of her, the tip of a tattoo showing above his collar.

Robyn heard Ben wail from upstairs and Gillian rose and went to him. Robyn walked down the path and sat in her car for a moment before deciding it wasn't too late to drive to Pickley to see the Penroses.

# TUESDAY 26 JULY

# 41

*Ben's mother in murder arrest* was the headline outside newsagents as Robyn drove to work. She was trying to pin down her own mood without success. There was the satisfaction of a case solved and a small but unpleasant part of herself which was happy to see Melissa humbled. The overriding feeling was the crushing sadness of the Penroses.

Graham was alone in the incident room, staring at the ceiling while on the phone, kicking to make the chair spin.

'No, I don't know. Yeah. You'd think so. No. I guess, OK, I'll put you across.' Graham held the phone out. 'Janice wants a word, Guv.'

Robyn walked to her desk wishing she could have this conversation in private.

'Hello, Janice.'

'Hello, Robyn. How are you?'

'Fine, I'm fine, thanks. And you?'

'Yes, thank you.' The voice had a brittle edge.

'You've heard the news then?'

Ravi and Chloe walked in carrying canteen bags. Robyn braced herself for Janice's answer.

'What did you expect from her? But now Ben's on his own so I need to know where he is, he can't stay in a children's home, he should be here …'

Robyn interrupted. 'Janice, he's not in a children's home, he's gone to foster parents.'

'I suppose anywhere will be better than with her.' Janice took a deep breath. 'We've applied for a declaration of paternity to get Josh's name on Ben's birth certificate. Then, we won't even need to go through formal adoption but it all takes time.' She paused for a second. 'And Josh hasn't even met his own son yet. Can you arrange something?'

Robyn massaged her temple. 'I'll see what I can do, Janice. Neither you nor Martin can approach Ben. Josh'll have to go on his own …'

The voice at the other end dropped to a soft whisper. 'Robyn, he can't go on his own. You saw what happened to him, this has been such a shock …'

'I'll do what I can.' She dropped her voice. 'You know I will.'

'I know. Thank you. I'm sorry about Martin – he's, he's just a bit …'

Robyn stood up. 'Janice, don't worry about it. I'll call you when I've got some news.' She handed the phone back to Graham.

Chloe was loitering by Robyn's desk. 'Is this a bad time, Guv?' She didn't wait for an answer. 'I just wanted to know what was going to happen to me now Ben's been found?'

'Well, it depends.' Robyn saw a little light go out behind Chloe's eyes. 'Normally, you would go back to Uniform. But, I'm an officer down now. Do you want to stay?'

Chloe nodded. 'Definitely, Guv.'

Robyn managed a smile. 'In the time you've been here, you've done a good job. I'm happy to speak to the superintendent about a transfer. You'll have to fill in a stack of forms and there's a lot of training. You need to be prepared to work hard.' Chloe's beaming face was too much: all she could see was Janice stuck in the shabby room at the police house. It still seemed harsh that one person getting their dream job happened because someone else was going to prison.

After a morning of cataloguing evidence and making calls, Robyn met Josh and Martin in the lobby. After she'd told Martin he would have to stay in the car, they drove to the edge of Barton, Martin a glowering presence in the back, Josh fidgeting in the front. Their destination was a semi-detached, one in a long avenue of identical houses. A good place to bring up a child. Robyn wondered how many confused children had been through this blue door, to be fostered, like Ben.

Robyn got out, walked around and opened the door for Josh. Crossing the pavement, she crunched the first golden leaves under foot and opened the gate of number seventeen before she realised she was on her own: Josh hadn't moved from beside the car and looked as if he was about to be sick.

When she walked back, she didn't dare touch him. 'Do you want to do this, Josh?'

Martin opened the car door and stood beside Josh. He turned his son's shoulders towards the house and gave him a gentle shove. 'Go on. You'll love him. He's yours.'

Josh's trainers scuffed the paving stones as they approached the gate. A woman with a pram hurried past.

'Yes, Josh?' Robyn paused with her hand on the catch.

Josh opened his mouth to say something, then nodded.

Without giving him a chance to change his mind, Robyn stepped up the path and rang the doorbell.

# 42

Robyn dropped a pile of forms onto Tracey's desk. 'There are the last of the expenses for the Ben Chivers' investigation. I've also put a request in for Chloe Talbot to transfer to CID.' The heady floral notes of Tracey's perfume were making her dizzy.

Tracey flicked through the papers and slotted them into a series of plastic wallets. 'Thanks. Bet you're glad it's over. I've been wondering what you're going to do to top this last week.'

'I was going to start with an early night.' The clock showed four twenty-five.

'Good idea. Oh, I know what I was going to say to you. A friend of mine does makeover parties, where you get your colours done. She tells you what sort of clothes and things suit you and she brings accessories and make-up to try. I thought it might be right up your street and a bit of a treat, after everything recently.'

Robyn's first thought was resentment at the interference. The second was to wonder if this same friend had recommended Tracey's neon top and leopard-print skirt combination. The third was she should be grateful someone was taking a positive interest. 'Thanks, Tracey, maybe you could give me her details?'

Tracey reached into her handbag for her phone and scribbled a name and number onto a Post It note. 'Here. The superintendent's taking an interest in what happened to your car, by the way.'

Robyn wasn't sure whether this was a good thing or a bad thing if it meant more officers being disciplined because of her. 'Right, I'm going to go home now, via the DIY store and start redecorating.'

'So the house is getting a makeover as well?'

'Been meaning to do it for years. Now I've started changing it seems to be the right time to change other things too.'

Tracey's face was in shadow, her voice was soft. 'No going back then?'

Robyn nodded, feeling a lump in her throat. She leant forward, brushing a strand of hair out of her eyes. 'Just because something isn't easy, doesn't mean it isn't right.'

*Robyn Bailley will return ...*

# Book Club Questions

1. How prepared is Robyn for the changes she has decided to make?
2. Do you understand why Robyn makes the changes she does?
3. What kind of psychological changes does Robyn go through and what do you think causes these?
4. What does Robyn learn about herself through the novel?
5. Who do you consider is most supportive to Robyn and why?
6. Where do you consider Ben would get the best upbringing and why?
7. Which characters have reasonable justifications for their actions and why?
8. How effective is the police culture in examining attitudes to sex, sexuality and gender?
9. The story is set in a medium-sized town. How do you think reactions would change if it were set in a city or a village?
10. The novel was written 2013–2015. What changes would you expect to see in people's reactions to Robyn if the book had been written now? Or in the 1970s?

# Acknowledgements

Because this is a first book, there was a lot I didn't know. I'm very grateful to all of the people who provided support, advice and encouragement to get this book published.

Thanks first to Mum and Dad for letting me grow up in a house full of books.

The very first people to meet Robyn were my writing group, Scribbles. They read the story in instalments over two years and were a constant source of support and critique. Particular thanks to Alan, Kate and Lorna for being there all the way through and to Terry for saying what needed to be said.

When I came up with the idea for Robyn, I was very lucky to meet and tweet with people who were happy to share their stories and experiences with me, which I have tried to reflect honestly. Special thanks go to Kyle and Anna for their patience with my questions. Also, thanks to Anna E for her knowledge of the police service.

A lot of people have read early drafts of this book and were kind enough to take the time to give their thoughts. My tutor, Chris

Wakling gave good advice (and saved a life). My fellow course participants Alice, Catherine, Dawn, Elin, Grace, Heidi, Julietta, Kate and Moyette have been a source of constructive criticism mixed with laughter. Judi and I have pursued literary aims together and it's a joy to have her friendship, comments and all the shared wine.

Huge thanks go to the Womentoring Project, a brilliant idea that introduced me to the fabulous Fanny Blake, whose experience, advice and ongoing back-stiffening has been invaluable.

I'm very grateful to Rachel Singleton at Impress Books who spotted the potential of the book and for her comments and suggestions.

Finally, there are people who are nothing to do with writing and who helped the book along by reminding me there is a real world out there. Thank you to Mel, Janet and Rashmila for making me laugh like a drain on a regular basis and to Jenny for her particular insights and her constant belief in my success.

# About Alex Clare

After nearly twenty years of being a committed corporate person, Alex Clare was made redundant. She had always enjoyed writing, studying fiction part-time through the Open University and managing to complete a novel in her commuting time, though no one had ever read it. Now, with lots more time on her hands, there was the opportunity to take writing more seriously. She began to enter competitions and joined a writing group, which encouraged her to try out new genres and styles.

After a period focusing on short stories, she wanted to try another novel. Inspiration came from watching Parliament debate the Equal Marriage Act in 2013. Astounded by the intensity of feeling generated, she created a fictional world to explore some of the issues and attitudes. Now working again she is writing her second Robyn Bailley story, in her usual place on a London commuter train.

Twitter feed: @_alexandraclare